BY ALL MEANS

Alan Alexander

A Fiske and MacNee Mystery

Acknowledgments

Thanks to Emma Quinn for the cover design and to Neale Stidolph for allowing us to use his photograph of the Aberdeen skyline.

Thanks, too, to the friends and family who read early drafts and provided comments that improved the final version.

CHAPTER ONE

'When did we last have two separate murders on the same weekend?'

Detective Chief Inspector Vanessa Fiske and Detective Inspector Colin MacNee sat opposite Campbell Esslemont, head of CID in North East Constabulary, early on Monday morning. Vanessa had spent most of the previous two days on an offshore oil-drilling platform. Colin had been at Grampian Royal Hospital. They had both been investigating sudden and unexplained deaths that they assumed were suspicious. Confirmation from the duty pathologist was expected later in the day.

'Never in my time, Vanessa'. The detective chief superintendent was budget holder for CID and he was already worrying about the cost of running two parallel murder enquiries. His time went back nearly thirty years. Few others in the force had longer memories, so it was safe to assume that it hadn't happened before.

'I can't tell you how petrified I was about getting into that helicopter,' Vanessa said. 'I read somewhere years ago how much less safe they are than fixed wing planes. But I loved it! Now I know why Russian oligarchs and the like have helicopters as well as private planes. Land the things anywhere, fly in straight lines from here to there. Great!'

Esslemont pursed his lips to signal that she should get on with it.

'Late on Friday afternoon, during a routine health and safety check of the rig - it's called Vermont One, by the way, its American operators call all their rigs after States that don't have major oil fields - an inspector found a body. The dead man wasn't a regular member of the rig's crew. He was a senior engineer from the States, sent over to perform an independent, or at least quasi-independent, safety check on all the rig's systems. Apparently this happens a few times a year, usually unannounced, with the results reported directly to the company's Audit and Risk Committee. He'd been on the rig for a few days and seemed to have established positive relationships with senior management and the resident engineers. Nothing negative reported. No fights, disagreements or spats. At first, they thought it was an accident. The body was lying at the bottom of an inspection chamber used to examine the drilling gear, and a guard-rail was bent in a way consistent with someone having toppled over it. The rail had been in perfect condition last time it was inspected, a couple of weeks ago.'

'So why did they think it wasn't an accident?' Vanessa made eye contact with Colin as the DCS asked the question. They both knew that he was hoping not to have to mount a full scale murder investigation, always expensive, but likely to be ruinous to his budget if it involved frequent visits to an oil rig more than a hundred miles north east of Aberdeen. Not to mention the possibility of running two investigations simultaneously.

'The medics on the rig noticed severe bruising on the back of the neck and shoulders, consistent with being struck, or pushed very hard, from behind. We should hear what the pathologist thinks very soon. Also, there was no sign of his hardhat, which is suspicious in itself. But there's no doubt that, at the very least, we have a suspicious death.'

'Colin?'

MacNee was a little apprehensive. He was looking at his first turn as Senior Investigating Officer on a major case, and his first murder, since he had got his promotion. He didn't count the few days he served as Acting SIO on the so-called Balmoral murder a couple of months before he was made up to Inspector, but he thought his performance on that case, both before and after his temporary promotion, had helped his career. He needed to get this one right, from the start.

'On Saturday morning, just before the shift change at eight o'clock, a nurse at GRH went for a pee in a staff loo in the main surgical block. He took out his phone to call his partner, dropped it - he said his hands were still wet because the hand driers are useless - and when he bent down to pick it up he saw two feet partially visible under a cubicle door. The door was locked, so he stood on the toilet bowl of the next cubicle and looked over. He knew right away that the man, whom he didn't recognise, was dead. He called security, they had a look and called us. I was on duty and I got there just after half past eight.'

'Has he been identified? And do we know the death is suspicious.'

'No ID yet, sir. There was nothing on the body to tell us who he was. No wallet, which is odd. So we don't know if he was a patient, a relative, a member of staff, or a contract worker. I've got Williamson and Todd working on it and they should be able to eliminate some possibilities quite quickly.'

'Cause of death?' Esslemont prompted.

'Again, we need to wait for the pathologist's report. He's doing two PMs, so it might be this afternoon before we have anything definite. But nobody had touched the body before I got there, and from the position and attitude I'd be surprised if he had died from natural causes. He looked as if he had been stuffed into the cubicle and there were scuff marks on the door that suggest somebody climbed over it to get out, probably after locking it.'

'Can we put a name to the oil platform body?' There was just a touch of exasperation in Esslemont's question. He clearly didn't want to have to tell the press that he had two unidentified murder victims on his hands.

'Harvey Jamieson, from Shreveport, Louisiana. We've been in touch with the American Embassy and the company has contacted the family. Married, three grown up children. We expect his wife to get here late this afternoon to do the formal identification.'

'Christ almighty!' Esslemont said, 'Two murders, one weekend. I was always taught never to believe in coincidence. Any reason to think they're related?'

'Very unlikely, sir,' Vanessa looked at Colin who shook his head. 'But we'll keep an open mind on it.' It was a well-worn cliché, but it would do for now.

*

Detective Constables Todd and Williamson, working on the identity of the hospital body, quickly established that he wasn't a patient or a member of staff. The hospital's computerised admission and discharge system kept meticulous records of the comings and goings of patients. The human resources department could check quickly which employees had used their electronic swipe cards to record arrival and departures over the previous forty-eight hours and there were no anomalies. It was just possible that a staff member had come into the hospital and forgotten to swipe. However the system, which had been introduced by the new private sector management company in the face of strong opposition from staff and unions, was used by human resources to verify attendance and by payroll to calculate wages and salaries, especially overtime. The detectives decided to exclude the possibility that the dead man was a member of staff until they had checked up on relatives and other members of the public, and, more importantly, contract staff.

'About three years ago', Duncan Williamson told Colin MacNee, 'the Health Board, against its better judgment, the chief executive says, was instructed by the Scottish Government to contract out the hospital's management. It was hugely controversial politically. I was still in uniform then and I had to police the union demos protesting against it. But it went ahead, and things became even more heated when an American health management organisation - an HMO - was announced as the preferred bidder.'

MacNee interrupted. 'Fascinating stuff, Duncan, but is it relevant?'

'Bear with me, boss. Eventually, the contract, for twenty-five years, was awarded to the HMO. It's called Hedelco - Health Delivery Corporation. They kept on most of the management, but the performance of the hospital is monitored, on a daily basis, by a team of number crunchers and lawyers from the states. They have a suite of offices on site and they are obsessively secretive. It's not a happy place, and Stewart and I are being blocked at every turn as we try to find out who they had on site on Friday and Saturday.

'For fuck's sake, we're investigating a murder in a major public building!'

'That's the point. Hedelco regard it as a private corporation. Their local people have to refer everything back to the States and you don't have to spend much time there to realise that the local management are shit scared of Hedelco.'

'But they don't own it. We own it. The National Health Service owns it. These money grubbing bastards need to know that. Who do I talk to?'

Colin MacNee was angry that the enquiry was being obstructed, but he also knew that he was showing his political leanings. As a serving officer, he had to be politically neutral, but his liberal views on race, gender and public service were well known to his colleagues. He had great respect for those police officers who, in the face of the usual stereotyping, became openly left wing after leaving the service, even to the extent of running for public office or taking the Labour whip in the House of Lords. His wife, Janet, was an NHS GP and, since his promotion had increased their income to the point where they could afford reliable childcare, she worked full time in a community health centre.

'Hedelco's local boss – "Chief Contract Management Officer" he calls himself - is Bernard - stress on the "nard": really pisses him off if you get it wrong - Donovan. I'd only been with him for two minutes when he told me about his MBA from Harvard. As my granny would say, if he was chocolate he'd eat himself. Very good at giving nothing away, though. Says he has to check everything with Head Office. Can't give out information without their approval. He's your man. You may need reinforcements, though.'

*

DCI Vanessa Fiske had a flat in Aberdeen, but for a few months she had been living with her - she was never sure how to describe him - boyfriend? partner? lover? - in his rather bigger apartment overlooking the harbour. Neil Derrick, a commercial lawyer in the oil business, had been less than sympathetic when Vanessa had confessed to being frightened by the prospect of flying by helicopter to the crime scene.

'For God's sake, Vanessa. You're a senior police officer in the oil capital of the UK. You really can't expect to restrict you investigations to places you can drive to. Anyway, the police use helicopters for all sorts of things.'

'I know that! But I've been quite clever, so far, about avoiding going up in the bloody things. Even when I was on royal protection I managed to negotiate myself out of airborne assignments. And budget cuts make it quite easy, most of the time, not to use them. But I've got a probable crime scene that happens to be a hundred miles offshore and I can hardly send Colin because I'm frightened to go on a chopper. He's a friend, and he's very loyal, but it would get out. So I'll just have to take a beta blocker and go for it!'

Going for it had meant a one hour flight from Dyce to Vermont One. It had been a lovely bright autumn day with very little wind and the conditions helped her to enjoy the experience. Circling round the rig and then landing on its helipad had been dramatic and her excitement had communicated to the two scenes of crime officers she had taken with her, and to her newly recruited Detective Sergeant, Sara Hamilton. But this was work, and potentially a very difficult case. She needed to assess the situation before sending for some uniformed support to take statements from the staff on the rig.

*

DI Colin MacNee had been sitting in the reception area of Hedelco's suite of offices rather longer than the urgency of a murder enquiry could tolerate. The young woman at the desk - locally recruited by the sound of her accent - was smiling at him in a way that was intended to be both apologetic and encouraging, but his patience was exhausted.

'Miss Archibald, I need to speak to Mr Donovan. Now. I assume that he is behind that door. I don't care how important his international call is. Either you go in there and tell him I have to see him right now, or I will. You might remind him that this is almost certainly a murder enquiry and that he is coming very close to obstructing the police.'

The door was opened by a man of about forty-five with close-cropped fair hair and wearing the unmistakeable uniform of corporate America. The jacket of the single-breasted suit was a little too tight, the trousers a little too short. The button-down, double-stitched collar contained the regulation anonymous, but to the British eye, faintly military tie, with the stripes sloping down from right to left. He stuck out his right hand - no shirt cuffs, so a half-sleeve shirt.

'Mr MacNee. I'm so sorry you've had to wait. How can I help?'

Smarmy bastard, Colin thought, let's make sure he understands the ground rules.

'It's Detective Inspector MacNee, Mr Donovan, and I've just been telling your secretary how perilously close you're coming to obstructing my enquiries, so perhaps we should speak in private.'

Donovan had the look of a man whose authority was rarely challenged. He was finding it difficult to process such a direct and aggressive approach from someone much younger than himself. MacNee thought that it was as much the perceived disparity in their salaries as in their ages that made his attack incomprehensible to the American, but this was his turf, not Donovan's.

'Yeah, sure.' Donovan said, indicating the open door to his office. 'Why don't you step this way, Inspector?'

Colin was a little disappointed not to be able to hear anything sarcastic or patronising in the use of his rank. The American had, apparently, decided to play it straight.

'Mr Donovan...'

Donovan interrupted. 'Please call me Bernard' - stress on the second syllable - 'Inspector.'

This time there was an edge, an attempt, Colin thought, to establish some kind of complicity between them.

'I'll stick to Mr Donovan, sir, if you don't mind.' This was becoming some kind of comedy of manners, so Colin turned sharply to the purpose of his visit.

'I'm investigating a probable murder, Mr Donovan, and I need your co-operation. We have a body found in this hospital, which your company manages on behalf of the National Health Service. He was neither a patient nor a member of the hospital staff. We think it unlikely that he was a relative or a member of the general public. I need to know what contract or visiting staff you had on site on Friday. And I need to know whether or not they are all accounted for.'

Donovan smiled indulgently, much as a nursery school teacher might when a toddler asked for a sweetie. 'I would like to help, Inspector, I really would. But we at Hedelco have protocols respecting the privacy of our staff and of information regarding them. I can't simply ignore them without first seeking approval from head office.'

'Mr Donovan, please tell me, without regard to your so-called protocols, if you have the information I need.'

'Quite possibly, Inspector, but that does not mean I can make such data widely available.'

Colin MacNee was struggling to maintain his composure. This man seemed to think that he was in an episode of *Law & Order* rather than at the sharp end of a real murder enquiry. 'I'll take that as confirmation that the information is available to you, Mr

Donovan, and I will make one more formal request that you hand it over to me. If you refuse, I shall do two things. Number one:' Colin was quite deliberately using American phraseology. 'I will arrest you for obstructing my enquiries. Number two: I will immediately seek a court order for the release of the information. I need hardly tell you that will lead Hedelco, already not the most popular organisation in Scotland, to sustain some real damage to its reputation. Your choice. You have fifteen minutes.'

With that, DI MacNee left Donovan's office, but not before he had thrown his card on to the desk.

*

As soon as they stepped off the helicopter on to Vermont One, DCI Fiske and her colleagues were issued with high visibility jackets, heavy duty, non-slip boots, and hard hats. They had been met by the Offshore Installation Manager, the most senior member of the crew. He introduced himself, in an accent that was Scottish but not Aberdonian, as Alex Randall, and then took them to his office, a cramped space with walls covered in diagrams, rosters, meteorological charts and a couple of family pictures.

As she sat down, on one of the four hard chairs that looked to have been brought in specially, Vanessa asked, 'Does everybody have to wear this gear, especially the hard hat, all the time?'

'Except when they are in social, recreational or sleeping areas, yes. Why do you ask?'

'Because when the body was found there was no sign of a hard hat. And it was in an operational area. Any idea why that should be?'

'None at all, Inspector. Harvey Jamieson was an experienced offshore engineer who knew the rules. If he knew he was going into an operational area, he would have been wearing his hat.'

Fiske noted the conditionality of Randall's answer. 'So, if he did know, he would have put on his hat and your people would have found it, either still on his head, or nearby. Unless it had been removed.'

'I suppose so.'

'And if he didn't know, we would have to conclude that he found himself in an operational area unexpectedly. If he had been forced to go there, for example.'

'Maybe. I have no idea why he was there. He had already done his checks on that inspection chamber a couple of days ago. If he had wanted to re-examine something there, he would have gone fully equipped.'

'So... Either he went there voluntarily, fully equipped, and the hat was removed after he died. Or he was coerced and went there without it. If the former, he was followed. If the latter, he probably knew his murderer. We need to examine his effects, Mr Randall, to see if his hard hat is among them.'

*

Bernard Donovan considered whether to try to stall Colin MacNee for a bit longer, but a quick reflection on his relationship with his bosses in America convinced him that an arrest and a court order would do him more harm than the unauthorised release of information in the course of a murder enquiry.

MacNee was still in the outer office when Donovan called him back.

'In the circumstances, Inspector MacNee, I think I am prepared to take local responsibility for the release to you of the information you require. It will take about a half-hour to assemble it. If you would like to wait, I'm sure that Sharon will provide you with a hot beverage.'

'Thank you, Mr Donovan, but I have to go to the crime scene. You have my mobile number. You can call me or text me when the information is ready and I'll come and get it. It's likely that it will raise questions that I'll need you to answer.'

The staff toilet where the unidentified body had been found was still decorated with crime scene tape and guarded by a female PC. The scenes of crime officers and the forensic team had done their work and their report would be on Colin's desk when he got back to HQ. He was under pressure from hospital management, albeit at a less exalted level than Bernard Donovan, to allow the toilet to come back into use, but he needed to have a last look at it before authorising the removal of the tape.

He wanted to think about how the unidentified victim had got to where he had been found. It seemed likely that he had been killed in the toilet. There was no evidence of any kind of scuffle in the corridor outside and no signs of the body having been dragged into the toilet. These conclusions were tentative because the relentless focus on cleanliness and infection control that had characterised hospitals since the near-epidemic of MRSA meant that the corridors, including the floor, had probably been cleaned more than once since the body was left in the toilet cubicle.

Colin went back into the corridor to see if anyone going into the toilet could have been seen, other than by anyone passing by. It looked as though the nearest CCTV camera was about a hundred metres away, where the corridor got to the hospital's main stair well. The value of any footage it had recorded would depend on where it was focused. The most likely target was the lifts and stairs rather than the corridor, so if the dead man and his assailant had been caught on camera, it wouldn't have been as they went into the toilet. Not useless, but less valuable than a direct shot of their arrival at the crime scene.

Two wards were entered from the corridor between reception and the staff toilet and both had half-glass doors. It was possible that the dead man had been seen walking towards the toilet and someone might recognise him from a photograph. Colin hoped not to have to use a *post mortem* picture, but that would depend on whether he was a contract worker and whether Hedelco had a photograph on file.

*

Harvey Jamieson's effects were in his cabin, neatly hung up in the small wardrobe or stored in the drawers beside the bed. There was no high visibility jacket or boots because he had been wearing them when the body was discovered. There was no sign of a hard hat.

'Would he have brought his own hat or would he have been issued one when he arrived?' Vanessa asked.

'These guys like to travel as light as possible, so he would have been issued with his safety gear when he got here, just as you were.' Randall said, as he double-checked under the bed.

Vanessa looked at the small desk in the corner of the room and said, 'We'll have to take that laptop, Mr Randall. Standard procedure with a suspicious death. We'll return it when our forensic IT people have examined it for anything that might help with the investigation'.

Randall looked concerned. 'But it's not his property, Chief Inspector. It belongs to Ebright Offshore Drilling. It's likely to contain commercially sensitive information. I don't think I can let you remove it from company property.'

'I'm afraid you don't have a choice'. Vanessa had already checked that the laptop was powered down. She unplugged it and dropped it into the large evidence bag that DS Hamilton had pulled from her backpack.

One of the SOCOs was collecting all Jamieson's effects while the other prepared to seal off the room. It would have to be forensically swept, but the first priority was to examine the inspection chamber where the body had been found.

'When was the last change of personnel on the rig? My understanding is that offshore workers typically work two weeks on and two weeks off, with a quarter of staff changing each week. Is that right?'

The significance of the question wasn't lost on Randall, and it showed on his face. 'Yesterday afternoon, about an hour or so before the body was found.'

'Why am I not surprised?' DCI Fiske said wearily. 'Brilliant timing, and no accident, I'd guess. I need a list of everyone who left the platform yesterday, together with all the personal and contact information you have. If you don't have the details, I need to know immediately who has. I also need a list of those who were here yesterday and stayed aboard, together with all personal details. They'll all have to be interviewed, starting tomorrow, as soon as I can get some uniformed officers here.'

*

Bernard Donovan texted Colin MacNee about twenty-five minutes after he left to go to the crime scene. The message said that he had the information and that MacNee would want to see it urgently.

'As well as the permanent Hedelco staff here,' Donovan said, 'We had four people on site from Head Office. I've located and spoken to three of them, two of them are still in Aberdeen, the other was at Heathrow en route back to Washington. But nobody can find the fourth, Peter Keller. I think he may be your man.'

Colin took out his iPhone and passed it to Donovan. 'Is this him?'

The picture of the dead man had been sent to Colin's phone by the pathologist.

Donovan lifted an iPad from his desk and handed it to MacNee. The colour image was of very high quality and Colin had no doubt that it was the same man.

'What was he doing here?'

'He's - was - what we call a Process Monitor. Part of a team that goes round the various facilities that Hedelco manages and assesses the efficiency of the way we deliver our product.'

Colin tried not to show his distaste for Donovan's corporate jargon. Some time, if an opportunity arose, he might tell him that health care was a service, not a product, but for now he needed to collect as much information as he could about Peter Keller, whom he had seen, where he had been, in the four days leading up to the day of his death. And he needed to know exactly how he had died.

CHAPTER TWO

On Sunday evening, a couple of hours after getting back from Vermont One, Vanessa phoned the MacNees' to speak to Janet. Her call was answered by Emma, the MacNees' elder daughter, eight years old, and a great fan of Vanessa.

'Hi, Vanessa! Daddy said you'd been up in a helicopter and you landed on an oil rig. Was it really, really exciting?'

'I'll let you into a secret, Emma. I was terrified about going up in the helicopter. Neil called me a wimp! But I loved it. I'll tell you all about it when I see you. I'm coming to look after you when your mummy and daddy go out for their anniversary. Is your mummy there?'

'Vanessa! How are you? Home safe?'

'I'm OK. Feeling a bit foolish about being scared of the helicopter, but I've done it now. I need to see you in your professional capacity. Tomorrow, if possible.'

'You really ought to go to your own doctor. Any reason why you shouldn't?' Janet was aware of an embarrassed, eloquent silence. 'Oh, Christ, Vanessa. You've been here for the best part of a year and you've never bothered to register with a doctor?'

'I know, I know. Haven't got round to it. I'm really very fit and healthy and I could have seen the MO in an emergency. Will you see me? Please. Better still, will you take me on as a patient?'

'One thing at a time. I'll fit you in at the end of afternoon surgery. About 4.45?'

'Thanks. See you then. Can I have a word with Colin?'

Vanessa and Colin had a brief chat about their meeting with Esslemont the next morning. 'He's not going to be happy about running two separate murder investigations at the same time.' Colin said.

Vanessa laughed. 'I heard about a top executive years ago who had cards printed to be sent out to customers. They read: "Thank you for your letter, which has not been selected for reply." Maybe the DCS could introduce a similar triage system when there's too much serious crime. Speaking of triage, how are things at the hospital? Going well?'

'American managers who like to keep everything confidential because they think they own the NHS. They've been giving Duncan and Stewart the runaround. I may have to bang the table a bit tomorrow.'

'Funnily enough, I had to remind the rig manager about our powers of evidence gathering. He tried to use company ownership as a reason to prevent me taking the dead man's laptop. They're an American company, too.'

'Let's try to meet up for a drink some time this week,' Colin said. 'Right now, I'm being harassed by two small but very powerful girls.'

*

The *post mortem* reports on the two bodies came in early on Monday afternoon. The cause of death for Keller, the hospital body, was unexpected and unusual, and when Colin MacNee read it he knew that this was going to be a long and complicated investigation. It was a detailed report, covering the external condition of the body, the state of the internal organs and of the brain, the contents of the

31

stomach, and evidence of old injuries and surgical procedures.

However, there was a key passage that would determine the direction of MacNee's enquiries.

> *My conclusion is that the immediate cause of death was cardiac arrest precipitated by intravenous lethal injections to the left arm. Toxicological analysis suggests that the deceased had been injected with the following drugs, probably sequentially and in the order given below:*

> · *Sodium thiopental/pentothal*
> · *Potassium chloride*

> *These are two of the three drugs commonly used in jurisdictions where lethal injection is the statutory form of judicial execution. They are used in many jurisdictions, including several states of the USA, and China.*

> *Sodium thiopental (sometimes known as pentothal) is an ultra-short acting barbiturate, often used for anaesthesia induction and for*

medically induced coma. A 5gr dose will cause unconsciousness in 10 seconds.

Potassium chloride stops the heart and the intravenous lethal injection dosage is conventionally 100mEq (milliequivalents).

Death would have occurred within ten minutes of the administration of the second injection.

The deceased had also sustained a blow to the head. This may have induced concussion to an extent that would have facilitated the lethal injections.

As soon as he finished reading, MacNee called DC Stewart Todd into his office and showed him the report. Todd looked shocked, but he knew immediately what he would be asked to do. He had to find out how, and where, the murderer might have acquired enough pentothal and potassium chloride to kill.

*

The cause of Harvey Jamieson's death on Vermont One was more straightforward. He had multiple injuries consistent with a fall from a height of more than six metres and it was likely, as the medics on the rig had guessed, that he had sustained a blow to the back of the head before he fell. Bruising on the torso was consistent with trauma caused by hitting a hard, horizontal object – probably the guard rail – in the course of the fall.

The pathologist was unwilling to say definitively which of Jamieson's injuries had killed him, but it was clear that his death had not been accidental. Time of death was estimated as between 1500hrs and 1900hrs on Friday afternoon. The final helicopter shuttle, taking rotating crew off the platform, had left Vermont One at 1800hrs.

When she finished reading the report, Vanessa called DS Sara Hamilton into her office.

'How are you getting on with locating the crew members who left the rig on Friday?'

'Randall gave me a list of names and contact details. They keep them on the rig in case of accident or illness. There were twenty names, and Aisha and I are working our way through them. So far, we've located and spoken to sixteen of them and we've told them that we may need them to be formally interviewed. They're all over the place, though, mostly in Scotland, but a couple in the north of England and one in Bristol. I've got somebody checking to see if any of the names come up in criminal records.

'What about the four that you haven't located?'

DC Aisha Gajani knocked on the open door and Vanessa beckoned her in.

'Hi, Aisha. What have you got?'

Aisha was a recent recruit to CID, the first woman in her Glasgow Pakistani family to have gone to university and the first woman from her local community to join the police. She helped Esslemont tick his diversity boxes, but no allowances had been made in taking her on. She had spent three years on the beat in Fraserburgh before applying for CID. She was tough, more experienced than her youth suggested, and very bright.

'I've still not spoken to four of the guys who left the rig on Friday. Three of them I'm not worried about. Their names and addresses check out and I've spoken to partners or flatmates. So I expect them to phone back. If they don't, I'll keep trying. But there's one that's a problem. His name is Thomas Nuttall and the address and phone number on record are in Wallsend, near Newcastle. The number is unobtainable, so I checked it and, apparently, it doesn't exist. Or at least it's never been allocated. Nothing from his mobile, either. I got on to Northumbria Police in Wallsend and asked them about the address. It used to exist, but it was demolished two years ago. The site was to be redeveloped, but the recession put paid to that.'

'Sounds as though Mr Nuttall, if that's his name, doesn't want to be found. Good work, Aisha. You carry on with that. See if Randall, or his head office, can help. Sara…'

Aisha interrupted. 'Sorry, Boss, this may be nothing, but I Googled the name Nuttall, and one of the areas where it's concentrated is Aberdeen. More than 1600 people, in and around the city.'

'Right. It may be coincidence, but we should be ready to follow up if none of the other lines of enquiry produces anything, so see what the operators of the rig have on him, and we'll take it from there.'

Vanessa turned back to DS Hamilton. 'How are uniform getting on with the interviews on the rig?'

'Nearly finished, I think. It's forty people, but the interviews are pretty short and we managed to get four PCs out there. It's overtime for them and most of them were up for the adventure. They've all got iPads, so we should have their interview notes quite quickly. I'll have a quick scan and let you know if there's anything significant.'

'Thanks, Sara. Ordinarily, I'd give you a hand with that, but I've got an appointment away from the office that I can't miss. Should be back by six o'clock, though. Will you still be here?'

'My boyfriend's picking me up at seven. Quick pizza and a film. So I'll be here till then.'

*

The *post mortem* findings on Keller were serious enough for DI MacNee to report it to his immediate line manager, DCI Fiske. He caught her just as she was finishing discussing with Hamilton and Gajani their progress on the Jamieson murder.

'Christ, Colin, this looks like a professional hit rather than an opportunistic mugging gone wrong. The killer probably removed the personal identification to delay the investigation. Have you spoken to the pathologist. Is he absolutely sure?'

'Not only have I spoken to him, I've been to see the body. The bruises to the head are very clear, but the needle pricks to the vein had to be pointed out to me. There was a small amount of blood encrusted around them that'll show up on the photos, but it was swabbed off during the PM and the marks were very clear. The pathologist says that when he saw the blood on the arm, and the needle marks, he decided to get a tox report quickly, so he sent the blood samples to the lab and then completed the PM. That's how the results appeared in his report. Good thinking on his part, I thought.'

'Indeed'. Vanessa looked thoughtful for a moment. 'We'll need to go to Esslemont with this. And he'll want to brief the Chief, if he can drag him away from buffing up his c.v.' Everybody knew that the Chief

Constable was applying for the top job in the new combined Scottish police service that the Scottish government, against all professional advice, had decided to set up.

'I'll see if I can set something up for early this evening. Say, six o'clock. That OK for you? I just think that this is so out of the ordinary run of murders that people outside North East Constabulary may begin to take an interest. And we need to keep the details out of the public domain.'

'The Press Office, which is to say Harry Conival, is working on a press release. Or two press releases. They can't decide whether to issue a statement about both murders, or one on each. I doubt whether anybody there has had to deal with two suspicious deaths simultaneously, any more than we have. What do you think, Boss?'

'My instinct is to treat them separately, just as we would have done if they had happened a couple of days apart. Some of the hacks might ask if we think there's any connection. But we can play a very straight bat to that. And we don't need to have a press briefing – yet – so they won't be able to push us too hard.'

Colin knew that Vanessa's recent experience with the press hadn't been entirely positive. They had put her under some pressure during the Balmoral murder case by digging into her private life. And she had come out of that case with a nagging doubt about whether she could trust Harry Conival. But he was the duty press officer and she had no credible reason to ask for him to be replaced. She had also decided, first appearances notwithstanding, that he was pretty good at his job.

'I've got to go. I've got an appointment'. She nearly said 'with your wife', but didn't, just in case Janet hadn't mentioned it. 'Could you let the press office know we want two press releases? I'll see you at six and we can approve them then.'

*

Vanessa looked up from an old copy of *Hello!* as Janet MacNee came into the waiting room.

'Hi, Vanessa. Come through.'

As Vanessa sat down in the consulting room, Janet closed the door and asked, 'So what can I do for you?

'I think I may be pregnant.'

'Oh! Why do you think that?'

'I've missed a period for the first time since I was fourteen. I'm usually as regular as clockwork. And a certain amount of queasiness in the morning. I wasn't really all that scared about the bloody helicopter. I just didn't want to throw up over my colleagues!'

'I assume you've done a test?'

'Positive. Five weeks, it said.'

Janet smiled. 'If you can give me a sample, I'll check and then I'll examine you. Espccially important since you haven't seen a doctor for at least a year.' The tone of disapproval was unmistakeable. Vanessa tried to look sheepish.

'But let's assume that you are, as my ever-sensitive husband would put it, up the duff. How do you feel about it?'

'I couldn't be happier! It'll cause problems, of course, but we'll deal with them. And I'll have to think about when to take my maternity leave. But I've got a great role model in Chris Jenkinson, so I know it can be done.'

Chris Jenkinson, Vanessa's informal mentor, had recently been promoted to Deputy Chief Constable. If the most senior female officer in Scotland could combine career and family, so could she.

'You said "we". Does Neil know?'

'I thought I'd wait for confirmation before talking to him   But I remember you told me the first time I met him that he wanted children, so I think he'll be happy. We have discussed it, in principle.'

Janet laughed. 'Just make sure he doesn't hug you too tight when you tell him.'

Vanessa was six weeks pregnant.   Janet booked her in for a scan at eight weeks and agreed to take her on as a patient.

*

DCS Esslemont looked appalled. 'Is the pathologist absolutely sure?'

'I asked the same question,' Vanessa said. 'But there seems to be no doubt."

'This is no run-of-the-mill murder, if there is such a thing.' Colin MacNee said. 'It looks like a hit. It was well-planned and expertly executed, if you'll excuse the pun. Given what the pathologist has said in his report, and confirmed when I spoke to him, the killer could have been in and out of that toilet in about two minutes.'

'But didn't the report say that it could have taken up to ten minutes for the heart to stop?'

'Yes, sir, it did. But remember that he was unconscious within ten seconds of the first injection, and the pathologist says that the pentothal would have kept him unconscious until cardiac arrest killed him. The cocktail was designed to ensure that condemned murderers don't wake up before they're dead. So as long as he was unconscious, and locked in the cubicle, the killer could be gone very quickly.'

'But we now know who he was?'

'Peter Keller, a Progress Monitor, whatever that is, employed by Hedelco, to inspect their systems, which could mean anything. I need to talk to Donovan, Hedelco's manager at GRH, to find out exactly what he was doing there. My working assumption has to be that he was killed for some reason connected with his job.'

Esslemont assumed his thinking position, head thrown back, eyes to the ceiling, hands steepled on his chest. 'I'll have to brief the Chief in rather more detail on this than we usually do this early in a murder enquiry. Summaries to his staff officer are unlikely to be enough. We don't need to say anything to the press about the cause of death, but we all know it will get out. And given that it involves an American company engaged in a very controversial enterprise it may turn political. Have we seen a draft press statement yet?'

Vanessa looked at Colin and then said, 'We're expecting Harry Conival to bring them up any minute. They were beating themselves up in the press office about whether to put out one statement or two. I decided two murders, two statements, just as we would have done if the bodies hadn't been found within twenty four hours of each other.'

'Good. And what about the oil rig body. Definitely murder?'

'Oh, yes, no doubt at all. On the face of it, it looks a bit more straightforward than Colin's case. Blow to the head and a six metre fall on to a steel platform. Multiple injuries. Possible, but not likely, that he might have survived if he had been treated immediately. One of the people who left the platform after the murder appears to have laid a false trail and we can't find him. That's where we're concentrating our efforts for now'.'Wasn't – what was his name? – Jamieson some kind of systems auditor. Didn't you tell me that this morning?'.

Vanessa nodded, and then realised where the DCS was going. 'Same kind of job as Keller was doing at the hospital. Both working for American companies. I'll work on finding out if it's anything other than coincidence. Like you, sir, I don't really believe in coincidence, but from where I'm standing now, I can't see a material connection.'

As they walked down the corridor outside Esslemont's office, Vanessa asked Colin if there was any significance in the fact that the killer had used only two of the three drugs that usually comprise the lethal injections used for executions.

'I asked the pathologist that', Colin said, 'and the answer is horrible. The third drug, given after the pentothal and before the potassium chloride, is pancuronium bromide. It's a paralytic. It ensures that the victims don't twitch while they're dying. Might upset the witnesses. I don't suppose our killer gave a shit about that.'

*

Later that evening, while they were sipping champagne to celebrate Vanessa's pregnancy, ('The last drink I'll have for God knows how long', Vanessa said, happily), Neil and Vanessa turned, as they often did, to discussing their day.

'Esslemont may be a man for the quiet life, but he's not daft. He spotted the similarities in the jobs of the two victims right away. I need to look into that, but I'm not sure I know where to start. Colin's talking to Hedelco's top man at GRH – the Chief Contract Management Officer – to find out exactly what the man murdered at the hospital was doing there. "Progress Monitor" tells us fuck all.'

'When I'm doing contract negotiations,' Neil said, 'I have to ensure that we've done the "due diligence", to use the jargon. It's about trying to ensure that we don't get any surprises further down the line. You know, the kind of thing that the government didn't bother to do when deciding on the West Coast rail franchise. One of our first steps is to find out who owns the companies involved. I would start there.'

CHAPTER THREE

'What exactly was Keller doing in the Hospital?' MacNee asked.

DI Colin MacNee and DC Duncan Williamson had been waiting for Bernard Donovan when he arrived at his office at eight o'clock on Tuesday morning. Colin had discovered, in a casual conversation with the smiley but not very bright receptionist, his habitual arrival time. Donovan had been surprised to see them there, which was exactly what Colin intended.

'He was a Progress Monitor, as I told you. Hedelco manages this hospital on fairly tight profit margins and we need to know we are doing things right. If we do them wrong it costs us money'.

'With respect, Mr Donovan, that tells me almost nothing. I have a murder victim who died in this hospital and I am working on the assumption that his death has something to do with his work, so I need to know exactly, and probably in some detail, what he had been doing in the days before his death.'

'That's one big assumption, Inspector. I'm guessing from the fact that you couldn't immediately identify him that his billfold was missing, so why can't it just be a shakedown gone wrong?'

'I can assure you that it wasn't. I can't tell you why I'm sure because it might compromise the investigation if I did. So, I'm asking you again, what was Keller doing here?'

Williamson had seldom seen his boss quite so aggressive and irritated, but after his rant in the office about privatising the NHS, he was impressed rather than surprised. He was taking detailed notes, and he was sorry he couldn't get tone and tenor into them.

'I should really get on to Head Office and maybe also the Health Board about this.' Donovan was fiddling uncomfortably with his tie, disturbing the neat arrangement of the Windsor knot and the button-down collar. 'Our contract with the Health Board has a number of very tight confidentiality clauses and I'm reluctant to breach them.'

Colin got up from his chair and leaned across Donovan's desk until he was closely enough in the American's face to show how serious he was, but not close enough to be accused of intimidating behaviour. 'We've been here before, sir, and I really don't want to have to lean on you again. I will simply remind you that a murder enquiry almost certainly trumps any claims of confidentiality that you or your masters might make. I will speak directly with them if necessary, but I really don't think I should have to.'

The colour returned to Donovan's face as MacNee resumed his seat. He stopped fiddling with his tie and began to pass a pen from hand to hand. The detectives waited. Donovan seemed to come to a decision, but not one with which he was entirely comfortable.

'Keller was engaged on what is called a technical audit. He was examining, in detail, a selection of the hospital's procedures and outcomes. We are…were… required to give him unrestricted access to wherever he wanted to go and to whoever he wanted to speak with.'

'Who decided what he would examine?'
'He did, possibly with guidance from Head Office.'

'And how did he report and who to?'

Donovan was looking more and more uncomfortable. His movements were coming close to squirming. He said nothing.

'Mr Donovan?' Colin MacNee's prompt had a little touch of menace in it.

'I don't know exactly who he reported to. As I understand it, he filed his reports by encrypted emails back to Head Office and his laptop was programmed to immediately delete the emails after receiving confirmation of delivery.'

'And where is his laptop? It wasn't with his body and it wasn't with his belongings at the hotel.'

'I have no idea. I never saw him without it. I'd be surprised if the hospital CCTV hadn't picked him up carrying it around. But I haven't seen it since the last time I saw it over his shoulder on Thursday morning'.

'Mr Donovan, you are Hedelco's Chief Contract Management Officer here. I find it very difficult to believe that you have no idea what Keller had investigated and what he had found.'

'He wasn't allowed to talk to me in detail about his work but from the questions he asked me, he seemed to be concentrating on some processes that were close to failure and which might – I say might – have endangered patient safety.'

*

While MacNee and Williamson were talking to Donovan, DCI Vanessa Fiske was on a shore to ship radio call with Alex Randall, the Offshore Installation Manager on Vermont One.

'When did Jamieson arrive on the platform?'

'Late on Sunday afternoon. He was scheduled to do a full five days of audit and inspection and he would have left on the last helicopter on Friday'.

'We've done a preliminary analysis of his laptop and we've found some draft reports, some of which detail serious safety and maintenance failures, but nothing dated earlier than Friday, the day he died. He must have prepared more reports than that. He would hardly wait to write them all up at the end of his visit.'

Randall was silent, and Vanessa wondered, as did DS Sara Hamilton, who was listening in and taking notes, if he was considering carefully whether he should answer. The silence continued.

'Mr Randall', Vanessa prompted, suppressing a belch that she hoped wasn't a sign that she was going to be sick, 'I hate to sound like a cliché cop on a TV show, but this is a murder enquiry, and if you know anything that might help us, you really shouldn't hold back.'

'No. He would have filed his reports daily by encrypted email. His laptop would have automatically deleted the emails after confirmation of delivery'.

Vanessa thanked Randall, and just as she was ending the call, he interrupted her.

'His hard hat turned up in a refuse skip. It's quite badly damaged. Will I send it to you?'

Vanessa said that he should avoid handling it too much, place it in a plastic bag, and send it by the next helicopter. She signed off, and with as much nonchalance as she could muster, rushed off to the loo.

*

When she got back to her office, Vanessa found a yellow sticky on her screen asking her to return a call from Neil Derrick.

'Hi! I'm feeling like shit, so make it quick.'

'Just thought you'd like to know, somebody at the oil company that operates Vermont One has a sense of humour. I thought that Ebright sounded too like an oven cleaner to be a sensible name for an offshore drilling company, so I Googled it. "Ebright", or to be totally accurate, "Ebright Azimuth" is the highest point in the state of Delaware: 447 feet. Only Florida has a lower highest point.'

There was sometimes an endearing Boy Scout geekiness about Neil, but Vanessa wasn't in the mood.

'Fascinating. Maybe it will come up in a pub quiz and you'll win a pint of lager.'

'Funny name for a business that's drilling thousands of metres under the sea. But I'm a commercial lawyer and I know that Delaware is a well-known corporate haven.'

'Neil, what the fuck is a corporate haven'.

'It's a place where you register your business if you want to make it very difficult for anybody to find out much about it. Delaware set up as a corporate haven at the end of the nineteenth century to attract businesses from New York. And it's worked for them.'

Vanessa took a sip of fizzy water. 'I'll bear it in mind'.

'You do that, darling. Meanwhile, I may do a little digging. In my lunch hour, of course. See you tonight.'

*

Vanessa was considering another loo run when Sara Hamilton came in carrying a printed pdf file.

'This just came in from Northumbria. It's a copy of Thomas Nuttall's Ebright ID. It was with a bundle of clothes stuffed under the seats of a changing room in a menswear store in the Metro Centre in Gateshead. It was found early this morning, but Christ knows how long it's been there. I've been on to Northumbria and they've sent somebody to the shop to see if anyone remembers him. Trouble is, if he bought new stuff on

Saturday, he may have been seen only by Saturday staff. On the plus side, it must be quite unusual for someone to buy a complete new outfit and then say they'll just wear it. So the shop's computer should have details of what he bought.'

'He'll be long gone. But it'll do no harm to circulate what we think he's wearing. I have a feeling that this trail is going cold very quickly. Remember that little nugget Aisha came up with, about all the Nuttalls who live in Aberdeen? Maybe it would worth her while to spend half an hour with the electoral register – and remind her, not that you'll need to, she's really on the ball – that she should look at the unedited version, not the one that people can buy for marketing and the like and that you can ask to be excluded from, and see if she can find a Thomas Nuttall of the same sort of age as our man'.

*

The Aberdeen office of Ebright Offshore Drilling was on a small business park just off the main road to Inverness. It occupied one floor of a 1990s prefabricated steel and glass block looking out on a pond populated by some ornamental carp and bordered by some ill-kept grass and shrubbery. Vanessa and

Sara pulled into a visitors' space in the car park and, as they got out of the car, Sara said, 'Boss, are you OK?'

'I'm fine. Why?'

'None of my business, I know, but I just wondered about all that running to the loo. If you've got an infection or something, you shouldn't be at work.'

'I haven't got an infection, Sara. Don't worry about me. I'm touched that you care.'

When they got to reception, Vanessa showed her warrant card and introduced herself and DS Hamilton. 'We have an appointment to see Mr Wootten.'

The receptionist smiled faintly, dialled a number, said that Chief Inspector Fiske was here, came round the desk and asked the detectives to follow her. They walked through a long open-plan office, with people working at computer screens to the sound of nondescript music of the kind played to waiting customers by call centres, to what seemed to be the only enclosed space on the floor. A discreet plate on the door read: 'T R Wootten: Europe Manager'.

The receptionist knocked and an American accent called, 'Come!' Vanessa thought that this was unusual. Her experience of the hail-fellow-well-met style of Americans in Aberdeen led her to expect Wootten to come out from behind the desk to welcome them. Her surprise was even greater when she entered the office and saw, sitting at the desk and showing no sign of getting up, a woman of about her own age, wearing a red silk blouse, a gold choker at the neck and large gold hoop earrings drawing the eye to her beautifully cut hair.

'Hi. I'm Tammy Wootten. How can I help you?'

Vanessa was careful not to show her surprise and wondered why she hadn't known she was coming to see a woman. 'We're investigating the death of Harvey Jamieson on Vermont One and I have some questions about what he was doing there. The platform manager, Alex Randall, couldn't tell us much so I thought I should speak to you before contacting your head office in the States.'

Tammy Wootten seemed guarded. 'What is it you need to know?'

'We need to have details of what work he was doing on the platform between his arrival on Sunday, and Thursday. We have some knowledge of what he was doing on the day he was killed – Friday – because we've analysed the contents of his laptop, but we need the full picture. I understand…'

Tammy Wootten interrupted. 'Yes, Inspector, I know that you have Harvey's laptop and we need to have it returned to us immediately. It is, after all, our property.'

Vanessa tried not to bridle. 'It may ultimately be your company's property, Ms Wootten, but for the moment it's evidence and therefore the property of the investigation of a murder. I understand that standard procedure is for someone doing Harvey Jamieson's job to file reports as encrypted emails each day and that these emails are then automatically deleted from the laptop.'

Tammy Wooten, with a look of some hostility, nodded.

'We need to see these emails. If you have copies here, that would be very convenient. If they have gone to your Head Office we'll need to go there. In a last resort, of course, our technical people can probably find them on the hard disk. That would be laborious and time-consuming and I need to move this investigation forward.'

'They would have been addressed to Head Office, not here. These reports go directly to the Audit and Risk Committee. I would only see them if the Committee decided that any local action needed to be taken.'

'Fine. Whom do I have to contact in the States?'

'I would prefer that you went through me. I will get in touch with Head Office and let you know their view'.

Vanessa smiled. 'I know you can't be expected to be up to speed on Scottish police procedure, Ms Wootten, so let me enlighten you. We don't conduct enquiries, especially murder enquiries, through intermediaries. I will contact the appropriate people at Ebright's head office directly, and if we have to speak to people there, I will either go to the States or arrange a videolink with the help of colleagues in the local police. However, examination of the emails may make that unnecessary, but I can't reach a conclusion on that until I've seen them.'

'But you don't know that Harvey's death was work-related?'

'It is a working assumption. We are also investigating other possibilities, which is why, as I'm sure you know, I've had a team of officers on Vermont One interviewing everyone who was on the rig while Jamieson was there, and another team tracing those who left the day he died'.

'All right, Inspector. I'll let you have names and contact details. We'll email them to you.'

'Within the hour, please.'

*

'Thomas is a less common name these days than it used to be'. DC Aisha Gajani was waiting for Fiske and Hamilton when they got back from Ebright's offices. 'I found only three Thomases among the Aberdeen Nuttalls. Our man is, according to HR records on Vermont One, forty-two years old, born on 23 February 1970. Two of the Thomases I found on the electoral roll were much older than that. The other was born on 23 February 1970, at Aberdeen maternity hospital, to James and Marion Nuttall, of Torry, both still alive.'

'Good work, Aisha', Sara said.

'That was the good news. The bad news is that Thomas Nuttall died just over a year ago, of leukaemia.'

Vanessa sighed. 'Identity theft. Or, to be exact, identity appropriation. This murder was premeditated. We just need to know why. Sara, have you had time to look at the interview notes from the rig?'

'I asked the PCs to flag up anything out of the ordinary or that might be linked to Jamieson's death. One of the men interviewed says he saw a heated argument between Jamieson and somebody who sounds a lot like Nuttall. This witness thinks this was late on Thursday, the evening before Jamieson was killed. Nothing else flagged up, but I'm going through the notes just in case.'

'Fine. Aisha can give you a hand. But I doubt you'll find anything of interest.'

*

Neil Derrick was a senior commercial lawyer working for an Aberdeen firm of solicitors specialising in the oil industry. He had started his career as a criminal lawyer, representing petty criminals in crown courts in the South of England, where he had qualified after doing a first degree in Scotland. He had got into commercial law when a colleague asked him to help with a complicated criminal fraud case. A facility with numbers that he had shown since he was a schoolboy had turned out to be very useful. That facility had also helped him to become quite an accomplished bridge player, a talent that he had yet to reveal to Vanessa. Commercial work was intellectually demanding and more quickly lucrative than criminal work – oil companies, as well as other industrial clients he had worked for before moving to Aberdeen, paid a lot more than legal aid – but he sometimes missed the buzz that came from following the evidence and from the analysis of human frailty that came with crime.

His interest in crime had, of course, been rekindled when he fell for a senior police officer. Vanessa liked to bounce ideas off him when she was in the middle of a case, and they were close enough, especially now, to talk in detail about her cases, even the most sensitive and confidential ones. He had, so far, been careful not to get involved without Vanessa asking him, but the oil rig murder was quite close to home, so he thought he might do a bit of research. And, when he had mentioned to Vanessa earlier in the day that he might do some digging, she hadn't objected.

Neil caught Vanessa on her mobile while Sara Hamilton was driving her back from Ebright.

'What's the name of that company that manages the hospital?'

'Hedelco – Health Delivery Corporation. Why?"

'Just checking something. Tell you tonight. How are you?'

'I'm fine. It's always better in the afternoon' Sara Hamilton gave Vanessa a knowing smile for which she was rewarded with a 'Don't go there' look.

*

'The usual?' Colin MacNee was at the bar of the pub round the corner from HQ and Vanessa was sitting at a corner table. Her 'usual' was a large glass of Sauvignon Blanc, so he was surprised when she said she'd rather have a mineral water.

'Not like you, Vanessa, especially after a hard day at the coal face'.

Vanessa gave him a bewildered look. 'You mean you don't know? Janet must take patient confidentiality more seriously than I would! I'm pregnant, Colin. Some champagne the other night with Neil when I told him was my last drink for quite a long time.'

'Well, if champagne was in order, so are congratulations!'

He leaned over and hugged her and gave her a kiss on the cheek. 'Emma and Cat are going to be almost as excited as you, if they can get over the fact that they can't have you as a second mummy. And I couldn't be happier for you and Neil'.

'Thank you, Colin. Just keep it to yourself for now. I have to work out when to take my leave, and I certainly want to get this oil rig murder out of the way before I go. I can't keep it hidden, so to speak, for very long, anyway. I think that Sara has guessed. But she'll be discreet.'

'How's that going?'

'I wanted to talk to you about that. When we spoke on the phone on Sunday night, you said something about being given the runaround by the American managers at GRH.'

'I persuaded the local guy to stop pissing me about, but it was a tedious business. A lot of stuff about confidential inspections, encrypted emails that are automatically deleted…'

Vanessa banged her glass down on the table. 'Christ almighty, I had a really difficult conversation this afternoon with a rather formidable woman who runs the Aberdeen office of the company that operates the platform, Ebright Offshore Drilling. She tried to tell me that I had to hand over the laptop that the rig manager didn't want me to take as evidence. But what's really interesting, is that she confirmed the procedure that had been described to me on the rig. The dead man's protocols as an inspector required reporting by encrypted emails that are automatically deleted.'

'So Esslemont's instinct may be right. Our two murders may be connected. But I still don't see how.'

Vanessa drained her glass. 'I think I should go home and start knitting bootees. But we'll have to talk to the DCS first thing tomorrow.'

*

When Neil got home, Vanessa was lying on the sofa watching Reporting Scotland on the BBC. He leaned down to kiss her and then sat and massaged her feet.

'What would this programme do without, crime, football and quirky highlanders? And the Nats want a Scottish Six O'clock News! God help us! Good day?'

'I had a really difficult contract to deal with but I think I sorted it. At least until the other side's lawyers crawl all over it. But I also did some light digging into Ebright and Hedelco.'

'Go on.'

'Do you mind if I have a drink, even when you can't?' She shook her head.

Neil poured himself a glass of South African Pinot Noir and sat down in an armchair facing Vanessa.

'I wanted to find out who owned Ebright Offshore Drilling. I've never had to deal with them – Vermont One is the only platform they operate in the North Sea, though they're after a license to drill in the North Atlantic, west of Shetland - so I did some basic computer searches. The kind we do as a matter of course when drawing up contracts. They used to be a independent company registered in Rhode Island, but about two years ago, after they posted a successful strike in Alaska and the one in the North Sea, they were bought by a private equity conglomerate registered in Delaware.'

'The well-known corporate haven,' Vanessa said.

'So glad you've been paying attention, DCI Fiske.' She threw a cushion at him in response to that.

This firm is called Burtonhall, and there's almost nothing they're not into. Oil, copper, wheat futures, armaments, private security, precious metals. You name it, they make money from it. But they are pathologically secretive. Took me some time – and I'm an expert – to find out who runs it. They have some really big names on their board. A former US Secretary of State, our last prime minister but three, a Russian oligarch, an allegedly corrupt politician-cum-businessman from Indonesia, and a guy who is, according to *Forbes*, the sixth richest man in America. Incorporation in Delaware fits with their extremely low profile.'

'A culture of secrecy isn't, in itself, evidence of wrongdoing', Vanessa said, a touch primly.

'Keeping an open mind, I see. Very commendable.' Vanessa looked for another cushion, but couldn't find one, so she said, 'Watch it, sunshine!'

'How about this, my sweet? Burtonhall also owns Hedelco. Acquired it last year at a knock-down price because it wasn't doing awfully well. They've stripped out most of the loss-making businesses – that's what private equity companies do – and they're now trying to make what remains profitable. And that includes the contract at GRH.'

'Neil, you're wonderful, but you know that already. I'm going to have to talk to Colin and then we'll both have to have a session with Esslemont. I have a feeling that this is going to turn into a very big deal indeed.'

CHAPTER FOUR

Burtonhall's corporate headquarters was a modern building of modest size, set in dense woodland just outside Wilmington, Delaware. The architecture, as those who knew both buildings had often noted, was strongly reminiscent of the CIA Headquarters building at the George Bush Centre for Intelligence in Langley, Virginia. Burtonhall's was on a smaller scale, but it had the same grandiose architectural signatures: the main entrance with the glass arched roof, the paved approach, the grassy courtyard with rustic benches, even a Burtonhall logo that echoed the CIA crest set into the entrance floor of the old CIA HQ. The similarities, which were not accidental and were intended to evoke a mixture of confidence, mystery and awe, were underscored by the array of antennae, aerials and microwave receivers on the roof, though these were rather less discreetly placed than those at Langley.

The strongest influence on the design of the building, completed in 2010, had been that of Cy Packard, the Chief Executive Officer of Burtonhall. Packard, a CIA veteran, had come to Burtonhall after running private security and protection operations in Iraq and Afghanistan, under contract to the Pentagon, and security for oil companies in the former Soviet republics of central Asia. He had commissioned the design of the building, supervised the architects, overseen the building contractors, and convinced the Board that an instantly memorable, but discreetly located, corporate HQ was the best way to give confidence to investors and the workforce. Insofar as they ever allowed themselves a joke at the expense of the CEO, Burtonhall employees said that he had had to be restrained by the Chairman of the Board from naming the building, in huge letters engraved on a granite tablet, "Packard House". As it was, its existence was announced by a small sign, easily missed by passers-by, saying simply, "Burtonhall".

On the Tuesday morning after the discovery of the bodies on Vermont One and at GRH, Packard was in his office, interrogating his director of security and head of human resources. The office was minimalist – a huge glass-topped desk, white bookshelves and occasional furniture, two upright armchairs, also in white wood, facing the desk. No ornaments or executive toys. The walls were decorated with photographs, professionally taken and elegantly posed, of the members of the Board. All but one of these was 12 inches by 10. The exception was the 18 by 12 portrait of the Chairman, a former United States Secretary of State famous for his aggressively interventionist style in defence of the perceived interests of the USA. Anyone moderately well-informed about current affairs, or even any casual reader of the major international news magazines, would have recognised other faces, too: a former UK prime minister, a Midwestern billionaire backer of the Republican Party, the former vice-president of a South East Asian 'republic', a Russian oil oligarch and ally of Vladimir Putin. It was a display of corporate power intended to impress and to intimidate all those who entered here.

Packard's management style was based on knowing everything about everything. Burtonall had a huge range of interests all over the world. Its main business was profit maximisation in order to increase the returns to the private equity investors who, collectively, had given it $40 billion to manage productively. The CEO insisted on seeing, daily, a one-page report from each of the businesses in which Burtonhall had a major interest. These were known, in a conscious echo of his time in intelligence, as 'sitreps'. One of his frequent responses to the information they contained, was to descend, unannounced, on local management if he thought they were underperforming or bringing unwelcome publicity. The company maintained a private jet, twenty miles away at Philadelphia International Airport, for the purpose.

'Come on, guys! How often do my sitreps bring me news of two murders? We've only got two businesses in Scotland and I'm looking at a dead body in each of them on the same fucking weekend. What's going on? What's the connection?'

Jack Eisner, Burtonhall's Director of Security, looked up from the sitreps. 'I just don't know, Cy. I've had no security concerns about either of these businesses. But I can see that it looks like one hell of a coincidence.'

'Yeah, you could say that! And here's another couple of things to add into the coincidence mix. Both of these businesses are giving me some concerns. Vermont One is way short of the production targets we promised. And the profit margins from managing that goddam socialised hospital are so thin you can hardly see them. None of that is known outside of this building, and I'd like to keep it that way. I need to be sure that we're managing this on the ground. Who's handling PR for these operations?'

Don Hamnett, the head of HR, looked uncomfortable. 'Hedelco has no local PR function. We took it out to reduce overheads and safeguard profits. The press relations of the hospital are looked after by the Health Board.' Packard looked pained. 'And PR for Vermont One is handled by local management. Tammy Wootten.'

'I really don't want to wind this up by flying to Aberdeen unless it's absolutely necessary. Apart from the fact that you don't know if they're connected, Jack, what details have you got on these killings.'

'Absolutely none. Only what's in the sitreps.'

'Christ, I don't pay you not to know about this kind of thing. You need to get over there, find out what the fuck is going on, and get back here by the end of the week, if possible. You can be in Aberdeen by tomorrow noon their time. And I want progress reports at least every day. More often if you turn up anything I should know, which is everything.'

*

The local press in Aberdeen had got wind of the hospital murder by the Saturday afternoon and of the body on Vermont One by Sunday morning. The North East Constabulary press office had confirmed that the two bodies had been found and that the deaths were being treated as suspicious. The need to wait for the *post mortems* to be completed made it possible to fend off questions about how the victims had died. None of he local crime reporters or the general reporters who worked as stringers for the nationals made any connection between Hedelco and Vermont One. A couple of the brighter sparks had expressed some scepticism about two murders on the same weekend being a coincidence. One of them had also mentioned the American connection to both of the crime scenes, but that was as far as it had gone, until early on Wednesday morning.

Harry Conival, the press officer assigned to both murder investigations, took a call from a financial reporter on one of the London-based broadsheets.

'Thanks for taking my call, Mr Conival.' That was two more surprises, Harry thought, on top of a call from a finance hack: a polite journalist and one who called him "Mr".

'Pleasure. What can an almost innumerate PR man do for you?'

'I was talking to one of my colleagues on the news desk about the two suspicious deaths over the weekend. Wouldn't normally interest me, but when he showed me the reports from our stringer and from the agencies, I couldn't help noticing that one body was found in a hospital run by Hedelco and the other on a platform run by Ebright.'

'That's right.' Harry had no idea where this was going.

'Do the investigating officers know that these companies are both owned by the same private equity company, Burtonhall?'

Harry had only the vaguest understanding of what a private equity company was, but he was experienced enough to know, first, that he should respond non-committally, and, second, that Fiske and MacNee had to be told. It was for them to decide if this information, if it could be confirmed, was relevant to their enquiries.

'I'll need to check on that, and come back to you, Mr ... I'm sorry, I didn't catch your name, not used to dealing with new customers.'

'Aaronson. Ben Aaronson'. He gave his mobile phone number and Harry promised to get back to him quickly, possibly within the hour.
*

Fiske and MacNee were already in Esslemont's office discussing how best to respond to the information that Hedelco and Ebright were owned by the same company. There was no reason to believe that this established a connection between the two murders, especially given the very different causes of death. However, as the DCS immediately pointed out, they needed to be able to respond effectively if they were. His first suggestion was that the two investigations should run in parallel, with two SIOs, reporting to him as Head of CID in overall charge.

Vanessa, partly because of her past slightly abrasive relationship with Esslemont, but mainly because she didn't think it would work, had to find both a tactful way of arguing against it and a viable alternative. Ideally, she would have liked to discuss it with Colin, but it was vital that they make a decision quickly.

'Sir, given your wider management responsibilities, wouldn't it be better, and more economical ('Nice touch, that', Colin thought.), if we simply brought the two murder investigations together, with me as SIO and Colin as Deputy SIO? We would each continue to lead our own part of the enquiry, with our own team in the field, but with regular broader team meetings and combined administrative backup. That would make it easier to record information and to identify and investigate any substantive connections.'

Vanessa was uneasily aware that she was employing a style of argument and vocabulary that the DCS sometimes called 'Met speak', in a disparaging reference to her training and experience in London. Colin MacNee nodded his assent, but before the DCS could respond, Harry Conival appeared at the door.

'Sorry to interrupt, but I've got something that you should know, if you don't already.' Vanessa had noticed before that Harry, who called her "Vanessa" or, if he wanted to be formal, "Chief Inspector", or, if he wanted to annoy her, "hen", never called Esslemont either "Sir" or "Chief Superintendent". She assumed that this was to emphasise his position as a civilian outside the chain of command, but she had never asked him. However, it was the kind of cussedness that would be wholly consistent with his general outlook: he had his job to do and the police had theirs. As long as his work supported theirs he could get away with quite a lot.

Harry told them about Aaronson's call.

'Thanks, Harry. As it happens, we did already know, but we didn't think anybody else did. What have you told the reporter?'

'Just that I'd get back to him within the hour. What do you want me to say?'

'Give us ten minutes and we'll give you a line. Vanessa or Colin will let you know and you can draft a release, if we think that's the way to go.'

Harry nodded and left, heading not for the press office but to the car park for a smoke.

Vanessa decided to get in first. 'That doesn't establish a connection, sir, but it does put the possibility in the public domain, or it will do when it goes up on the paper's website. We should pre-empt that by saying that we've established a possible connection between the murders, that it will be one among several lines of enquiry, and that we are now engaged in a single joint investigation. We'll still be reporting to you, and through you to the Chief, as you rightly suggested might be more necessary than in the case of an 'ordinary' murder.'

She was pushing her luck, or pressing the advantage that Harry's information had brought her. She was also laying on a little flattery. Esslemont looked a little peeved, but he was a man for choosing carefully where to stand and fight.

'All right. Get it done. We should get a press release out before Harry's deadline. Up to him to finesse depriving the reporter of an exclusive.'

*

As they walked back to the detectives' room next to Vanessa's office, Fiske and MacNee discussed who they needed on their team.

'I've got Sara and Aisha and you've got Duncan and Stewart. We probably need another DS and we need to be able to deploy uniform to do the legwork. Could you come up with a plan, Colin, with some idea of who should be doing what?' Colin nodded and Vanessa went on. 'Neil suggested that we might need some real financial experience on this, someone who can find their way quickly through company accounts, annual reports and the like. We need to know pretty quickly if there's anything in Hedelco, Ebright or indeed Burtonhall that might go to motive for these murders. And we need someone to analyse the content of these encrypted emails.'

They had reached Vanessa's office. 'One more thing. We need to find out what happened to Keller's laptop.'

*

Soon after arriving in Aberdeen from the Met, Vanessa Fiske had followed the advice of her former boss and sought out a senior officer to be her informal mentor. Her relationship with Assistant Chief Constable Chris Jenkinson continued after Chris was promoted to become, as a Deputy Chief Constable, the most senior woman police officer in Scotland, and Chris had recruited Vanessa into the Women's Police Network Scotland, an informal support group that helped individual women officers deal with discrimination and prejudice, as well as lobbying to make equal opportunity a reality rather than an aspiration.

On Wednesday evening Chris and Vanessa were driving together to Perth for a WPNS meeting. They spent the first part of the journey catching up and talking about the agenda for the meeting. As they approached the ring road round Dundee, Vanessa took a deep breath.

'I have some news, Chris, and you're only the second person in NEC that I've told.'

'You're not leaving, I hope.

'Nothing like that, no. I'm pregnant. Just over six weeks.'

'Well, I didn't expect that. I want to say "Congratulations" but I suppose I should ask if you're happy about it.'

'Very. Neil and I decided quite quickly that we wanted kids. I'm no spring chicken and we didn't expect it to happen so soon. I need to work out when to take my maternity leave and how I'm going to deal with the so-called "work/life balance". I can't think of anyone whose advice I'd value more than yours.'

'I'm not going to pretend it's been easy or that my life is perfect. But it's been OK. The hardest thing has been not having my husband here all the time. You won't have to deal with that.'

Chris had a son in secondary school and a daughter in primary. Her husband, a history professor in Manchester, spent weekends and university vacations in Aberdeen.

'Let me give you two pieces of advice. Make your maternity leave as short as you can and try to find reasons to come into the office - without the baby - occasionally. Maternity leave is supposed to have no effect on your career, but don't bank on it. You'll be surprised by some of the attitudes your pregnancy will flush out. And make sure, before the baby is born, that you have absolutely reliable childcare in place. Colleagues will promise support, but it'll disappear the first time you take an unscheduled day off because childcare has fallen through. I managed to avoid that, but I've seen women try to do it on a wing, a prayer and granny, and it doesn't work!'

'One granny's in Warwickshire and the other's in Devon, so that's not on! Thanks for the advice. I may want to talk about it again.'

'Any time! I'm really pleased for you.'

Vanessa smiled and involuntarily rubbed her stomach. 'Can I ask you a personal question that you might not want to answer?'

Chris grimaced. 'Go on.'

'Arc you applying for the Scotland job?'

Chris guffawed. 'God, no! Not for me, not now. But I don't mind the Chief thinking I am. He's frightened to ask me in case he doesn't like the answer. Keeps giving me knowing looks. Great fun.'

*

As Chris Jenkinson parked the car opposite the Salutation Hotel in Perth, Vanessa's phone rang.

'Sorry to phone when you're off duty, Vanessa, but I thought you'd want to know.' It was Harry Conival. 'I've just had a call from the crime reporter of the *Gazette & Times* asking me to confirm that the guy murdered at GRH - Keller - was killed by lethal injection, and I don't know what to tell him, because I don't know whether he was or he wasn't. I said I'd get back to him before the first edition goes to press.'

'Did he say where he got the information?'

'He said something about a reliable source. Nothing more specific. Is he right?'

'He is, as it happens, but I was hoping to keep the details out of the public domain for a bit longer. Can you stall him until we have a press briefing tomorrow?'

'I can say I couldn't find you. He won't believe me and he'll run with his exclusive anyway. And what's this about a press briefing? Did I know about that?' Harry's questions were heavily ironic.

'Sorry, Harry. Just decided on it. Can you get a note out to the usual suspects? Let's make it noon. That'll make it harder for the hacks to complain about short notice.'

Vanessa hung up and turned to Chris to apologise.

'Don't worry about it. Problem?'

'Possibly. I've been sitting on some details about the GRH murder - cause of death - because it's so out of the normal run that I think it might be key to the case. Now Harry Conival's had a reporter on asking to confirm it. Somebody's leaked it. I hope it's come from someone involved in the *post mortem*, because if it hasn't, it has to be someone on my team.'

'But why? What's in it for them?'

Vanessa looked, and sounded, really fed up. 'About a hundred quid, I think. That's the current going rate.'

*

Colin MacNee spent the rest of the afternoon, after the meeting with the DCS, going round the other Detective Chief Inspectors trying to identify a Detective Sergeant who might be attached to the murder investigation. He needed an experienced detective with skills in either financial investigation, or information technology, or both. IT was more likely, and hoping for one person with both kinds of expertise was just daft.

It became clear pretty quickly that there was no-one in NEC with the kind of forensic accountancy skills that the information about the ownership of Hedelco and Ebright suggested might be necessary. In the past, such specialised knowledge had had to be brought in from a much larger force, more often than not Strathclyde, but occasionally the Met or West Midlands. A call to the fraud squad in Glasgow produced a couple of recommendations of detective inspectors who might be up for a short-term secondment if they could be released. A formal request would have to come from Esslemont.

More than one DCI identified NEC's in-house computer nerd, Detective Sergeant Don "Dongle" Donaldson, as someone who could break into any computer and who was a genius at recovering deleted files and deciphering encrypted ones. Colin went to see him in his office, more like a lab, in a satellite building in the centre of Aberdeen which housed a variety of specialist units: computer crime; forensic anthropology;

photographic and video analysis; voice recognition.

'DS Donaldson...'

Donaldson interrupted. 'Call me Dongle, everybody else does. What can I do for you, Inspector?'

Colin smiled. 'The first thing you can do is tell me why you're called Dongle.'

'Maybe because I'm the key to all computers? Or maybe because a guy called Don Donaldson who's into computers just invited the nickname. I can't remember, but I don't mind it. Helps me to stay doing what I'm good at and what I enjoy. We've nailed quite a few bad buggers on the basis of my ferreting about in their hard drives. What's your problem?'

Colin outlined the investigation of the two possibly related murders, emphasising the similarities in the jobs the victims had been doing and the identical protocols that appeared to have governed their reporting back to the USA.

'We've got one laptop and we're trying to locate the other. We're also trying to get copies of the encrypted reports that the dead men had already sent back. But we're dealing with some very edgy and secretive people and they're likely to try to block us, so we need to know if the deleted and encrypted emails can be recovered.'

'Almost certainly, but it may take some time. Two or three days, possibly. If you think you can get copies from the recipients quicker than that, I'm not your man. Assuming you can't, the fact that you've got one laptop is really helpful. If they were both issued by the same organisation, it's almost certain they both used the same encryption and deletion software. Crack one, and we crack the other, if you find it.'

'The companies are separate but share an owner, a private equity company that stays well away from publicity.'

'Still likely that they use a common IT system. Cheaper that way. And as I understand it, private equity is a byword for cost reduction and profit maximisation. I read that in the *Economist* and I've just shared with you the full extent of my knowledge.'

Colin liked Dongle's style. 'Do you want me to bring the laptop here or do you want to join our happy band at HQ?'

'Better for me to work on it here, where I've got all my magic tricks. I'll look after it. I've got a safe here for when I'm not working on it, so it'll be secure.'

'I'll get it to you by the end of the day, first thing tomorrow at the latest. We'll check that you're here before we bring it.'

*

As soon as Keller had been identified as the GRH body, DC Duncan Williamson went to hospital security to collect the CCTV recordings for the five days that Keller had been there. Because of the nature of his work and the secrecy with which it had been done, it wasn't possible to put together a definitive account of where he had been. They would have to look at all the recordings. There were twenty CCTV cameras recording 24 hours a day: 2400 hours of recordings that might enable them to build up a picture of where Keller had been. They needed to know when his laptop had disappeared.

Because of staff shortages it was unlikely that the work could be covered entirely, or even mainly, by CID. Colin decided that analysis of the recordings could be done by uniformed officers supervised by Williamson. He already had a high definition picture of Keller. He had enough copies of it printed for distribution to the officers who would examine most of the footage and he had, from Donovan, a detailed description of the bag containing his laptop that, Donovan had said, Keller always had over his shoulder. Colin told Williamson that he should personally and urgently examine the recordings from the camera at the end of the corridor that led to the crime scene. He needed his findings by the end of the day.

*

Jack Eisner, Burtonhall's head of security, touched down at Aberdeen Airport on a BA flight from Heathrow just after 1030 on Wednesday. He had caught an overnight BA flight from Dulles International Airport with plenty of time to make a connection to Aberdeen just before nine. He had called Tammy Wootten at Ebright just after eight and then Bernard Donovan at GRH.

Eisner arrived at Ebright just after 1100 and went immediately to Wootten's office.

'What the fuck is going on, Tammy? Cy Packard is going postal. He needs to know whether the Vermont One murder is related to the one at the hospital. What can you tell me?'

Wootten's response to this was curious. 'Why should they be related? Nobody's suggested that they are anything but coincidental. It's a big city. Two murders on a weekend can't be that unusual.'

'This isn't New York City, Washington or Phillie. And even if you were right, and you're not, it stretches coincidence a bit that both deaths happened in facilities owned by Burtonhall.'

Wootten was obviously shaken. 'I had no idea the hospital was owned by Burtonhall.'

'It isn't. It's managed by an HMO - Hedelco - that Burtonhall bought last year. But you haven't answered my question. What can you tell me about Jamieson's murder?'

'Not much. He was found dead at the bottom of an inspection chamber and the autopsy confirmed he had been murdered. The police have been here asking what he was doing on the platform. I've told them to get in touch with head office. But they've got his laptop and they're refusing to return it.'

'What was he doing on the rig?'

'An independent audit of all systems and processes. It's done without notice a couple of times a year. Reports go straight to Ebright's Audit and Risk Committee in Providence. I thought they went to Cy as well.'

'If they do, he didn't tell me, and I think he would have, before sending me here. What had Jamieson found before he was killed?'

'I don't really know. I only spoke with him twice, once when he stopped by when he arrived, and once by radio last Wednesday.'

Eisner was becoming irritated by Wootten's reticence. He had a short fuse at the best of times and jetlag didn't help.

'So what did he tell you?'

'Not much. These guys aren't supposed to reveal their findings to local management.'

'Why were you talking to him?'

'I was trying to find out if he had come across anything that might affect production. He wasn't very forthcoming, but he didn't sound happy.'

'Why were you concerned about production rates?'

Wootten shot him an angry look. 'Because it's my job?'

The interrogative inflexion showed her irritation, but Eisner wasn't about to let it go.

'Tammy, Packard told me that Vermont One isn't meeting its targets. If Jamieson had discovered why, I need to know.'

'That's all I know.'

Eisner didn't even try to hide his scepticism, but decided to move on.

'Have the press been on to you?'

'Only to ask for background on Jamieson.'

'From now on, you don't talk to them. You refer them to me and I'll decide whether to call in the PR professionals.'

*

By one o'clock, Eisner was in Hedelco's offices at GRH, talking to Bernard Donovan.

'Keller clearly wasn't happy with some of the things he turned up. He didn't want to go into detail - he's not supposed to reveal his findings to anybody outside head office - but he told me that if we didn't deal quickly with some failings that could affect patient safety, we would be at risk of contractual penalties or statutory intervention.'

'What the fuck does that mean, Bernard?'

'It could mean inspections by the Health and Safety Executive and Healthcare Improvement Scotland, which means the goddam government. They can slap improvement orders and fines on us. And that would cost money. Cy wouldn't like that.'

'Bet your life! He's already concerned about profit margins here. Are we looking at losses?

'Not unless the inspectors come in.'

'OK. Let's make sure they don't. Who else knew about Keller??

'My top team knew he was here. He may have spoken to some of them.'

'How much do the police know?'

'Not much. They know he was a inspector and he had found some things that concerned him.'

'The press? The health board handles that side of thing, I believe? In future, refer all enquiries to me. I'm going to do some digging around to find out what's going on.'

*

At about the time that Eisner was leaving Donovan's office, the Chief Constable's staff officer took a call from the office of the First Minister in Edinburgh.

'Good afternoon, Inspector. Paul MacIver, Special Advisor to the First Minister. The First Minister would like a word with the

Chief Constable. When would it be convenient for her to call?'

CHAPTER FIVE

At the team meeting at 0830 hrs on Thursday morning, DCI Fiske was joined in Conference Room 5 by Esslemont, Colin MacNee, Sara Hamilton, and the three DCs who had been attached full time to the investigation: Duncan Williamson, Stewart Todd and Aisha Gajani. 'Dongle' Donaldson had been persuaded out of his hideout and was introduced all round, and the pathologist who had conducted the *post mortems* had agreed to be at the end of a telephone line if any questions arose about cause of death, time of death or related matters. DI Andy Hanna, on secondment from Strathclyde Police Fraud Squad would arrive later.

'Right,' Vanessa said, 'We need updates on the main lines of enquiry. I'm tempted to say that shouldn't take us long, because were getting nowhere fast, but I'm never defeatist.'

As the slightly uncomfortable laughter subsided, she turned first to DS Sara Hamilton. 'Sara. You and Aisha have been following up the nearest thing we've got to a lead, Thomas Nuttall, or whatever his real name is'.

'Newcastle Police talked to people at the store where his clothes and ID were found and the cashier remembered him. She was surprised when he asked to borrow scissors to cut the labels off the clothes he'd bought so that he could wear them. He paid cash – nearly £150 – and she didn't notice at the time, but remembered when prompted, that he wasn't carrying anything when he left. The shop was busy and she let it go. The barcode scanning system gave us a pretty detailed description of what he bought and we think we've got him on CCTV. Not a particularly good image, but better than nothing. We've circulated his description and photographic are trying to enhance the image so that we can put that out as well. Network Rail are sending over DVDs from the CCTV at Aberdeen and Newcastle stations and we're checking with the bus companies as well. It's all a bit labour-intensive, boss, so we could do with some more bodies.'

'More bodies is the last thing we need, Sara, but I know what you mean. I'm using uniform to go through the hospital videos, so they may be able to do the rail and bus footage as well. As most of you will know from the file notes, it's almost certain that

Thomas Nuttall is not his real name. We believe that he has appropriated the identity of a Thomas Nuttall who died about a year ago. This makes Jamieson's death look planned, as was Keller's. Your opportunistic killer doesn't go around with syringes and lethal drug cocktails. So we've got two planned killings. Enough coincidence, already.'

Esslemont pursed his lips: not a man for levity where murder was concerned.

'Stewart, what have you discovered about the availability of the drugs found in Keller's body?'

'Just because they're used to execute people doesn't mean they're difficult to get. I raked around the Internet a bit and found several sites offering to supply both potassium chloride and Pentothal. You have to be a wee bit careful, though, or you'll end up with potassium choloride, which is a substitute for salt rather than a murder weapon. The sites looked pretty accessible, with minimal checks on purchasers, mainly in Eastern Europe and the Americas. I checked with our drugs squad and then with the SCDEA and they said that the only risk in sending for the stuff through the post would be its interception by customs, and in the absence of intelligence that's unlikely. The guy I spoke to at the SCDEA also said that if the purchaser could provide a medically-related identity, that would make it even easier. The message is that these drugs aren't all that hard to get and that the suppliers are unlikely to co-operate with us.'

Vanessa said that this was such an unusual cause of death that it was unlikely that the Scottish Crime and Drug Enforcement Agency would know any more about the drugs' availability than her team did, but she commended Todd for his thoroughness.

Duncan Williamson reported on progress so far with the 2400 hours of video material he had collected from GRH. There were multiple sightings of Keller between Monday and Friday and in all of them he had his laptop bag over his shoulder. He was having them brought together on one DVD so that people at the hospital could identify the locations. This might give them a way into what he had been investigating.

'The last sighting of him was at four o'clock on Friday afternoon, coming out of the lift at the end of the corridor leading to the toilet where his body was found. He was on his own, and he was carrying his laptop. He appeared to walk towards where he was killed. We're now trying to identify everybody who came out of these lifts or up the adjacent stairs between three and five on Friday. But it's a painstaking business. There are six wards and various other units that are accessed from that stairwell and lift, so there's a lot of traffic. We may need to use face recognition technology to match images with hospital personnel records.'

Colin MacNee snorted. 'Hedelco are going to love that. Please can I have the job of telling Donovan?'

Vanessa laughed, weakly. 'A bit below your pay grade, Detective Inspector. But what you can do to earn your keep, is take over this meeting while I go to the loo'. She was already on her way, looking a little pale. If Sara Hamilton still had any doubt about what was 'wrong' with her boss, they vanished.

'You all know about the ownership connection between Hedelco, who manage GRH, and Ebright, the operators of Vermont One. We don't know if that has any bearing on the murders, but we can't ignore it. Given that the most difficult financial document any of you ever deals with is your overtime claim, or maybe your credit card bill, we've called in some help. DI Andy Hanna will get here later today on a two-week secondment from Strathclyde. He'll be analysing the financial state of Hedelco, Ebright and their parent company, Burtonhall, to see if anything crawls out that might throw some light on why these two men ended up dead on our patch.'

DCI Fiske came back in, apologised for her abrupt exit and took over.

'You've all met Dongle Donaldson…Christ, do I have to call you that?'

'I might not answer if you don't, boss. It's who I am now. I've almost forgotten my real name.'

Everyone, except Esslemont, laughed, and Vanessa pressed on.

'Dongle knows more about hard drives than anyone you've ever met. He's already working on Jamieson's laptop and we hope that will give us access to the encrypted emails he sent back to his head office. I'm also trying to get copies of them sent to me from Rhode Island, but for Ebright, like Hedelco, the default response is "no". That makes me very suspicious and very determined. Anybody fancy a small wager that these murders have a corporate connection?'

Vanessa consulted her notebook. 'Right. Most of you are in the middle of lines of enquiry and you should carry on. Duncan and Stewart, leave the uniform boys and girls to get on with the video evidence. You need to talk to Hedelco's senior staff at GRH – Donovan's "top team", as he calls them – and find out what they know about what Keller was doing between Monday and four o'clock on Friday. We can then compare anything you find out with the video evidence of where he went. Might help to establish motive. Aisha, could you try to find out when and where the real Thomas Nuttall's identity records were accessed. When did someone apply for a copy of his birth certificate? Check out the usual suspects for unlawful access to his national insurance number. That sort of thing. He needed a false identity, probably for some reason as well as murder. Check out what he had to produce to get the job on Vermont One. See what you can find.'

DCI Fiske looked at the DCS, who nodded.

'I've called a press conference for noon today. I wouldn't have done so except that some information about this enquiry has got into the public domain when it shouldn't have. If you've seen the *G & T* this morning you'll know what I'm talking about. Either there's a leak, or someone let something slip inadvertently. If any of you thinks you may be the source, you need to tell me. In any case, I'm going to try to find out, and if anyone's at it, God help them!'

*

Jack Eisner, Burtonhall's Director of Security, was an ex-FBI agent who had taken early retirement from the Washington office of the Bureau in his early fifties. He had met Cy Packard occasionally, during joint operations with the CIA, and had contacted him to see if there was a possibility of his working for Burtonhall. They had a lot in common, especially their view that corporate information should be protected at all times, even, and this was slightly odd for former law officers, from the forces of law and order. Their operating principle was: hand over nothing voluntarily, but avoid enforcement action.

After his meetings with Tammy Wootten and Bernard Donovan. Eisner considered how to go about finding out more about the investigation into the deaths of Jamieson and Keller. On his way across the Atlantic, he had remembered that a former FBI colleague had gone to a similar job to his in an American corporation that was engaged in a huge and controversial development in the UK. As soon as he had Internet access at Heathrow, he went online to find the company, and details of where it was operating.

The Last Corporation (Company motto: "Last shall be First") was the corporate embodiment of a flamboyant Philadelphia property magnate, Ewan Last. It had interests all over the world and had, over the last few years, been engaged in developing a major leisure complex not far from Aberdeen, on the fringes of the Cairngorm National Park. The development was controversial, fiercely opposed by some, because of its environmental impact; strongly supported by others, because of the investment it brought to the region. Its methods, however, had been pretty universally deplored, and in the North East of Scotland it was hated by its opponents just as much as Hedelco was by its detractors, and for largely similar reasons.

Eisner's Internet search brought up details, in news reports, of The Last Corporation's dealings with public and private organisations in and around Aberdeen. His former colleague's name rarely appeared. That was no surprise. However, Eisner reckoned that if anyone could put him in touch with people who could tell him what was going on with the GRH and Vermont One enquiries, it would be someone in the Last office in Aberdeen.

"Hi, my name's Jack Eisner and I'm trying to locate an old colleague of mine, Frank Mancuso. I think he works for the Last Corporation and I'm on a flying visit here and it would be good to meet up.'

The receptionist who took Eisner's call was well trained. 'I'll try to help, sir. Please give me your name again, and a contact telephone number, and we'll get back to you within the hour.'

Eisner was impressed. She had been friendly and apparently helpful, but she had neither confirmed nor denied that Mancuso worked there. Mancuso was now in control. It would be up to him to decide whether to make contact.

Eisner had a shower to try to stave off the worst effects of jetlag. Flying business class helped, but he was still beginning to feel shitty. As he was towelling off, his cell phone rang. It was Frank Mancuso.

'Jack! Are you in Bonnie Scotland?'

'Better yet, Frank. I'm in Aberdeen, and I wondered if you'd be free for a drink or some dinner this evening. It would be good to catch up and there's something you might be able to help me with.'

'Name it.'

'Not on the phone. It's kind of sensitive.'

They agreed to meet in the bar of Caledonian Hotel in Union Terrace at 6.30 that evening.

*

Before the press briefing at noon, the NEC press office issued what Vanessa Fiske had come to call 'a Harry Conival Special': a briefing that gave an impression of openness, but made public only what the investigating officers wanted known. In this case, it was limited to information already in the public domain, and it was crafted in a way designed to influence the line of questioning Vanessa and Colin would face.

SUSPICIOUS DEATHS ON THE VERMONT ONE OIL PLATFORM AND AT GRAMPIAN ROYAL HOSPITAL

North East Constabulary is investigating two suspicious deaths. Both are now being treated as murder.

The body of Harvey Jamieson, of Shreveport, Louisiana, USA, was discovered late on the afternoon of Friday October 5 on the Vermont One Oil Platform, operated by Ebright Offshore Drilling, approximately 100 miles north east of Aberdeen. The cause of death was a blow to the head and a fall from a height of about six metres.

The body of Peter Keller, of Biddeford, Maine, USA, was found at Grampian Royal Hospital at about 8.00 a.m. on Saturday 6 October. The cause of death was a lethal injection.

The investigation is being led by Detective Chief Inspector Vanessa Fiske and Detective Inspector Colin MacNee and is pursuing a number of lines of enquiry, including the fact that both Ebright Offshore Drilling and Hedelco, the company that manages GRH on behalf of the Health Board, are owned by the same company, Burtonhall Inc.

Vanessa began the press conference by referring to the briefing paper and saying that she had nothing to add to it, but she was ready to take questions.

'My answers may, of course, be limited by the need to keep some information confidential in the interests of the investigation, but I will try to tell you as much as I can.'

The first question came from the *G & T* reporter who had broken the story about the cause of Keller's death. 'Can you tell us what drugs were used to kill Mr Keller, Chief Inspector?'

Vanessa smiled. 'I'm really sorry not to be able to answer the very first question, but no, I can't.'

The reporter came back. 'It's an unusual cause of death, isn't it? Do you think that it's what might be called a professional hit.'

'Not a phrase I would use. But we are working on the assumption that Mr Keller's murder was planned. It was not an opportunistic killing, or a killing in the course of another crime, such as a mugging.'

Vanessa moved on. 'Ben Aaronson, *Financial Post*. You said that you were pursuing the common ownership line. Do you believe that this will lead to the motive for either or both of these killings.'

'As I said, it's one line of enquiry among several. We thought it wise, when we learned about the ownership of the two companies, to bring the two enquiries together. We have added to the team a financial expert on secondment from the Strathclyde Police Fraud Squad. If there's anything there, we hope he'll help us to find it.'

'David MacKay, *BBC Scotland.* Are you looking for one killer or two?'

'Two. The timelines make it impossible that the victims were killed by the same person. Both murders took place on Friday afternoon or early evening and the timings of helicopter shuttles from Vermont One would have made it impossible for the same person to commit both murders.'

No-one asked what the dead men had been doing, so Vanessa didn't mention the two laptops, one taken as evidence and one missing. Nor did she have to tell the hacks about Dongle Donaldson. Just as well, really, as she still couldn't say his name without laughing.

It had lasted little more than twenty minutes and Vanessa was about to close by saying that further statements would be issued and press briefings arranged as appropriate when the man from the *G & T* stood up.

'Chief Inspector, would you care to comment on the possibility that the drugs used to kill Mr Keller were similar to those used in executions in the United States?'

Only those who knew her really well, like Colin MacNee, would have known that Vanessa was a little thrown, for her reply was crisp and conclusive.

'As I said, I can't comment on that.'

As they left the briefing room, Vanessa said to Colin, 'Somebody is feeding him information. If we were in a spy novel, I'd say we had a mole.'

*

Frank Mancuso was at the bar of the Caledonian Hotel drinking a cocktail when Jack Eisner arrived.

'Jack! How the hell are you? Good to see you. Drink? I've been trying to train bartenders in this goddam city to mix a decent whisky sour, but they don't seem to want to learn. They probably think it should be illegal to drink anything but Speyside malt, but I can't get a taste for it. Too full on!'

'You ought to try the Islay malts, full on and industrial strength!'

'So what brings you to Aberdeen?'

Eisner told Mancuso that he was here to find out what he could about the investigation into the two murders that had happened at the weekend because both of them had happened on facilities operated by Burtonhall companies.

'Cy Packard – remember him – is fit to be tied and wants me to get ahead of the police, or at least to give him a heads up on where their investigation is going. I don't have a lot of time, so I need a contact, somebody who might, for a consideration, give me some inside information. I thought you might be able to help.'

'Why me?'

'Well, we're old colleagues. But more importantly, because Last Corporation has had the kind of rough time here that can only be smoothed out by good PR. And that means two things: contacts and information. I need contacts so that I can get information for Cy.'

'Not my bag, Jack. Like you, I'm security and I don't know jackshit about PR.'

Eisner looked at him incredulously.

Mancuso smiled broadly. 'But I may know someone who does. Tell me where you're staying and I'll get a name to you by tomorrow morning.'

*

'Boss, can I have a word, please?' Colin MacNee caught up with Vanessa in the corridor outside the briefing room.

As they went into Vanessa's office, she asked what was on Colin's mind.

'It's work-related, but personal, and I really need your advice.'

Vanessa looked concerned.

'I know you're busy, so I'll come right to the point. You know that we decided after I got my promotion that Janet could go back to work full-time. Well, it's not working out. We can't get reliable childcare. We've bounced from one unsuitable childminder to another. We need someone who can be there when Emma and Cat get out of school, even if there are some days when one of us can be there. We've both got unpredictable jobs. I can't always get away and Janet can hardly walk out on a patient.   I've nipped off a couple of times, but people are beginning to notice…'

Vanessa grinned. 'Slow down. Colin. And no, I'm not grinning because I find it funny. I'm grinning because this is a reprise of a conversation I had the other night with Chris Jenkinson after I told her I'm pregnant. Best I can do is to give you the advice she gave me: find reliable childcare.   Easy in principle, I know.   In practice, a bit more difficult.'

'We can't afford a nanny, and I don't think I could live with myself if I had to tell people we had one. But we need someone that we don't have to check up on all the time, that we know will be there when they should be.'

'How about an *au pair*?   Board, lodgings and pocket money. Less than that probably, once they've met the girls. They're so lovely an *au pair* would probably pay you!'

Colin laughed. 'Well seen you don't have to live with them. How would we go about it? What kind of person could we get?'

'There are agencies. Or you could advertise. English language students from Europe.

American graduate students writing up their dissertations. Aussies travelling the world. I've known lots of people who've had *au pairs*, including DCC Jenkinson. It's one of the possibilities that Neil and I will have to consider.'

'I'll talk to Janet. And the girls. Mind you, I don't think I'd relish being interviewed by Emma and Cat. Thanks, Boss. I'll let you know how it goes.'

*

In Wilmington, Delaware, Cy Packard was reading a brief message from Jack Eisner, setting out what he had done so far in Aberdeen and saying that he hoped, later in the day, to be able to report progress in finding a source that could give him the inside track on the two murder investigations, when his phone rang.

'It's the Chairman, Cy', his secretary said, 'Putting him through.'

'Mr Chairman! What can I do for you?'

'You can tell me what the hell's going on in Scotland. You must have known this couldn't be kept under wraps. We have the kind of investors who scan the Web every day, or have people who do it for them. I've had the financial advisors of three of them on to me in the last twenty-four hours, as well as several members of the board. Nobody threatening to withdraw funds. Yet. But they're getting edgy. They saw Burtonhall as a safe, anonymous fund that would make money without making headlines. So what gives?'

'I don't know yet. But I've got Jack Eisner over there now, and by the weekend I should know how much damage, if any, these two murders are going to do us. Ebright and Hedelco, or rather Vermont One and that fucking hospital, aren't the strongest businesses we own, so anything that affects their performance causes me concern. I don't know whether we'll need to do anything, but I'm on it.'

'Glad to hear it', the Chairman said drily. 'How bad are things?'

'Vermont One is some way off the production levels we promised investors, but that may be temporary. We've been shielded a bit by the rising price of Brent Crude. The hospital is just about breaking even. Wouldn't take much going wrong to put it in the red.'

'Look, Cy, we have some real heavy hitters on the Board and I wonder if we should use them. I know it's a while since James stopped being prime minister, but he still has access. Maybe we should see if he can do anything to help.'

'Maybe. But not yet. I need to get a firmer handle on this than I have so far before we take any initiatives. We still don't know how big it's going to get.'

'Keep me in the loop. If this goes viral I need to be ready.'

*

It was nearly noon when, just as Vanessa and Colin were starting the press briefing, Eisner took a call in his hotel room from Frank Mancuso.

'Jack. You didn't get this from me, but the name you want is Martin Gilbertson. He's a press officer at the council we had to apply to for planning permission for the development out near the Cairngorms. He was very helpful to us and he seemed to have connections in the local police. There were a number of demonstrations against our complex and it was really useful to know in advance what police tactics were likely to be. We had to compensate him, but his rates were reasonable. I'll text his private cell phone number to you.'

As soon as he ended the call, Jack Eisner dialled Cy Packard's direct line at Burtonhall HQ. It would be early morning in Wilmington, but Packard was usually at his desk by seven. The call was picked up by Packard himself: his staff didn't get there until eight.

'How's it going, Jack? Your email last night told me zilch.'

'That's because there was nothing to tell. I think I'll do better today. Meantime, I need some background.'

'On what?'

'Did you send Jamieson and Keller in to get some data that would allow us to pull out of these businesses. I need to know what I'm dealing with here.'

'Hell, no. I didn't even know they were there until they were killed. Ebright and Hedelco deployed them.'

'Just another coincidence, then?'

'I'm not sure I like your tone, Jack, but yes. No conspiracy.'

'The Brits only have two possible explanations when things go tits up, Cy: cock-up and conspiracy. So if it's not conspiracy…'

'Who's responsible for the cock-up? That's what you're there to find out.' He hung up.

*

The First Minister of Scotland was the kind of woman who is usually described as 'formidable'. She had moved against her predecessor in a well-planned coup, removed him, and had been FM for just over a year. Her nationalism was uncompromising and it was generally believed that she would stop at nothing – or almost nothing – to achieve her goal. She was resolute in the defence of Scottish interests as she saw them and believed that every confrontation she could engineer with the UK government made it more likely that she would win a referendum on independence. Her colleagues respected and feared her in equal measure. Her opponents found it difficult to lay a glove on her. Her nickname, of which she was very well aware, was 'Eva'. She affected to believe that the reference was to Eva Peron. Others had quite another Eva in mind.

Paul MacIver, the FM's special adviser, was never far from her side. He was adviser, enforcer, fixer and spokesperson. He organised her diary, ensured that the maximum publicity attached to all her appearances, worked to make it unnecessary for her to dirty her hands with party management, and listened in to every telephone call she made or received. It was said that nobody liked him, not even his family, but most people feared him. And he was anonymous, hiding in plain sight. Even the best informed Scots would have been hard pressed to put a name to a photograph of him.

'You need to try to close this down.' MacIver was alone with the FM just before she was due to speak to the Chief Constable of North East Constabulary. 'Scotland's oil and Scotland's health service, both at the mercy of an American private equity company? If the opposition had any brains, you'd be struggling already. Make sure you don't hand this one to them on a plate.'

'How can I be seen to interfere in operational policing?   You persuaded me to go right over the top about police independence when that royal aide tried to interfere in the investigation of the Balmoral murder. I can't ask the chief constable to limit the enquiry.'

'No, but you can work on him to keep the investigation limited to the murders.   The detective leading the enquiry announced today that she's added a financial expert from Strathclyde to her team.   That means she's going to poke around in the accounts of Hedelco and Ebright. Possibly Burtonhall, too. You should come on as a local MSP. He knows you're FM and, as always, he'll want to be helpful. He also knows that you'll have the final say in the appointment to the Scotland   job.   Perfect   conditions   of suggestibility.'

Her look was a mixture of outrage and complicity. 'I'll ask him for an update and take it from there. He's very unlikely to reveal anything about our conversation. He's too ambitious for that, which is more or less what you just said.'

*

'First Minister! It's always good to hear from you. How can I help.' The Chief Constable was striving for, but not quite achieving, the right balance between authoritativeness and obsequiousness.

'I'm speaking to you mainly as one of your local MSPs, Chief Constable. Is there anything more you can tell me about these murders, apart from what's been in the news? I see you've brought the two investigations together. Rather worrying. I don't know how many deaths make a serial killer, but I hope you can reassure my constituents.'.

'A connection between the deaths is only one of several lines of enquiry. These may be two quite separate...events...and the...commercial connection may be a coincidence or even a red herring.' He was choosing his words carefully, trying to protect the independence of his force while reassuring the FM and safeguarding his own position.
'You must act as you see fit, but it seems to me that the focus should be on the deaths and who caused them - the purely criminal aspects that bear on community safety, rather than on the businesses - both very important to the area and to Scotland - where they happened to occur.'

'Quite. Quite. It is, as you suggest, First Minister, a matter of balance rather than exclusiveness.'

'Good. We may be in touch again on other matters in due course. Thank you for your time.'

In Aberdeen, the Chief Constable thought the conversation would have done his prospects no harm. In Edinburgh, Paul MacIver was satisfied that subtle pressure had been applied, but that the transcript, if it became public, would seem innocuous.

*

Late that evening, text messages were received on two disposable, untraceable mobile telephones. One was on the bedside table in Jack Eisner's hotel room. The other was in the briefcase of Paul MacIver.

They read, respectively: *07147 284183* and *Back at base. What next?*

CHAPTER SIX

On Friday morning, a week after the murders, DCs Williamson and Todd arrived at Bernard Donovan's office at GRH. Sharon Archibald, Donovan's nice but dim secretary, offered them coffee and asked them to wait. Colin MacNee had told them Donovan would make them wait, even if they arrived exactly at the agreed time, and he had told them not to accept a delay of more than five minutes.

'You know what he's like, Duncan, so you know what I mean. Making you wait is an assertion of his status. Don't put up with it.'

In the event, within a couple of minutes Donovan came out to invite them into his office. They sat down and Sharon brought the coffee in.

'As I understand it, gentlemen,' Donovan said, 'You need to speak to the members of my top team. I'm happy to facilitate that, and to that end, I have asked them to meet you in our board room in about ten minutes.'

Williamson and Todd looked at each other and then at Donovan.

'Together?' Williamson asked. 'You've set up a meeting for us to talk to your top people, together?' His tone was an mixture of incredulity and contempt.

'I thought that would be an efficient use of your time. And ours, if it comes to it.' Williamson expected him to say that time was money.

'Mr Donovan, we are grateful to you for providing us with a room where we can talk to your people, but Stewart and I will interview them individually. When they arrive, we will ask one of them to wait – we are happy to take your advice on who that should be – and tell the others that we will ask for them when we need them. Perhaps Miss Archibald could call them for us? That would mean that we would only need her extension number. I assume that there is a telephone in the room? Also, we will need about ten minutes on our own before your people arrive, so please ask Miss Archibald to let them know that they should meet us at nine-thirty.'

Donovan did not look happy, but he was smart enough, given his possession of an MBA from Harvard, to know that any resistance would be met by a reply that reminded him that this was a murder investigation and that he should not obstruct the officers in their conduct of it.

'Fine,' he said, with pained resignation, 'But I really don't know what you expect to learn. None of my people had much to do with Keller, so I don't see what you can get from them beyond what I've already told Detective MacNee.'

Both detectives were aware, as they agreed later, of Donovan's nervousness, but neither could decide whether it came from fear of what his people might tell them, or from his general apprehension about how his handling of the whole thing would be regarded at head office or by Burtonhall. They didn't yet know about Donovan's visit from Eisner. If they had, they would have put Donovan's edginess down to that.

'We still have to talk to them, individually. So who should we see first?'

'Probably David Masur. He's my Ops Director. Keller would have touched base with him after he met me. Let me take you to the board room.'

When Donovan had left, Stewart Todd asked his colleague why they needed time on their own before they began the interviews.

'Why do you think, Stewart? To search the room for bugs. We could hardly send the sweep squad in, but we can at least look in the most obvious places. Donovan is so concerned to watch his arse that I wouldn't put it past him.'

The board room was simply furnished: a table with eight chairs, a sideboard with a tray of glasses and bottled water, a data projector mounted on the ceiling and pointing at a screen on the end wall opposite the door, a flipchart stand and, beside the screen, a small whiteboard. The detectives reasoned that there had probably not been enough time for the installation of any sophisticated electronics, so they looked under the furniture, in the sideboard and behind it, and behind the screen and whiteboard to see if there was anything that might be a microphone. They found nothing.

Duncan Williamson picked up the handset of the phone and thought he detected a tiny delay before he heard the dial tone. He took a Swiss army knife out of his pocket and unscrewed the base plate of the phone. He beckoned Todd and pointed to a small component attached magnetically to the inside of the casing.

'Don't like the look of that', Todd said. 'Will I go and get Donovan?'

'No. We'll deal with him later. I'll disconnect it.' Williamson pulled a pair of latex gloves out of his inside pocket. The device was wired into the phone simply enough for him to remove it and drop in into an evidence bag. 'We'll see if forensics can lift any prints.'

*

The interviews with Donovan's top team took just under an hour. None of those interviewed had had much more than passing conversations with Keller: brief chats in the corridor or over a coffee in the canteen. None of them had been directly involved in any of his inspections or discussions with clinical and other staff in the hospital. Nothing they told the detectives was particularly sensitive, only information about what areas of the hospital's operations Keller had been looking at. This left them wondering why anyone had thought it worthwhile to bug the room.

At the end of the session, Williamson and Todd drew up a list of Keller's areas of interest, as mentioned to the team members. There were four: diagnostic procedures, including radiography, CT scans and MRI scans; usage of operating theatres; laboratory procedures; and sub-contract management. They now needed to check whether these corresponded with what they knew, from CCTV footage, about Keller's movements in the hospital.

*

While Williamson and Todd were at the hospital, a truck driver collecting a rubbish skip from outside a house under renovation in Garthdee, on the south side of Aberdeen, noticed a laptop half buried by kitchen cupboard panels and other rubble. He pulled it out and found a label on the bottom: *Property of Hedelco Inc. If found, please return to Hedelco Inc., Boston Ma., USA, or to local police.* The driver took it to the nearest police station. The duty sergeant recognised the name Hedelco from internal bulletins and from the press and immediately contacted CID. The laptop was in the possession of DCI Fiske's team within an hour.

Vanessa assumed that the laptop was Keller's so she asked Dongle Donaldson to have a look at it. While he was examining it, she sent the serial number and the asset register number from the laptop to Donovan, for onward transmission, if necessary, to the USA, with a request for confirmation that it had been issued to Keller.

'Sorry, Boss,' Dongle said, 'This isn't going to help you. The hard disk's missing. Been removed quite carefully, by the look of it, by somebody who knew what they were doing.'

'Probably at the bottom of the Dee by now. We're going to have to put pressure on Hedelco.'

'But if you were just going to throw it in the river, why would you remove it? Why not just dump the whole laptop?'

'So whoever disposed of the laptop wanted to keep the hard disk?'

'It's possible.' Dongle smiled. 'So much for the bad news. Now the good stuff. I've decrypted some of Jamieson's emails.'

'Put it in a file note, Dongle, and I'll see it later. I need to spend some time working out how to prise Keller's emails out of his bosses in America.'

*

'Thank you for coming up, Campbell.' The Chief Constable came out from behind his desk and indicated to the DCS that he should take one of the low armchairs by the occasional table at the end of his office. 'We need to have a word about this double murder enquiry that Vanessa Fiske is running. Doesn't seem to be making much progress, if the reports that Richard has been getting are anything to go by.'

Inspector Richard Fleming was the Chief's staff officer, to whom Esslemont had been sending daily reports prepared by Vanessa or by Colin MacNee. Esslemont regarded Fleming as a young man in a hurry and he thought it likely that he was putting his own spin on the reports before passing them on.

'That's hardly fair, Sir. These American companies have been less than fully co-operative. Vanessa's putting on as much pressure as she can, and I've just had a call to tell me that she, or rather Donaldson the IT man, has cracked the encryption on Jamieson's laptop. That may give us a motive for his murder. Less success on Keller. We've found his laptop, but minus the hard disk. We're also pursuing the Nuttall connection...'

The Chief held up a hand. 'Yes, yes, I know all that, but I've had a call from the First Minister, expressing concern as a local MSP that we may have a serial killer on the loose.'

'Oh, come on, sir. I hope you told her that serial killers usually have the same MO for all their victims and...'

Esslemont was relieved to be interrupted again, because he had realised that he was sounding unnecessarily defensive and, possibly, not supportive enough of his staff.

'I did', the Chief said, 'but that was just an excuse for the call. She really wanted to talk about what she described as the "commercial" aspects and to suggest that we should concentrate on the purely criminal matters raised by the murders.'

'But so far they're inseparable. We can't wish away the fact that the outfit that runs GRH and the company that operates Vermont One are owned by the same corporation. I'm sure that when you were in CID you were always very suspicious of anything that the outside world might describe as a coincidence.' The Chief might have regarded that as a cheap shot. It was well-known that he hadn't been particularly successful in CID and had made his career in uniform and in administration, supported by the occasional high profile secondment to the Home Office and the Police Colleges in both Scotland and England.

'I'm not suggesting that you wish it away, only that you handle the commercial aspects sensitively. These companies bring a lot of investment and support a lot of jobs.'

Esslemont was trying not to bridle. 'You know my views about political meddling in operational policing, Sir, and I would hope that you share them.'

'Of course I do. But it won't do any of us any good to get on the wrong side of the First Minister.'

Esslemont knew that this meant that it wouldn't do the Chief any good, but he let it go.

'Just make sure you don't step on any unnecessary toes. Vanessa Fiske's a good officer - that's why we promoted her - but she can be abrasive. Keep an eye on her.'

Esslemont decided not to respond. 'Thank you for keeping me informed, Sir. I'll make sure we handle the investigation properly.'

*

As soon as he left the Chief's office, Esslemont went to see DCI Fiske.

'The Chief's had his ear bent by the First Minister. She thinks your investigation should concentrate on the purely criminal aspects of the case, rather than the "commercial" side. Somebody's pointed out to her that the murders are connected with two of her government's flagship areas, the NHS and the oil industry.'

Vanessa snorted. 'And how does she propose we should separate them?'

'She told the Chief she was concerned, as a local MSP, that we might have a serial killer on the loose, but even the Chief saw through that. I said that until we can establish motive, the criminal and commercial aspects are inseparable. I'm not suggesting that you should change your approach, which I think is right. But keep me informed.'

'Do you think the Chief is covering his back, sir?'

'You don't really expect me to answer that, do you, Chief Inspector?'

*

Vanessa Fiske had one more go at Donovan in an effort to get his bosses to release Keller's emails. It got her nowhere. Donovan had passed her request to Head Office and been told that the emails were commercially sensitive and could not be released to a third party. Her only recourse was to seek an order from a court in the United States. She knew that that would be a lengthy process, possibly involving appeal procedures if either side was unhappy, which seemed not unlikely, with the decision made at the first hearing. She needed to get some legal advice to determine whether there was any procedure that might get her the emails without going to court.

North East Constabulary's legal adviser, Fiona Marchmont, was both a solicitor and a member of the Faculty of Advocates. She had been an academic lawyer, teaching at Aberdeen University, but after she had had her children, she had decided to take on something that used her talents, but on a basis that was a little closer to normal office hours than was possible at the Bar. Vanessa had taken her to a couple of meetings of the WPNS and she had developed a very high opinion of both her legal competence and her judgment.

'Fiona, between you and me, I'm getting nowhere fast with this investigation, mainly because I'm being blocked at every stage by the Americans. Is there anything I can do, short of a court action in Massachusetts, to force Hedelco to tell me what was in Keller's emails?

'If you go to court, you'll still be there when you draw your pension, so we need to find another way. I think there may be a political solution to this, but it's risky and, might raise issues between the UK and Scottish governments.'

'Go on.'

'We need to get the US authorities to intervene to put pressure on Hedelco, and/or their parent company, to release the emails voluntarily. I use the word loosely! That will need to involve the Foreign Office and, probably, the legal attaché in Washington. Our masters in Edinburgh won't necessarily like that, but under the current devolution settlement there's no other way. But we might finesse it by going through the Law Officers in Edinburgh - probably the Solicitor General - and getting them to persuade the Advocate General to talk to the FO.'

Vanessa laughed. 'Who or what is the Advocate General. Sounds like something out of Gilbert and Sullivan.'

'You should see him in full fig!' Fiona said. 'He handles cross border legal issues on behalf of the UK government and there's an ongoing working relationship between him and the Scottish Law Officers. Do you want me to sound him out?'

'Probably. But I'll have to run it past my boss first. I'll get back to you.'

*

Late on Friday afternoon, just after the end of the working day, Jack Eisner dialled the mobile number that had been texted to him the previous day. Martin Gilbertson, a senior public relations officer at Mid-Aberdeen Council, answered with a simple 'Hello'.

Eisner was equally cautious. 'I need some information on how the police are doing in their enquiries into last weekend's two murders. You don't need to know who I am and we don't have to meet, but we do need to trust each other. I need to know that anything you tell me will be kosher. And you need to know that you will benefit from passing it on. I'm sure you understand what I'm saying.'

No names; no introductions. A simple act of collusion that, they hoped, would get each of them what they wanted.

'Use only this mobile. Don't try to contact me any other way. I'll deliver to you by text. I suggest you get a disposable phone, what I think you call a burner. You'll deliver to me as I specify by text. Do we understand each other?'

'Perfectly,' Eisner said. 'But I don't have a lot of time.'

'You'll have something by tomorrow morning, possibly by midnight tonight. Don't turn in too early.'

Eisner already had a burner. He texted the number to Gilbertson.
*

It had been a hard and frustrating week. Just after half past six on Friday Vanessa Fiske was in Neil Derrick's flat with her feet up, drinking a glass of mineral water and watching *Reporting Scotland* on the BBC. They had briefly reported on her press briefing the previous evening and, as she had made little progress since then, there would have been nothing to tell them even if they had shown any continuing interest. The bulletin had just moved on to sport - Forres Mechanics had been drawn against Partick Thistle in the League Cup - when Neil came in, kissed Vanessa, poured himself a glass of wine, and slumped in a chair.

'Tough day?'

Vanessa tried to smile but soon abandoned the attempt. 'I'm getting nothing but nothing from both Ebright and Hedelco. I'm not so worried about Ebright, because we've got Jamieson's laptop and Dongle has recovered the emails and decrypted them. We've also got Keller's laptop, but its hard disk is missing and Hedelco say that they can't release the fucking emails because they're commercially sensitive. I could go to court, but we'd probably be grandparents before we had a decision. Fiona Marchmont's trying a political route via the Advocate General, but it's a mess, and I don't really know where to go next.'

'What did Dongle come up with?' Neil asked.

'Lots of technical stuff. Jamieson kept using the phrase 'run to failure' to describe how some of the systems on Vermont One were being operated. I think I can guess what that means but I'm not sure I understand the significance. He also criticised the amount that was being spent on maintenance and the effect that this might have on production.'

'Anything else?'

'He said that he thought the operational managers on the rig were taking risks with health and safety. That part of his reports was less firm, seemed to be based on impression rather than hard evidence, but he obviously thought that his concerns were serious enough to be reported to the Audit and Risk Committee. And he said that the offshore unions were becoming uneasy about the conditions that their members sometimes had to work in.'

Neil refilled his glass and brought the Highland Spring over for Vanessa. 'That's quite a list. I'm no expert, but if Jamieson was right there must be a risk, at least, that the rig would have failed an official inspection and would have to be shut down. Can't see Ebright, and more importantly, Burtonhall, being very happy about that. It's what's called a red risk, one that endangers the business, and the Audit and Risk Committee would want to mitigate it.'

'Hardly a motive for murder, though, unless you get deep into the kind of conspiracy theory that seldom explains this kind of crime. Who would have known what Jamieson had found, except the people who read his encrypted emails? This murder had to be committed by someone already on Vermont One, most likely "Thomas Nuttall", and if he did it, why did he do it? As I said, I'm getting nowhere fast.'

'What about the financial expert you brought in from Strathclyde? Anything from him?'

Vanessa sighed. 'Mainly generalities. He's been through a load of public domain stuff on the three companies and, as he put it, there's no smoking gun. He doesn't think they're making much money, but he doesn't see anything that might make Ebright pull out of the North Sea or Hedelco fail to break even, at worst, in their management contract at GRH. Nor does he see anything illegal. Nothing hidden, no money laundering, nothing like that. He's going to see if he can get access to banking records, but he doesn't seem hopeful.'

Neil shook his head. 'They're American companies, the parent company registered in Delaware, so I'd guess he'd have as much trouble getting bank records through legal processes as you will getting Hedelco's emails. It should be possible, though, to get a hold of the prospectuses sent out by Burtonhall to likely investors. They're not quite public documents, but they're not secret or confidential. Financial journalists quite often get copies. They would give you an idea of what Burtonhall expected of the two companies. You might mention that to him.'

'I will. But if any of your contacts have them...'

'OK, I'll ask around. Now, do you want to go out to eat?'

*

Jack Eisner received Gilbertson's first text message in the middle of the evening.

> *Police investigating fin posn of rig co, hosp co and parent co. Have emails sent from rig. Have some idea what Keller was investigating at GRH. Looking for Thomas Nuttall as prime suspect in rig murder. Contact from First Minister re commercial aspects.*

Eisner immediately called Cy Packard.

'Cy, they're digging deep into the company. You need to tell me if they're going to find anything that might produce the kind of publicity here that I'll have to manage. Because if they are, I'll need some professional PR help.'

'Hell, no, Jack. If they're relying on stuff that they can Google, we're in the clear.'

'Is that supposed to make me feel good? We're not talking some hick police operation here. The detective leading the investigation is pretty smart, and she's called in specialist help. And we need to assume that the press is digging around as well. Nobody will be relying on Google.'

'Hedelco will refuse to release the emails without a court order and if the Scottish police go to court they'll be there till hell freezes over. And by that time, they'll have nailed somebody for the murders and we'll be home free.'

'Cy, don't be so fucking naive! Ask yourself if you'd be happy to tell the Board that's your strategy. If the Scottish First Minister is taking an interest, so will other politicians. You need a better handling plan than waiting for it to go away.'

'Don't tell me how to do my job! Just make sure we don't get any bad publicity.'

*

On Sunday, the *Globe*, sister paper of the *Financial Post,* ran, on its business pages, a piece by Ben Aaronson about the financial position of Ebright and Hedelco. Neither was making a lot of money on its Scottish operation, but there had been little sign that they would pull out. Aaronson speculated about the murders, and about whether they were connected, given the common ownership of the two companies by what he described as the 'highly secretive' private equity company, Burtonhall:

Burtonhall, registered in Delaware to minimise the possibility of public scrutiny of its operations, has forecast, in its prospectuses to investors, profits from all its investments within three years of acquisition.

This, of course, includes Ebright and Hedelco, and it implies that if profitability is not achieved within the promised timeframe, Burtonhall will disinvest to protect returns to investors.

Vermont One, the oil platform where American engineer Harvey Jamieson was murdered a week ago on Friday, began production just under two years ago and its profitability is unclear. Oil experts say that its financial performance has been, to an extent, shored up by the steadily rising price of Brent Crude. Sources suggest that

Jamieson was undertaking a technical audit of the rig. If he had found anything that might adversely affect the platform's performance, that would be a real concern to its operator, Ebright, and to its ultimate owner, Burtonhall.

The management contract for Grampian Regional Hospital, awarded to Hedelco eighteen months ago, was highly controversial politically and it is thought that Hedelco trimmed its margins very tightly to secure the contract, which runs for twenty-five years. Operational management of the hospital remains in the hands of local clinicians overseen, 'aggressively', according to doctors and unions, by a small team of American lawyers, accountants and contract managers.

For differing reasons, the health service and the oil industry are central to the policies of the Scottish Government, and therefore to the independence project, so it would be surprising if the First Minister and her colleagues were not watching the situation very closely.

Aaronson went on to list the big names on the Burtonhall board and to suggest that the presence of so many high-profile political figures, added to the concerns of Scottish ministers, made it unlikely that the two murders would remain "purely a matter of criminal investigation".

*

On Sunday Morning, Paul MacIver, Special Adviser to the First Minister, was in his flat in Edinburgh's New Town. He had just been out to the newsagent in Howe Street to collect the Sunday papers and he was working through them, his practised eye quick to pick up anything that was relevant to his job or to his other activities.

Most of the Scottish titles had already relegated the double murder story to the inside pages and the UK papers, with the exception of Aaronson's piece in the *Globe,* ignored it entirely. It was possible, and from MacIver's point of view, highly desirable that other papers would, on Monday, pick up on the *Globe* piece and run with it. Contrary to his advice to his boss, he needed both the press and the police to continue to pursue what she had called the "commercial" aspects of the double murder enquiry in Aberdeen. If that didn't happen spontaneously, he would have to give it a push.

MacIver got up from his kitchen table and fetched his briefcase from the living room. He took out his disposable mobile phone – he didn't watch much television or read American detective stories, so he probably wasn't familiar with the term "burner" – and brought up on the screen the text that he had received on Thursday night. It was time to move things on.

CHAPTER SEVEN

'The General Register Office issued a certified copy of Thomas Nuttall's birth certificate last May. It was ordered by a Simon Mathieson and it was sent to an address in Glasgow. Turns out that the address is one of these private mailbox services that will give you an address without a box number, because lots of organisations won't send stuff to a box number. I've asked Strathclyde to take the enhanced picture of Nuttall – the one from the Gateshead CCTV footage – to the shop and see if anyone recognises him as Simon Mathieson. They should be co-operative. Their business depends on staying on the right side of the law. I expect to hear something soon'.

DC Aisha Gajani was reporting to the Monday morning meeting of the enquiry team.

'Anything on his NI number?' DCI Vanessa Fiske sounded a little weary, partly because of how she was feeling, and partly because of her frustration that the investigation wasn't moving as quickly as she would have liked.

'We've been on to the usual suspects and leaned on them a bit. It looks as though one of them – a private enquiry agent, also in Glasgow, as it happens – got Nuttall's NI number from a contact in the DWP and supplied it, "for the usual consideration" (Everybody here was getting good at ironic quotation marks, Vanessa thought), by telephone to someone with a Glasgow accent. Again, this was a few months ago, probably at about the same time as the birth certificate was obtained.'

'Well, that narrows it down to the quarter of a million or so men with Glasgow accents. Progress at last. Thanks, Aisha. Duncan?'

'We now have a pretty clear idea of the areas of hospital operations that Keller was investigating and what we learned from Donovan's "top team" (There it was again. Vanessa smiled.) seems to be confirmed by the CCTV footage. We put all the Keller sightings together and Donovan's people identified where he was in most of them. Now we need to know what significance to attach to what he was looking at. It wouldn't half help if we could see his emails.'

'I'm working on that', Vanessa said, 'But it's not easy. Anything else?'

'Far be it from me to praise uniform. Nobody in CID had much time for me when I wore one. But one of the PCs who was looking at the footage was alert enough to notice that in several – not all – of the sightings the same so far unidentified male was also visible. May be nothing, but I'm having the images enhanced and we'll see if anyone, or any system, can recognise him.'

Vanessa grinned. 'I shall ignore your descent into chippiness, Duncan, and simply say good work. When do you expect to have the pictures?'

Williamson said he would have them later that morning and that his first port of call would be the HR department at GRH.

'So we'll have enhanced CCTV images of possible suspects for both murders? That puts us in a better place than we were when I clocked off on Friday. But we still need more on motive. The Jamieson emails help, but even there we're dealing with inference rather than evidence. I now need to take some advice on what we know about Keller's activities at GRH'.

'I mentioned his areas of interest to Janet at the weekend.' Colin MacNee was speaking for the first time, and DCS Esslemont greeted his introduction with a sharply raised eyebrow. Esslemont was old school in every possible way, and he would never have considered discussing details of his work with his wife. But these were different times, so he let it go, and simply listened to what DI MacNee had to say. After all, he hadn't objected to Fiske's taking advice from her partner on the financial issues.

'She was struck by the fact that three of the four areas Keller seems to have been looking at - diagnostic procedures, usage of operating theatres, and laboratory procedures – are what she described as "manageable", for which read capable of being rationed to control expenditure or, if you're a cynical sod like me, to maximise profit. You can't do that so easily with, for example, A & E or intensive post-operative care. But you also can't do it without affecting quality of care and, probably, outcomes for patients. So, any recommendation that affected the ability of the Hedelco people to manage expenditure in these areas would, I guess, hit the bottom line.'

'What was the fourth area?' Esslemont spoke for the first time.

'Sub-contract management. And again, that's an area where management pressure can be applied to costs, sometimes in areas that directly affect patients, like transport, though it's not something that a medic like Janet would know much about. Hedelco's operation at GRH includes a contract management section, some managing their contract with the health board, but some engaged, as one of the "top team" put it to Duncan and Stewart, in holding subcontractors' feet to the fire.'

Esslemont frowned. 'But if Keller was killed because of what he had turned up, who benefited? As you often ask, Vanessa, "*Cui bono*".'

'The answer to that, sir, just might be Burtonhall and its investors.'

'How so?'

'Well, Keller was reporting directly to Hedelco's head office in Boston, not to Burtonhall, whose interest is entirely on what Colin called the bottom line. They promise investors that all of their companies will be in profit within three years. If Hedelco wanted to avoid contract penalties, or the threat of government inspection, they might intervene in a way that delayed profitability. Burtonhall is, apparently, famously hardnosed when it comes to returns to its investors.'

'Or they might decide to disinvest, which might leave the health board, and the government, with a real problem. We need to see these emails. And we need to find out what Burtonhall knows.'

'Boss.' Stewart Todd held the same rank as Duncan Williamson, but when they worked together, as they often did, he usually deferred to Duncan's seniority, so this was his first intervention. 'One of Donovan's "top team" mentioned that Burtonhall had sent somebody senior over to find out what's happening with Hedelco and Ebright. Maybe you could talk to him.'

'Thank you, Stewart. Do we have a name?'

'Sorry, no. That's all I got. But Donovan should know.'

'Or Tammy Wootten at Ebright. Let's talk to them both. Colin, get on to your friend Donovan. I'll tackle the lovely Tammy.'

*

As soon as she got in on Monday morning, Fiona Marchmont, NEC's in-house lawyer, spoke to a senior civil servant in the Solicitor General's office in Edinburgh. She explained the problem of obtaining the emails that Peter Keller, who had been murdered at Grampian Royal Hospital ten days before, had sent back, in encrypted form, to his employers in the United Sates.

'The Senior Investigating Officer believes that the emails may help to establish a motive for the murder, but Hedelco, the company that manages the hospital on behalf of the NHS, and who employed Keller and sent him to do some kind of technical audit of the hospital's systems, are refusing to hand them over. Going to court is really out of the question. It would take forever. So I need some help to find a political solution.'

'What do you have in mind?'

Fiona Marchmont had dealt with Gavin Aikman before. She had found him not exactly unhelpful, but reluctant to take any action until he was absolutely satisfied that it was right legally, administratively, and politically. Being ultra-cautious had got him to his current level. He wasn't going any further, but that didn't mean he was prepared to take more risks. On the contrary, and rather like DCS Esslemont, he wanted to serve out his time until retirement, doing his job ('entirely to his own satisfaction', Fiona thought, remembering an apocryphal performance appraisal), making no waves, and causing no difficulty for his superiors.

'We need to get the US authorities to put some pressure on the company to release the emails "voluntarily". That will need some help from the Foreign Office. I can't approach them directly. Cross-border sensitivities make it important that we do this absolutely by the book. We're investigating two murders, possibly related, both of American citizens, and both involving US companies working in Scotland. I need the Advocate General's office to talk to the FO and persuade them to get the Embassy in Washington – they still have a legal attaché, I hope, even after so many rounds of cuts – to intervene with the appropriate Federal and State officials.'

'Is that all?' Aikman asked drily.

'I know it's a tall order, Gavin, but can you help or not?'

'I'll have to talk to my masters, but I can't see any reason not to approach the AG's office. Give me a couple of hours. I'll try to get back to you by lunchtime. Early afternoon at the latest.'

'Thank you. You should know, by the way, that the First Minister is taking an interest, ostensibly because she's a local MSP, but probably because of the importance of US investment in Scotland.'

'I'm glad you told me that. I shall need to tread carefully.'

*

'I got the *au pair* job.'

Shelley Mehring was a PhD student from Oklahoma, registered at Robert Gordon University in Aberdeen. She had completed all of her course work and her three years of registration and was now writing her dissertation. Her topic was the multiplier effect on the regional economy of foreign investment in the North east of Scotland and one of the companies she had studied was the Last Corporation. Her contacts there had led to an expenses-only internship, but she needed to find a paying job until she could complete the thesis.

Frank Mancuso, head of security at Last Cairngorm, had taken her on as a personal assistant and general gopher, and when she told him about the advert in the postgrad newsletter – "Professional couple seeks *au pair* to provide reliable, stimulating childcare for two bright but demanding primary schoolgirls" - he had encouraged her to apply. It offered pay at just above the legal minimum wage, board and lodging.

'That's great, Shelley. We'll miss you here at Last, but it sounds like just what you need. If the kids are in school, you should have plenty of time to work on your dissertation. That, and board and lodgings, make it a no-brainer. Go for it! What do the parents do?'

'She's a family doctor and he's a detective with North East Constabulary. They seem very nice. I said I'd let them know by the end of today. I'll stay here until the weekend, if that would help.'

Mancuso smiled. 'No, it would probably be best if you started as soon as they want you.'

*

As they left the team meeting, Colin MacNee caught up with Vanessa Fiske.

'Thanks for your advice last week, boss. Turned out that Janet got a similar steer from the senior partner in her health centre. Probably because she's been taking more of the strain than I have, and because she can be very decisive, she took action. She approached both universities and asked them to put a note in the email they send out every week to their postgrads. That went out on Thursday – before I had even told her about our chat – and by Saturday lunchtime, five c.v.'s had been emailed to us, all with photos and testimonials.'

'Anyone promising?'

'We showed the pictures to Emma and Cat and then we told them which three we had decided to talk to. They all came round yesterday, and we think we know who we want.'

They had just reached Vanessa's office and Colin handed her a copy of Shelley Mehring's c.v. – or "Resumé" as it was headed.

'She looks OK. Did the girls like her?'

'They liked them all. They can spot someone that will spoil them as twenty paces! But when we talked to them afterwards it was pretty clear that she had their vote. Just as well, really, since Janet and I had pretty well decided.'

'So when can she start?'

'She's interning at the moment – at Last Cairngorm – so we hope she can start right away. Things arc pretty fraught, but Janet can take a couple of days off this week to show her the ropes. It's such a relief!'

*

Fiona Marchmont called just after one o'clock. Vanessa was beginning, somewhat tentatively, to eat an egg and cress sandwich from the canteen. She had stopped feeling sick a couple of hours before and she had chosen egg and cress because that was what she fancied. But she hadn't taken account of the smell produced by boiled egg, even when it's mixed with mayo. Still, perseverance was in her nature, and she was hungry. She swallowed a mouthful and picked up the phone.

Fiona wasted no time on pleasantries. 'We've got a meeting with a senior official at the FO tomorrow morning at eleven. I talked to someone in the Crown Office this morning and he's just got back to me to say that they've agreed to a meeting with the Advocate General's people. They want me there to explain why we need them to intervene. And I want you there to tell them, directly, why it's so important that you get these emails.'

'Christ, Fiona, you don't hang about, do you? I'll talk to Esslemont, and if he agrees, which he will, but I have to give him his place, I'll get admin to book us on a plane. Might have to be quite early, though.'

'That's fine. Bob can get the kids off to school, and it's his turn to be home for them tomorrow afternoon'.

'Bit of a military operation having kids and a job. I've just been talking to Colin MacNee. He and Janet are taking on an *au pair*.'

'We thought of that, but we're managing on the basis of my flexitime and the goodwill of his colleagues at the university. Why so interested?'

'Always concerned for my colleagues.' She rang off.

*

'Aisha's just heard back from Strathclyde about Nuttall. She's following up on his application to Ebright, so she asked me to let you know what they've come up with.'

Vanessa had managed to finish her sandwich and was sipping a cup of camomile tea. 'Go on, Sara.'

'They sent a PC to the mailbox shop where Nuttall's birth certificate was sent to Simon Mathieson. He doesn't have a box there any more – he only rented it for three months, from mid-April to mid-July – but one of the staff said he recognised the picture of Nuttall as someone who had had a box there. He couldn't say for sure whether Nuttall was the person he knew as Mathieson, but he was pretty certain he had been there.'

'Better than nothing, I suppose, but hardly conclusive. I guess we have to find Mathieson, if that's his real name. I suppose it's too much to hope that he's already known to us?'

'I checked the databases for both Nuttall and Mathieson. Nothing known. Aisha is asking Ebright what checks they make before taking someone on, but uniform have checked all the names we collected on Vermont One and from Ebright and nobody has come up with a record'.

'I assumed that was the case. Someone would have told me if anything had popped out. Bloody slow progress, this. Not much better on Keller, though I've got a meeting in London tomorrow that might help with the emails. Get Strathclyde to do what they can on Mathieson.'

DC Aisha Gajani appeared the door.

'You know, Aisha, you sort of materialise rather than just coming in. What've you got?'
'Well, Nuttall, or whoever he is, first applied for a job with Ebright in late May. His address was at the mailbox shop we already know about, but it's quite feasible that his

mail was being picked up by Mathieson, because you can have multiple names listed for the same box. I've just checked with the shop again, and one of the names listed for the box rented by Mathieson was, you guessed it, Thomas Nuttall. You would have thought that Mathieson, if it was him, would have applied for the birth certificate in Nuttall's name, but he didn't. Maybe he didn't think ahead to the point where his new identity would apply for a job. Or maybe he thought that Register House might cross-reference to Nuttall's death certificate. Whatever, it's another link between Nuttall and Mathieson.'

'And Ebright?'

'They do a basic criminal records check after they've decided to offer someone a job. Nuttall came up clean. I've seen his application and he claimed experience, which Ebright didn't verify, in offshore work. Since Nuttall is dead, I thought I'd see if any of the major employers ever had a Simon Mathieson on their books. Might take a while. Should I carry on with it?'

Vanessa spread her hands in front of her and shrugged. 'Might as well. Can't do any harm. And it might help us find him. Now I need to get the DCS to sign off on my trip to London tomorrow. He'll have to inform the Chief.'

*

Jack Eisner was in his hotel room drafting an email to Cy Packard at Burtonhall HQ when Vanessa Fiske knocked on his door. Colin MacNee was with her.

'Good afternoon, Mr Eisner. I'm Detective Chief Inspector Vanessa Fiske and this is Detective Inspector Colin MacNee.' They both showed heir warrant cards and Eisner beckoned them in.

'We understand that you work for Burtonhall, Mr Eisner, and we would like to ask you some questions. We are investigating the murders at Grampian Royal Hospital and on the Vermont One oil platform, both of which are managed by companies owned by Burtonhall. Are you happy to talk to us?'

Eisner looked uneasy. 'Sure. But I don't know what I can tell you. I've only been here a few days.'

'Let's start with what you do for Burtonhall.'

'I'm the Director of Security. I report directly to the CEO and he asked me to come over to see if I could help with the PR aspects of the unfortunate events at the hospital and on the rig.'

Colin MacNee looked at him with distaste. '"Unfortunate events"? There have been two murders, Mr Eisner. This isn't a Lemony Snicket adventure.' Colin caught a glance from Vanessa and backed off.

'How much do you, and Burtonhall generally, know about what the two dead men, Jamieson and Keller, were doing here?'

'Almost nothing. Cy Packard, the CEO, takes a close interest in all Burtonhall's investments. That's why he sent me over. To find out what's going on and to protect our reputation.'

'Come on, Mr Eisner. You're pretty high paid help for a PR man. Let me ask you directly, have you, or your Mr Packard, seen the emails that Peter Keller sent from the hospital?'

'No. Burtonhall is not involved in the day-to-day management of the companies it owns. Any reporting would have been directly to Hedelco. And Ebright in the case of the Vermont One.'

'Could you get them if you wanted to?'

'I guess Cy could get them. But they would be commercially sensitive. We'd want to keep them confidential.'

Vanessa looked unimpressed. 'I'm sure you would. But if you haven't seen the reports, why are you here?'

'Reputational damage can go to the bottom line. I'm here to try to prevent that happening. And with senior politicians taking an interest, the press coverage will continue. We need to manage that.'

Colin was about to intervene but Vanessa touched his arm.

'Thank you, Mr Eisner. Please let your CEO know that reputational damage, as you put it, might be less if he ensured that we have sight of Peter Keller's emails to Hedelco. And please let us know if you intend to leave Aberdeen.'

Eisner had already opened the hotel room door. As they walked down the corridor, Colin again started to speak.

'Let's talk in the car, Colin.' Vanessa said, firmly.

As she got into front passenger seat, Vanessa said, 'Spit it out. I think I know what it is.'

'How the fuck does he know that the First Minister has stuck her oar in?'

'How indeed? He seemed much more certain than press generalisations would justify. We need to find out who's leaking, and why?'
As Colin started the car, Vanessa turned to him. 'And what was that about Lemony Snicket?'

'The girls have been reading it. You get sucked in. You'll understand eventually.'

*

Not long after the detectives left his hotel room, Eisner reached for his burner to read a text.

DCI trying to get emails. Mtg 2moro in London Foreign Office to discuss getting US govt to help.

Eisner immediately sent this information in an encrypted email to Packard. The response was almost immediate. Packard would talk to his Chairman. It was time to deploy the ex-PM.

*

At 21.30 that evening, one of Mancuso's security staff, doing his routine round of inspection at Last Cairngorm, found a suspicious package at the bottom of the indoor ski slope. The slope was housed in one of the buildings that had caused most controversy when the development was under consideration for planning permission by Mid-Aberdeenshire Council. As he had been trained to do, he immediately left the building and began to contact security control by radio. As he was walking away, he was lifted off his feet by the blast from a huge explosion. Apart from some bruising and a sprained wrist, he was unharmed. As he got up, he looked back to see the ski slope building engulfed in flames. As he hurried to the security control room, there was a loud crash as the roof collapsed on to the slope.

*

That same evening, 130 miles south west, in Cumbernauld, the duty IT Manager at Mercury Fulfilment, a US-owned warehousing and distribution centre, providing services to several online retailers, began to get calls from customers who had been unable to order items, and from staff unable to dispatch them. The IT system had become unresponsive. It was failing to accept valid credit and debit cards, returning postcodes as unrecognised, declaring stock items, even when they were clearly visible to warehouse staff, unavailable, and refusing to allow returning customers to log on, apparently because their passwords were invalid.

The IT manager quickly realised that his systems had been hacked into. He called the chief executive and told him that the company was under cyber attack and that if he did not close down the system entirely, the whole business would be at risk.

Customers worldwide began to email and telephone to complain. When the message,

"Mercury Fulfilment apologises for the temporary unavailability of its services. We hope to be back online very soon" appeared on an otherwise blank website, messages began to trend on Twitter and other social media asking "WTF is going on at Mercury?"

The first response of the company to press enquiries was to play down the significance of a 'glitch' in its systems, but as soon as the IT specialists in press, television and radio got involved, the words 'cyber attack' became the entirely accurate shorthand for what had happened to Mercury Fulfilment.

CHAPTER EIGHT

James Michael Roskill - "James" to his
colleagues and fellow investors in Burtonhall
and the other companies whose boards he
adorned, "Mike" to his family and his oldest
friends, "RosKILL" to the protesters and
campaigners who remembered nothing about
his career except the two short and bloody
wars in oil-rich Central Asia that his
government had waged in defiance of
international opinion - had served as Prime
Minister of the United Kingdom for a little
under four years. Before that, he had been
Foreign Secretary for six years and, since
leaving office and resigning from parliament,
he had shown little restraint in using his
influence and access in the interests of the
businesses through which he was in the
process of becoming very rich.

For much of Roskill's time at the Foreign
Office, and throughout his premiership, Sir
Justin Carey had been Permanent Secretary
at the FO and head of the diplomatic service.
Carey was nearing retirement and could look
forward to immediate elevation to the House
of Lords when he left. Despite the
restrictions on the practice of senior civil
servants using the so-called "revolving door"

between government and private business, it was well known that he was looking around for directorships that would draw on his wide experience of government and international affairs but, more significantly, provide him with a supplement to his already generous pension.

When Eisner told Cy Packard about the meeting at the FO, he immediately called Burtonhall's chairman.

'Richard, the Scottish police are going to the British Government tomorrow to get them to ask the Feds to put pressure on Hedelco to release the emails that their man sent back from Aberdeen. We need to prevent that. I don't need to tell you why.'

Richard Seaton had served as Secretary of State under two presidents. His second term had coincided with Roskill's premiership. They could hardly be described as soul mates: Seaton was a hardcore conservative Republican and Roskill had spent his entire career ducking and weaving around the centre ground of British politics. But their political interests had coincided around what had become known as "liberal interventionism" and they had become very close during the Central Asian wars.

'What do you need me to do, Cy?', Seaton asked, in a tone that suggested that he already knew.

'I need you to talk to Roskill and persuade him to talk to Carey at the British Foreign Office. Carey should be able to call off the dogs.'

'I'll do what I can.'

*

'James, I know you usually need more time before you try to intervene on our behalf with your high level contacts, but this is serious, and it's urgent. We need you to prevent the Brits going to the US government to get them to put pressure on Hedelco to release the emails that their man sent back from Aberdeen.'

'Not easy, Richard. If this were a simple commercial matter, I would have no reservations about speaking to Carey. But it's a criminal investigation into a particularly unpleasant murder - two murders if we include Vermont One - and it crosses the devolution line. Even after two hundred years, you Americans know how sensitive what you call "intergovernmental relations" can be. There's a lot of press speculation here about the interest the Scottish First Minister is taking in the police investigation. I'm not sure I want to get into the middle of this.'

'Not like you to be so squeamish. I've been approached by several members of the board and, more importantly, by some very big Burtonhall investors. They're getting nervous about the publicity this is generating. We need to try to close it down.'

'As I say, I'm not comfortable with this. I don't even know whether I can reach Carey.'

'Come off it. Burtonhall pays you handsomely. That should help you to be comfortable. And of course you can speak to Carey. He worked for you for the best part of ten years. Not to mention that you went to school with him. I'm asking you to do this not only for Burtonhall, but as a personal favour to me.'

There was silence and then Roskill muttered something that might have been, 'OK.' And the line went dead.

*

Vanessa Fiske and Fiona Marchmont met at Aberdeen airport at six o'clock on Tuesday morning. As they headed for the gate to catch the 0630 flight, Vanessa made a quick detour to pick up the Aberdeen *Gazette & Times, The Times* and *The Guardian*. On Monday, the papers had picked up Aaronson's story in *The Globe*, but they had done little more than what Harry Conival contemptuously described as 'copying out'. If they were going to do any serious follow-up, it would be today.

The running was being made by the *G & T*. The chief crime reporter had a piece about the slow progress on the double murder enquiry and about the difficulty faced by the investigating officers in getting information from the American companies that owned or operated the 'facilities' ('When did we start using that Americanism?' Vanessa thought) where the bodies had been found. He rehashed the stuff about ownership and the recruitment to the investigating team of an expert in company accounts. But it was his closing paragraph that made Fiske angry, and frustrated that she wouldn't be able to talk to Colin MacNee or to Esslemont until she got to London.

It was already widely known that the First Minister is taking a close interest in the case. However, the G & T *can reveal that detectives have approached the UK government to get them to intervene with the Americans to persuade the two companies directly involved – Hedelco and Ebright Offshore Drilling – to release emails that the murdered men are believed to have sent back to their head offices in the USA, in encrypted form, before they were killed. Reliable sources say that a high-level meeting will take place today (Tuesday) at the Foreign Office in London to discuss this. It will be attended by the senior investigating officer, DCI Vanessa Fiske, and by North East Constabulary's legal adviser, Fiona Marchmont.*

As they strapped themselves in, Vanessa passed the paper to Fiona. 'You can skip most of it. It's bog standard space filler. But look at the last paragraph. Somebody is giving out confidential information. And I think I know who it is.'

Vanessa hadn't noticed the reports, only in the *G & T* because the news had broken too late for the early editions of the London-based papers, of the explosion at Last Cairngorm and the cyber attack on Mercury Fulfilment.

*

DC Duncan Williamson was trying to persuade Bernard Donovan at Hedelco's GRH office, to let him compare the enhanced picture of the hospital murder suspect with the pictures held on the HR database of male employees of the same apparent age.

'Here we go again, Detective Williamson. You can't really expect me to let you roam freely in the personal records of our employees. I wouldn't be surprised if your Data Protection Act made that illegal. I have no wish to be unhelpful. Indeed, my head office has instructed me to co-operate as much as I can with your inquiries. But we do have a duty of care to the people who work here.'

'Duty of care?' Williamson thought. 'He's been doing what the Americans call "lawyering up".'

There was no point in taking this on if there was another way.

'Mr Donovan, if our IT people could find a way to compare the pictures you hold with the picture of the suspect without accessing any other information, not even the identity of the people in the photos, would that work? If we got a match, we would ask you to identify the suspect.'

'Can that be done?'

'I really don't know. But if it can, will you help us?'

Donovan smiled. 'Let me think about it. I'll give you an answer when you let me know it can be done.'

'Next stop, Dongle Donaldson', Williamson thought, and dialled his number.

*

Paul MacIver read the morning papers in his flat before setting off for the First Minister's office in St Andrews House on Calton Hill. The Scottish titles, with deadlines later than the Northern editions of the London papers, all led with the explosion at Last Cairngorm. There was no more than a news brief about the computer problems at Mercury Fulfilment in any of the papers. That was a story, MacIver thought, that could be labelled "developing".

None of the reports gave a definitive cause of the explosion, mainly because the fire and rescue service, and the police, were saying very little, and because Frank Mancuso, Last Cairngorm's security chief, had ensured that the guard who had been reporting the suspicious package when the blast went off, and who was suffering from shock, was kept well away from the press.

Speculation about sabotage, even terrorism, would start before the evening papers hit the street and would probably be the main story by the time the television and radio news broadcasts went on air in the early evening. Making any kind of link between events at Last and at Mercury would take a little longer. MacIver smiled and thought carefully about how he would advise the First Minister to respond.

*

On the flight to London, between sips of fizzy mineral water and trying not to think about the cooked breakfast that was being served to most of the passengers, Vanessa Fiske went over with Fiona Marchmont the reasons why she needed early sight of the Hedelco emails. Fiona tried to anticipate the objections that might be raised by Foreign Office officials and their legal advisers and to formulate answers to them. She emphasised, again, that any intervention would have to be political. Even if it involved the legal attaché in Washington, that route would be quasi-political because it might involve the US Attorney General and his opposite numbers in Massachusetts, where Hedelco was registered, Rhode Island, where Ebright had its HQ, and possibly in Delaware, because of Burtonhall's ownership of the company.

'This is far from a done deal, Vanessa. The fact that they were persuaded to set up a meeting so quickly is a good sign, but it will all depend on who's represented and at what level. It's not impossible that the final decision will be taken by the Permanent Secretary, or at least be run past him. So we might not have this sorted today.'

Fiona was suddenly aware that Vanessa had lost concentration and had gone very pale. She was just about to put out her hand to grasp Vanessa's arm when Vanessa lurched forward, grabbed a sickbag from the seat pocket, and retched into it, trying, unsuccessfully, not to draw the attention of other travellers. Fortunately, the middle seat of three was unoccupied, with Fiona at the window and Vanessa on the aisle.

Fiona moved into the middle seat and put her arm round Vanessa's shoulder and whispered 'Are you all right?'

'I'm fine. As you probably guessed when we spoke last night, I'm pregnant. Nobody at work knows except Colin MacNee and Chris Jenkinson, and now you. My DS has worked it out and everybody else is speculating on why I keep nipping off to the loo. So I'll have to go public soon, but I thought I'd wait until I have a scan next week'.

'So you're about six or seven weeks? First three months are the worst, as you probably know. I take it you're happy.'

'Yes, we are. And thank you for confirming that I've got another six weeks of this to look forward to.'

'My pleasure. Worth it, though. I've done it three times.'

Vanessa laughed. 'I may come to you for advice. My mum's a long way away, and my sister shows no sign of breeding. Then again, neither did I, as far as anyone could tell.'

*

Dongle Donaldson and Duncan Williamson were sitting in Bernard Donovan's outer office in the Hedelco Suite at GRH.

Sharon Archibald, as always, offered them a 'hot beverage' and, as always, Duncan declined, with thanks.

'You know, Sharon, I'm spending so much time here that you should name this seat after me. A nice little brass plate saying, "The Detective Constable Duncan Williamson Chair", would be nice.'

'Oh, you'd really have to speak to Mr Donovan about that, Sergeant', Sharon said, with her usual sweet but vacant smile.

Fortunately, Donovan came out of his office at that point, so relieving Duncan of the need to explain the joke.

'Come in, gentlemen, please.'

'This is Detective Sergeant Donaldson, Mr Donovan…'

'Just call me Dongle,' Donaldson interrupted, 'Everybody else does.'

Williamson had hoped to avoid having to explain Dongle's nickname, but it was now inevitable, so he did.

'Not much about computers and databases that Dongle doesn't know.'

'OK', Donovan said, 'So what has he come up with?'

Dongle sat forward on the seat he had taken facing Donovan, who had sat down behind his desk.

'Well, Mr Donovan, most HR databases are, in fact, two databases that can be related to each other. They're called relational databases. Have you heard the term?'
Donovan nodded, and said, 'Go on.'

'Commonly, one database is composed of the photographs, usually in jpg format, and one holds all the other, more personal and confidential information. In normal usage they appear to be one database – if I called up your file, I'd see all your personal details and your picture – but they can be detached from each other and interrogated separately. So, if your HR records are set up that way, we can do the exercise that Duncan described to you earlier today.'

'Would you have to go through everything?'

'No. We would search for all male employees in a particular age range, in this case, between thirty and fifty and download the pictures to a single file. We would then run it through our facial recognition software to see if we have a match.'

'And no other information would be accessed?

'Absolutely none.'

'I'll ask our IT manager to come up. She'll be able to confirm if our records are arranged in the way you describe.'

*

Janet MacNee and Shelley Mehring, the MacNees' new *au pair*, were sitting at the MacNees' kitchen table drinking coffee. Shelley had phoned Janet on the previous evening, Monday, to accept the job and Janet had asked if she would like to come round early on Tuesday so that they could both take the girls to school.

'I've taken a couple of days off to show you the ropes. I'll have to introduce you to the head teacher and to the girls' teachers. And we'll have to fill in all sorts of forms to make it possible for you to pick them up from school. So if we took them to school together we might be able to sort all that out in one go.'

When they got back from the school, Janet had shown Shelley her room, usually a guest bedroom. It was perfectly clean and tidy, with a supply of towels laid out on the bed. Then they had viewed Emma and Cat's room, which was a mess, with toys and books all over the place, and duvets, Emma's with pictures from *Anne of Green Gables* and Cat's showcasing *Spongebob Squarepants*, hanging off both of the bunk beds.

Janet didn't apologise. 'Please don't be tempted to tidy up for them. They're supposed to do it themselves, but Colin's the only one who can persuade them to do it. I think he bribes them, but he denies it, says he relies solely on charm.'

'If I get involved, it'll be as a joint operation with Emma and Cat', Shelley said.

'You'd think you'd already started, Shelley. That sounded a bit like the police-speak Colin sometimes brings home. Which reminds me of something I have to emphasise, and I hope you won't mind that I do.'

Shelley looked apprehensive.

'Nothing to worry about. It's just that both Colin and I do jobs where confidentiality is really important. We want you to be part of the family, so it's likely that you'll hear us talking about work. I think that asking you to sign a confidentiality agreement or something would be over the top, but I need to tell you that anything you hear shouldn't be repeated outside the house.'

'That's absolutely fine, Janet', Shelley said, 'I understand'.

'Good. So now let's go through a typical week in the lives of Emma and Catriona MacNee.'

*

Vanessa and Fiona took a taxi from Paddington Station to Whitehall and walked through the ornamental arch into King Charles Street and the Classical splendour of George Gilbert Scott's main Foreign Office building. They identified themselves at the entrance. Vanessa showed her warrant card and introduced Fiona as her colleague. The porter on reception asked them to wait while he made a phone call. A couple of minutes later, a young man in shirtsleeves and a college tie came down to meet them and conducted them up the spectacular Grand Staircase.

They were taken to a small but elegant room, furnished as a board room and with pictures from the government art collection on the walls. They were not the kind of old masters that command millions at auction, but they were high quality English landscapes, completely in keeping with the opulence of the Scott interiors they had seen as they made their way up from reception. The room was already occupied. Four men rose from their seats as Vanessa and Fiona entered.

'Good morning, Detective Chief Inspector Fiske, Ms Marchmont. Welcome to the Foreign and Commonwealth Office. I'm Gerald St Clair, Assistant Secretary with responsibility for relations with the United States. Let me introduce my colleagues. David Horner is one of our lawyers and he served for some time as legal attaché in Washington. Nigel Inchholm is here representing the Advocate General. And Commander Kenneth Bancroft is from Special Branch, attending at the request of the Permanent Secretary and the Commissioner of the Metropolitan Police.'

Vanessa and Fiona shook hands all round, and then Vanessa turned to St Clair. 'I recognise that it's your meeting, Mr St Clair, but may I ask what interest Special Branch has in this case?'

St Clair looked at Bancroft, who took off his half-moon spectacles and polished them. He prepared himself to speak, much like a ham actor in a 1950s provincial repertory theatre.

'There are *aspects*' - the emphasis was partly declaratory and partly conspiratorial - 'to this case that are of interest to HMG. Sir Justin, the Permanent Secretary, asked us to observe this meeting because he takes the view that the ownership of the facilities in which the murders took place is both largely irrelevant and, having consulted the Commissioner, likely to lead to a waste of police time, both here and, if the FCO does what you want, Chief Inspector, in the United States.'

Vanessa remembered what Neil had told her about the membership of the Burtonhall board. Sir Justin has been got at, she thought, almost certainly by James Roskill.

'I'm not sure on what evidence Sir Justin has taken that view, Commander Bancroft, but I strongly disagree with him. I am leading an investigation into two murders that occurred within hours of each other, in establishments owned or managed by two separate American companies that are subsidiaries of the same holding company. I have been unable to establish motive and I believe that access to the emails sent back to the United States, in encrypted form, by the murdered men, may help me to do so.'

'What makes you say that, Chief Inspector?' This was St Clair, and the note of scepticism in his question was unmistakeable.

'First of all, both men were doing similar jobs, auditing the performance of systems in the hospital and on the oil platform. Second, Ebright tried to prevent me from taking as evidence Harvey Jamieson's laptop computer, which was among his effects on

Vermont One, and Hedelco, who run the hospital, have refused to release copies of Peter Keller's emails to them. Third, the emails recovered from Jamieson's laptop and decrypted by our experts, contain evidence that he had discovered practices that might adversely affect the profitability of Vermont One. Fourth, circumstantial evidence about Keller's movements in the hospital also suggests a concern with the performance of processes that might affect the bottom line. At the very least, I have to investigate whether commercial concerns may have played a part in these murders. To do that effectively, I need to see the emails.'

'But there are other lines of enquiry?', Bancroft asked.

'Of course. We have CCTV images of possible suspects for both murders and we are actively pursuing these avenues. As we speak, one of my team is attempting to persuade Hedelco in Aberdeen to allow us to compare one of these images with pictures held on the hospital's HR database. I don't know at this point if they are being any more co-operative than they've been so far. But these are parallel enquiries to those concerning the commercial issues. They are not a substitute for them. The various strands of the enquiry are inseparable.'

'So, exactly what would you like the FCO to do?', St Clair asked.

Vanessa sensed the beginning of a runaround. 'I am advised by Fiona that if we attempt to get access to these emails by purely legal means, by going to court, the process could take a very long time. I need help to persuade these companies, Hedelco in particular, to hand them over "voluntarily". That would be a political and diplomatic route to the same end. So I am asking the FCO to use its connections in Washington, possibly via the legal attaché, to exert some pressure.'

David Horner, the former legal attaché, spoke for the first time. 'It's not unheard of for us to help in this way, but it's not common practice. The difficulty here is that it would involve both federal and state authorities, so we would have to persuade our American friends, in the Justice Department and the FBI, to act on our behalf with the state authorities in Massachusetts and Delaware, possibly also in Rhode Island. That's very complicated and would take some time, though not as long as going to court, I grant you.'

'What if we limited our efforts to Hedelco? The Keller emails are in their ownership and any court action would be against them rather than their parent company. We have most of Jamieson's emails, so we could put Ebright to one side for the purposes of this exercise and so limit the state level intervention to Massachusetts.'

'Administratively, that would simplify matters, certainly,' St Clair said, 'But Sir Justin would still need to be convinced that your need was great enough to justify any action by us. David?'

'Yes. If a request like this had come to me I would have been more hopeful if it had involved only one company and, in particular, only one state. In this case, too, the process might be assisted a little by the fact that the administrations in Washington and in Massachusetts are of the same party.'

Vanessa thought that of the four men she was trying to persuade – in effect, only three, because Inchholm from the Advocate General's office was carrying no more than a watching brief – Horner was the only one who was trying to be helpful.

'So,' Vanessa said, reaching for a glass of water and suppressing a belch, 'Can we go after Hedelco?'

St Clair signalled the end of the meeting by closing his folder. 'I shall put it to Sir Justin and get back to you as soon as I can.'

'Thank you, Mr St Clair. Now, I wonder if you could direct me to the nearest ladies' room.'

*

'I think we may have a match.' Dongle Donaldson and Detective Sergeant Anil Jasthi of the Video Analysis Section had been watching as Anil's video recognition software compared the enhanced CCTV image with the file of photographs from the GRH HR database. There were more than eighty male employees in the 30-50 age range and it took an hour to do the comparison.

'How sure are you, Anil?' Dongle asked. 'I need to be able to tell MacNee how confident we are that we can identify this guy.'

'Pretty sure.'

'How sure?'

'Well over 90 per cent.'

'I'll phone MacNee.'

*

Williamson and MacNee gave the picture of the employee matched with the CCTV image to the senior HR manager and went for a coffee in the hospital canteen. She would go through the files related to the employees whose photos had been compared until she identified the match. It wouldn't take long, and she agreed to text Williamson as soon as their suspect had been identified.

'His name is Andrew MacIlwraith and he worked here for less than a year as a porter.'

Maggie Melvin from HR had texted them less than an hour after they left her office. She now sat at her desk with three pictures spread in front of the detectives: the enhanced CCTV image; a jpg from the file that had been drawn from the HR database; and a print from MacIwraith's file.

'You said, "worked". When did he leave?' Colin MacNee asked.

'He was dismissed in July after a final warning for inappropriate behaviour towards patients. He lodged an appeal and then withdrew it just before the initial hearing.'

'So what was he doing back in the hospital a fortnight ago?'

'No idea. But you have to remember that we don't security check everybody who comes in. We would have known he was here only if one of his former workmates or, conceivably but not likely, a patient, had recognised him and reported it.'

'Do you have an address for him? He's probably long gone, but somebody might know where he went.'

The address was a sub-let council flat in the Mastrick area of Aberdeen. Nobody there remembered MacIlwraith, but one of the neighbours thought he might have gone to Glasgow.

CHAPTER NINE

Vanessa Fiske and Fiona Marchmont were back in Aberdeen by late afternoon. Vanessa had phoned Esslemont's office from Heathrow to say that it was imperative that she see him before the end of the day.

'Productive trip?' Esslemont asked. No-one else was present.

'Don't know yet, sir. The people we met need to talk to the Permanent Secretary, and I think that he may have been got at. But before I go into detail, there's a rather more urgent matter that we should discuss.'

Esslemont leaned forward. 'Oh?'

'Somebody is leaking information on the murder investigations. Some of it is appearing in the press – did you see the *G & T* this morning? – and some of it is getting to people with an interest in what we're doing but no right to have it.'

'Go on.'

'The first thing was the enquiry to Harry Conival asking him to confirm that Keller had been killed by lethal injection. I had deliberately kept that detail back. Then there was the fact that reporters, and Eisner from Burtonhall, clearly knew about the Chief's call from the First Minister. At the press briefing, it was clear that the *G & T* reporter knew what drugs had been used to kill Keller. I had withheld that, too. And I suspect that Sir Justin Carey, the Permanent Secretary at the FO, had been lobbied by Burtonhall, almost certainly by Roskill, who's on the Burtonhall board, about our meeting there this morning. If they knew about the meeting before the *G & T* story appeared, and I think they did, they didn't get it from the lawyers or from the FO. It came from here.'

'What makes you think that the Foreign Office had been lobbied?'

'For one thing, the fact that Special Branch were represented at the meeting, ostensibly to observe on behalf of the Permanent Secretary and the Commissioner of the Met.' Vanessa noticed a expression of real irritation cross Esslemont's face, but she carried on. 'For another, the clear reluctance of the senior FO official who ran the meeting to reach any decision without consulting the Permanent Secretary.'

'Did you form a view about the interest of the Met?'

'I asked that, and Bancroft – from Special Branch – said that the Commissioner thinks that the ownership of the businesses where the murders happened is irrelevant and pursuing that line of enquiry would waste police time. I didn't believe a word of it.'

'No. And none of the Met's business anyway. I'll manage my resources as I see fit.' Esslemont was more than irritated. He felt that his territory was being invaded, but he let it go and turned to the leak.

'Let's suppose you're right. How do you propose to identify the source? All the facts you mention were known to a lot of people here, and you know how leaky this building can be. I can see that this might damage your investigation, but I don't know what we can do about it, other than to warn people, once again, to be discreet'.

'Strictly between you and me, sir, I have shrewd idea who we're after, but I can't work out why it's happening.'

'I have a feeling you're not ready to give me a name. So what do you propose?'

'I need to work out how to confirm my suspicions. I'll come up with something, relevant to the investigations, but known only to you, me, possibly the Chief, and my "suspect". Then if it appears where it shouldn't, we'll know. Once I have a plan, I'll tell you who I think we're after.'

'When?'

'Tomorrow, sir. I'm not having my investigation compromised for any longer than that.'

*

Colin MacNee was waiting for DCI Fiske as she left Esslemont's office. She told him that there was no decision yet from the Foreign Office, but that she was hopeful that they might agree to help with the Hedelco emails. She asked what had been happening in her absence.

'You should get the details on the grunt work on finding our suspects from Sara and Aisha, and from Duncan and Stewart on their ongoing relationship with Donovan at

Hedelco.   But you probably don't know much about the two overnight attacks.'

'I saw something about Last Cairngorm on a TV screen as Fiona and I were rushing through Terminal 5. Nothing to connect it with our enquiries, is there?'

'Well...'   Colin tailed off, with an inflexion that Vanessa recognised. He had something on his mind.

'Come on, Colin, I know that look. Let's have it!'

'Nothing direct, boss, but the bomb at Last wasn't the only "attack" last night.   There was a really serious cyber attack at Mercury Fulfilment in Cumbernauld at about the same time.   Completely knocked out their IT systems, which puts them temporarily out of business.'

'I'm not with you. If these are crimes, they're not for us.   They're for specialist units: counter-terrorism, special branch, the high-tech boys.'

"I've lost count of the number of times you've told me, and everyone else on your team, not to believe in coincidence. Or at least to look very sceptically at anything that looks like coincidence.'

Colin knew Vanessa well enough to recognise when she got it. There was an almost visible light bulb glowing above her head.

'Hedelco, Ebright, Last and Mercury. All American companies with major investments in Scotland. All involved in major crimes within a couple of weeks. You're not going to tell me that Burtonhall owns Last and Mercury as well…?

'Alas, no! But if our murders aren't just murders, but crimes with a economic motive of some kind…'

Vanessa held up a hand. 'Slow down, Colin. You're in danger of getting ahead of the evidence. But your off-the-wall questions have paid off before, so I'll think about it and we can talk again in the morning, after the eight-thirty meeting.'

As she headed for her desk to check her emails, Vanessa thought that Colin might, unwittingly, have given her a way of flushing out the 'mole'.

*

In Edinburgh, on Tuesday morning, while Fiske and Marchmont were on their way to the FO, Paul MacIver was briefing the First Minister on the attacks on Last Cairngorm and Mercury Fulfilment, and bringing her up to date on the murder investigations in her constituency.

'Counter-terrorism and Special Branch are involved in the Last Cairngorm investigation and the high-tech crime specialists from Strathclyde are at Mercury. There's no doubt that the explosion and fire at Last were caused by a bomb. No-one killed or seriously hurt – the place was closed and very quiet when it happened – just minor injuries and shock to the security guard who spotted the package containing the bomb and was calling it in when it went off. Clear, too, that Mercury has been subject to a targeted and sophisticated attack on its systems. Their official position is that they'll be up and running again quickly but some people I've spoken to say it'll be weeks, not days.'

The First Minister shook her head. 'I never thought I'd have to ask this, Paul, but has anyone claimed responsibility?'

'No. No warning, no calls to the Press Association, none of the stuff you remember about Northern Ireland.'

'Do we know any more?'

'No, we don't, and what I'm about to say, I wouldn't say outside this room – yet.'

The FM nodded for him to go on.

'Hedelco, Ebright, Last and Mercury. All American companies with major investments in Scotland. All involved in major crimes within a couple of weeks. And, before you ask, there's no obvious link between Last and Mercury and Burtonhall. We don't know the motive for these two attacks, we don't have any idea who's behind them, and we don't yet know who killed Jamieson and Keller…'

'I feel a "but" coming on.'

MacIver shot her a sardonic grin. 'But…we can speculate on the effects of all four crimes. They could adversely affect inward –and indeed continuing – investment in Scotland. And that means jobs, the feel-good factor, and the referendum. So we need to ensure that every effort is made to solve them quickly.'

'So what do you advise?'

'I don't think you should get directly involved, especially since your call to the Chief Constable got into the public domain so quickly. I'll talk to the Justice Secretary and he and I will maintain close liaison with the police, probably through ACPO. We'll keep you well briefed. You'll be expected to answer questions on the attacks in Parliament tomorrow. I think you should pre-empt that by making a statement. I'll draft something bland but statesmanlike. I'll limit it to Last and Mercury. You shouldn't raise any possible connection with the two murders. If the opposition does, you can bat them off'.

*

At the 0830 team meeting on Wednesday morning, DCI Fiske needed to be brought up to date on the Glasgow end of the investigation and on any progress made in identifying and finding a suspect in the death of Peter Keller at GRH.

'Probably better to hear from Duncan first, boss,' Colin MacNee said, 'because what he and Stewart discovered in their latest wrangle with Donovan may affect how we proceed in Glasgow.'

Vanessa nodded.

'Dongle' - DC Williamson nodded towards Donaldson, who, was sitting at the end of the conference room table staring intently at his laptop - 'came up with a way to compare the enhanced picture of the unidentified man in the CCTV footage with the employee photos held on the Hedelco HR database without accessing any confidential information. That kept Donovan happy. Our suspect is Andrew MacIlwraith, formerly employed as a porter at GRH, who was dismissed last July for inappropriate behaviour towards patients. No more details, except that he lodged an appeal and then withdrew it at the last minute. Nobody knows what he was doing at GRH at the material time and all we discovered at his previous address was that neighbours think he may have moved to Glasgow.'

'Have we been on to Strathclyde about him?'

'Not yet, boss. We only identified him late yesterday afternoon and   we thought you might want to think about him in relation to what's come back from Strathclyde about Nuttall and Mathieson.'

Vanessa turned to DS Sara Hamilton who indicated that the update on Nuttall-Mathieson should come from DC Gajani because she had been liaising with Strathclyde.

'This is hardly definitive, boss', Aisha said, 'but the people at the mailbox shop recall only one person accessing the box rented by Mathieson but with Nuttall's name also listed against it. So they may be one and the same. Trouble is, we don't know which one to look for first.'

'Well, logic points to looking for Mathieson, because we're pretty certain that Nuttall exists only as a result of identity theft.   And the Nuttall birth certificate went to Mathieson.   Trouble is, that doesn't prove that it was Mathieson who assumed Nuttall's identity, so we need to find out whether Nuttall had a separate existence in Glasgow. Not easy, and since we appear to have a confirmed sighting of Mathieson at the mailbox shop, we should start with him.'

'The suspect in the Keller murder, Andrew MacIlwraith, is also thought to be in

Glasgow.' DI Colin MacNee had decided to assert himself, gently, as SIO in the GRH murder. 'So it looks as though, on what the Chief calls "the purely criminal aspects" of these killings, the centre of gravity of the enquiry is moving to Glasgow. We can't continue to rely on Strathclyde making enquiries on our behalf.'

Vanessa belched discreetly and took a sip from a glass of fizzy water. 'No, we can't. Sara, you and Aisha should go down to Glasgow and see if you can locate Mathieson, MacIlwraith and, if he has a separate existence, Nuttall. I'll talk to the DCS about backfilling by in bringing a couple of people from some of the other CID teams.'

*

'I think it's Richard Fleming, sir.'

Esslemont looked shocked and sceptical. 'The Chief 's staff officer? I don't like the bugger, Vanessa, but I can't see why he would risk his career for a few quid slipped to him by a hack. What makes you think he might be the source?'

'I've looked carefully at the details that have got into the press, into the public domain, and into the hands of interested parties without a legitimate reason, and I've cross referenced them to the people here who knew about them. As you said yesterday, that's quite a number.'

She passed him a handwritten A4 sheet. 'That shows the pieces of leaked information, each with a list of the people here who knew about it. The only names that appear against all of them are mine, yours, the Chief's, and Fleming's. It wasn't me, sir, and I assume it wasn't you.'

Esslemont gave her a sarcastic smile. 'Thank you for the vote of confidence, Chief Inspector!'

'And I think we would both want to give the Chief the benefit of any doubt, which leaves only Fleming.'

'But why, Vanessa, why?

'I really don't know, sir. I'm only going where the evidence takes me.'
Esslemont sighed. 'Fleming's a bit too sure of himself, and he can be a supercilious sod, but I don't think he's corrupt. If it's him, there

must be a reason other than personal gain. There must be an innocent explanation. We can't just confront him.'

Vanessa took back the sheet of paper. 'No, we can't, but events the other night may give us a way of confirming my suspicions. Nobody has linked the bomb at Last Cairngorm with the cyber attack on Mercury Fulfilment and no-one has linked either with our murders. However, the fact that all four crimes involve American firms make it legitimate for us to talk to counter-terrorism to see if they have any intelligence that would make connections that might assist our investigation.'

'So what do you suggest we should do?'

'I think you should go to the Chief and get his support for an approach to counter-terrorism, emphasising the need for absolute secrecy. We can assume that Fleming will either sit in on your discussion with the Chief or be told by him what's happening.'

Esslemont nodded.

'Then we wait. And on previous form, we won't have to wait long.'

*

At Holyrood, the First Minister rose at 1230 hrs and read the statement prepared for her by Paul MacIver.

> *Members will already be aware, from press and media reports, of the explosion at Last Cairngorm on Monday evening and of an apparent cyber attack the same evening on Mercury Fulfilment in Cumbernauld. The appropriate authorities are investigating, North East Constabulary and Scottish counter-terrorism unit in the case of Last and the Strathclyde Police computer crime specialists at Mercury. At this stage, we have no reason to link the two incidents.*

> *There was no warning before either incident and there has been no claim of responsibility.*

> *The Justice Secretary is keeping closely in touch with the investigation and I will, of course, keep parliament fully informed.*

The questions that followed were, in the main, straightforward requests for information that the FM didn't have. She responded by accepting the need to give frequent reports to parliament and by recognising the concerns of members in all parties. It was bland, emollient, and even, as Paul MacIver had intended, statesmanlike.

She was about to resume her seat when the Presiding Officer called the name of a Labour member for Glasgow, a man known for his contacts in Strathclyde Police, and his visceral dislike of the First Minister.

'These two companies are American owned, and one of them has been involved in a very unpopular development in one of the most beautiful parts of Scotland. There have also been two murders recently on premises owned or operated by other US companies, one of which is just as unpopular as the Last Corporation. Does the First Minister have any reason to believe that there is anything to link the events covered in her statement with the murders?'

The FM got to her feet. 'No.'

Her questioner rose again. 'In that case, can she explain why officers from the North East Constabulary murder investigation team are arriving in Glasgow today to continue their enquiries?'

The best the FM could do was to say that this was clearly an operational matter and therefore the responsibility of the Chief Constable. But the question had unsettled her because her briefing had not anticipated it. And it had put into the public domain the possibility that Paul MacIver had not wanted to raise outside her office.

*

'Harry Conival's just had some calls asking us to confirm an MSP's claim at Holyrood that we're linking the murders with the Last and Mercury attacks. I've told him to say that we are simply following up in Glasgow leads from the normal course of our enquiries.'

DCI Fiske wanted to reassure the DCS that the question to the FM was not the result of a leak and would not get in the way of their efforts to identify the source of the stories that had got out since the murder enquiry started.

'Could have come from any number of sources, sir. And it doesn't in any way compromise the investigation. Strathclyde were already helping us. The most likely source is somebody in Strathclyde Police. The MSP in question is known to have good contacts there, and there's little doubt that it's the FM he's after, not us.'

Esslemont grunted. 'Even so, it adds to the mix and it's a potential distraction. And the Chief may use it as a way of deflecting attention from his office if you're right about where the leaks have been coming from.'

'But the defence is that this 'leak' is not in any way confidential. I would have announced it at the next press briefing. May even be helpful to our "strategy" by raising the possibility of a link to the Last and Mercury incidents.'

'I'm not sure whether you're just being devious, Vanessa, or looking on the bright side. In any case, I spoke in confidence to the Chief this morning and he agreed that we should approach counter-terrorism, as long as we do it discreetly. Our man was there taking notes.'

Vanessa noticed that at no point in the conversation had Esslemont mentioned their "target" by name. He wasn't entirely comfortable about what they were doing. She was still a little surprised that he had gone along with it.

*

Sara Hamilton and Aisha Gajani got off the train in Glasgow early in the afternoon. They were met by a DC from Govan Police Station who drove them first to their hotel - one of a no-frills chain - and then to the station, where they were found a couple of desks and introduced to the people and systems they needed to know.

On the train, they had discussed how they should approach the search for Mathieson and MacIlwraith. They decided to assume that Mathieson and Nuttall were one and the same. They knew that neither Mathieson nor MacIlwraith had a criminal record. That didn't mean that nothing was known about them. Police intelligence on individuals who had not yet been placed on the 'system' might help. If that turned up nothing, then they would be into a laborious trawl through other databases, some open to the public, some not - electoral register, council tax rolls, school and college records, national insurance files, even the phone book. From the CCTV pictures, they knew the approximate age of the suspects. That would help, but perhaps not much. Their only possible leads were that MacIlwraith's records at GRH had contained a previous address, from several years back, on the south side of Glasgow. The mailbox shop was in the same general area. That was why they had arranged to be based in Govan.

Govan Police Station is the most secure in Scotland, where suspects arrested under terrorism and security legislation are held. The Major Crime and Terrorism Investigation Unit is based there and officers from the Unit had been called in immediately by NEC to lead the investigation at Last Cairngorm. DCI Fiske, and her superior officers, would come to regret that they had not considered, when Sara and Aisha arranged to be based there, the propensity of the press to add two and two and make five.

CHAPTER TEN

Esslemont had seen the Chief Constable late on Wednesday morning, soon after Vanessa Fiske had named the Chief's staff officer as her suspect. Just after five o'clock, Harry Conival took a call from the chief crime reporter on the *Gazette & Times*.

'Afternoon, Harry. I've just had a tip, from a usually reliable source, that your DCI Fiske is talking to the counter-terrorism boys about a possible link between her two murders and the explosion at Last Cairngorm. Anyone there care to comment before we put it up on the website?'

'Give me half an hour, Jason, and I'll get back to you. I'll need to talk to Fiske.'

'Twenty minutes would be better. We want this to go up before the evening news bulletins.'

'I'll do my best.'

Harry caught Vanessa just as she was clearing her emails before going home.

'Harry, issue a flat denial. We have not contacted counter-terrorism about either murder, and we have no present intention of doing so.'

'You do know that that won't stop him. It'll go up in the next half-hour together with your denial, and unless you take out the word 'present' they'll use that as a justification for their story. It's a weasel word, and Jason Sime will spot it a mile off.'

'There are moments, Harry, when I know what we pay you for. Take it out. If anything changes on this, the last thing the reptiles will be concerned about is that I denied it today.'

*

While Harry was talking to Jason Sime, Jack Eisner's burner alerted him to the arrival of a text.

NEC tecs talking to counter-terrorism re poss link between murders and Last explosion.

It was just after 12.20 hrs in Wilmington, Delaware, when Cy Packard read an encrypted email from Eisner passing on what his source had told him. Packard called his Chairman, who called Roskill, who called Sir Justin Carey at the Foreign Office, who called the Commissioner of the Metropolitan Police, who called the Chief Constable. Didn't somebody once say, the Chief thought, that a lie can be half way round the world before the truth has got its boots on?

The Chief took the call, on his personal mobile, at 17.49 hrs. The *G & T* put the story up on its website at 17.58 hrs.

It was short, but its prominence on the website suggested that it would be a splash on the front page of the print edition next day. So it proved. Sime had worked hard to give credibility to a story that had been strongly denied. He had picked up on the MSP's question to the First Minister and had got Strathclyde Police to confirm that two officers from the team investigating the hospital and oil rig murders were now located at Govan, the base of the Scottish Counter-Terrorism Squad and the major crimes unit. The story didn't say that Hamilton and Gajani were there to pursue a terrorism link, but the implication was clear enough for other reporters to pick it up. The script for Vanessa Fiske's next press briefing was being written.

*

As soon as he had reassured the Commissioner that there was no known link between the Jamieson and Keller murders and either the explosion at Last or the cyber attack at Mercury, the Chief asked his secretary (Fleming had left for the day) to summon DCS Esslemont and DCI Fiske to his office. When they arrived, he offered them a drink – accepted by Esslemont, declined by Vanessa – and sat down with them at the occasional table that he used for semi-formal meetings.

'I had a call from the Commissioner of the Met to tell me that he had a report from the Foreign Office to the effect that wc were linking the Jamieson and Keller murders to the explosion at Last and that we were talking to counter-terrorism. I told him it was rubbish and he seemed to accept that it was.'

'When did you receive the call, sir?' Vanessa asked.

The Chief picked up his mobile. '17.49. Why?'

'Because the story didn't go up on the *G & T* website until 17.58. Which means that the story we planted wasn't given to Sime exclusively. I doubt he has access to the Permanent Secretary at the Foreign Office.'

'I suppose this means we have to confront Fleming.' This was Esslemont. 'And I need your authority, sir, to suspend him from duty pending further enquiries.' The Chief nodded. 'I think we should let him report for duty tomorrow morning and then ask him to come to see me and Vanessa. We won't know how to proceed until we see how he reacts.'

'You better run it past Chris Jenkinson as well. She has management responsibility for personnel matters, so she'll have to know that a suspension is on the cards. What a bloody mess! I can't begin to guess what made Richard do it.'

'We'll try to find out,' Esslemont said. 'But I rather think the "how" will be as important as the "why".'

*

Despite feeling queasy, Vanessa was in her office very early on Thursday morning.

Inspector Richard Fleming was usually at his desk in the anteroom to the Chief's office by 0730 and she needed to be available as soon as the DCS arrived just before eight o'clock. Neil drove her to police HQ before going to work.

When her phone rang at 0755, she expected to hear Esslemont's voice, but it was Fiona Marchmont, calling from home as she got her kids ready for school.

Between the shouted enquiries about the whereabouts of shoes, schoolbags and lunches, Fiona told Vanessa that Gavin Aikman in the Solicitor-General's office had called the previous evening.

'I know you need your sleep, so I decided to leave off phoning you until this morning. Nothing you could have done last night anyway. Gavin had a call from St. Clair to say that he had just been given the go-ahead by the Permanent Secretary to instruct the legal attaché in Washington to try to get the Hedelco emails released to you. As discussed, no action on Ebright or Burtonhall, though I think we can expect the latter to take an interest. You and I will need to get together to prepare the brief.'

'Thanks, Fiona. Did Gavin say when St. Clair phoned him?'

'I think it was about six o'clock last night. The decision seems to have taken St. Clair by surprise. He wasn't expecting it before the end of this week or the beginning of next. Why?'

'I'm constructing a timeline on a related matter.'

'Very cryptic!'

'Can't say more now, but you'll have a shrewd idea what's going on before you leave today.'

As Vanessa put the phone down, Esslemont came into her office.

'Fleming's on his way down. I think you should join us.'

*

The Association of Chief Police Officers (Scotland) terrorism lead was a Deputy Chief Constable from Lothian and Borders and he was reporting to the Justice Secretary and Paul MacIver at the First Minister's office every morning at 0830 hrs. Their first meeting had been on Wednesday, before the FM's statement to Parliament. There had been little of substance to report. By Thursday, the investigation had moved on, but not very far.

'We are now absolutely sure that the explosion at Last Cairngorm was not an accident.' DCC Grant Ingram spoke as he placed his uniform cap on the coffee table that separated him from his political masters. 'The device was unsophisticated but very effective and it had been placed to cause the maximum amount of structural damage. There are no immediate clues as to where it was assembled. Our experts, and the fire and rescue people, think that it was the kind of device that can be assembled from instructions available on the Internet.'

The Justice Secretary looked at MacIver and then at Ingram. 'Do we know how it got there, when it was planted?'

'No we don't, and because the complex isn't yet fully operational – won't be until next month – there is very little CCTV footage, and none of the building that was targeted.'

MacIver was taking notes, but he looked up at this, and asked if that meant there were some pictures.

'There are a couple of cameras at the entrance, but they're panning cameras, which means they don't provide a complete record of who comes and goes. Like the ones you see on Edinburgh buses.'

'I assume you are examining the footage to see if it yields anything useful.' The Justice Secretary was looking a little pained as he anticipated his meeting with the FM.

'Of course. But please don't get your hopes up. Nearly everybody who comes in is carrying some kind of backpack or bag, and we'd have to be very lucky to identify a suspect.'

'Has anyone claimed responsibility?'

'We've had the usual crank calls. We're looking into all of them, but there's nothing serious so far, so we have no idea what the motive was. We are checking with all UK jurisdictions and with Europol to see if there is any intelligence that might help, but there is really very little progress to report.'

'What about Mercury Fulfilment?' MacIver asked. 'Are you any further forward there?'

'Not much, I'm afraid. This was a very clever attack by people who knew exactly what they were doing and which systems they wanted to knock out. Mercury has a default system that kicks in if their main IT processes fail. They immobilised that as well.'

'Do we know where the attack originated?' The Justice Secretary asked. 'As I understand it, attacks like this can be mounted from anywhere in the world.'

'That's right. First indications, and don't ask me how the hi-tech people know this, are that it came from somewhere in the UK. Again, as with Last, there's no obvious motive, nothing "commercial", for example. That leaves us with other possibilities: cyber-vandalism, for instance, or a form of terrorism. The investigating officers from Strathclyde's computer crime branch are meeting the counter-terrorism people today.'

The Justice Secretary closed his file and stood up. He extended his hand to DCC Ingram and said he would see him tomorrow. 'Let's hope you have more to report then.'

*

'Sit down, Inspector Fleming.' Esslemont's tone was cool and formal. Fleming could have been in no doubt that this was a serious matter.

Esslemont and Fiske were sitting rather uncomfortably side by side behind Esslemont's desk. Fleming took the chair that had been positioned on the other side. He was in uniform and he had removed his cap and tucked it under his arm as he entered the room. He now placed it on the desk in front of him.

'Inspector Fleming, I have asked DCI Fiske to take notes. I would also like your consent to record our discussion.' Fleming nodded.

'We have reason to believe, Inspector, that you have been communicating confidential information, acquired in the course of your duties here, to people not authorised to have it.'

Vanessa caught a momentary look of concern cross Fleming's face, but he recovered quickly.

'I have no idea what you're talking about, sir. I take my duties, and my oath as a constable, very seriously, and there is no way that I would act inconsistently with that.'

'Pompous bastard!', Vanessa thought, but said nothing.

'DCI Fiske, please tell Inspector Fleming what you told me yesterday.'

Vanessa described the information that had been leaked and the fact that Fleming had known about all of it. She passed to him a copy of the analysis she had given Esslemont.

Fleming tried a laugh, but it was unconvincing. 'Proves nothing, Chief Inspector. I doubt if that's something you'd rely on in court.'

Vanessa decided not to respond to his reference to the caution given in England before an arrest. He was being snide about her training and experience in the Met.

'Nice try, Inspector, but there's more. Yesterday, the DCS asked the Chief to sanction an approach to the counter-terrorism unit to discuss a possible link to the murders of Harvey Jamieson and Peter Keller. Only four people knew about the approach - until the *G & T* broke the story - the Chief, the DCS, myself, and you.'

Fleming shifted uncomfortably. 'Journalists don't reveal their sources. They'd rather go to prison. It could just be speculation.'

'Come on, Richard!' Esslemont sounded irritated. 'Don't treat us as idiots. We know you did it. We now need to know how and why.'

Fleming stayed silent.

Vanessa leaned forward, and looked intently at Fleming. 'Can you explain how the Chief had a call last evening, before the *G & T* story went up on their website, from a very senior officer in another force, asking him to confirm or deny that we were involving counter-terrorism?'

Fleming's face became suddenly pallid. He reached for a glass of water, took a sip, and composed himself.

'I don't think I want to say any more until I take advice, sir.'

'All right, Inspector. I have to inform you that you are now suspended from duty, with immediate effect. DCI Fiske will go with you to your office, so that you can collect any personal items, and then conduct you out of the building. We'll need to speak to you again very soon.'

*

In Glasgow, DC Aisha Gajani and DS Sara Hamilton were on a crash course on good old-fashioned detective work. They had begun by contacting the collators in every major police station in the city to ask if anything was known about Mathieson or MacIlwraith. They were looking for the kind of intelligence that may turn out to be useful but that can't be recorded on official databases. They drew a complete blank. As far as they could tell, neither man had come up on anybody's radar. Nor did they get anything by floating the name of Thomas Nuttall. They would need to interrogate the semi-public databases and Aisha knew, from looking for Nuttall in the Aberdeen electoral register, that that could be a laborious and time consuming task.

Aisha and Sara were sitting drinking coffee at the desk they shared in Govan Police

Station. They had their working files open in front of them with the enhanced CCTV pictures of their suspects on top of the other notes they were accumulating before inputting them to the case log in Aberdeen. One of the local CID officers walked past them, stopped, and came back. He pointed to the picture of MacIIwraith.

'I think I know him. I was at Glasgow Uni with him. Didn't know him well, but he was a bit of a firebrand, always involved in demos. I don't think he even finished his degree. Too busy campaigning for Scottish independence, or Scotland's freedom, as he put it.'

Sara and Aisha looked at each other and then at their new colleague. Sara thought she should double-check his recollection before going any further.

'I don't suppose you remember his name, do you...? Sorry, I don't know your name.'

'Cameron Ritchie. Everybody calls me Cam. I'm a DC with the drugs squad. If you're quite young and you've got a degree, they put you on drugs. I wonder why.'

Sara and Aisha smiled and Sara looked hard at the picture of MacIlwraith to remind Cam of her question.

'Aye, I do. MacIlwraith, Andy MacIlwraith.'

'Would he be about your age, thirty or so?'

'Twenty-nine, but I've had a hard life.' He smiled. It was a nice smile, Aisha thought.

She was taking notes, but she looked up and asked, 'Do you have any idea where he lives? It's not a very common name, but if we can avoid the usual trawl through Google, electoral roll and so on, it wouldn't half speed things up.'

'I don't. But I think he came from somewhere outside Glasgow, maybe Ayrshire or Lanarkshire.'

'Thanks'. She paused and smiled. 'Cam. I'm Aisha and this is Sara.'

'You're welcome. Let me know how it goes. Maybe we could have a drink some time, Aisha.'

'That would be nice.'

Cam Ritchie walked away, Aisha blushed slightly, and Sara said, 'I think you just pulled, girl.'

*

Janet MacNee got in from work most days around half past five. On Thursday, she noticed, even as Emma and Cat were jumping all over her, that Shelley Mehring was pre-occupied, her usual enthusiasm and bounce almost totally absent. Janet put it down to some problem with her thesis and got on with preparing the girls' tea.

Colin got home just as Shelley finished reading the girls a story and she came into the living room where he and Janet were having a glass of wine before supper. Janet held the bottle up to ask Shelley if she wanted a glass. Shelley shook her head and said, 'No. Thanks. There's something I need to talk to you about.'

Colin and Janet looked at each other anxiously.

'You're not thinking of leaving us, Shelley, are you?' Janet said.

'No. Nothing like that. I'm really enjoying the job and the girls are lovely.'

'What then?'

Shelley looked very worried. 'You know that before I came to you, I was working as an intern for a man called Frank Mancuso at Last Cairngorm.'

Colin grinned. 'Yes, and he gave you the kind of reference that glows in the dark.'

Shelley nodded and smiled weakly. 'Well, he called me on Tuesday and offered me money to tell him anything I heard you talking about that might affect Last, especially the investigation into the explosion. He also mentioned the two murders. When I said no, he threatened me.'

Colin sat forward, and felt a restraining hand on his arm. 'How, Shelley? How did he threaten you?'

She was close to tears. 'He said that if I didn't do as he asked he would tell the university that I had falsified the Last data that I'm using in my dissertation, and make sure that my PhD registration was cancelled so that I wouldn't get my doctorate.'

'When did he say that?'

'He called me again today, while the girls were at school. I said I would think about it, but the more I did, the more I was convinced that I should talk to you about it.'

Shelley was sitting on the sofa opposite the MacNees. Janet got up and sat beside her, putting an arm round her shoulders. 'You did the right thing, Shelley. Thank you.'

'Yes, absolutely. Thank you, Shelley. You know I'm going to have to follow this up, though? I'll make sure this doesn't come back on you. If Mancuso approaches the University, which he won't, I'll speak to them on your behalf. Your job's safe, and so is your degree.'

'There's something else. When you offered me the job, I said that I would work for Mr Mancuso until the end of the week, so as not to leave him in the lurch. I was really surprised when he said it would be best if I started here right away. I think I know why now.'

'If he contacts you again, let me know right away,' Colin said. 'Get me on my mobile, and if I don't answer, send a text.'

*

DCI Fiske spent the second half of Thursday afternoon in Fiona Marchmont's office working on the brief to the Foreign Office for onward transmission to the legal attaché in Washington.

'We need to make it very clear,' she told Fiona, 'that the Hedelco and Ebright lines of enquiry are not the only ones we are following. Details of our request will be passed to Scottish ministers and, given the First Minister's concern that we should limit ourselves to the "purely criminal" aspects of the murder cases, we need to show that other lines are being pursued just as vigorously.'

Fiona agreed. 'Do you think it would be wise to say that, in the event that your enquiries lead to a resolution of the murder cases, you will immediately let the FO know, so that the US initiative can be put on hold?'

'Don't see why not. Shows willing and it wouldn't prevent us from resuming pursuit of the emails if we need to.'

'I'll email a draft to you before I leave today. If you're happy with it, I'll get it to St Clair, with a copy to Gavin Aikman, tomorrow morning.   Now, what was that about constructing a timeline? Is it something to do with Richard Fleming being suspended.'

'Got it in one! We're almost certain that Fleming has been leaking information. Remember that story that appeared in the *G & T* about our visit to the Foreign Office. There were other leaks and Esslemont and I did a bit of what might be called "entrapment" and we think we've got him. He's taking legal advice'.

'But why? Fleming is an arrogant little shit, but he was clearly on the fast track to a command rank. Why would he jeopardise that?'

'That's what we need to know. That, and how he was passing on the information. We know it was getting to places other than the *G & T*.'

'Was this connected to Carey's sudden decision to assist?'

'Very probably, but I never look a gift horse in the mouth.'

*

Colin MacNee phoned Vanessa Fiske just as she and Neil were settling down for a relaxing night in. They had ordered a Thai take-away and Neil had borrowed a box set of a Danish crime serial for Vanessa to pick holes in.

'I'm really sorry to disturb your evening, boss, especially after the week you've had, but I need to see you. Can I come round for half an hour?'

'What's this about, Colin?'

'I'd rather tell you face to face, and I'd like to bring Shelley Mehring, our *au pair* with me.'

'Didn't she work at Last before you took her on?'

'Yes, she did.'

*

Paul MacIver had advised the First Minister that there was no point in her making another statement in Parliament that day. This meant that the first opportunity would be the following Tuesday. By then, he hoped, things would have moved on to the point where it might be possible to make some real political capital out of the various investigations underway in Aberdeen and beyond.

For now, a press statement setting out how the Justice Secretary was keeping abreast of the enquiries would be enough. MacIver was just a little disappointed that the Foreign Office – or "the Westminster Government", as he preferred to say – had not been more obstructive. He had a slight feeling that things were not entirely under control. Further diversionary tactics might be necessary over the weekend.

*

As soon as she heard what Shelley Mehring had to say, Vanessa decided that the 0830 hrs team meeting would need to be postponed until the early afternoon. She and Esslemont had arranged their next meeting with Richard Fleming for eleven o'clock on Friday morning and in the normal course of events that would have followed the team meeting.

But it was urgent that she and Colin speak to Mancuso, because she thought it very unlikely that there was no connection between Mancuso's attempt to get an inside track on the investigations and Fleming's activities. Shelley had told them that Mancuso usually got to his office at about 0830 hrs. They would be waiting for him when he arrived.

Vanessa was unaware of another benefit of having the team meeting in the afternoon: it gave Sara Hamilton and Aisha Gajani a few more hours to follow up on the lead they had on MacIlwraith. They would be joining the meeting by video link. Sara expected to be on a train back to Aberdeen for the weekend by five o'clock. Aisha had decided to stay in Glasgow, ostensibly to see her family, but mainly so that she could meet Cam Ritchie in a bar in the Merchant City.

CHAPTER ELEVEN

The Last Cairngorm complex, twenty miles
west of Aberdeen, was still a crime scene.
Four days after the explosion, officers and
specialist scene of crime investigators were
searching the ruins of the indoor ski slope.
Their search had been delayed until
Wednesday morning as they waited for the
Fire and Rescue Service to declare the site
secure and the collapsed building safe to
enter. DI Colin MacNee drove DCI Vanessa
Fiske up to the main gate just before eight
o'clock on Friday morning.   It was a
horrible morning, with driving rain, and the
spectacular beauty of the Cairngorms
invisible through the mist. Vanessa was
feeling rotten.   She had had no breakfast,
convinced that she wouldn't have been able
to keep it down, especially as Colin drove the
twists and turns of the Deeside road.   She
sipped from a bottle of fizzy water. She
hadn't mentioned to Colin that she had a sick
bag stuffed into her handbag.

One side of the double gate was open, with
entry barred by a line of three traffic cones.
As Colin drew up, a security guard came out
of a small granite gatehouse.   Before the

guard could say anything, Colin brought his window down and held up his warrant card.

'Detective Inspector Colin MacNee, North East Constabulary. This is Detective Chief Inspector Vanessa Fiske. We're here to see Mr Mancuso.'

'He's no' here yet.' The guard had a broad Aberdeenshire accent that reminded Colin of his father.

'We'll wait. Where's his office?'

The guard pointed to a one storey building about twenty-five metres into the site. 'That's the security control block. The boss has an office in there. He's generally here before quarter past.'

Colin thanked him and he removed the cones to let the car through. He parked at the far end of the building, having noticed, as they passed, a parking space "Reserved for F Mancuso". They would be able to see him as he drove in.

'Mr Mancuso, can we have a word?' Vanessa spoke as she and her colleague approached Mancuso, both holding up their warrant cards. 'DCI Fiske, and this DI MacNee. Is there somewhere we can speak privately?'

Mancuso looked apprehensive but tried to bluster. 'I'm pretty damn busy here, for reasons you know about, so I hope this won't take long.'

Colin MacNee was unimpressed. 'It'll take as long as it takes, sir. Now where can we talk?'

They followed Mancuso into the building and through to his office, which was on a corner, near where Colin had parked, with a view of the whole complex.

Mancuso poured himself a coffee and offered cups to the detectives. Colin said, 'Black, please, no sugar', and Vanessa said she would stick to water.

'So, what's this about?'

'It's about you putting pressure on Shelley Mehring to tell you what she hears in the course of her work for my colleague and his wife...'

'I've no idea what...'

'For Christ's sake.' Colin was angry, but he was trying to keep it in check. 'Spare us the injured innocence. There's a wide choice of things we can charge you with, and we may still choose one, but what we're really interested in is why you wanted Shelley to spy on me.'

'I don't know what you're talking about.'

'Look', Vanessa took a sip of her water and belched discreetly, 'I've got two murders to solve, and I don't have time for you to fuck me about. So just tell me what you hoped to learn, and why.'

Mancuso mumbled inaudibly.

'Didn't catch that.'

'It wasn't for me.'

*

DC Aisha Gajani was already at the desk she was sharing with DS Sara Hamilton, sipping from a large beaker of coffee, and looking very pleased with herself.

'I've found something very interesting about MacIlwraith and I've done it without having to access any of these.' She was looking at Sara's list of the databases they might have to interrogate. 'We may still need them to find him and, because of what I've got, it may be even more urgent that we do. Come and have a look at this.'

Sara stood behind Aisha and looked at her computer screen. It showed a page of a tabloid-sized newspaper with a large picture of what seemed to be a demonstration. Two young men in the foreground held placards. A group of six or eight supporters stood behind them, some carrying what looked like leaflets. The placards read, "SFP says: SET SCOTLAND FREE."

'Read the caption.'

Sara leaned forward.

> *Scottish Freedom Club chair and secretary, Simon Mathieson and Andy MacIlwraith, lead a demo outside the Union against Scottish Secretary Fraser's visit to Tory club.*

'Christ, Aisha, good work! Where did you get it? And how?'

'It's from the university student newspaper about ten years ago. It's all archived online and it's got a pretty good search function. I started to think about what Cam said. If he's twenty-nine he must have graduated seven or eight years ago, so I went to the archive and searched for MacIlwraith, starting in 2000. He comes up a lot in reports of demos and debates, but that's the only picture. And it establishes a connection between MacIlwraith and Mathieson.'

Sara Hamilton whistled in appreciation. 'And if Mathieson is Nuttall, we've also got a link between the two murder suspects. Does the face match our enhanced picture?'

'Possibly. There's ten years between them, but there are clear similarities: shape of face, prominent nose, but he had a full beard in 2002. We'll need to get the photographic analysts to look at them, but I think we should work on the assumption that we're looking at Nuttall.'

'You're probably right. I'll need to speak to the boss before the team meeting. And, as you said, we'll need to find MacIlwraith and Mathieson and see if they're still in touch. This may be a breakthrough. Or it may be nothing.'

*

'It's got to be Eisner,' Colin MacNee said as he and Vanessa Fiske drove away from Last Cairngorm and back to Aberdeen. 'They must know each other, and the timeline points that way.'

'What timeline?'

'This can't be about the explosion, or not just about the explosion. Mancuso started setting Shelley up last week. It was information about the murder investigations that he was after.'

Vanessa closed her eyes and leaned back on the headrest. 'We need to talk to Eisner again for another reason, too. You've probably heard that Richard Fleming's been suspended. Esslemont and I are pretty sure he's been leaking information and I think some of it has been getting to Eisner. We planted a bogus detail about the investigation that only Fleming knew about, other than me, the DCS and the Chief. It got back to the Chief in very short order from the Met Commissioner. It was pretty obvious when I went to the Foreign Office that they had been got at. I think they were lobbied by

Burtonhall and I think Burtonhall went to them again to verify our phoney fact, and then the FO talked to the Met.'

'So when do we go to see Eisner again?'

'I've got to interview Fleming again as soon as I get back, so it'll have to be after the team meeting.'

Vanessa's phone rang. It was Sara Hamilton.

'Boss, I think Aisha's found something really important.'

Vanessa listened as Sara outlined what Aisha had found.

'Thanks. This may be the nearest thing we've had to a real lead. Email the picture to me so that I can see it on my phone and get it to photographic analysis and see what they say about the possibility that it's Nuttall. Go through Dongle Donaldson. I can't remember the name of the DS who ran the video recognition software that identified MacIlwraith, but Dongle will. We'll talk about this in detail at two. Is your video link set up?'

'Not half! You should see the kit they've got here. We could do a video link to Mars.'

*

DCI Fiske collected Inspector Richard Fleming and his lawyer from main reception at eleven o'clock and took them to an interview room where DCS Esslemont was waiting for them.

'Thank you for coming in, Inspector Fleming. You are here voluntarily to help us with our enquiries into the unauthorised release of confidential information. Once again we would like your consent to record our conversation.'
The lawyer touched Fleming's arm. 'I'm David Wozniak, Richard's lawyer, and I don't think I'm prepared to let him agree to that until you charge him with something. And I'm not sure you should have taped the previous interview. I'll need a copy of that tape.'

'Certainly. And you should know that we want to question your client under caution. He is suspected of misconduct in public office. Other charges may follow. Now, I assume you will want to talk privately. We'll leave you to it. Dial 555 when you're ready to continue.'

Ten minutes later, Esslemont and Fiske were back in the interview room. Wozniak said that he had advised his client to answer questions that did not incriminate him and that he now accepted that the interview would be recorded.

Esslemont nodded to Vanessa Fiske.

'We're pretty sure,' she said, 'that you were the source of the confidential information that appeared in the press and some also seems to have got to other unauthorised people. However, my main concern is that these leaks have hindered my enquiries into two murders. I need to know who you spoke to other than the ..'

Fleming interrupted. 'I did not speak to any reporter.'

Vanessa responded sharply. 'So who did you speak to?'

'No comment.'

'Look your career is over and although I'm curious about why you risked so much, my immediate interest is in how people of interest to my investigations got sensitive information if you didn't speak to them. Who was the intermediary?'

'No comment.'

Esslemont stirred. 'This is pointless. I'm releasing you on condition that you return for further questioning when I request you to do so. Meanwhile we will pursue other enquiries and get started on a report to the Procurator Fiscal. Good morning, gentlemen. DCI Fiske will see you out.'

*

'What other enquiries did you have in mind, sir?' Vanessa was standing in the door to Esslemont's office.

'We need to have a good look at Fleming's life: who are his friends, what does he do in his spare time, does anyone have a hold over him? And we need to do it quickly and discreetly. Who have you got?'

'I really can't spare anybody, sir, but I can see your point. As long as it was only for a day, a couple of days at most, I could put Williamson on it.'

'Do it. And brief him very carefully.'

*

Vanessa Fiske's plans for the team meeting had been made almost irrelevant by her conversation with Sara Hamilton. All the other strands of the investigations would still have to be covered, but the priority was to discuss and assess the new information about Mathieson, Nuttall and MacIlwraith. Williamson, Todd, Dongle Donaldson, Andy Hanna on the last day of his secondment, and an administrative assistant to take notes, were on three sides of the table in Conference Room 5. Sara Hamilton and Aisha Gajani, sitting uncomfortably close together in Govan Police Station's video suite, were on the flat-screen television on the wall above the fourth side of the table. Colin MacNee sat beside Vanessa, on her right.

Vanessa had just brought up on the computer screen beside her an enlarged version of the photograph from the student paper when Esslemont came in and sat at the end of the table, facing the television screen.

'Aisha found this picture in the online archive of the Glasgow University student newspaper. It shows Andrew MacIlwraith, our prime suspect in Peter Keller's murder. It also shows someone called Simon Mathieson, and that was the name given by the person who requested the late Thomas Nuttall's birth certificate from the General Register Office. We believe that Mathieson and Nuttall are one and the same, and if they are, we are also looking at the prime suspect in the murder of Harvey Jamieson.'

'The picture on the screen is exactly as Aisha found it. The guys In the video analysis section are doing what they can to enhance it. That may make it possible to compare the image of Mathieson with the pictures of Nuttall from his Ebright ID and the CCTV images. No guarantees, boss, but we may be able to tell, with an exact percentage accuracy, if it's the same person in both images.'

'Thanks, Dongle. And please note that I've just said your name without laughing. When will we have something from video analysis?'

'This afternoon, I think. Anil Jasthi said he would email his results as soon as he has them. Might even come while we're still here.'

'Aisha, first of all, good work. This is the first thing we've seen that looks like a breakthrough.' Everyone in the room rapped the table in appreciation. Aisha smiled, and blushed a little. 'So where do these two guys live? You wouldn't want to leave the job half done.'

Fiske's tone was light but the question was serious. Sara Hamilton answered. 'One of the DCs here knew MacIlwraith at uni and thinks he lived outside the city, Lanarkshire or Ayrshire. We're working through the appropriate databases for these areas and, of course, for Glasgow. We've got a number of hits on the names and we now need to check ages. We're assuming that both our suspects are in their early thirties, so we should have it narrowed down by later today.'

'OK. Once we know how many possibles we've got we'll have to decide how to identify our men. I'd like to avoid bringing in people solely on the basis of name and age, so we may be into surveillance and, if we are, we'll need to rely on Strathclyde for support.'

DI Colin MacNee turned to Andy Hanna. 'Anything on the financial side to report before you leave us?'

'Not much. I managed to get hold of the prospectuses Burtonhall sent out to possible investors. They were a bit more bullish about the likely performance of Hedelco and Ebright than the current numbers support, but that's common enough and nothing to kill for. You could just about find a motive in an attempt to prevent adverse operational reports coming to light, but it would be a stretch.'

'We'll only get that if there's really negative stuff in the emails Keller sent back before he was killed.' Colin looked at Fiske in a way that expected a response.

'The Foreign Office has agreed to help us to get them without going to court. I'm just about to sign off the brief that Fiona Marchmont and I have prepared. I had hoped to get it off yesterday, but something came up. It'll go today, so we can't really expect an answer from Hedelco until the middle of next week.'

'They'll resist,' Andy Hanna said. 'It'll depend on whether the Yanks have any leverage and if they're prepared to use it to help us.'

'Thanks for all your help, Andy. We'll call you if we think you can assist further.'

'There's one more thing. Just for fun, I had a rake around the public domain information on Last and Mercury...'

Esslemont stirred. He had said nothing so far, but that wasn't unusual when he sat in on a team meeting. 'A bit outside your brief, Inspector.'

Hanna had the unfazed look of a man who'd soon be on his way. 'Yeah, probably. I'm sorry. I was pushing the envelope a bit, but you may still want to hear what I found.'

Esslemont looked at Vanessa, who nodded.

'As far as I can tell, Burtonhall doesn't have a financial interest in either of them, but there's some cross-membership on the boards. James Roskill's a non-exec on Mercury's board, and Richard Seaton chairs Last's Remuneration Committee. Nothing sinister in that, but interesting. As far as financial performance is concerned, Last is on a knife edge - the up-market leisure sector isn't doing well in the recession. Mercury, like many Internet-based businesses, is making money hand over fist. Their employment practices, however, are, to use their preferred euphemism, "robust". Their car park in Cumbernauld is known as "Picket Plaza". Up to you to decide if any of that is useful.'

'Interesting, but not immediately relevant,' Vanessa said. 'I'll think about it. Now, if there's nothing else, Colin and I need to go and talk to Eisner again.'

*

In Edinburgh, Paul MacIver was preparing for the weekend. The First Minister had spent most of the day in Fife, trying to ensure that her government took the credit for the fact that the sun had come up that morning and for the likelihood that it would set in the evening. MacIver had been at her side throughout, ensuring that the press picked up the best soundbites, keeping her increasingly regal progress to time, identifying for the security team known troublemakers so that they could be kept well away from microphones and cameras.

In the middle of the afternoon, as DCI Fiske was about to close the team meeting, the FM left her last engagement - the opening of an new hi-tech component plant that had received much public subsidy and provided very few jobs - and set off for her constituency in the North East. MacIver asked the political editor of the *Glasgow Banner* to drop him off at Leuchars so that he could catch a train to Edinburgh. He intended to be a little indiscreet so that a "helpful" exclusive would appear in the Sunday edition of the paper.

*

As the murder investigation team was gathering their papers together for the end of the meeting, Dongle Donaldson looked at his phone. 'Hold on, boss. I've just got the enhanced image of MacIlwraith and Mathieson. Anil's emailed it to you. You might want to call it up.'

Vanessa logged on, went to her email and opened the attachment. Anil Jasthi had done a good job. The faces of the two principals were much sharper and the supporting cast were now distinguishable from each other. The team looked closely at the new image. The likeness between the MacIlwraith in the student paper and the MacIlwraith identified from the hospital CCTV was compelling, that between Mathieson and Nuttall less so.

'Anil is running the facial comparison software over both pairs of images. Later this afternoon he'll be able to tell us how certain he is that the two MacIlwraiths are the same person and that Mathieson is also Nuttall. His report should be waiting for you when you get back from talking to Eisner.'

*

'Before you and Colin go to see Eisner, I need a word.'

Esslemont had intercepted Vanessa as she left the conference room and was now walking towards his office. Vanessa followed. The DCS asked her to close the door. He logged on to his computer and brought up the enhanced image of MacIlwraith and Mathieson at the Scottish Freedom Party demonstration outside the university union. He picked up a pen and pointed to a young man in the middle of the line of students standing behind the two suspects.

'I think that's Paul MacIver.'

Vanessa looked closely at the screen. She had never met MacIver and she couldn't recall having seen a picture of him.

'The FM's special adviser?' Her tone was incredulous. 'Are you sure, sir?'

'Pretty sure. I've met him occasionally when I've had meetings with the First Minister in connection with constituency matters. He's ten years older now, and he's put on a fair amount of weight, but I think I'd be prepared to swear in court that that's MacIver.'

'So we have evidence that the FM's closest aide was a "known associate" ' - the quotation marks were audible - 'ten years ago of the prime suspects in two murders. What do you suggest we do?'

'Nothing yet. I just want you to be aware. If you find that the connection is anything other than historic and you think it may be relevant to your enquiries, we'll have to decide how to proceed. Meanwhile, keep me very closely informed.'

*

One of Vanessa Fiske's administrative support team had arranged for her and Colin MacNee to see Jack Eisner at the Ebright building at four o'clock. Tammy Wootten was less than warm in her welcome, but she said that as she had some shopping to do, they could use her office.

'I need to speak to you about your interest in my investigation.'

Eisner looked at Fiske and said nothing. As the press often say of murderers about to be sentenced, he showed no emotion.

Vanessa went on. 'I believe that you have received confidential information and I need you to tell me how you got it.'

'I don't know what you're talking about.' Eisner poured himself a glass of water from the jug on Wootten's desk.

'Have you been in touch with Frank Mancuso at Last Cairngorm?'

Eisner looked uncomfortable.

'I've known Frank for a long time. Naturally, when I came to Aberdeen, I got in touch. We had a drink.'

'Nothing more?' Colin MacNee's tone had become much more aggressive. 'So why did he try to set up Shelley Mehring, who works for me and my wife as an *au pair*, to pass on information that she might pick up at our house? It can't have been about the explosion at Last Cairngorm. Why did you want an inside track on our murder investigation?'

Eisner shook his head, but said nothing.

'We also know that Mancuso attempted to blackmail Shelley.'

'I'm sorry, inspector, but I can't help you.'

'Can't or won't?

Eisner smiled. 'Does it matter? There's no more I can say.'

'Mr Eisner, you work for an organisation which finds itself a lot closer to two murders than it would like. You came here to try to prevent what you call "reputational damage" to Burtonhall Inc. I don't think a blackmail charge that involved you would help you in your mission.'

Eisner looked more worried. Vanessa pressed her slight advantage.

'I believe that on Wednesday you passed a piece of sensitive information to Cy Packard, your CEO. Very few people in North East Constabulary knew about it. I need to know how you got hold of it.'

'If I did, and I'm not saying I did, the communication would be commercially confidential, just like the emails you're trying to get the Federal government to force Hedelco to release.'

Colin looked at Vanessa and shook his head almost imperceptibly. They both knew that they couldn't ask him directly about Richard Fleming. But they also knew that they had indirect confirmation - nothing admissible as evidence but enough to inform their enquiries - that Eisner had got information and had passed it on to Packard. They already knew, pretty well, what Packard had done with it. But they still had no clear motive, either criminal or commercial, for the murders at GRH and on Vermont One.

*

Vanessa was about to leave for the weekend when DS Anil Jasthi phoned to say that he was more than 95 per cent certain that the two MacIlwraith images were of the same person. The other comparison yielded results that were less conclusive, but Anil still put the likelihood that Mathieson and Nuttall were one and the same at over 75 per cent. She would consult the DCS, but Vanessa thought that was enough to arrest them, if they could be found and positively identified.

Sara Hamilton sent an email just before rushing for her train to Aberdeen. She and Aisha had found addresses for three Andrew MacIlwraiths and two Simon Mathiesons. They had found no Thomas Nuttalls. Strathclyde surveillance officers would provide new pictures of all five men by the time she got back to Glasgow on Monday. Aisha had told her mother she would visit on Saturday afternoon and then gone to her hotel to get ready for her date with Cam Ritchie.

CHAPTER TWELVE

Paul MacIver was pleased with the result of his off-the-record chat with the political editor of the *Glasgow Banner*. The headline on the front page of the Sunday edition was the first thing that caught his eye as he collected the papers from the newsagent on Sunday morning. It had a "Banner *EXCLUSIVE*" strap line and it read: *"Cops and pols at odds on attacks on US firms"*.

With no sign of any arrests following the murders two weeks ago at Grampian Royal Hospital and on the Vermont One oil rig, highly placed sources have told the Banner *that very senior political figures at Holyrood are becoming frustrated at the refusal of the police to consider the possibility that Scotland may be the target of a concerted campaign to undermine and deter US investment. Both murders happened at locations owned or managed by subsidiaries of the American conglomerate Burtonhall Inc.*

Within days of the killings, two other American-owned businesses in

Scotland, Last Cairngorm and Mercury Fulfilment, were hit. Last's leisure complex near Aberdeen was bombed and, on the same evening, Mercury's warehouse at Cumbernauld was the target of a devastating cyber attack that knocked out all its IT systems. Last was due to open fully within weeks, but that is now unlikely. Mercury's claim that it would be back online "within days" has proved to be wildly optimistic.

Sources say that the police investigations are concentrating "too exclusively" on the purely criminal aspects of all the investigations. They say that "at this very sensitive time", which is code for "in the run-up to the Independence referendum", greater priority should be given to the possibility that opponents of independence may be attempting to destabilise the Scottish economy.

There is also some frustration that the UK authorities have been less than fully engaged with the investigations. Initially, the Foreign Office was reluctant to intervene with the Americans to help North East

Constabulary detectives get access to emails thought to be vital to their enquiries. Assistance was given only after detectives agreed to restrict their request to the company, Hedelco, that runs the hospital where Peter Keller was murdered.

There has already been one piece of collateral damage. Lack of progress on the murders has made it almost certain that the NEC Chief Constable is no longer considered a serious candidate for the top job in the new all-Scotland police service.

It may be an exclusive today, MacIver thought, but the other papers will follow it up tomorrow. By Tuesday, when the FM was due to report again to Parliament, the political temperature should rising nicely. And a certain amount of turmoil inside NEC might also keep the pot boiling.

*

On Friday afternoon, Sara Hamilton had given the addresses of three men called Andrew MacIlwraith and two called Simon Mathieson to the area commander at Govan Police Station and requested, on behalf of her

SIO, DCI Vanessa Fiske, that photographic surveillance be mounted at each address. The object was to eliminate those individuals whose descriptions and photographs did not match those of the suspects in the GRH and Vermont One murders.

The MacIlwraiths located by the data searches undertaken by Hamilton and Gajani had addresses in the Springburn area of North East Glasgow, in Saltcoats on the North Ayrshire coast, and in Carluke, in South Lanarkshire. The Mathiesons were in the West End of Glasgow, near the University, and in Uddingston, a suburban town just South East of the city. Two officers in plain clothes and trained in long distance camera surveillance were sent to each address on Saturday morning, with instructions to identify and describe the men living there. On the basis of the descriptions, it proved possible, acting on information on the suspects provided by the murder investigation team to the Strathclyde officers, to eliminate one MacIlwraith and one Mathieson. The surveillance photographers at the Springburn and Uddingston addresses were stood down.

The photographs of the two remaining MacIlwraiths and of Mathieson were waiting for DS Anil Jasthi when he got to his office in Aberdeen at eight o'clock on Monday morning. By 0930 he had eliminated the MacIlwraith in Carluke as a possible match to the hospital murder suspect. He phoned Vanessa Fiske.

'Morning, boss. I've got a 95 per cent match on the Saltcoats MacIlwraith and 90 per cent on Mathieson/Nuttall. That's about as good as we ever get with this software. Up to you to decide if it's enough for arrests.'

'Thanks, Anil. I'll talk to the DCS, but I think Colin and I are looking at a trip to Glasgow and Ayrshire.'

*

Vanessa Fiske was relaxing with a good book on Sunday afternoon. She hadn't read the papers, so she hadn't seen the *Banner*'s exclusive when DC Duncan Williamson texted her to say that he would like to come round to see her. Vanessa's partner, Neil Derrick, groaned when she told him that Williamson was coming round to report on his enquiries into Richard Fleming.

'You had a bloody hard week last week, and I'd be surprised if next week is any easier.

And we have to go to GRH for your scan on Tuesday. Couldn't you at least take a weekend off?'

She put her arms round his neck and kissed him. 'I'm sorry, darling, I really am. But the tempo of these cases has suddenly been cranked up a notch or two, and I'll probably have to go to Glasgow this week, perhaps tomorrow, with an overnight and back on Tuesday. Don't worry, I'll be back in time for the scan. Wouldn't miss it! But the sooner I can get these murders out of the way, the sooner we can start some serious planning.'

'When's Duncan coming round?'

'He's on his way. Be here in about twenty minutes.'

Neil let Duncan in and then went to his study, leaving the two detectives alone in the living room.

'So, Duncan, what have you got on our Inspector Fleming?'

'It wasn't easy, boss. Fleming lives in Stonehaven. It's a small enough town for things to get around pretty quickly, so I had to be careful not to raise too much interest. I started with the local sergeant. He told me that Fleming kept a fairly low profile. He lives on his own in a flat overlooking the sea and, so far as the sergeant knew, he hasn't been in a relationship while he's lived there, which is a couple of years.'

Vanessa interrupted him. ' "In a relationship" is an odd way to put it.. I would have expected you to say "had a girlfriend" or even – what's that term I've heard people use?- a "bidey-in".'

'Well, that's the point. No-one's very sure about Fleming's sexuality. The sergeant said that the talk around the station was that he might be gay, but that he wasn't doing anything about it because he's very ambitious, and it might slow his progress.'

'Well, he won't have to worry about that any more! If he's gay, he'll be able to come out with impunity. But perhaps not immediately, if he ends up in prison. Go on.'

'He hasn't taken much part in local life, except the occasional pub quiz. I went to the *Dunottar Castle* and had a word with the licensee who, like many publicans, likes to keep on the right side of the police. I emphasised the need for confidentiality and asked him what he knew about Fleming. Again, the answer was not a lot, but there is one thing that may be significant. Apparently, his regular team captain in the quizzes was a guy called Martin Gilbertson who lives just outside Stonehaven in a village called Fetteresso. Gilbertson works in public relations at Mid-Aberdeenshire Council.'

Vanessa sat forward. 'Does he, indeed? So he would have contacts in the local press.'

'Yeah. But there's something else. According to my source, he sometimes had on his team somebody from Last Cairngorm, an American with something to do with security.'

'Good work!'

'The American hasn't been seen in the pub for some time, and nor has Fleming. But Gilbertson still drinks there most nights. Nothing heavy, just a pint or two after work. The licensee considers him a regular.'

'I need to speak to Gilbertson, but I don't know when. There's a lot going on!'

'Before I go,' Williamson said, 'Have you seen the front page of today's *Banner?* If you haven't, you should. There may be some shit flying in the office tomorrow.'

*

After she had read the *Banner* front page online, Vanessa knew she would have to make some phone calls. Duncan Williamson's report on Fleming had made it urgent that she speak to Esslemont, as did the likelihood that she would have to go to Glasgow to arrest her two prime suspects. That would need the co-operation of Strathclyde Police, both in supporting the early morning visits to the suspects' homes and in applying for warrants to search them. She would need to see Colin MacNee to tell him that MacIlwraith, the suspect in the murder of Keller at GRH, had been located in either the Glasgow area or in North Ayrshire and that he would be heading the team that arrested him while she picked up Mathieson/Nuttall.

She knew that she should also be in the office early enough to call DCC Ingram at Lothian and Borders to brief him in advance of his daily meeting with the Justice Secretary. She was in some difficulty, however, in knowing how much to tell him. If she gave him all the details, and if he then had to brief the First Minister, and if the connection between the suspects and Paul MacIver wasn't merely historic, her investigation might be compromised. Her instinct was to keep her report to Ingram very general, but she would have to discuss it with Esslemont. She might be able to delay her report until later in the day, and the fact that Parliament did not sit on Monday might also buy her some time.

She knew, also, that the *Banner* report would, as Duncan had predicted, cause the shit to hit the fan. The Chief would be incandescent and would demand a report in person from Esslemont, who would want her support, and possibly Colin MacNee's as well.

And then there were Fleming and Gilbertson. She would have to talk to Gilbertson before she and the DCS interviewed Fleming again, and it was possible that she might have to have another go at both Eisner and Mancuso.

Vanessa had just finished making notes covering all that needed to be done next day when Neil came in from his study. She looked at him and smiled weakly as she reached for the phone.

CHAPTER THIRTEEN

As she drove into work on Monday morning just after seven o'clock, DCI Vanessa Fiske needed to take her mind off the huge amount she had to do before going to GRH for her scan at four o'clock the next day. She thought about the cliché, much employed by the press, of the "dawn raid". It was a certainly a cliché, but the process was effective, maximising the surprise (and so ensuring that the press would report after the event rather than in real time, except when the police saw some advantage to having the whole thing filmed), and minimising the possibility that the target would be alerted to the fact that his house had been surrounded by cars he didn't recognise, full of people, some in uniform, some not, he didn't know.

She was a little unsettled by the fact that, although she would be in charge of the arrests, she was not in control of the logistics. She was relying on Strathclyde CID to organise the vehicles and the officers needed to make simultaneous arrests, at 0530 hrs on Tuesday morning, in the West End of Glasgow and in Saltcoats or Carluke. She needed to be able to decide when Mathieson/Nuttall, and whichever

MacIlwraith she decided to bring in, would learn that the other had been detained. Vanessa remembered the Prisoner's Dilemma scenario, from a course at Bramshill during her time in the Met, but she had never been able to use it in a real investigation. As a way of putting on pressure during questioning, it might be very useful, but only if she could choose at what point to offer each the opportunity to incriminate the other.

As she parked, Vanessa began to think that she might already be over-complicating the process of arrest and interrogation, and she knew that this was because she had very little to go on. These men would be arrested, and their homes and workplaces searched, on the basis of enhanced CCTV images and a relationship that they had had when they were students nearly ten years ago. It was possible, though unlikely, that they had had no contact with each other since then. However, it was vital that their arrests came as a complete surprise and that the search warrants were executed immediately. Unfortunately, nothing was known, or hadn't been when Vanessa left the office on Friday, about where either man worked. DC Aisha Gajani had stayed in Glasgow over the weekend, and she had agreed to do some digging, possibly informally assisted by Cam Ritchie, on Sunday.

But the arrests would not take place for nearly twenty-four hours. There was an awful lot to do before then.

*

Detective Chief Superintendent Esslemont's car was already in the underground car park when Vanessa arrived, and as she climbed the stairs to the CID floor, she saw DI Colin MacNee drive in. The place reserved for the Chief was unoccupied but, Vanessa thought, not for long. She had to talk to the DCS before they both got the inevitable summons to the Chief's presence.

As she walked towards her office, Esslemont came out of the lift carrying a coffee in a paper cup, and a bacon roll. He looked slightly sheepish, not something she had seen before.

'Left very early. The wife wasn't up to make my breakfast.' Vanessa's expression made him look even more sheepish. He knew his younger colleagues called him 'old school'. Maybe they were right. What he didn't know was that Vanessa's expression had as much to do with the taste of morning sickness as with distaste for his benighted sexism. 'We need to talk.'

'Oh, yes, sir. We do.'

*

'These guys don't seem to have any hinterland.' DS Sara Hamilton had just got back to Glasgow and Aisha Gajani was telling her what she had discovered about their suspects.

'Hinterland? Hinterland? What are you on about?'

'Sorry, Sarge. I had this sociology lecturer at uni who was always on about how "hinterland", the things in the background of people's lives, helps to explain their behaviour. Hadn't thought about it for years, but Cam took the same course and he reminded me...'

'Cam? I see...'

Aisha looked a little embarrassed. 'Anyway. We couldn't find any record, anywhere, of the Saltcoats MacIlwraith or Mathieson being employed anywhere, at least not recently.

And they're not on benefits. The Carluke MacIlwraith is a primary school deputy head in Biggar, so we'll know where to look if he's our man. Which I doubt.'

'We need to know how they survive, but we can't risk poking about any more. The Boss is going to arrest them first thing tomorrow. We need to join the team meeting by video at two.'

*

'Duncan Williamson dug up some interesting stuff about Fleming, sir. But before we get on to that. I need to talk to you about how I should report to DCC Ingram.'

'And I need to talk to you about yesterday's *Banner*. We should get our story straight before the Chief calls us in.'

'Maybe we better do that first. His car wasn't in the car park when I got here, but he's usually in his office by eight.'

Esslemont looked at his watch. It was 0740. 'So where did the story come from? Not here. Too much political detail. And we've stopped up our leak. Unless there's another one.'

'I spoke to Harry Conival last night and he's pretty sure this was planted by somebody quite highly placed in Edinburgh. He wasn't prepared to guess who, but he said that it was unlikely to be a minister, though maybe somebody close to ministers.'

'The Chief won't want to talk about the reference to him and the Scotland job, but he'll have a go on the bits about lack of progress on the murders. What can we tell him?'

'We can tell him that arrests are imminent, but I don't think we want to be forced to tell Ingram that. If there is a connection between my suspects and Paul MacIver, any indication that we arc about to detain suspects for the murders could make it very difficult to pursue any line of enquiry that involved conspiracy or collusion. I don't know whether MacIver is of interest to us, sir, but all my instincts tell me to that we should act as though he is. Otherwise we risk giving him an opportunity to cover his tracks.'

Esslemont snorted. 'The trouble with that approach is that it just underlines that no progress is being made. But we may have to put up with a bit of bad press as the other papers follow up. We'll have to persuade the Chief to support that line. If he does, I'll phone Ingram and tell him that we are pursuing several lines of enquiry. It's pretty weak, but since the First Minster can't report to Parliament until tomorrow afternoon, we might get away with it.'

Vanessa nodded. 'We still need to talk to the Chief about MacIver. Let's assume that when we arrest my suspects tomorrow we find something, anything, to link them to MacIver. In any murder case, we would follow up known associates, even if only to eliminate them. No exceptions.'

'Yes. You're right. We need to get the Chief on board this morning. Who knows, he may be more amenable if he's convinced he's out of the running for the top job.'

'Then there's the stuff about the links between the murders and the attacks at Last and Mercury? Completely the opposite of the First Minister's line to the Chief. What's that about?'

'I have no idea. After we've seen the Chief, you can spend some time applying your *cui bono* test and see what you can come up with. If he

raises it we can say, honestly, that we don't understand what the *Banner*'s "sources" are on about. And if things get really heated, I'll play the "no political policing" card. He'll like that.'

Esslemont's phone rang. It had just gone eight o'clock. He smiled wryly. 'Here we go!'

*

Esslemont and Fiske were in the Chief 's office for about half-an-hour. For ten minutes they were the audience for the Chief Constable's rant about the irresponsibility of the Press, the attempt, as he saw it, by anonymous politicians to influence the conduct of a double murder investigation, and the cravenness of indirect personal attacks through the media. This last was the nearest he came to mentioning the reference to his own ambitions.   He seemed to relax after he had vented his anger, and they turned to more immediate and more sensitive matters.

'How is thc investigation going, Campbell?

Esslemont sat forward in his chair. 'A bloody sight better than the *Banner* would have people believe, but we can't say so today. Vanessa?'

He turned to DCI Fiske and indicated that she should take over.

'Sir, I intend to arrest two prime suspects first thing tomorrow, one for each of the murders. I believe they know each other and that they may have acted together. My difficulty is that I still have no clear idea of the motive, or motives, for the killings. I hope this will be clarified by questioning and by searching the homes and, if we can find them, the workplaces of the suspects.'

'So, we can convey that to the politicians via Ingram and get them off our back?'

'Not yet, sir. Bear with us.' Esslemont nodded to Vanessa to go on.

Vanessa described to the Chief the possible link between the prime suspects and the First Minister's closest political adviser and the possibility that there was some connection to the murders.

'Liaison on this to the First Minister is from DCC Ingram to the Justice Secretary and MacIver, so I really need your support to make my report to Ingram today very general and unspecific. I don't even want to promise him better news tomorrow. So we'll take some stick in the media for the next twenty-four hours. I don't see any alternative.'

The Chief shook his head. 'I don't like it. I don't like it at all. But we may have to swallow hard and do as you suggest. But before I sign off on it, I need to hear the possible scenarios after the suspects are in custody.'

'If we find nothing that links either suspect to MacIver, we'll issue a formal statement describing in general terms, but not naming, the men who've been detained in connection with the murders. It's not perfect, for a link might still emerge under questioning, but it's the best we'll be able to do.

'And if you do find evidence of a connection?'

Vanessa looked at Esslemont. They hadn't had time to discuss these 'scenarios' before they were called into the Chief's office. Esslemont nodded.

'Then we'll need to arrange to brief the First Minister without MacIver there. Not easy, as you know, for she seldom goes anywhere without him. I suggest we arrange it through Special Branch and the Permanent Secretary to the Scottish Government. There is no-one else who can insist on a private meeting, and no-one else who can insist that it takes place in his office rather than hers. And Special Branch can use unspecified matters of security to gain access.'

The Chief looked worried. 'And MacIver?'

'We'll detain him while the FM is with Sir James.'

*

Vanessa left Colin MacNee to agree the logistics of the arrests with Strathclyde while she drove out to the offices of Mid-Aberdeenshire Council to talk to Martin Gilbertson. She had decided to turn up unannounced. When she got to reception she was directed to a small annex to the converted private villa that served as the corporate headquarters of the council. The sign on the door said 'Press and External

Relations' and beside it there was an intercom button.

'I'd like to speak to Martin Gilbertson, please.'

A woman's voice said, 'What is it regarding?'

'It's a private matter.'

There was a pause and then, 'Name, please.'

'Vanessa Fiske.'

'Representing?'

'I think he'll know the name.'

There was a click and silence. Vanessa was trying hard not to get pissed off, but, as she stood in the chill of an autumn east wind, it was a struggle.

She began to wonder why she had decided to spare Gilbertson the possible embarrassment of a visit from a senior police officer. One flash of her warrant card, or a call to the council chief executive, would have cut through all this crap and saved some time.

'Please come in.' There was a buzz and a click. Vanessa pushed opened the door and was met by a tall man in his mid-thirties. He was in shirtsleeves and he extended a hand and said, 'Ms Fiske, please come through.'

She thanked him and followed him to a small office. The partition walls were thin, and their conversation, if it was conducted in anything much louder than a whisper, would be audible in the general office, where three women and a teenage boy sat at their desks.

As she sat down, Vanessa said, quietly, 'You know that it's Detective Chief Inspector Fiske?'

Gilbertson nodded.

'This is a sensitive matter, Mr Gilbertson, and, at this stage, a confidential one, so it's important that we are not overheard.'

'There should be no problem if we don't raise our voices.' This was said in a tone that Vanessa's father would have described as "oleaginous", but she decided to take it at face value.

'I need to know the nature of your relationship with Inspector Richard Fleming.'

'Not a name I immediately recognise, Chief Inspector.'

'Yes it is.' Vanessa spoke very quietly, but with a mixture of certainty and menace. 'I do not have time, in the middle of a major murder investigation, to be pissed about, so answer the question.'

Gilbertson made a show of recall. 'Oh, Rich Fleming! It was the rank and the Sunday name that threw me. I've met him now and again in the *Dunottar Castle* in Stonehaven. We've been on the same quiz team a couple of times.'

'With Frank Mancuso of Last Cairngorm, I understand.'

Gilbertson looked shaken. He saw that DCI Fiske was not simply on a fishing trip and he needed to calculate quickly how much she might know and how much he should say.

'We've had the occasional meal together and I think we went to see the Dons at Pittodrie once.'

'I think that he's been feeding you confidential information that you've been passing to people, like Mancuso, who are prepared to pay you for it.'

Vanessa was chancing her arm, but Gilbertson's reaction to her second mention of Mancuso, told her she had hit home. She pressed on.

'We think you passed information about policing plans to Mancuso during the demonstrations against Last's development of the leisure complex and I think you've been in touch, more recently, with someone, whose name you may not know but I do, with an interest in the locations of the murders I'm investigating. So this is serious, Mr Gilbertson. You should talk to me.'

'I don't think I want to say any more before I take advice.'

'That's your right, but I should tell you that we know the source of the information that has got out. And I would advise you, very strongly, not to attempt to contact anybody' - she placed an unmistakably meaningful emphasis on the word - 'in North East Constabulary.'

Gilbertson was no longer the confident PR man who had opened the door to Vanessa a few minutes before. 'Am I suspected of a crime?'

Vanessa could scarcely conceal her contempt. 'Of course you are. I'm just not ready to charge you yet. I'll find my own way out.'

*

When she got back to HQ, Vanessa went to see the DCS. She told him what Williamson had discovered about Fleming and Gilbertson and about her meeting at Mid-Aberdeenshire Council.

'We need to speak to Fleming again, but we need to try to establish a clear and continuing connection between him and Gilbertson. I really don't see how we can find time to do it before Wednesday. I have to get to Glasgow later today ready for the arrests tomorrow morning, then I've got to get the suspects back here. We'll interview them separately as soon as we get them here. At the same time, Hamilton and Gajani, with a little help from Strathclyde, will be searching their homes and workplaces, so we may want to talk to them again, depending what they turn up.'

'So couldn't we find an hour to speak to Fleming late tomorrow afternoon? We need to resolve this soon, or decide whether to call in the Police Complaints Commissioner.'

'Ah. Sorry, sir, I have to be somewhere else at four o'clock tomorrow. Not work related, but unavoidable.'

'Can't you postpone it?'
Vanessa took a deep breath. 'I'm pregnant, sir, and I have to go to GRH for a scan. Hardly anybody here knows, though some will have added two and two. I decided not to "go public" until we have the results of the scan.'

Esslemont looked nonplussed, unsure how to react, riffling through his memory of the personnel manual to find the appropriate response. Vanessa decided to help him.

'Neil and I are delighted about it, sir, so you an to say "Congratulations"...if you want to.'

'Yes, well, congratulations, Vanessa. Hope everything is OK. No doubt you'll want to discuss arrangements...in due course...'

'We could ask Fleming to come in on Wednesday afternoon. Three o'clock?'

'What's wrong with Wednesday morning? I really don't want this dragging on.'

'Priorities, sir. I may have to be in Edinburgh on Wednesday morning, early.'

'To pick up MacIver?'

'If we have enough to go on. By the way, sir, I've been thinking about what we told the Chief, and I think it may be simpler to arrest MacIver before he leaves home and then get Ingram to brief the First Minister. I can get uniform to pick me up at 3.30 and drive me to Edinburgh. I don't think MacIver will leave home before six.'

'Fine. I'll let the Chief know.'

CHAPTER FOURTEEN

In Wilmington, Delaware, on Monday, while Vanessa Fiske in Aberdeen was telling the DCS that she was pregnant, Cy Packard, the Chief Executive Officer of Burtonhall Inc., was sitting at the head of the board room table in his company's headquarters. On a television on the opposite wall, the Chairman, the Honorable Richard Seaton, in Washington DC, and Jack Eisner, in Tammy Wootten's office in Aberdeen, were on a split-screen video link. On Packard's left, the first two chairs were occupied by Burtonhall's general counsel, Magnus Friedkin, and Charlie Fillmore, the Chief Investment Officer, Packard's most senior adviser. Opposite them sat Caleb Adams, CEO of Hedelco, and his legal adviser, Joanna Morse, both of whom had flown down from Boston the previous evening in order to be at this eight o'clock meeting.

At each place there were two plastic folders, one clear, one green. The clear folder contained a thin portfolio of papers. The longest document was Fiona Marchmont's formal request to the Foreign and Commonwealth Office for diplomatic assistance in persuading Hedelco to release to DCI Fiske copies of the emails sent back to Hedelco by Peter Keller during his technical audit in the four days before his death at GRH. This was covered by copies of the minute from the FCO to the Legal Attaché at the British Embassy in Washington, the note from the attaché to the Department of Justice, the DoJ's request for assistance from the Massachusetts Attorney General, and the state A-G's formal request to Hedelco for the release of the emails. The green folder held copies of Keller's emails.

'Magnus', Packard said, 'What do you advise?'

Friedkin, a small man in a dark business suit with an almost invisible silver grey stripe through it, a light blue shirt, and an unremarkable dark silk, self-coloured blue tie, placed his pen on top of the unopened folders. 'As you are all probably aware, this is not a legal issue. If the Scottish police thought that they had any chance of a quick resolution of this issue through due process, we would be preparing for our day in court.'

He allowed himself a slight smile as he used the legal cliché. 'But we're not, because this is essentially political. And we can use that adjective with both a lower case and an upper case p. It's political with a capital P because it involves, internationally, two governments, and, domestically, two levels of government. It's political with a small p, because it raises policy issues for Hedelco and, ultimately for Burtonhall.'

Richard Seaton's disembodied voice resonated from the flat screen on the wall. 'What policy issues, specifically?'

'Well, Chairman, we're here because Hedelco, following Burtonhall practice, has refused to release these emails because they are commercially sensitive and therefore privileged. I wouldn't like to guess whether that claim would stand up in court, though I am prepared to say that if the murder had happened in Boston, and the request had come from the Boston police, I would have advised compliance on two grounds. Number one, they would probably have got an order from a judge quite quickly compelling us to release the emails. Number two, the Boston *Globe* and every news programme in the state would have trashed our reputation if we had resisted.'

'So the issue is whether the policy is to be defended at all costs?'

'I would rather say "in all cases".'

Packard sat forward. 'A policy is a policy. We take a strong position on confidentiality because that's what our investors expect.'

'What our investors expect, Cy,' Seaton said, 'is a good return on their money and as little publicity as possible. We're already taking a reputational hit in the UK and I think I speak for the whole board when I say I don't want it to get any worse. We've got politicians as well as the press taking a very close interest in this. I'm not convinced that refusing to release the emails is worse than handing them over.'

Caleb Adams, the Hedelco CEO, indicated that he wanted to speak. Packard nodded.

'I've never believed that confidentiality should be defended in all circumstances, irrespective of the content of the document. You've all seen the emails. Some of what Keller was reporting might affect the financial performance of the hospital. That would certainly interest the press and, by extension, public opinion. If you think Obamacare is politically charged, try messing with the British National Health Service.'

'What are you saying, Caleb?' This was Seaton again.

'I'm saying that we risk a campaign against us for not revealing what's in the emails. The fact that Keller was doing some kind of audit is already public knowledge. If the publicity continues, there's also the possibility of formal action. Politicians could order an inspection of the hospital and that could lead to enforcement action and contractual penalties.'

Joanna Morse, Hedelco's legal adviser, spoke. 'Aren't we in danger of forgetting why the Scottish police want to see these emails? It's clear from their brief to the UK government that they haven't been able to find a motive for Keller's murder. They also go out of their way to say that they are pursuing other lines of enquiry. As Caleb says, we've all read the emails. I can't see anything in them that amounts to a motive for killing Keller.'

'So, what would you advise?', Packard asked.

'I think I should draft a response to the state Attorney General saying precisely that. We see nothing in the emails that goes to motive and therefore no reason to depart from our policy on confidentiality. That might buy us some time until we see if any other lines of enquiry produce results.'

Packard looked unconvinced and said, 'Only until the press here – The *Globe*, the *Post*, the *Times* – and the television people, as Magnus said, decide to go for us for failing to co-operate in the investigation of the murder of an American citizen abroad.'

'Cy, can I say something?' This was Jack Eisner. 'My confidential informant has gone to ground, so I don't have any further details about the murder investigation, but it seems to me that Joanna's suggestion is worth considering. What we do know is that some officers from Aberdeen are in Glasgow and, according to the press, though this is denied by the police, they are working with the anti-terror squad who are investigating a major bomb attack on Last Cairngorm and a cyber attack on Mercury Fulfilment. If that line of enquiry comes up with anything, our emails will become much less significant.'

'Timescale?' This was the first intervention by Charlie Fillmore, the Chief Investment Officer. 'I can keep the lid on this as far as investors are concerned for a few days, but no more. The sovereign wealth funds in the mid-east haven't weighed in yet. When they do, it's a whole new ball game.'

'Can we go with Joanna's suggestion and see if it buys us forty-eight hours?' Eisner said. 'By that time things may have moved on here, and I might have been able to raise my source.'

'Richard?' Packard looked at the screen.

'OK. But we'll have to meet again on Wednesday.'

*

'Jason Sime.'

'Good afternoon, Jason. You don't mind if I call you Jason?'

The caller to the *G & T* newsroom spoke with an American accent that Sime thought he could place to somewhere in the North East of the United States.

'That depends a bit on who you are.'

'My name is Mark Dinsdale and I work on the crime desk of the Boston *Globe.* In the United States. Massachusetts.'

'I know where Boston is. But how do I know you're who you say you are?'

'Fair enough. I'd really like to talk to you about the two Americans murdered in Aberdeen. So why don't you go online, check out the *Globe*'s number and call me. You'll recognise my voice and we'll be able to talk. How's that sound?'

*

The office of the Attorney General for the Commonwealth of Massachusetts received Joanna Morse's email late in the afternoon after the meeting at Burtonhall. She had stayed in Wilmington to get it signed off by Friedkin and Packard before getting a cab to Philadelphia International Airport to catch an early evening flight back to Boston. Caleb Adams had decided to stay until the meeting scheduled for Wednesday. Joanna would join by video link.

The response attached to the email was brief and to the point and it surprised no-one in the AG's office. The AG forwarded the email

303

and its attachment to the Department of Justice in Washington. From there it went to the British Embassy, the FCO and, just as the car that was driving her to Glasgow crossed the Friarton Bridge near Perth at half past ten in the evening, to Vanessa Fiske's BlackBerry.

By the time the car reached Stirling she had read the attachment. 'Fuck it! Hedelco has told the Attorney General to piss off. According to their legal adviser, there's nothing in Keller's emails that "goes to motive" for Keller's murder, so they see no reason to depart from their company policy on commercial confidentiality. She also notes that we are following other lines of enquiry. She trusts that these will be productive and that there will be no need to pursue the matter further with Hedelco. Patronising cow!'

'Just doing her job, boss.' Colin MacNee said. 'And you did say in the brief that you would not pursue the emails if other enquiries led to a resolution of the case.'

'Bloody hell, Colin! Why do you have to be so fucking reasonable? I'm trying to keep a lot of balls in the air here, and I think I just dropped one. And we don't know that this little jaunt won't turn out to be a wild goose chase.'

'No, we don't. But we also don't know it will. There's nothing to be done about Hedelco just now, so put it to the back of your mind until we see what tomorrow brings.'

'Christ, that's like something from *The Sound of Music*!'

Colin said nothing, so she apologised for being bad tempered, leaned back in her seat, and closed her eyes.

*

The last edition of the Boston *Globe* came off the press at midnight Eastern Daylight Time, just as Vanessa Fiske and Colin MacNee were getting into the cars that would drive them to the known addresses of Simon Mathieson in the West End of Glasgow and Andrew MacIlwraith in Saltcoats.

Dinsdale's story, with an 'Exclusive' tag, was on the front-page, below the fold, with a continuation to page seven. The headline, *'Mass Company Blocks Investigation of Maine Man's Murder'*, was as bad as Cy

Packard had feared. The details of how Peter Keller had died all but guaranteed that the story would be picked up throughout the Eastern seaboard and possibly beyond. The unpopularity of Hedelco in Scotland was laid out and put in context with a description of how the National Health Service works and why the company's take-over of the management of GRH had been opposed by staff and unions.

The murder of Harvey Jamieson on the Vermont One oil platform (*'run by another New England-based corporation, also owned by Burtonhall'*) on the same day as Keller's and its *'so far inconclusive investigation'* was also covered, with a clear implication that the two killings might be connected to each other and, through the ownership of the companies, to Burtonhall.

Dinsdale had been a bit more tentative in the way he covered the Last explosion and the Mercury cyber attack, but the suggestion of a concerted campaign against US companies in Scotland was unmistakable.

Neither Hedelco nor Burtonhall had been prepared to comment and the Attorney General's office had failed to return the reporter's calls.

Beside the continuation on page seven, in a box, there was a short piece by Jason Sime, described as "*the reporter who broke the story of how Peter Keller died*". Sime profiled Detective Chief Inspector Vanessa Fiske, "*The detective who solved the fifty-year old Royal Balmoral murder earlier this year'*" and said that she was unlikely to be put off by Hedelco's refusal to hand over the emails. When she had a murder to solve, she had a reputation for "*letting nothing stand in her way.*"

If Vanessa had seen that after she stepped out of the shower at 0445 hrs., she might have felt less bleak as she dressed, threw up in the toilet, grabbed a bottle of fizzy water, and went down to meet the team from Strathclyde Police that would accompany her to the West End.

CHAPTER FIFTEEN

Strathclyde Police had traced Simon Mathieson to a first floor flat in a Victorian sandstone tenement in Ruthven Street, off Byres Road, the main thoroughfare through Glasgow's fashionable and, in an apologetically Scottish sort of way, Bohemian, West End. The area is home to students, mainly those attending Glasgow University, less than half-a-mile away, recent graduates, and young professionals renting flats while they try, against the economic odds, to save for a deposit to buy their own place. It's not a cheap area, a fact that raised again in DCI Fiske's mind the question of how Mathieson managed to maintain an address there. DS Sara Hamilton and DC Aisha Gajani had found no record of employment for him, either currently or in the previous three years. They now knew, however, that Andrew MacIlwraith had worked as a porter at Grampian Regional Hospital for about a year until a few months before, but that was the only record of his having been gainfully employed. They also knew that neither suspect was receiving social security benefits.

Fiske and MacNee had spent their short night in a budget hotel on the south side of the River Clyde, almost in the shadow of the high-level Kingston Bridge. Hamilton and Gajani had been staying there since their deployment to Glasgow and they were waiting with Colin MacNee in reception when Vanessa came out of the lift.

'Morning, all', she said, with unconvincing brightness. 'Are they here?

'Two unmarked cars, one to take you and Sara to the West End and one to take me and Aisha to sunny Saltcoats, jewel of North Ayrshire.'

'Don't be cynical, Colin. It doesn't suit you.'

'Have you ever been to Saltcoats, boss?' MacNee didn't wait for an answer. 'Four Strathclyde officers and two SOCOs will meet you at Mathieson's address at half past five, and a similar team will meet me and Sara at MacIlwraith's place at six. So we should be on our way back to Aberdeen just in time to miss the Glasgow rush hour.'

'Search warrants?'

Sarah Hamilton pulled some papers from her backpack and handed them to Vanessa, who examined them, put one in her bag and gave the other to Colin.

'OK. Let's do it.'

*

Ruthven Street is a one-way street with vehicular entry only from Byres Road. Just before five-thirty, two unmarked cars drove into the street and stopped, in the middle of the road between two lines of parked cars, outside Mathieson's address. The third car, in the livery of Strathclyde Police, parked across the entrance to the street. There was unlikely to be much traffic so early, but if any vehicle tried to turn in from Byres Road, the uniformed driver would wave it on.

DCI Fiske and DS Hamilton, accompanied by the four Strathclyde officers, went into the building, using the entry code that had been provided by the building's management company. The Scenes of Crime Officers waited in one of the cars. They would start work in the flat as soon as the arrest had been made and the search warrant served.

The arrest of Simon Mathieson, on suspicion of the murder of Harvey Jamieson, took only a few minutes. After he had been cautioned, he was taken to Govan Police Station, about ten minutes away, while DCI Fiske, assisted by DS Hamilton and the SOCOs, did an immediate search of the two-bedroom flat. A full forensic examination would be done later. For the moment, Vanessa was looking for a computer, documents, mobile phones, memory devices and anything that might link Mathieson to Vermont One, to Andrew MacIlwraith, or to Paul MacIver.

DS Sara Hamilton opened a door leading off the hall, expecting to find a bedroom. Instead, she walked into a windowless box room measuring about 2.5 by 1.5 metres. There was a built in desk along the left-hand wall, behind the door. On the desk there was an array of IT equipment: computers, hard drives, modems, wi-fi hubs, scanners, boxes of memory sticks.

'Boss, you should see this.'

Fiske came across the hall from the living room. 'Rather more than your average home computer set up. There's a laptop in one of the other rooms and we'll take that to Dongle. But I'll have to ask the hi-tech boys from Strathclyde to deal with this. We'll need to know why a man with no record of paid employment could afford this amount of kit. And we'll need to know what he's been doing with it.'

*

Andrew MacIlwraith's address in Saltcoats was less easy to secure. It was on an estate of semi-detached council houses, some of them sold to their tenants under the right to buy scheme. Colin MacNee noticed that the percentage still in council ownership was, on the face of it (the clue was the replacement front doors on those that were now owner-occupied), higher than in similar estates in the major cities. It was an economically depressed area, with an unemployment rate higher than the Scottish average. If MacIlwraith had been living here as a student, Colin thought, as Cam Ritchie had suggested, he had probably inherited the house, either as tenant or owner, from his parents.

The target was on a stretch of the road with houses on only one side. It faced on to a slightly unkempt open space where, even this early, a couple of people were out walking their dogs by the light of the street lamps that flanked the path through the "park". Just before six o'clock, to the obvious curiosity of the dog walkers, three unmarked police cars drove into the street. MacNee's car stopped directly outside MacIlwraith's house. Its front door hadn't been replaced. The other two cars stopped laterally across the road to prevent vehicles driving past.

Unlike Mathieson, MacIlwraith was reluctant to open the door. Colin MacNee rang the bell and rattled the letterbox. A sleep-muffled voice from inside said, 'OK, OK, I'm coming. What's going on?'

Through the letterbox, MacNee said, "Police, please open the door!'

Looking into the house through the slot, MacNee saw a man in pyjamas turn and rush back into one of the rooms.

'Break it down!"

One of the Strathclyde officers was carrying a battering ram, known in the trade as the FBK or 'fucking big key', and within seconds, the door was swinging open, the lock broken and the jamb splintered.

'Mr MacIlwraith, don't do anything stupid. I'm Detective Inspector Colin MacNee of North East Constabulary, and I'm here to arrest you on suspicion of the murder of Peter Keller at Grampian Royal Hospital. I also have a warrant to search these premises.'

MacIlwraith was sitting at a laptop computer in a back room. MacNee assumed that he was trying to delete incriminating files. MacIlwraith didn't know about Dongle Donaldson, Colin thought. More significantly, if he didn't know that deleted files were recoverable, he was unlikely to be responsible for the cyber attack on Mercury Fulfilment. No link there, then.

MacNee told MacIlwraith to get dressed - 'Do it where I can see you' – and one of the Strathclyde officers handcuffed him.

'I'll be here for about half-an-hour, so take him to Govan and we'll pick him up later.'

As MacIlwraith was being taken to one of the cars, the SOCOs went into the house, and lights began to go on in neighbouring houses. MacNee was always impressed, and a little bewildered, by how quickly news of an arrest got around. Usually, little knots of spectators assembled within minutes and the first of them was coming together, most in nightwear and dressing gowns, just as the car left the street on its way back to Glasgow.

Colin MacNee turned to his colleague. 'Aisha, can we rely on the custody officer at Govan to ensure that MacIlwraith and Mathieson don't see each other?'

'I think so, boss. Sara spoke to the Area Commander yesterday. Mathieson should be on his way to Aberdeen before MacIlwraith gets there. I've asked Sara to send me a text when he's off the premises. I can then give the driver the all clear.'

'Good.' She's really on the ball, Colin thought, misses very little. Must speak to the DCI about her.

'Right. Let's collect the obvious stuff.'

They both pulled on latex gloves and Aisha produced a bundle of evidence bags of various sizes.

*

The first car to Aberdeen left Govan Police Station at 0730 hrs. DCI Fiske was in the front passenger seat. Mathieson, handcuffed and silent, sat in the back with DS Sara Hamilton. The driver who had brought Fiske and MacNee from Aberdeen the previous evening took the car on to the M8 at the junction just north of the station, easing into the already thickening morning traffic. He crossed into the outside lane and headed towards the city centre, and after a few miles took the slip road on to the M80 towards Stirling. From there he would take the M9 and the A90 to Aberdeen.

The car was doing a steady 75 mph towards Cumbernauld and, as she caught sight of the Mercury Fulfilment logo on a huge hangar-like building just off the motorway, Vanessa's mobile buzzed. She took it out of her bag, looked at the display and said, as quietly as she could consistent with being audible, 'Hi, Harry, what can I do for you?'

Harry Conival, the press officer assigned to the investigation, apologised for phoning at this hour. 'I knew you had an early start but when I spoke to Duncan Williamson about this he said you'd want to know. It seems that Jason Sime is, probably without knowing it, being very helpful to you.'

Vanessa, who had had nothing to eat but a cereal bar, wasn't in the mood for Harry's sometimes elliptical style of communication. 'What are you talking about? I've got a murder suspect in the back of the car, and I'm knackered.'

'He called me last night and told me to have a look at the website of the Boston *Globe*. They've run a front page story about how that health company is blocking your enquiries into the murder of an American citizen. And there's also a wee piece by Sime that's very nice about you.'

'That is interesting. How did they get the story?'

'A *Globe* reporter phoned Jason, and it went on from there. But what you'll really like is the possibility that this will go big in the States. Jason's contact told him that the local TV stations in Boston have picked it up and he thinks that other papers, and maybe the networks, will run with it. The *Globe* went to Hedelco for a quote, but they refused to comment.'

'Thanks for that. It's what? About 3.30 in the morning over there, so nothing's likely to develop for a few hours. I'll be in the office by about half-past ten. I'll talk to you then.'

Before she leaned back on the headrest and tried to sleep, Vanessa texted Colin MacNee. As the SIO on the Keller case, he needed to know.

Boston paper having a go at Hedelco for blocking us. Maybe first time you've been grateful to the reptiles.

*

It was nearly 10.30 when they reached the outskirts of Aberdeen. Vanessa had dozed a little, but rather regretted it as she reached for her fizzy water to try to wash away the acrid taste of sleep. She thought about how she would use the rest of the day. Neil would collect her at 3.30 in the afternoon to go to the hospital. That left four and a half hours to work on the case. She didn't want to interview Mathieson until MacIlwraith arrived from Glasgow, and she reckoned that that wouldn't be until between 11.30 and noon. In any case, she couldn't talk to him without his lawyer present. His solicitor, whom he had phoned before they left Govan, was unlikely to get to Aberdeen before the early afternoon.

She wouldn't be ready for a full session with him until Dongle had looked at his laptop, but the clock had started ticking on the time she could hold him without charge as soon as she had arrested him. She had no idea how long the hi-tech unit at Strathclyde would need before they gave her a preliminary analysis of the computer equipment. When his solicitor arrived, she could question Mathieson about his theft of the identity of Thomas Nuttall but she would have to play for time until she got the other evidence.

She would also need to bring DCS Esslemont up to date and talk to Colin MacNee to co-ordinate their interviews with the suspects. And she would have to decide, by the end of the working day, whether they had enough evidence to arrest Paul MacIver. She would have to come back in after her scan. Neil wouldn't be happy.

*

Harry Conival had been on the internet monitoring the morning news programmes on the Boston affiliates of the four major US television networks and the websites of the other major East Coast newspapers in New York, Philadelphia and Washington. The Hedelco story was growing legs.

'I can't see how they can go on refusing comment for very long. One of the TV stations is reporting that Hedelco's chief executive is out of town, in Delaware for a meeting at Burtonhall, their parent company. Their legal adviser is in Boston, but she's unwilling to say anything until she gets a steer from her boss. It's not quite a feeding frenzy, but they'll want it to go away.'

Vanessa sipped her peppermint tea and belched discreetly. 'The quickest way for them to make that happen is to let me have the emails.'
Harry grinned and began searching in his pockets for his cigarettes. 'Fancy a small wager that you'll have them by tonight?'

*

At 11.15, Colin MacNee and Aisha Gajani led Andrew MacIlwraith through a back entrance to North East Constabulary HQ and down a flight of stairs to the cells. There were two groups of holding cells, one on each side of the stairwell, so the suspects could be isolated from each other. The custody officer had been told that each suspect should not know of the other's arrest and that the arresting officers were awaiting the arrival of their solicitors before interviews could begin.

Aisha and Sara had supervised the transfer of the evidence taken from the suspects' homes to a secure conference room. A patrol car took two laptop computers and five disposable mobile phones to Dongle Donaldson's 'lab' with a request from DCI Fiske for a preliminary analysis of their contents to be delivered to her as soon as possible, and certainly before three o'clock. DCs Williamson and Todd were drafted in to help with a first examination of the notebooks and other documents collected from the addresses in Glasgow and Saltcoats.

While her team looked for evidence to connect the suspects to the murders and to each other, Vanessa Fiske briefed the DCS.

'Not a lot to say until we've talked to them, sir, and we're waiting for their briefs to get here. When do you need to update DCC Ingram?'

'I've told him I'll phone before nine tonight. And, if we need to, we can talk to him again before he sees the Justice Secretary and MacIver at 8.30 tomorrow morning.'

'Ah, MacIver. I hope we can finesse that before you speak to DCC Ingram today, but I won't know until we've had a first trawl through the stuff we picked up after the arrests and Dongle has done a preliminary analysis of the computers and phones.'

'When will that be?'

'Who knows? But I'll be back after my hospital appointment, hopefully by about five or five thirty.'

Esslemont smiled and raised an eyebrow. 'Does your partner know that?'

Vanessa was surprised. The DCS almost never showed any interest in the personal lives of his staff, but she looked a little guilty as she replied, 'Not yet.'

Esslemont looked at his watch. 'Anything else? I've got to speak to the Chief.'

'One thing. From our first search, we've got the bank details of both suspects. Just cheque books and cards. No statements, though we might get them from their laptops. If we don't, I'll need to get transaction details going back at least two or three years.'

'Not until they're charged. Why do you need them?'

'Because neither of them has any visible means of support. No paid employment for years, except for MacIlwraith's short spell at GRH, and no benefits. Somebody's subsidising them. I want to know who.'

'Let's see if we get enough to charge them. And, some time today, we need to talk about Richard Fleming. We can't just leave him dangling.'

Vanessa didn't see why not, but she said nothing.

*

'Well, boss, your boys definitely know each other.'

Dongle Donaldson had phoned at 2.30 to say he was on his way to HQ. He arrived carrying a rucksack containing the two laptops and the five mobile phones, and as he spoke he was laying them out on the conference room table.

'There have been calls back and forth between both of MacIlwraith's burners and two of Mathieson's. Easy enough to discover that once I had found the numbers. There are some pretty cryptic texts, too, though fewer than I'd expect. I'll put them all in my report and you can see if you can make anything of them. I can't identify who owns the phones that messages went to that aren't between the phones I've got, but you might want to see one that was sent by Mathieson in the week after the murders.'

Fiske and MacNee stood on either side of Dongle and leaned in to see the display on the phone.

Back at base. What next?

'Sounds a bit military.' Colin MacNee said. 'Tells us bugger all until we know who it went to, though. Anything else, Dongle?

'Nothing obvious, but I've got a lot still to do on the laptops. I can tell you that there's been quite a lot of email traffic between our two boys and some between both of them and two other email addresses. I'll get the IP addresses and then I'll start on requesting the internet search histories. Should have something for you by six o'clock or so.'

'I've got a meeting at four,' Vanessa said, 'but I'll be back about five, five thirty at the latest. Mathieson's brief is here, but it's all very circumstantial so far. We need some physical evidence. When will the SOCOs be here?'

Sara Hamilton took out her phone. 'They're on their way. I'll find out where they are.'

The SOCOs had just passed Laurencekirk. 'They'll be here in about half a hour and it sounds as though we'll need some time to sift through what they've got.'

'Right, you can do that while I'm at the...while I'm out. In the meantime, I'll have a session with Mathieson about Nuttall.'

*

Neil Derrick dropped Vanessa off at NEC HQ at 5.15. Before she got out of the car, she closed her eyes and took several very deep breaths. The time she had to question the suspects before she would have to charge or release them was ticking away. She knew she had the right men and she had to decide what, if anything, to do about MacIver. She had to put the results of the scan to the back of her mind.   She leaned over and kissed Neil. She couldn't say when she'd be home.

She took the lift to the fourth floor and went to the conference room.

'Anything?', she asked, as she poured herself a coffee from the vacuum jug on the side table.

'You bet!', Colin MacNee said. 'You might want to sit down while we go through it.'

Colin started with the physical evidence from MacIlwraith's house. He passed to Vanessa a small evidence bag containing two syringes and another that held a small cardboard box with printing on it in Cyrillic script.

'Do we know what the syringes were used for?'

'One of the SOCOs is standing by to take it to the lab to see if there are any identifiable traces. Even if there's not, the box may be the physical evidence that makes some of the circumstantial stand up.'

'How?'

'One of the SOCOs did Russian at university. The writing on the box says "Sodium thiopental". And there are dosage instructions for rapid inducement of unconsciousness.'

'Right. Well, you know where to start your questioning of MacIlwraith. Anything else?'

'You know about the bank details. We're waiting for Dongle to come up with the contents of the laptops. And there's a message for you to call the hi-tech specialists at Strathclyde. Mathieson has been a lot more careful, possibly a lot brighter, than MacIlwraith. There are notebooks from both locations, but I can't find anything immediately incriminating, or even interesting, in the stuff from Mathieson's flat, except Nuttall's birth certificate, and we knew about that already.'

'Good to have it as evidence, though.'

'Yeah, it is. And have a look at this.'

Colin handed Vanessa a transparent evidence bag containing an open notebook. The page visible through the plastic was a list of letters and numbers. The numbers were obviously telephone numbers, some landline and some mobile. Each set of numbers had letters beside them.

'That's from MacIlwraith's place. Look carefully, boss. One entry stands out. It's different from the others.'

Vanessa examined the list. Most of the numbers had two or three letters against them, apparently the initials of the contact. But one read:

FMAD 07413 569150

'That one?' Vanessa pointed to the number

MacNee nodded. 'Two of MacIlwraith's burners and one of Mathieson's made calls or sent texts to that number. We need to know who owns it.'

'I think I know. But proving it is going to take this investigation into very scary territory.'

CHAPTER SIXTEEN

Early yesterday morning, as I have already reported to Parliament, officers from the North East Constabulary, assisted by officers from Strathclyde Police, arrested two men, one in Saltcoats in North Ayrshire and one in Glasgow. The arrests were in connection with the murders, at Grampian Royal Hospital and on the Vermont One Oil Platform, of Peter Keller and Harvey Jamieson, respectively. I was unable yesterday to give the names of the arrested men, but since they have now been charged, I can tell Parliament that Andrew MacIlwraith, aged 31, was arrested at his home in Saltcoats and subsequently charged with offences relating to the death of Mr Keller. Simon Mathieson, aged 32, was detained at his home in Glasgow and later charged with offences relating to the death of Mr Jamieson. Other charges are under consideration and a further report will be submitted by North East Constabulary to the Procurator Fiscal.

The First Minister paused, looked closely at the paper from which she was reading her statement, and took a deep breath.

Early this morning, acting on evidence and information arising from the arrests of MacIwraith and Mathieson, and other enquiries, officers from North East Constabulary, assisted by officers from Lothian and Borders Police and other specialist officers, arrested a third man, at his home in Edinburgh, also in connection with the murders of Mr Keller and Mr Jamieson. The man is currently detained at NEC headquarters in Aberdeen. Charges are expected, but because they have not yet been laid, I am not able to tell Parliament the name of the arrested man.

I should also tell Parliament that NEC officers, assisted by specialist officers, are actively pursuing the possibility that the arrested men may be able to help with enquiries into the recent explosion at Last Cairngorm and the cyber attack on Mercury Fulfilment in Cumbernauld.

*I will, of course, keep, Parliament
fully informed of any developments.*

The First Minister, her face drawn and pale,
resumed her seat and waited, with some
apprehension, for questions from her political
opponents.

*

DCI Vanessa Fiske, DI Colin MacNee, and
DCS Campbell Esslemont were with the
Chief Constable in his office, watching the
First Minister's statement. Harry Conival
was also there, as were the NEC legal
adviser, Fiona Marchmont, and the Chief's
Acting Staff Officer.

The investigating officers were already
aware, from the picture DC Gajani had found
in the student newspaper and Esslemont's
identification, that the arrested men knew, or
had known, Paul MacIver. The key pieces of
evidence that had convinced Fiske, and
persuaded the DCS and the Chief, that
MacIver should be arrested, had come from
Dongle Donaldson's analysis of the laptops
and mobile phones found in the homes of
MacIlwraith and Mathieson and from
Strathclyde's hi-tech unit's preliminary

examination of the equipment found in the Ruthven Street flat.

The email accounts of the two men showed frequent and numerous messages to and from a Hotmail account with an IP address in Edinburgh. The emails were not obviously incriminating, but the pattern of traffic suggested that the accounts had not been active during the time when MacIlwraith was believed, on the basis of the hospital CCTV, to have been in Aberdeen and when Mathieson alias Nuttall had been on Vermont One and then in Newcastle. Also, there was a spike in traffic to and from MacIlwraith's account in the days following the explosion at Last Cairngorm. Mathieson's account had shown increased activity after the cyber attack on Mercury Fulfilment. All of this was circumstantial, as was the notation against a mobile phone number in the notebook found in MacIlwraith's house which might refer to the First Minister's Special Adviser.

In seeking support from the DCS and the Chief to arrest MacIver, Vanessa had conceded that all or most of the evidence gathered was circumstantial.

'Taken together, though, it's indicative and certainly enough for an arrest and a search warrant.' She had looked first at Esslemont and then at the Chief and continued. 'It's what our American colleagues would call "probable cause".'

Esslemont had nodded. The Chief, much more concerned than the DCS about the politics, had probed a bit further.

'I think I need to be able, if the question arises, to assure…' He paused to rephrase. 'To be able to give assurance that such an arrest and search was more than a fishing trip based on what you admit is wholly circumstantial evidence. Are you looking for anything specific or only for evidence which, in general, ties MacIver to the two other suspects?'

'I understand the delicacy of your position in this, sir. But I believe that a mobile phone number in MacIlwraith's notebook to which there have been calls and texts from two of MacIlwraith's disposables and one of Mathieson's, may be a disposable phone owned by MacIver. I need to find that phone. And now that there is the beginning of a link to Last and Mercury, I need access to his computer.'

Vanessa's confidence that they had not only got the right men but had uncovered a criminal conspiracy had been bolstered by the discovery, among the hardware collected from Mathieson's flat, of the missing hard disk from Keller's laptop. This established a further likely link between MacIlwraith and Mathieson, and it made irrelevant whatever decision Hedelco and Burtonhall might make on the release of Keller's emails. Dongle Donaldson would recover them and decrypt them. As it turned out, the need to limit the damage to the companies' reputations from the media coverage of their refusal to hand over the emails, had convinced Packard, Seaton and their colleagues to announce that they would be complying with the request for the emails as soon as possible. The question remained why they had resisted for so long.

'Here we go,' Harry Conival said, as the Leader of the Opposition rose to ask the first question. 'I'm offering odds on him blowing it and letting her off the hook.'

But this time, Harry had got it wrong.

*

'Will the First Minister comment on the rumours circulating here and in Edinburgh's New Town to the effect

that the third man in this case is personally known to her?

A camera focused immediately on the FM, who was clearly struggling to maintain her composure. She glanced at the Justice Secretary, who shook his head, almost imperceptibly.

'Clever question', Vanessa said, 'Especially that reference to the New Town.'

'How so?' asked the Chief.

Vanessa looked at Harry, aware that she might be about to encroach on his territory. 'Because some time today, some media outlet or some blog will say that the arrested man has been "named locally" as Paul MacIver.'

The First Minister was getting to her feet.

I cannot comment on rumour, especially in connection with an ongoing police investigation.

The Labour Leader was rising before the FM had resumed her seat. He was striving to appear both statesmanlike and cmollient.

I understand, and support, the First Minister's position, Presiding Officer, so perhaps I can turn to another matter. Colleagues in this Chamber, and members of the press, have noted today the quite unprecedented absence from her side of her special adviser, Mr Paul MacIver. Is he perhaps indisposed?

The Chamber was silent, except for a low hum as members whispered to each other. The FM did not move. She was rescued by the Presiding Officer, who reminded members that questions should relate to the substance of the First Minister's statement. But the damage was done. The arrest of Paul MacIver was almost in the public domain.

*

'If any of you hasn't already guessed what I'm about to tell you, you don't deserve to be detectives, so I may have to recommend that you return to pounding the beat.'

DCI Fiske was opening the team meeting at six o'clock on Tuesday evening. She needed to bring them up to date on the arrests, on the first round of questioning and on the preliminary analysis of the evidence gathered from the suspects' homes. She also had to put in place contingency plans for getting to Edinburgh by six o'clock on Wednesday morning if she got approval, from the DCS and the Chief, to arrest MacIver.

'I'm pregnant. Eight weeks.' There was a ripple of applause and some drumming of fingers on the table. 'Colin already knew because I had to explain the inexplicable when I asked for a fizzy water rather than my usual half-pint of Sauvignon Blanc when we went to the pub last week. And Sara, who's spent a lot of time in my company over the last couple of weeks, has given me the odd knowing look but has, I think, remained shtum. So, thanks to them for being discreet. And I had to tell the DCS why I couldn't conduct an interview with him late this afternoon.'

Esslemont smiled, and Vanessa went on.

'I had to go to GRH for a scan. I know you will all be delighted to know that everything seems fine. In fact, more than fine, because it's twins. Came as a bit of a shock, and I shall be investigating their father's background to discover if there's anything I should have known. However, there's nothing like a double murder investigation to remind a happily expectant mother that there's still more than seven months to go. The work goes on, as I said to Neil as he dropped me back here after a cup of sweet tea.'

She was suddenly aware that she was, quite involuntarily, rubbing her stomach, so she leaned both hands on the table and turned to the business of the meeting.

'Colin. You arrested MacIlwraith in what you picturesquely described as the Jewel of North Ayrshire and you and Aisha interviewed him this afternoon'.

'Yeah. And we got more out of his house than we've so far been able to get out of him. He refuses to tell us what he was doing with the syringes. No residues in them, by the way, so the lab can't discover what they were used to inject. Claims he has no idea how the sodium thiopental box with the Russian script came to be in his bedroom, hidden at the back of a drawer.'

'Did you ask him what he was doing in GRH while Keller was there?'

'We showed him the enhanced CCTV images and asked him to identify himself but, on the advice of his solicitor, he said "no comment". So if he wasn't prepared to admit he'd been there, there seemed little point in pursuing the matter any further. He did look very nervous and shifty, though. But it's quite difficult to use that as evidence.'

Esslemont leaned forward so that he could see Colin. 'What did he have to say about the emails and texts?'

'Nothing, sir. He wouldn't tell us who the texts from his burners went to and he simply "no commented" on the emails.'

DCI Fiske intervened. 'Neither MacIlwraith nor Mathieson has been told that the other is in custody, though we should assume that their lawyers have met in the canteen and exchanged a few words. I'd really like to question them some more before we decide to charge them. Their statutory twelve hours expires about now, but the custody officer has agreed, because of the time it took to get them here, to extend that by another twelve hours, so we'll have to charge them by early tomorrow, or release them, and that's not an option.'

'What about Mathieson?' Esslemont asked.

'For reasons already explained, I haven't been able to talk to him yet about the Jamieson murder. I'll do that as soon as we're done here. Before I went to the hospital, I interviewed him about Nuttall's birth certificate. He admitted that he had applied for it – he could hardly deny it – but refused, on the advice of his solicitor, to say why he wanted it.'

'Have we got enough to charge them?' The DCS was beginning to sound a little impatient, probably because he knew there was other business to be considered.

'Fiona thinks we've got enough to charge them with conspiracy to murder and that after further interviews, when we've put to them all the evidence gathered from their homes, we'll probably be able to add murder to the sheet.'

*

As they left the Chief's office after they had decided to arrest MacIver the next morning, DCS Esslemont asked DCI Fiske whether she thought she had to make the arrest personally.

'Absolutely, sir. Why wouldn't I? I'm the SIO and I can't duck the responsibility of making the highest profile arrest this force will see in a long time. If it goes political, I need to be able to tell the Chief, and you, that it was all done exactly by the book.'

'I see that, but you've been working really hard on this and I just wondered whether, given your condition, you might want to avoid getting up at three o'clock in the morning to go to Edinburgh.'

Christ almighty, Vanessa thought, he's gone from old style to Neanderthal! She had to nail this here and now.

'Sir, I'm not ill, I'm pregnant. I'm also a senior professional police officer in the middle of a difficult, high profile case. I haven't decided when to take my maternity leave but I'm not taking it now.'

Esslemont seemed genuinely surprised, even shocked, by her response. 'I just thought you might welcome a good night's sleep before interviewing MacIver tomorrow. I wasn't questioning your commitment or your ability to do your job.'

'With respect, sir, that's not how it sounded. If I go home now, I can get five hours sleep and possibly a bit more on the way to Edinburgh. We'll have MacIver back here by ten o'clock. His lawyer will take a bit longer, so we might be able to fit in another session with Richard Fleming. It's a lower priority, but it needs to be done.'

'I'll try to set that up for eleven.'

'Thank you, sir. We really ought to get that sorted now that we're linking the murders to the Last and Mercury attacks. We'll need to be sure that Fleming's connection to Mancuso, Last's security chief, was purely social. And we still don't know why Fleming was feeding information to Gilbertson.'

Vanessa hadn't set out to demonstrate that she was completely on top of her job, but that was the effect. Esslemont got the message, wished her good night and success in Edinburgh, and turned towards his office.

*

By half-past-eight, Vanessa had finished her second interview with Mathieson. It had been no more productive than MacNee's questioning of MacIlwraith. She had decided not to bring up what she already knew about the search history on his computers. She had suggested to Colin that he should also hold back on this when questioning MacIlwraith. They had preliminary analyses from Dongle and from the Strathclyde hi-tech unit, but she wanted to see the full reports before she confronted the suspects. She also needed some early indication of what was on MacIver's computers.

When she was done, Vanessa checked with Fiona Marchmont and with the lawyer in the procurator fiscal's office and then instructed the duty chief inspector to formally charge McIlwraith and Mathieson with conspiracy to murder. She asked Fiona to see if she could arrange for their first court appearance to take place on Wednesday afternoon, ostensibly so that she could be present, but also because she wanted an opportunity to question Mathieson again when she got back from Edinburgh. Colin MacNee would interview MacIlwraith again as soon as he had all the details from the computers. Both Dongle and the Strathclyde people had said that their full reports would be emailed by eight o'clock on Wednesday morning. Admin support would confirm their arrival to DCI Fiske as she travelled back from Edinburgh.

By ten to nine, Vanessa was sitting on the sofa in their flat while Neil Derrick made her a pasta.

'I really need to get to bed. I'm being picked up at half-past-three and a slightly surreal conversation with Esslemont earlier makes it even more essential than usual that I'm on the ball tomorrow. It's been some day! Twins? Fucking twins! Is there any history of twins in your family, because there certainly isn't in mine.'

Neil paused in his stirring of the bolognese. 'I don't think so, but my mother is checking with her sisters and aunts. And I've had a little surf around the internet. Apparently...'

Vanessa interrupted him. 'I know. If there's no history, there's a greater likelihood of identical twins, which would mean that the ideal outcome of a boy and a girl is less likely. But, do you know what? I don't care! I'm shocked, shaken and very happy. I couldn't believe how professional I was after I went back to the office after the scan. That's what made Esslemont's "concern" so hard to take. As Chris Jenkinson said, pregnancy lays prejudices bare. Big news, big case. Let's have that pasta, then all three

344

of us are off to bed. You can make it four if
you like.'

CHAPTER SEVENTEEN

At DCI Vanessa Fiske's request, Harry Conival had called a press conference for 1430 hrs on Wednesday. The timing allowed Vanessa to be in court at two o'clock to see all three men charged and remanded. The call to the press conference was accompanied by a press release announcing that Paul MacIver, 32, of Edinburgh, had been arrested at his home that morning and brought to North East Constabulary Headquarters in Aberdeen. He had been questioned by DCI Fiske and subsequently charged with conspiracy to murder both Peter Keller and Harvey Jamieson. Further possible offences were being investigated, but no other charges had yet been laid. The press conference would be taken by DCI Fiske. DI Colin MacNee, as the Senior Investigating Officer on the Keller case would also be there, as would Detective Chief Superintendent Campbell Esslemont, Head of NEC CID.

Before the First Minister made her statement to Parliament, at 12.30 pm, Paul MacIver had, indeed, been 'named locally' as the man arrested in Edinburgh's New Town early that morning. The information had been posted immediately on most news media websites and there was febrile speculation about the political significance of the involvement of the First Minister's most trusted adviser in two murders and, possibly, other serious offences. The investigating officers had so far said nothing publicly about why the men had been killed, and the announcement from Hedelco and Burtonhall about the release of the emails had led the smarter journalists, especially Ben Aaronson of the *Financial Post,* to conclude that they had contained nothing that the police would recognise as a motive for murder.

Aaronson's conclusion, on the *FP* website, was clear and unequivocal:

The emails were posted on the Hedelco website as soon as they were released to the police investigating Peter Keller's murder, largely to limit the damage to the company's reputation, and to that of its secretive parent, private equity giant Burtonhall. US media had attacked them for obstructing enquiries into the death of a US citizen.

By asserting 'commercial confidentiality' as their reason for withholding the emails from the police, the companies may have been stating nothing but the truth. Whether it was the whole truth remains to be seen. Things might be clearer if the emails to Ebright, the owners of the Vermont One oil rig, where Harvey Jamieson was murdered on the same day that Keller died, were made public. For now, we must assume that, just as the Hedelco emails call into question the financial position of the Grampian Royal Hospital contract, the Ebright emails almost certainly show the precarious profitability of Vermont One. The government inspectors are already heading for the hospital. If the performance or safety of Vermont One were called in question, the possibility of Burtonhall pulling the plug on both of these substantial investments in Scotland would become very real.

As to the real motives for the murders, and any links there may be to other recent crimes in Scotland, police investigations continue. The North East Constabulary press conference this afternoon may clarify the political ramifications of this complex affair.

*

When Vanessa entered the briefing room she saw even more reporters than had turned out for her press conferences during the Balmoral murder investigation some months before. She was particularly aware of the line of cameras and microphone booms set up at the back, and she immediately spotted the logos of the BBC, ITN, Channel 5 and Sky News. Two of the four major American networks were also there, as were all the usual suspects, local and national.

She and Colin MacNee sat at a table on the raised dais at the front; Esslemont took a seat at the end of the front row of seats; Harry Conival hovered about by the door through which the officers had come in. As soon as the expectant hum had died down, Vanessa stood up and made an opening statement that did little more than rehash what had been in the press release.

She finished by saying, as usual, that she would try to answer questions as fully as possible, but that she might have to withhold some information in the interests of what was still an ongoing investigation.

Dozens of hands shot up. Vanessa nodded at Jason Sime of the *G & T*, in recognition of the piece he had written for the Boston *Globe*. 'I think you should have the first go, Jason, as the local boy.'

Sime stood up, looking slightly embarrassed. 'It's pretty clear from the Hedelco emails that there is no financial or commercial motive for the murders. And I assume that you've ruled out the possibility of two muggings gone wrong on the same day. We now know, that you've arrested and charged a very highly placed political figure. Are we looking at a political motive for these killings?'

'You know I try to resist descending into cliché, Jason, but I have to say that we are keeping an open mind on that.'

'What's the connection between MacIver and the other two men you've charged? Do they know each other?'

'We believe that there is a historic connection between them and we are investigating the possibility of more recent contacts.'

Vanessa pointed to another reporter.

'Kevin Bennett, *Glasgow Banner.* Can you tell us what contacts you've had with the First Minister in the course of your investigations?'

Vanessa glanced at Esslemont who gave her a look that suggested she should be careful.

'Early in the investigation, the First Minister spoke, in her capacity as a local MSP, with the Chief Constable. Also, at her request, we arranged for her to be briefed, daily, through the Justice Secretary, on progress with the various investigations underway.'

Bennett stood up. 'The FM told Parliament that the Justice Secretary was being briefed about the Last Cairngorm and Mercury Fulfilment attacks. Was he also briefed on the murders, and if so, are you connecting all of these crimes?'

Vanessa knew this was a good question. She considered quickly, but carefully, how to respond.

'In the first instance, it seemed sensible to use the briefings to report any progress on the murders, given the FM's constituency interest. More recently, we have begun to look at the possibility of the kind of connection you mention.'

Esslemont nodded. It was going to come out as soon as the press began digging into MacIver and sniffing around the Major Crimes Unit at Govan, so it was as well to put it into the public domain now.

'David MacKay, *BBC Scotland*. Who briefed the Justice Secretary? And was anyone else present during the briefings.'

Vanessa had been in this game long enough to recognise a question to which the questioner already knew the answer. If she dodged it, the reporter would simply come back with a second question naming the people he knew to have been present.

'The briefings were undertaken by a Deputy Chief Constable from Lothian and Borders and on all but one occasion the Justice Secretary was accompanied by a member of the First Minister's staff.'

'Was that member of staff Paul MacIver?'

Vanessa smiled. 'I'm sorry, but that's one of the things I can't tell you.'

From the back of the room, without invitation from DCI Fiske, a voice said, 'Thornhill, freelance. Was the DCC from Lothian and Borders Grant Ingram?'

'Yes.'

'And isn't he the ACPO lead on terrorism?'

'Yes.'

The media now had their story. There was a link between the murders and the Last and Mercury attacks. The possibility of terrorism was in play. And they believed that one of the suspects had been given confidential briefings on the course of enquiries that had led to his arrest. It was going to be very difficult, now, to separate the political and criminal aspects of the investigations.

*

'We've got means and opportunity, but we still don't have motive. The Hedelco emails are no more use than those Dongle extracted from Jamieson's laptop. MacIlwraith and

Mathieson did these murders, but if we don't come up with a convincing motive, the case is weakened, possibly fatally. Its circumstantial, and that will be a gift to the defence, even with the forensic evidence, such as it is, from their homes.'

Vanessa Fiske was opening the team meeting immediately after the press conference, and she wanted to use it as a brainstorming session to ensure that all possible leads and theories had been considered.

'What forensic have we got?' This was Esslemont, who had decided, because of the political and media interest, to attend all the team meetings.

'Not a lot. Colin?'

MacNee got up and went to the whiteboard, where he would write the key points as he went along. He always did this, because he always had, even if, as with the preliminary sweep of MacIlwraith's house, there was very little to report.

'The only potentially useful thing, so far as connecting the suspect to the murder is concerned, is the cardboard box with Cyrillic script that appears to have contained

Pentothal, one of the drugs used to kill Keller. The SOCOs found it behind a chest of drawers. Keller says he knows nothing about it, which is a bit odd, given that it's got his fingerprints on it. We also found a couple of surgical syringes, but they'd been cleaned and wiped. No prints, no residues.'

'Phones and computers?', DS Sara Hamilton asked.

'We got three disposable phones from MacIlwraith's place and' -- he looked to Vanessa for confirmation -- two from Mathieson's. Three of them -- two of MacIlwraith's and one of Mathieson's -- had calls and texts to the same number. The boss thinks it's likely that we've found that burner in MacIver's flat.'

Vanessa looked at Dongle Donaldson, who smiled and said, 'Right on the money, boss. We recovered two burners and a BlackBerry from MacIver's place. The Blackberry was issued to him by the Scottish Government, so is unlikely to incriminate him, but we're analysing it anyway. One of the burners is certainly the number that the texts and calls Colin mentioned went to. MacIver seems to have been more careful than the others: all texts had been deleted and the call logs erased.'

'So that connects MacIver to the others, but not directly to the murders.' Vanessa said. 'We need more and, at the risk of being boringly repetitive, we still need motive.'

'What else did you find at MacIver's place?' DC Duncan Williamson, like his colleague, DC Stewart Todd, was a bit pissed off not to have been more directly involved in the arrests, and was determined to contribute something to the investigation.

Vanessa was sensitive to the need to be inclusive in the interests of staff morale. 'Sorry you and Stewart have been a bit deskbound on this one, Duncan, but one of the purposes of this meeting is to allow those of you who've not been directly involved to look at what we've got and, I hope, point to things we may have missed by being too close.'

Esslemont looked impressed by the management style that lay behind Vanessa's response, but said nothing.

'As well as his burners, three of them, we found two laptops, now in Dongle's custody for analysis, one Scottish government issue, one not. Also, some bank statements, showing unidentified substantial deposits to an account different from the one that his salary goes into.'

'Didn't I see in the case logs something to the effect that neither of the other two suspects has, to use an old-fashioned phrase, any visible means of support? No job. No benefits.'

'That's right. And we need to know who's been subsidising them.'

'Maybe MacIver's been bankrolling them from the mystery deposits to his second account. How can we find out?'

'Good thinking, Duncan', Vanessa said, deciding not to mention that her mind had been going in the same direction. 'Speculative, but interesting. I think we may have to call Andy Hanna in again. That kind of forensic financial investigation is laborious and time-consuming and needs real expertise. I've also got a residual concern about the position of Burtonhall in all this. I don't think they're entirely off the hook, so Andy might be able to help with that, too.'

'What about all that sophisticated computer hardware you found in Mathieson's flat, boss? Do we know any more?' This was Colin MacNee.   'Weren't we supposed to have a full report from Strathclyde by the time you got back from Edinburgh?'

'We were. But it's taking a bit longer than they thought. Apparently, they need to see the laptop that Dongle's been analysing. They think that Mathieson may have had it configured to control the other computers and hard disks he had and that might have given him the capacity to launch pretty damaging cyber attacks. As soon as we're done here, a car is going to Glasgow with the laptop. They hope to get a report to me by early tomorrow. With a bit of luck, not to mention the persuasive skills of the DCS, we can arrange for Andy Hanna to bring the laptop back when he comes to rejoin the team.'

*

As they walked towards the interview room to question Inspector Richard Fleming not long after she had got back from Edinburgh that morning, Vanessa shared with Esslemont her developing thinking about Fleming's motive for passing confidential information to Gilbertson.

'I really don't think he was doing it for the money, sir. I think he may have been buying affection.'

Vanessa had often wondered what the phrase "looking askance" meant. Esslemont's reaction told her. His face showed disbelief and horror.

'Do you mean his relationship with Gilbertson was sexual? Is Fleming gay?'

'Not openly. But there are rumours, and nobody here, or in Stonehaven, where he lives, remembers him having a girlfriend. He lives a pretty solitary life and, sadly, given what's about to happen, he was dedicated to the job, and ambitious with it.'

'What about Gilbertson?'

'Nothing known. My guess is that he was in it for the money, selling information first to Mancuso, then to Eisner and finally, when he got greedy, to Jason Sime at the *G & T.'*

'Can you prove that?'

'Not yet. Not ever, in Sime's case. He'll never reveal his source. But we might crack Mancuso and Eisner. If either of them gives up Gilbertson, we can probably get a confession out of Fleming.'

*

Although the emails posted on the Hedelco website revealed no motive for murder, they confirmed that Keller had serious concerns about how the management of various procedures and processes at GRH, including those that Janet MacNee had speculated about - diagnostic procedures, usage of operating theatres, and laboratory procedures - might affect patients. In his reports on all of these, as well as on contract management, Keller had urged Hedelco to ensure that the risk assessment process properly considered the possibility of adverse effects on patients and the outcomes of their care.

In one of the decrypted emails, Keller had said:

> *I have found no conclusive evidence that patient care has been compromised. However, there is a danger that the pressure on unit costs that characterises the management of*

the hospital, will affect the capacity of clinical staff to offer the standard of care that is implicit in the outcome targets set for GRH by NHS Scotland.

That had been enough to produce *"Patients at risk at privatised hospital?"* headlines in two of the Scottish tabloids. There were also more thoughtful pieces in the broadsheets about the ability of the Scottish Government to guarantee the quality of care in hospitals that it had decided to have managed by private companies.

Within twenty-four hours of the emails becoming public the Government, through its independent inspectorates, responded. As Bernard Donovan had forecast to Jack Eisner, both Health Improvement Scotland and the Health and Safety Executive announced snap inspections at GRH. Damage to the reputations of Hedelco and Burtonhall had been limited. The focus now shifted to senior politicians, principally the First Minister and the Health Secretary. Their ability to maintain the confidence of the public in their stewardship of the Health Service was on the line. They found themselves, quite suddenly, as a direct result of a criminal investigation that they were even less able to influence than was generally the case, at the centre of a political and media storm.

*

By the time the team meeting ended, late in the afternoon, Vanessa was exhausted and ready to go home. She had been up since 3.00 am, had been to Edinburgh and back, arrested the First Minister's special adviser, interviewed both Mathieson and MacIver about the murders, and joined the DCS in a brief and inconclusive interview of Inspector Richard Fleming. She had negotiated another two-week secondment of DI Andy Hanna from Strathclyde and discussed with the Procurator Fiscal the possibility of further charges against the three arrested men.

She needed some time to think and she needed to talk to Neil about the financial aspects of the case: where MacIlwraith and Mathieson got the money to live on, where the substantial deposits to MacIver's account had come from, and the possible consequences for Hedelco, and Ebright, of the reports that Keller and Jamieson had sent back to the US. The trading position of these companies might turn out to be irrelevant to the murders, but with press, political and public interest in Last and Mercury showing no signs of diminishing, Vanessa wasn't yet ready to park it. Neil's insights into the financial world had been useful at the start of the investigation. They might be again.

For now, she needed a good night's sleep, preceded, perhaps, by a light meal out with Neil, and some gentle, unhurried sex. As she got into the car beside Sara Hamilton, who had volunteered to drive her home, she smiled at the curious mixture she felt of fatigue and sexiness.

CHAPTER EIGHTEEN

'It's going to be really difficult to find out where the money was coming from. I did a case once down south that involved illicit deposits to an account in a British bank. We managed to trace it back to an account in the some overseas tax haven – the Cayman Islands, I think – but we never identified the account holder, just a shell company with nominee directors.'

Neil and Vanessa were having breakfast on Thursday morning, a day after MacIver's arrest. Vanessa was feeling refreshed after her first good night's sleep of the week and, as she sipped her peppermint tea, she felt less queasy than she had for some time. She would have to brief Andy Hanna, who was arriving from Glasgow on an early train, so she was picking Neil's brain on the various financial loose ends that she wanted to tie up.

Neil poured himself a second cup of coffee. 'Mind you, we were using private investigators and forensic accountants. You may have more luck, with the full might and majesty of the law behind you.'

Vanessa snorted. 'Much good the might and majesty did me when I was trying to get these emails out of Hedelco. It was the press wot done it, in the end. And I'm not sure our interest in Burtonhall, Hedelco and Ebright is over now that the emails are out. Talk me through the possibilities for Burtonhall of what the two victims found.'

'Well, at the most strategic level, for a private equity company like Burtonhall, the two possibilities are investment or disinvestment, to hang in there or to sell up and invest the proceeds elsewhere. Because Hedelco holds a major contract with the government, selling the company on could be complicated. It might, depending on the terms of the contract, require the consent of the government. Ebright's simpler. It's wholly private sector and, because oil is a long term business, finding a speculative buyer, which is what Burtonhall was when they bought it, might be easier.'

'I know its not your area of expertise, but can you see the politics of this? I know the government will take flak on the effects of privatisation on the NHS, but in the cut and thrust of Holyrood, that's business as usual. Is there anything else? And is there anything that might link the politics of Burtonhall and its subsidiaries, to Last and Mercury?'

'Christ, Vanessa, I'm glad you didn't start on this last night. It would have put me right off!'

She smiled a contented smile. 'Glad I didn't. But I'm asking you now.'

'The common thread is inward investment and the effect that has on the Scottish economy. Ministers are likely to be very nervous about anything that puts that at risk. Worst case analysis? If Last, Mercury and Burtonhall all decided to pull out, or even to delay or curtail investment, it wouldn't be good for business confidence, and it would turn the spotlight on the government's management of the economy. And, in the run-up to the referendum, anything concerning the North Sea is really touchy. That, my darling, is the limit of my knowledge. If I think of anything else, I'll let you know.'

*

DS Dongle Donaldson was waiting for DCI Fiske when she got to HQ just after eight o'clock.

'Morning, Dongle,' Vanessa said, with only the slightest hint of a smile. 'You're an early bird. I hope this means you've got something for me.'

'Your admin people told me you were usually here by eight, and I have got something, but I'm not sure how important or significant it is. I haven't finished analysing MacIver's laptop – nothing of interest on the government one, by the way – but I've found some stuff that you should see.'

He opened the laptop and booted it up as Vanessa pulled up a chair beside him.

'He's a got a number of email accounts, mainly freebies – live.com, Hotmail, Googlemail and others - and one of them, damascus@easymail.com, seems to have been used to exchange emails with only one address: mike@exflt.com.'

'Fancies himself, doesn't he?' Vanessa said. Dongle looked puzzled. 'Paul? Damascus? Didn't you do RE at school?'

'Oh. Yeah. I see. But what's really interesting is that all the messages to and from mike@exflt.com are in code. Not encrypted like Jamieson and Keller, but not in clear either. I haven't broken it yet, but it doesn't look very difficult. It's alphanumeric – with numbers or groups of numbers representing letters and words. It's the kind of code that people who do really hard crosswords could break. And me, of course. I just wanted to ask if I should do it before I analyse the rest of the hard disk.'

'How long will it take?'

'Couple of hours, maybe. Should have it done by lunchtime, probably earlier.'

'Go for it. I'll be here or hereabouts all day. If you can't get me on the phone, send me a text.'

*

At Grampian Royal Hospital, as the two sets of inspectors tried not to trip over each other and negotiated an agreement to share their findings wherever possible, Bernard Donovan and his 'top team' sat around the Board Room table discussing what Donovan should recommend to head office.

'My instinct', Donovan said, 'is to get ahead of the inspectors. God knows how long it will take them to produce their reports and we are pretty clear from the emails where the problems are likely to be. I'd like to recommend to Caleb that we spend what's necessary to correct the faults. That way, we'll be able to respond to the inspections by saying, "Job Done". But I'll need to put some numbers on it.'

'I'll have to check this with the accountants.' This was David Masur, the Operations Director. 'But my back of an envelope numbers suggest that it will be well into seven figures. Maybe not two mill, but certainly well over one. Pounds, not dollars.'

Donovan whistled. The other members of the team studied their papers.

'That much?' Donovan asked. 'That's enough to put us in the red, at least for this year. Unless we can find a way of booking some of it against future years.'

'If we want to make an impact quickly, to be able to say we're already turning things around, the only way to do it, in all the areas Keller identified, is to take on more staff, or let existing staff do more hours, at overtime rates. That's where the cash goes, Bernard. That's why we've been managing these parts of the business so aggressively. That's why we are where we are.'

Donovan was pretty sure that Caleb Adams, the Hedelco CEO, would see the force of his argument. If there was a problem, it would be with Cy Packard at Burtonhall.

*

DCI Fiske had decided that none of the suspects should be interviewed again until she, MacNee and Esslemont had seen the full analysis of the computer hard disks and a report from the SOCOs on the evidence collected from Paul MacIver's flat. That left her with some time that she could use to try to draw a line under the distraction of the Fleming affair. She left a message with Esslemont's office to let him know she was going to talk to Jack Eisner and Frank Mancuso, requested a car from the pool, and drove first to Ebright's offices just off the Inverness Road.

'Thank you for agreeing to see me, Mr Eisner.'

'Pleasure. But, as ever, I don't know if I'll be able to help.'

'We'll see.' Vanessa smiled in away that she hoped was ironic. 'Perhaps we can work on the assumption that we both know that you obtained confidential information about my investigation. I need to know, entirely off the record, and for reasons internal to the force, where that information came from.'

Eisner looked Vanessa straight in the eyes and said, 'After that email fiasco, my boss, Cy Packard, sent out a note, to me, Tammy and Bernard Donovan, telling us that we should be as co-operative as possible with what he called "the local authorities". That includes you, Chief Inspector, but it does not oblige me to incriminate third parties.'

'Fair enough. What can you tell me?'

'Cy wanted me to try to get an inside track on your enquiries. I received a cellphone number on my burner. I reached an agreement with someone I've never met and that person provided me with some useful information.'

'I'm guessing you're not going to give me the name of your initial contact, but is there any reason not to give me the phone number?'

'Can't think of one.' Eisner reached into a drawer and took out a disposable phone, turned it on, wrote down a number and passed it to Fiske.

'Can we have an off-the-record conversation about what Packard thinks of what's been going on here with GRH and Vermont One?'

Eisner laughed. 'What does "off-the-record" mean in this context?'

'It means the conversation didn't take place and if anything it contains helps my enquiries it will do so in ways that only I will know about. Intuition always has a place in detective work.'

'OK. You're obviously aware that Burtonhall is in any business to make money and make it quickly. You've had financial experts crawling all over Hedelco and Ebright and it's no secret that, as of now, these businesses are marginal. Right at the start of this, Cy said to me that it wouldn't take much to push them into the red. I think he's now beginning to believe that the murders were the push. But he's got no idea why or who.'

'Cui bono?'' Vanessa thought. *'Cui bono?'*

'Thank you, Mr Eisner. I don't think I'll have to speak to you again.'

'Glad to hear it. I'm flying to Washington tomorrow afternoon.'

*

Frank Mancuso seemed rather less relaxed than Jack Eisner, probably because he wasn't leaving the area.

'How can I help, Chief Inspector?'

'We both know that for some time you've had access to confidential information from NEC HQ, going right back to the demonstrations against the Last Cairngorm development. I need to know who was your source. No. Let me be more direct. I need you to confirm that your source was Martin Gilbertson, Mid-Aberdeenshire's PR man.'

Mancuso said nothing.

Vanessa took out of her bag the piece of paper Eisner had given her. 'If I call that number, how likely is it that Gilbertson will pick up? Shall I try?'

Mancuso still said nothing. But he had gone very pale.

*

Donovan's conclusions were in Caleb Adams' inbox when he arrived at Hedelco HQ in Boston at 0730 hrs Eastern Time. Masur and the number crunchers at GRH had refined the figures and the recommended additional expenditure was £1.8m in the current year and over £3m in a full year. Fancy accountancy might spread some of this over several financial years, but it was clear that Hedelco would be losing money on the GRH contract for some time.

Adams spent a couple of hours going over the figures with his chief financial officer. They managed to trim the numbers marginally, but every time they tried to cut more deeply the risk profile changed to a point where the management at the hospital would be unable to say that they were dealing adequately with the recommendations expected from the inspectors. Hedelco's final recommendations went off to Packard at 1100 hrs ET / 1600 hrs GMT.

*

'How soon can we get Fleming in here?' Vanessa Fiske had gone straight to Esslemont when she got back from Last Cairngorm.

'I'll get Caitlin to phone his solicitor. I told him to be available at short notice, so I think he could be here this morning. What have you got?'
'Enough.'

'Enough for what?' The DCS was showing some signs of irritation at the lack of detail.

'Enough to get a confession, and probably a resignation, out of Fleming. Possibly enough to charge Gilbertson, though I'll have to talk to Fiona about what we can do him for.'

'What's the hurry, Vanessa? We need to deal with it, but we've got more important things on the go.'

'Exactly, sir. It's a distraction. I want it off my desk as soon as possible.'

*

'I can't tell you who <u>mike@cxflt.com</u> is, but I can tell you what MacIver was exchanging emails with him about.' Dongle Donaldson had his own laptop open on the conference room table beside MacIver's. 'Some of it's technical, some of it's economics, and a lot of it's political. And all of it's about American companies in Scotland.'

'Really?' DCI Fiske moved to stand behind Dongle so that she could see both screens. 'Have you transcribed them all?'

'If you look at MacIver's laptop, all you'll see, in every email, in and out, is a series of groups of numbers. If you look at mine, you'll see what I've made of them. Before I started I made copies, so that for evidence purposes I could give the originals and the deciphered versions compatible and recognisable reference numbers. The originals have a number followed by the letters "AC", for alphanumeric code. The deciphered versions have the same numbers but with the letters "DC", for deciphered.'

Vanessa laughed. 'Your sense of humour's quite near the surface, isn't it?'

'Yeah! I like a bit of fun. But it's clear and logical. A jury will love it.'

'A bit early for that, but let's have a look.'

Vanessa began to read the first exchange. mike@exflt.com appeared to be following up on a casual meeting with MacIver and was asking his views on the financial performance of American companies that had recently invested in Scotland. MacIver's response struck Vanessa as guarded, as though he was trying to establish the nature of his correspondent's interest.

'Before we go any further,' Vanessa asked, 'How would they have known what code to use, if this was the first exchange?'

'No idea, boss. No evidence. Could have been set up by text, or even, God help us, by snail mail. But if you put "How to encode messages" into a search engine, you'll be surprised at what comes up.'

There were a lot of emails, more than thirty, and Vanessa had time only to scan them quickly before going to talk to Fiona Marchmont about what she might charge Martin Gilbertson with, and then making the arrest. A quick scan was enough to give her the flavour. The exchanges had moved quite quickly – the emails had all been sent over a period of just under six months – from generalities about inward investment to discussions about how disruption to operations might affect measures of economic performance and, from there, to questions of the political repercussions. The latest emails seemed explicitly to link economic disruption to perceptions about the independence referendum, and MacIver seemed to take a view very different from that of his boss, not least in his willingness to consider what Dongle had deciphered, probably accurately, as "direct action", to achieve his ends. Perhaps, Vanessa thought, MacIver had not moved far from his days in the Scottish Freedom Party, or if he had, not in the direction that his public role suggested.

*

Despite Harvey Jamieson's concerns, no official inspections had been ordered on Vermont One. Ironically, given Tammy Wootten's efforts to get Jamieson's laptop back from the police, his emails had not become public. Ebright had all the messages that had been sent before the day of Jamieson's death. DCI Fiske and her team had them too, as well as the drafts that remained unsent on the hard disk.

The Hedelco case, and the release of the Keller emails, had caused Ebright's risk assessment staff to get senior management approval to send copies of the emails to Wootten, with a request for her recommendations. She reacted in the same way as Bernard Donovan at GRH. In the two major areas of concern - the high risk strategy of running some key components to failure, and the possible corner-cutting on health and safety, money would need to be spent, more on the early maintenance or replacement of sophisticated equipment than on improving the largely statutory aspects of health and safety. This would forestall the certain reputational damage and the possible negative financial consequences for Ebright of a snap inspection by the Health and Safety Executive and perhaps a temporary shutdown of the platform.

Wootten's strategy was to counteract the negative press reports about the performance of Vermont One, especially those by Ben Aaronson in the *Financial Post*, by demonstrating that local management was on top of any problems that the inspection by Jamieson might have uncovered. Ebright's management in the United States quickly approved her recommendations and passed them on to Burtonhall.

They arrived on Cy Packard's dcsk on the same day as Hedelco's recommendations on

GRH. Almost simultaneously, and in a way that made even an aggressive and unsentimental manager like Packard feel embattled, a long analysis piece by Aaronson cast doubt on the ability of Ebright to maintain the profitability of Vermont One in the face of the recent steady decline in the spot price of Brent Crude and the more serious forward prediction of further drops. Packard was looking at two loss making businesses in the Burtonhall portfolio. He hadn't seen that before and he was already calculating the possible effect on his annual bonus. He decided to talk to his Chairman and began to make contingency plans for an emergency board meeting.

*

'Sara, I need you to come with me to Mid-Aberdeenshire Council. I'll brief you on the way.'

DCI Fiske had just come from the office of DCS Esslemont where she had got his approval to arrest Gilbertson. They had decided to bring him in before they talked again to Richard Fleming. If Gilbertson was in custody it was more likely that Fleming would confess. Fiona Marchmont had eventually been persuaded that they had enough to bring Gilbertson in, but she made it very clear that Vanessa should try to persuade him to put his hands up.

'The PF will say that what you've got is pretty thin and may not sanction charges, but it's worth a punt.'

When they got to the council offices, they went straight to the annex where Fiske had met Gilbertson on her previous visit. Once again, the young woman who responded to the entry phone kept them waiting while she went to see if Mr Gilbertson was available. The fact that Vanessa and Sara were police officers cut no ice. She had her instructions. Like many members of the PR profession, her boss did a nice line in non-communication.

'Mr Gilbertson, I need to speak to you privately. This is my colleague, Detective Sergeant Sara Hamilton.'

He led them to the room with the wafer-thin walls where Vanessa had spoken to him the last time she had come to the council offices.

'How can I help?'

'Martin Gilbertson, I'm arresting you on suspicion of conspiring to commit corruption in public office.'

Gilbertson tried not to react, but the deliberateness with which sat down at his desk proved an inadequate cover for his obvious shock. He listened while Vanessa cautioned him and checked that he had understood. He nodded and began to speak.

Fiske interrupted. 'Please be careful, Mr Gilbertson, what I've just said is serious. DS Hamilton is here to make a verbatim note and you may be asked to sign it to confirm accuracy and timing.'

'I understand that, but there's some things you need to know.'

'I'm sure there are, but, believe me, it would be in your best interests to save them until we get to an interview room and you have consulted a solicitor.'

'But I know who planned the bombing.'

*

'Richard, we have Martin Gilbertson in custody on suspicion of conspiring to commit corruption in public office.' Vanessa paused to let the information sink in. 'I don't have to tell you that conspiracy is never a solitary crime.'

Fleming said nothing. He looked at his solicitor, who nodded.

'I would like to make a full statement. I shall also be resigning from the police service with immediate effect.'

DCS Esslemont leaned towards Fleming and looked straight into his face. 'You know that resignation will make disciplinary action against you impossible, but not criminal charges.'

'I'm aware of that, sir, and if I'm charged, I intend to plead guilty in the hope of reducing the penalty. Is also wish to co-operate fully with your enquiries.'

After Fleming had given a full account of his relationship with Gilbertson, which he insisted had not been sexual, Vanessa asked him if there was anything else.

'Such as?'

'Such as information going in the other direction, from Gilbertson to you, about matters of current interest to us.'

'I'm not sure I know what you're talking about, Chief Inspector.'

Vanessa was in no mood to be pissed about. 'Come off it! You're still a police officer and, until just a few days ago, you were in a very privileged position. You knew - you know - exactly what's going on here and I need to know if anything of interest to us came out of your relationship' - she tried to keep her use of the word neutral - 'with Martin Gilbertson.'

Fleming turned to his lawyer and they had a very brief, whispered conversation after which the lawyer asked if he could have a few minutes alone with his client.

Fiske and Esslemont left the interview room and, after telling the uniformed constable who was sitting outside to come and fetch them when Fleming and his lawyer were done, they went to the canteen.

Esslemont bought a coffee and a fizzy water and they found a table. 'What do you think?'

Vanessa sipped her drink. 'He's got something, sir. He's talking to his brief about how much it might buy him.'

'Any idea what?'

'Not really. But if you forced me, as Harry Conival might say, to choose a horse and put money on it, I'd go for the Mancuso connection.'

*

When the interview resumed, Fleming described an occasion in the *Dunottar Castle*, after a quiz night, when Frank Mancuso had too much to drink and began to talk about the 'big names' who had taken an interest in Last Cairngorm.

'I wasn't surprised to hear him talking about the First Minister, given her constituency responsibilities. And there were a lot of local celebrities - I'll give you a list if you need it - both for and against the development, and local politicians, local government people and police officers he claimed to have good relationships with. But then he began to hint about major international figures who had been, as he put it, "sniffing around". He was trying to be very discreet, or maybe very mysterious, but then he went to the bar and spent some time teaching the licensee how to make a Whisky sour. He came back with a very large glass. I think it tipped him over the edge.'

'Into what?' Fiske was becoming impatient. This was taking some time to get off her desk.

'Real indiscretion. The sort you get from someone who wants to impress.'

'Who was he trying to impress?'

'Difficult to say. Maybe me because of my closeness to the Chief. Maybe Martin as payback for the information he had supplied.' 'And that you had supplied to him.' This was Esslemont, who was equally irritated by the slow progress of the interview.

'Yes, and all of that will be in my statement. But Mancuso started talking about an old friend who worked for a huge American conglomerate and all the major political figures he knew.'

'Go on.'

'He then leaned forward, in a kind of cod conspiratorial way, and said that he was expecting a visit from people connected with a very important person. By this time, Martin and I were getting pretty fed up and Martin said Frank had had enough, took his keys off him, and asked the landlord to call him a taxi.'

'That's it?'

'Not quite. He became pretty incoherent, rambling on about his time in the FBI, contacts with the CIA, his closeness to Ewan Last - I didn't believe that - and then, as he staggered into his taxi, he leaned very close to me and Martin. We were more or less carrying him. He said just one word.'

'What was it?', Vanessa asked.

'Roskill.'

CHAPTER NINETEEN

'The deposits to MacIver's account came from a bank in the British Virgin Islands. Difficult to impossible to find the true identity of the account holder. BVI is a tax haven, highly secretive and if you set up an account there you don't want anyone to know it's yours.' DI Andy Hanna paused, just long enough to allow DCI Fiske to speak.

'So you set up a shell company with nominee directors and work out a way to give them instructions and pay them fees.'

'Very good, boss. Been doing your homework?'

'I have a live-in tutor. But if I wanted to set up that kind of account, where would I get the nominee directors? And how would I know I could trust them?'

'Law firms and accountancy practices in BVI, as in all the tax havens, offer nominee director services. They charge the kind of fees that only the seriously rich and the seriously criminal will pay and their business depends on absolute discretion and trust. The only industry in these places is looking after money for people who don't want anybody, especially the tax authorities, to know they've got it or where they've stashed it.'

'Can you try to find out who's using the account?'

'I can try, but I don't hold out much hope. I'll talk to some people in London, but if you've any other way in, you should use it.'

'What about the payments to MacIlwraith and Mathieson?'

'Better news there. The money came from MacIver, all right, but he tried to disguise the fact that he was sending it. A sum equivalent to the two payments went, from the same account that received the BVI money, by standing order each month, to an account in the name of the "SF Club". Apart from payments to MacIlwraith and Mathieson, and deposits to cover them, the account has been dormant for years. The signatories are MacIver and somebody called Morven Trask, but there's no evidence that she's had anything to do with the account in the last five years. I didn't go back any further than that. It's common practice for an account in the name of an organisation rather than an individual to have more than one signatory, with each signatory authorised to make transactions. Payments to MacIlwraith and Mathieson were made, by monthly standing order, from that account. It's not very sophisticated as a way of covering his tracks, but MacIver clearly didn't want people to know where the money was coming from.'

'Morven Trask? That name rings a bell.'

She turned to her computer and put the name into a search engine. 'She was a Nationalist MSP until the last election. Stood down to work full time for the Independence side in the referendum campaign. Almost exactly the same age as MacIver. He probably knew her at university. We'll have to talk to her'.

'There's one more thing, boss. The deposits from the BVI account only started about six months ago. MacIlwraith and Mathieson have been receiving deposits for a lot longer, at least three years, but for much smaller amounts.'

*

'Duncan, how do you and Stewart fancy a trip to Edinburgh?'

DC Duncan Williamson looked up from his computer. 'I'm up for it, boss, even though I know that there's only one answer to a question like that.' He grinned at Vanessa. 'Stewart will feel the same. What do you want us to do?'

'Andy Hanna's come up with a piece of information that may or may not be important. I want you two to find out which it is. Get a hold of Stewart and come and see me and I'll give you a briefing.'

*

'Right, Dongle. Let's hear what you've got from the laptops. We'll do MacIlwraith first, then Mathieson, then MacIver.'

'Thanks, boss. MacIlwraith's was the simplest. He's not the brightest wire on the circuit board, so he hadn't done much, effectively nothing, to cover his tracks. The search history brought up an impressive number of porn sites, a couple of dating sites...'

'Sad bastard!' Colin MacNee could be quite Presbyterian and judgmental. It didn't sit well with his generally liberal and relaxed attitude to other people's lives. Vanessa put it down to his having daughters.

'Go on,' she said, with a sideways glance at Colin.

'He's done a lot of research on lethal drug cocktails and on where he might get the ingredients. Visits to a number of sites in Eastern Europe enquiring about Pentothal and potassium chloride. He eventually ordered enough to kill, from a company in Russia - Ekaterinburg - and paid in Bitcoins. I guess he must have had help to set that up.'

'Probably from Mathieson', MacNee said. 'Was there anything on the box we found at MacIlwraith's to suggest where it came from in Russia?'

'I don't think so.' DC Aisha Gajani said. 'But it may have had the name of the manufacturer. We could locate it from that.'

'That would firm up the circumstantial a bit.' This was Esslemont.

Dongle looked to Fiske to see if he should continue. She nodded.

'Also, our boy had been raking around for instructions in bomb making. Mainly radical Islamic sites, but also some in the USA. He had even downloaded and saved some recipes. As I said, not very bright.'

'Let's get that to the Last investigation team. We need to know if any of the "recipes"' - Vanessa shook her head at the word - 'matches what they know about the Cairngorm bomb. Mathieson?'

'Almost nothing. He applied online for Nuttall's birth certificate, but we probably knew that already. No porn, no evidence of suspicious interests. Lots of traffic to legitimate sites - online magazines and blogs - dedicated to the Scottish nationalist cause.'

'The Strathclyde hi-tech squad have confirmed that his laptop was configured to control the various other computers and hard disks that we found in his flat. He had the capacity to mount the kind of cyber attack that crippled Mercury, but there's no conclusive evidence that he did it. They're still working on it.'

'Might take a while.' Dongle said.

'That's it?' Vanessa asked.

'Pretty much. If I dig up anything else I'll let you know.'

'What about MacIver?'

'He's been very careful. Nothing of interest on his government-issue laptop, but there's something, or possibly nothing, on his personal laptop. Over a short period, about five, six months ago, he did a fair bit of research into a number of international organisations - I think they're called NGOs, Non-Governmental Organisations - and charitable foundations. All working in the countries of the former Soviet Union, mainly in Central Asia. Doing good works, education, medical aid, development.'

'Doesn't sound directly relevant to any of our investigations.' Colin was itching to get back to some old-fashioned police work, like interviewing suspects, and he was showing some impatience with Dongle's laid back style.

'Maybe not, directly. But then I had a closer look at the sites. All of these organisations are connected to James Roskill. Most of them were set up by him or by the foundations and trusts that he's set up.'

'The ex-prime minister?' Aisha Gajani asked. 'I remember him from when I was a student. Went on a few demos against wars in Central Asia. Before I had to police them...I remember placards that said "RosKILL", with "KILL" in capital letters.'

DCI Fiske suppressed her interest. 'Might be worth a closer look. Let me have a list of the organisations with their URLs. Next meeting tomorrow, same time. Sir, can I have a few minutes?' Esslemont nodded. 'Colin, would you join us, please?'

*

'I'm really not sure what to make of this, sir, if anything.' Fiske was sitting beside Colin MacNee, facing Esslemont across his desk. 'I was a bit thrown, as you probably were, by that stuff about MacIver researching Roskill's good works, given what Fleming told us about Mancuso's drunken ramblings.'
She turned to MacNee. 'Sorry, Colin, I haven't had a chance to tell you about our latest interview of Richard Fleming.' She gave him a brief account of what Fleming had said. He nodded and took some notes.

'I'm going to spend some time this evening looking at the sites Dongle mentioned to see if anything leaps out at me. But if Roskill turns out to be of interest to this investigation, we'll have another layer of politics to deal with. I'd like to keep this between ourselves for now. If we decide to go any further with it, we'll have to brief the Chief.'

*

Esslemont had decided that less damage would be done to the force if they announced the charges against Richard Fleming quickly. The statement would also say that he had resigned from the police service with immediate effect. Vanessa Fiske's remark to Fleming that conspiracy was never a solitary crime made it inevitable that they would also announce the charges against Gilbertson. They decided to withhold the news until the men had appeared in court and been formally charged and released. That way, there was at least a chance that Fleming and Gilbertson could avoid the press and the photographers.

Harry Conival cobbled together a pretty anodyne press release and sent it out just in time to miss the main evening news bulletins. The release didn't say specifically that the charges related to the same offences, but that was a tiny piece of obfuscation that no hack more senior than a copy boy, or whatever the equivalent was in the digital world, would have any trouble with.

As expected, Harry's phone started to ring within minutes of the emailed press release going out. The questions were all about how the arrests and charges related to the murders and to the investigations at Last and Mercury.

Harry had agreed a line with Fiske - 'The offences came to light in the course of other enquiries' – that said everything and nothing, but it might keep some of the hacks happy until the next press briefing.

Jason Sime of the *G & T* was the first to ask the direct question that joined the dots. 'What's the connection between Fleming and Gilbertson and the head of security at Last Cairngorm, Frank Mancuso? They know each other, don't they?'

'No idea, mate.' Harry said, unconvincingly. 'I'll pass your enquiry on.'

'Who to?'

'DCI Fiske.'

'What about the anti-terrorism boys?

'I don't work for them,' Harry said, as he grabbed his cigarettes and headed towards Vanessa's office.

*

DCI Fiske spent an hour, late in the afternoon following the team meeting, looking at the Roskill websites that Dongle had identified from the recovered search history on MacIver's laptop. Most of them were promotional, describing the charitable foundations that Roskill had set up after he resigned as prime minister and left parliament. There were many examples of the good work being undertaken by NGOs and charities that he supported, either through his foundations, or in a personal capacity, as a board member or trustee. Almost all of them worked extensively, and some of them exclusively, in Central Asia. Conscience money, Vanessa thought.

Some of the sites reproduced articles about Roskill and his work for the foundations and other bodies. Their content was mainly related to the parts of the world where the work was being done, with only rare excursions into domestic political issues. The exception was the website of *The James M Roskill Public Affairs Trust*, an online archive of Roskill's public statements and press articles. Most of these related to his overseas work. A few were excursions into domestic politics. Only one was relevant to Vanessa's enquiries.

Just about six months before the murders (Vanessa was, as usual, relating everything to the date of the crimes under investigation), Roskill had given an interview to an international business magazine. The subject matter was wide-ranging, covering the domestic and foreign policies of his successors and trying, not altogether successfully, to avoid backseat driving. There was one passage, however, that changed Vanessa's approach from skimming to careful reading.

Roskill had been asked about the likelihood of Scotland voting to leave the United Kingdom and, after reviewing the state of public opinion on constitutional change, he turned to the economic effects of the uncertainty leading up to the referendum.

The independence campaign is majoring on the fact that, by their measures, Scotland's economy is performing better than the UK. However, if the performance of enterprises in Scotland, particularly those that depend on foreign capital, were to decline sharply, or if foreign companies withdrew or delayed investment, the terms of the independence debate would change. It could go either way: it could make people more defensive about Scotland's future and so more inclined to support independence; or it could make them more nervous and inclined to see the bigger UK economy as a safety net for companies operating in Scotland. I think the former is more likely.

Vanessa emailed the link to the article to MacNee and Esslemont.

*

DCI Fiske was just about to leave for the day when she took a call from DCC Chris Jenkinson, whom she hadn't seen since the evening of the WPNS meeting in Perth.

'Hi, Vanessa. I hear it's twins. Clever girl! Get it all over in one go, one pregnancy, one maternity leave. Couldn't be better! Would you like to have that discussion soon?'

'In principle, yes. But I've been trying not to think about it until this double murder enquiry is over.'

'But I knew you had made the arrests. That's why I decided to phone you. Is there a problem?'

'Not as such. I'm sure we've got the right people in custody, and we may even lay some more charges. It's just that it's kind of grown legs. You'll know it's already a bit political. Might be about to become more so. The DCS, Colin MacNee and I may have to have a session with the Chief tomorrow.'

'Possibly not the best day. The Justice Secretary is announcing who's got the top job at a press conference in Edinburgh at noon. I'd get in before that, if you can.'

'Understood! Can I get in touch when things are less fraught? I need to think about how I should plan things, and a chat with you will help to clear my head.'

'Fine. Look forward to it. Oh, and it would be nice to meet Neil some time. Come to dinner one weekend, when my husband's here.'

*

'Not the Cayman Islands, my sweet, the British Virgin Islands.'

Vanessa was hanging up her coat and shouting to Neil, who was searing a couple of salmon steaks, and, at more or less the same time, trimming some asparagus spears.

'That's where the money was coming from, a shell company with nominee directors, just as you said. Andy Hanna's trying to find out who really owns the account, but he's not very hopeful.'

'Nor should he be. Tax havens rely on secrecy. BVI, though, has been the target of a lot of investigative journalism, mainly about very rich expats avoiding tax, but if any big names had come up, we'd know.'

'What if the name was Roskill? Would that have made a headline?'

'Oh, I think so! Is that who you think was paying MacIver? But why?'

'I'm working on that. But if any of your old mates at Canary Wharf can help, I'd appreciate it. I have sexual favours to offer!'

She put her arms round Neil's neck and kissed him.

'I get them anyway…unless you're offering them to my old mates at Canary Wharf…'

A look was enough.

'As it happens, I spoke to one of the said mates today. I asked him if there was any unusual activity on the shell company front and he said that there's a rumour doing the rounds of the City to the effect that Roskill has been setting up companies and registering them abroad. He didn't know how many, and he didn't know where. Odd though that Roskill's name should cross both our desks on the same day.'

'Yes, it is. And I don't believe in coincidence, as you know. Now, serendipity, that's a whole other ball of wax. I need to phone Andy Hanna.'

*

Vanessa had arranged for Colin MacNee to join her at a meeting with Esslemont at nine o'clock on Friday morning and had asked the DCS to make a provisional arrangement to see the Chief Constable as soon as possible after their discussion. When she told Colin about the meetings, he had asked if he could have a discussion with her before they saw Esslemont. He was waiting for her when she got to HQ.

They collected coffees from the canteen and as they were walking back to Vanessa's office, she asked Colin what was on his mind.

'Roskill. But I need a whiteboard before we talk about him.'

Colin stood beside the small whiteboard in Vanessa's office, armed with a selection of coloured markers.

'Let's look at how many times Roskill's name has come up since the murders. As soon as we linked Vermont One and GRH to Burtonhall, we learned, from Neil in the first instance I think, that he's on Burtonhall's board. Then you approached the Foreign

Office for help in getting the emails. Sir Justin Carey, the Permanent Secretary, questions your need to see them and he's very close to Roskill. You suspected that Roskill had approached Carey twice – before you went to the FO and after you planted the story that nailed Fleming. Then we find that he's a non-exec on the board of Mercury Fulfilment, and Mancuso, albeit pissed, says he's showing an interest in Last Cairngorm. Dongle finds that MacIver's been researching Roskill's activities. Then you come up with that quote from him about how disinvestment by foreign companies might affect the independence debate. I think all that makes him a person of interest to us. We need to talk to him.'

'You're probably right. And there's more. The money that was paid into MacIver's account, and then passed on to MacIlwraith and Mathieson, came from an account in the British Virgin Islands. The account is controlled by a company registered in BVI and run by nominee directors. However, we don't know who's behind it. But Neil got a tip from a pal in the City yesterday to the effect that Roskill's rumoured to be setting up shell companies and registering them abroad. And you know how I feel about coincidence!'

Colin returned to the whiteboard. 'I've been thinking about the exchange of coded emails that Dongle found on MacIver's laptop. We know that damascus@easymail.com is MacIver. But we don't know who mike@exflt.com is.'

'I know that look! You've got a theory, haven't you?'

'Yep! I had a look at a biography of Roskill. He's James Michael Roskill, and although he was always know as "James" in public life, to his family and close friends he's "Mike"…'

'Bit of a stretch…'

'Bear with me. The other part of his email address is 'exflt'. It took me some time to come up with this – actually it was when a camera on the news last night zoomed in on the door of 10 Downing Street that I twigged – but the formal title of the PM is "First Lord of the Treasury". "FLT". So I think mike@exflt is Roskill. And the content of the later email exchanges is very close to the stuff in the interview you emailed to me and the DCS.'

'Makes sense to me! We'll have to convince Esslemont. And the Chief's looking at quite a difficult day.'

CHAPTER TWENTY

The First Minister had gone to ground. She hadn't been seen in public since she had answered questions in Parliament on the day of Paul MacIver's arrest. For a politician so determined to be in the papers and on the news as often as feasible, and daily if possible, her invisibility was already causing comment. The press had suggested that she was avoiding questions on the arrest of her closest adviser. She had cancelled a scheduled constituency surgery in Montrose on Saturday, and the Justice Department had said that the announcement of the head of the new unified police force for the whole of Scotland, and the introduction of the appointee to the press, on Friday at noon, would be handled by the Justice Secretary. This was the delivery of one of her government's election promises. Her absence was eloquent.

At noon, in a briefing room in St Andrews House on Edinburgh's Calton Hill, the Justice Secretary announced to a press conference that the Chief Constable of Lothian and Borders Police would be the first Commissioner of the new Scotland-wide force. For a few minutes, after speeches from the minister and the new appointee, the reporters observed the proprieties and addressed their questions to the Commissioner. They were predictable and unchallenging, about crime rates and the possible loss of local responsiveness, the effect of cost-cutting on crime detection and the visibility of the 'bobby on the beat.'

'Kevin Bennett, *Glasgow Banner.'* A shadow of apprehensiveness passed across the face of the Justice Secretary. The new Commissioner looked unconcerned. 'Hedelco, Ebright, Mercury, Last. Major American companies with big investments in Scotland. All targets of major crimes in less than a fortnight. All the good coppers I know don't believe in coincidence. What's your view, Commissioner? And yours, if it comes to it, Minister?'

The two men on the platform looked at each other. The Justice Secretary nodded. The Commissioner rose.

'I can't comment on ongoing enquiries. However, I will say that the creation of a Scotland-wide organisation will improve co-ordination, especially when links emerge between apparently separate crimes.'

Bennett was on his feet before the minister could call anyone else.

'Perhaps the Justice Secretary, who already has a nationwide remit, would care to comment. And while he's at it, he could tell us why the First Minister's not here. Is she afraid she might be asked about Paul MacIver?'

The Justice Secretary looked very uncomfortable and a little shifty.

'It would be inappropriate for me to say anything that might be interpreted as interference in operational policing...'

Sotto voce, a reporter said, to some laughter, 'Christ! He's dipping into the cliché bank!'

'...and we should concentrate here on the delivery of the government's commitment to a Scotland-wide police service.'

'Oh, come off it!' This was Jason Sime of the Aberdeen *Gazette & Times.* He identified himself and went on. 'I've been covering this story since the start and it's turning into the biggest news story Scotland's seen since the children were murdered in Dunblane. And it's as much politics as crime. How can you stand there and refuse to say anything about it?   And what kind of leadership is it that goes into hiding in the face of a developing national scandal?'

The Justice Secretary was gathering up his papers.

'Thank you, ladies and gentlemen.   Further information will be provided by police HQ and, as appropriate, by my office.'

The reporters were already on their phones and laptops, inputting copy for websites and early editions.   The broadcast journalists were facing cameras and microphones on the steps of St Andrews House.   From the Government's perspective, it wouldn't be pretty.

*

DCS Esslemont listened carefully to Fiske and MacNee as they described what they called "the Roskill connection".

'We certainly can't ignore it, but you don't have enough to approach him, much less confront him.   It may be that somewhere in what you've got there's a motive for these murders, and maybe a connection to Last and

Mercury, but you've still got some work to do to stand them up. We'll need to talk to the Chief. There are obvious political ramifications, on top of the fall-out from the MacIver arrest. And there are resource implications, if you're going to have to go to London and, possibly, further afield. If there is a connection to Last and Mercury, this is going to become even bigger than we already expected.'

'Should we see him this morning?' Fiske asked. 'The new Scottish police chief is being announced at noon. If the Chief's here, I assume that it's not going to be him. But it may not be the best time.'

Esslemont smiled sardonically. 'On the contrary! He'll be keen to show that it's business as usual. And an even higher profile for this case might be just what he wants, especially if he can be persuaded that we've got a better than even chance of cracking it, and getting convictions for both murders. Helping to nail the Last and Mercury cases would be a bonus. And there will be big jobs on offer in the new force.'

'Sir, so far only you, me and DCI Fiske know about the Roskill connection.' Colin MacNee was thinking about the "good old-fashioned police work" that would be needed before they could approach Roskill. 'If, as you put it, we're going to be able to stand this up, we'll need to put some people on it – DC's and DS's - so they'll have to be told why they're being asked to investigate Roskill, even if it's only from their desks.'

Vanessa Fiske thought she should underline the point. 'I've sent Williamson and Todd to Edinburgh to talk to a woman who's a co-signatory on the account that's been sending money to Mathieson and MacIlwraith. I'd like them on this because they've been feeling a bit out of it. Sara and Aisha can help, too. But we'll need to backfill to be sure all the local loose ends are tied up.'

Esslemont sighed. 'All right. If the Chief agrees that you should follow this up, I'll make sure you've got the bodies.'

*

'We're moving next week to a shop front location on Princes Street. We'll be a lot more visible when the campaign gets into high gear.'

Morven Trask was showing DCs Williamson and Todd into her office on the second floor of a nondescript building on Jeffrey Street with nothing to commend it except a wonderful view of the Art Deco detail of the back elevation of St Andrews House, where, just as they arrived, the Justice Secretary was announcing their new boss.

'Thank you for seeing us, Miss Trask.' Duncan Williamson said.

'No problem, and please call me Morven. I'm not sure how I can help you.'

Stewart Todd reached into his backpack and took out a clear plastic folder containing a couple of sheets of paper. 'This is a print-out of a bank statement in the name of the "SF Club". We found the account in the course of the investigation that led to the arrest of Paul MacIver. What can you tell us about it?'

'I was a member of the SF Club when I was at uni. It was, maybe still is, the student wing of the Scottish Freedom Party. I've had nothing to do with it for years. Not since I joined the SNP and got elected to the Holyrood in 2003.'

Either she doesn't know what we've got, Duncan Williamson thought, or she's very good.

'How was the SFP different from the SNP?'

'It was a splinter group. Split away after the failed referendum in 1979. Much more radical than the SNP. More left wing. Sometimes talked about "direct action". But they were all talk. That's why I left. At least the SNP had a plan, especially after the parliament was set up.'

'No contact at all?'

'I suppose I may have met some SFP members over the years.'

'Nothing more?'

'No.' She was beginning to look uncasy. 'What's this about?'

'Morven, according to the bank, you are a co-signatory on this account. The other signatory is Paul MacIver.'

She blanched. She looked genuinely surprised and shocked.

'I had completely forgotten about that. I agreed to be co-signatory when we...when I was a student. But Paul ran the account. He told me the bank needed two signatories.'

'Why you?' Duncan Williamson had picked up the folder and was making a show of examining the statement very closely. 'Why did MacIver ask you?'

She closed her eyes and leaned back in her chair, looking at the ceiling, as though she was considering how to respond. She seemed to come to a decision. She leaned forward, elbows on the desk.

'I had a relationship with him when we were students. It ended when I decided that the SFP weren't into serious politics. Paul stayed, at least for a time. We've hardly spoken since.'

'Hard to credit,' Stewart Todd said, 'What with you taking a high profile role in the campaign for independence and MacIver advising the First Minister.'

'There are Chinese walls between the government and the campaign. I'm on one side, he's on the other.'

If Stewart had known what an old-fashioned look was, he'd have shot her one. Instead he said, 'So, when did you last speak to him?'

'At last year's party conference in Aviemore. I bumped into him at the Leader's Reception. We exchanged pleasantries, no more. He keeps himself out of the limelight.'

'So, you're telling us that you've had nothing to do with this account, of which you acknowledge being a signatory, for more than ten years?'

'Yes.'

'When did MacIver leave the SFP?'

'I'm not entirely sure. He went abroad after uni - Canada, I think, Montreal. He was away for a couple of years, so I suppose he decided to join the SNP when he came back. He got a job on the *Glasgow Banner* writing editorials and political analysis. That's what brought him to the attention of the FM. She took him on when she was Finance Secretary.'

'Are you sure he left the SFP?'

Morven Trask was incredulous. 'He couldn't be in both parties. Could he?'

*

As they left Morven Trask's office just after one o'clock, Stewart checked the train times and found that they could be back in Aberdeen at 1546 hrs. He phoned Fiske's admin support and asked if the team meeting could be delayed until four. Confirmation came back as they descended the stairs to the concourse of Waverley Station.

For Fiske and MacNee, the extra time was welcome. They had arranged for Mathieson and MacIlwraith to be brought from the remand wing of Aberdeen Prison at one o'clock. Now they could arrange for them to be followed by MacIver at three. Fiske and Hamilton would interview Mathieson while MacNee and Gajani tackled MacIlwraith. Once they had discussed the product of these interviews, Fiske and MacNee would talk to MacIver.

'The weakest link in this, boss, is MacIlwraith. He's not very bright, as Dongle says. It's easier to understand how he dropped out of university than how he got in. I intend to put quite a lot of pressure on him.'

418

'That's fine. Just make sure you check the audio and video equipment before you start. And be prepared for his brief to shut him up if he begins to incriminate himself.'

'I always do. Doesn't do anybody's career any good to lose a conviction because of technicalities. I want him to incriminate the others. I don't care if he does it deliberately or by accident.'

*

MacNee and Gajani entered the interview room just after one o'clock. MacIlwraith and his lawyer were already there, accompanied by a uniformed constable who got up and sat outside the door as soon as the two detectives arrived.

As Colin MacNee sat down, Aisha Gajani switched on the recording equipment. Colin recorded the time and the names of those present and then turned to MacIlwraith.

'Mr MacIlwraith, how do you keep body and soul together?'

MacIlwraith looked at his solicitor, who nodded. 'I'm not sure what you mean, Inspector.'

'Well, as far as we can discover, and we're quite good at what we do, you don't have a paying job' - he put a slightly sarcastic tone on "paying" - 'and you don't get any social security benefits. No Job Seeker's Allowance, no sickness or disability payments. We've checked with the DWP and they have no record of any dealings with you. So how do you pay your way in the world? You know, food, bus fares, council tax, Internet connection, Sky tv, mobile phone. That kind of thing. We know you worked as a porter at GRH for a while, but that doesn't pay very much and what with rent and living expenses in Aberdeen, you wouldn't have saved much out of your wages.'

'I own the house and I have some savings, money my parents left me. And my needs are pretty modest.'

'Oh. I forgot to mention the laptop, state-of-the-art hi fi system, forty-four inch 3D ready smart tv. Must have been quite an inheritance. And, since you left the hospital in July, you've had no other regular source of income?'

MacIlwraith shook his head and Colin told him to answer "for the tape".

'Do you have a bank account?'

'I've got a current account with Santander and a savings account in a building society - Nationwide in Kilmarnock. You can check, if you like.'

'Oh, we have. There's about ten quid in Santander and a few hundred in the Nationwide. But you've got another account, haven't you? With the Co-op. That's the one I'm really interested in.'

The lawyer touched MacIlwraith's sleeve and shook his head.

'No comment.'

'The account I'm talking about is in your name, the correspondence address is your house in Saltcoats, and there's about five thousand pounds in it. Bit of advice, just in case you ever get out of prison. That's an awful lot of money to keep in a current account.'

The reference to a long prison sentence caused MacIlwraith to turn pale. But again, his lawyer shook his head.

'No comment.'

'Here's the thing. Every month £750 is deposited to that account. Did you know that? And you make regular ATM withdrawals from it. Sorry, to be accurate, regular withdrawals have been made using an ATM card in your name. And that card was among your effects when we searched your house.'

Before his lawyer could stop him, Maclwraith protested. 'Its only been 750 for a few months. It was only 200 before...'

His lawyer grabbed his arm and said, 'That's enough, Andy. Wait for the inspector to ask questions.'

'So it was! But that sounds like an admission that the account is yours and that you know about the deposits.'

'No comment.'

'Do you know who was making the deposits?'

'No comment.'

'Let's give you the benefit of the doubt. Let's assume that you don't know. Would you like to know? Because I'm in a position to enlighten you, but it would be in your interests for you to tell me rather than for me to tell you and hope that you'll confirm that we've got it right.'

'Can we have a few minutes, Inspector?' The lawyer was looking at Colin, his hand gripping his client's arm.

*

'I think you've got him on the run, boss.' DC Aisha Gajani had just come back from the canteen with two coffees. 'I think he's about to give up MacIver.'

'Let's not get ahead of ourselves. Even if he does, we'll still have to get him to tell us what he was supposed to do for the money. And we'll still have to implicate Mathieson.'

Vanessa Fiske stuck her head round the door. 'Are you done with MacIlwraith?'

'Not quite. He's consulting his brief. But he may be about to tell us who was sending him money. Mathieson?'

'Nothing so far. We're having a comfort break. He's pretty cool, though. Very sure of himself and determined to give us nothing. I'm thinking of letting Sara have a go at him, but if MacIlwraith gives us MacIver as the source of the money, we'll be able to apply more pressure.'

*

'You need to make a statement. Your approval ratings are dropping like a stone. You are risking taking the party and the fucking referendum down with you. I know it's hard, but life, and the government, goes on.'

The Justice Secretary had demanded to see the First Minister as soon as he left the press conference. She was at her official residence in Charlotte Square and there was a small knot of reporters, and a camera crew, hanging about outside.

'I know I should, but I need to know where the police have got to before I do.   Does

Grant Ingram know? Have you checked? Is he still being briefed? Is he briefing you?'

She was edgy, not completely in control, acting in a way that the Justice Secretary hadn't seen before.

'I haven't been briefed since MacIver was arrested, so I assume that the arrangement to keep us informed via DCC Ingram has lapsed because of the government's closeness to the action.'

'You mean me?' The First Minister was fiddling with a thread on the Scottish flag that stood by her desk. 'Should I speak to the Chief Constable?'

'He'll probably refuse to take your call, and I wouldn't blame him.'

There was a knock at the door and a secretary came in.

'I'm sorry to interrupt, First Minister. There's an urgent telephone call. It's Detective Chief Superintendent Esslemont from Northeast Constabulary.'

*

'We need to speak to the First Minister.'
Esslemont had just had reports from Fiske
and MacNee on the three men on remand.
Morven Trask's information on MacIver's
background added urgency to the need to
determine how deeply he had been involved
in the murders, in the Last explosion and in
the cyber attack at Mercury.

'She may wish to do the interview when she's
up here on constituency business. And I think
we should accommodate her. I'll phone her
and I'll ask her to make no public statements
bearing on the case until she's talked to us.'

*

'We have the beginning of a motive for these
murders and a glimmer of light about who,
ultimately, was financing the killers. We
know they were being paid by MacIver,
directly when they were on low pay,
indirectly when their pay went up - tripled, in
fact, about six months ago. But we need a lot
more before the Crown Office will be ready
to prosecute.'

DCI Fiske looked round the table at her
augmented team.

'Those of you who've been on the investigation since the start will know that information was being leaked in a way that compromised our enquiries. That's been dealt with, but it underlines the importance and sensitivity of what I'm now going to say.'

Esslemont gave her one of his almost imperceptible nods. She decided to regard this as support and encouragement.

'I have reason to believe that the men we have in custody were being funded by James Michael Roskill. Some of you are old enough to remember him as prime minister and I hope that the rest of you have at least heard of him. He is very high profile and our enquiries into his affairs will need to be sensitive and, to the greatest extent possible, secret. We are already working at the heart of the Scottish Government, so what we do will be under constant scrutiny, from politicians, from the press, from the public.'

'You mentioned motive, boss. Can you tell us any more?' DS Sara Hamilton already knew that some of her ongoing work was being passed on to a detective constable brought in from another team, but she was less sure what she was now expected to do.

'This is hypothetical, but based on evidence collected in the course of the arrests we've made. I think that MacIver, working through Mathieson and MacIlwraith, planned the murders as a way of destabilising the companies that operate GRH and Vermont One. We know that MacIver used to be a member of the Scottish Freedom Party. It's possible that he never really left it. He may have used his time in Canada to put distance between himself and his former SFP associates - who included MacIlwraith and Mathieson - so that he could, apparently, join the political mainstream.'

'I'm struggling a bit here.' Duncan Williamson said. 'Why would they want to "destabilise" businesses that bring investment and jobs to Scotland?'

Vanessa nodded. 'I know. It sounds perverse, but the radical fringes operate a different logic from the rest of us. There's a school of thought - if you can call it that - that says that demonstrating the fragility of inward investment will make people more likely to believe that Scotland should be running its own economy. It's a particular form of xenophobia. All our problems stem from the wicked foreigners, so we should try to make them leave. Then Scotland will be a truly independent nation. If the voters think that Scotland would be better off without foreign investment, the "logic" goes, they'll be more likely to vote yes in the referendum. As I said, perverse. But remember we're talking about people who'll kill and bomb to further their aims.'

'So does that mean that Last, and Mercury are part of this too?' Andy Hanna sounded incredulous.

'Possibly. I'm talking to the anti-terrorist unit and to Special Branch, and it's at least possible that they'll take over the investigation. Meanwhile, we have some serious legwork to do.'

'But what's Roskill's interest in this?'

'That, Andy, is what I want you to work on. I need you to find everything you can about Roskill's financial activities. The obvious question is how he might benefit from problems in firms owned by a company where he's a director. Sara and Aisha, I want you to dig as deeply as you can into the political activities of MacIver, Mathieson and MacIlwraith. How much contact has there been between them since university, where did they meet, who else was in their circle?

Crucially, did MacIver maintain his links to the SFP after he became "respectable".'

Aisha Gajani smiled. She quite fancied another trip to Glasgow.

'You'll be able to see your mother,' Sara Hamilton whispered, with heavy irony.

Stewart Todd was about to speak, but Vanessa pre-empted him.

'Stewart, I want you and Duncan to find out what MacIver was doing in Canada. What does Quebec, where he seems to have spent a couple years, have in common with Scotland? Please don't ask to phone a friend.'

'A separatist movement with a terrorist wing.' Stewart looked pleased with himself.
'So you should talk to the RCMP to see if they've got anything about him on file. Our intelligence services as well, though you may need to involve me or the DCS in approaching them.'

That left Dongle Donaldson.

'Dongle, when you are completely certain that you've extracted everything of interest from the phones and laptops, I need you to get close to the hi-tech boys in Strathclyde. I want to know whether they can establish a link between Mathieson and the cyber attack on Mercury. It's a missing link in the circumstantial case. We know MacIlwraith was looking at bomb making sites, so that's the beginning of a link to Last. All that geekware in Mathieson's flat wasn't just for playing computer games.'

CHAPTER TWENTY-ONE

'Did I hear you having a bad time in the loo this morning?'

Vanessa kissed Neil on the cheek. 'Yeah. Sorry if I woke you. Hasn't been bad this week, probably because I haven't had time for it. But my body knows it's Saturday and I'm supposed to be off!'

'Supposed to be?'

She looked a little shamefaced. 'I'm off duty, but on call. And I really have to go in to talk to Andy Hanna. Shouldn't take me more than an hour, if that. Especially if you've anything to tell me that might help him to cut some corners.'

Neil smiled. 'I'll make a fresh pot of coffee while you have a shower, then we'll talk about it.'

'Have you had a shower?'

'No.'

'Come and have one with me. I'll make it worth your while! Then you make the coffee while I get dressed.'

*

'I spent my so-called lunch break yesterday sitting in Union Terrace Gardens giving my mobile what my Glasgow auntie used to call "laldy". I spoke to a lawyer I used to work for who's now with the Serious Fraud Office. He'll talk to Andy off the record and point him towards some people in the City. He also said, and you may not like the sound of this, that there are some really smart investigative journalists working on globalisation and international financial dealings. They might be prepared to speak to him.'

'Oh, Neil! After all that stuff with Fleming, not to mention that bastard from the *Graphic* who tried to blackmail me during the Balmoral murder investigation, I'll need a very long spoon before I sup with the reptiles. They always want a *quid pro quo.* And I can hardly go handing out exclusives!'

'I'm not about to tell you how to do your job, but it might not be in your best interests, maybe not in the public interest, for you to deal in moral absolutes.'

Vanessa's post-coital glow disappeared. 'Moral fucking absolutes! I'm just trying to be consistent in the messages I send my team, as well as making sure that I'm procedurally squeaky clean. This is so high profile that...'

'Take it easy! Bad choice of words. I was simply trying to point out that you can't afford to rule out anything that might help you to close this case.'

'Easy for you to say!'

Neil decided to move on. 'My contact specifically mentioned Ben Aaronson of the *Financial Post.* Wasn't he the guy who unearthed the fact that Burtonhall owns Hedelco and Ebright?'

Vanessa nodded. It was the first time Neil had seen her in anything approaching a huff. 'You dug that up too.'

'I did, but the fact that Aaronson got it shows he's good. And he's not on the *FP*'s staff. He's freelance, which allows him to be more radical.'

'Radical?'

'Apparently he spends part of his time working with a "collective" of financial reporters who expose the seamier side of international finance. His particular interest is in who uses tax havens, offshore accounts, and offshore companies.'

'Really?'

'Yes.'

'Did you mention Roskill?'

'Of course not! I did say that the investigation had already reached into some pretty high places. If he checks, hc'll see that you've charged the First Minister's adviser and that you had a meeting at the FO. He may also know that Roskill's on the Burtonhall board. But if he knows you're going after Roskill, he didn't get it from me.'

*

'I need you to go to London. Whether you go today, tomorrow or Monday is up to you. If you can arrange to see any of the people whose names my partner has produced over the weekend, then go. Admin will make travel arrangements and find you a hotel. I'd leave the SFO guy until you can reach him in his office. But I guess the reptiles - sorry - journalists might be prepared to meet you tomorrow.'

'Can't I just phone them, boss?'

'I really don't think so. You may need to prove you're not recording what they say and that they're talking only to you. Difficult in either an audio call or by video. My guess is that if Aaronson or any of the others agrees to talk to you, they'll want to do it in a public place in the open air. Weather forecast's good for the next few days in London.'

Andy Hanna took the list of names and numbers from DCI Fiske and started to enter them in his smartphone.

'Is that wise?' Vanessa asked.

'More secure than a wee bit of paper, or writing them down anywhere else. The phone's password protected and my contacts are encrypted. Dongle would be into it in no time, I grant you. Not many Dongles about, though. And I'll delete them as soon as I'm done.'

'The things you learn in police work. Please tell me if I begin to show signs of geekiness.'

'What's the order of priority in this? If I was coming back with just one piece of evidence, what would you like it to be?'

'That's easy! Who are the signatories and who are the beneficial owners of the account that's paying MacIver? And anything, repeat anything, else about James Michael Roskill, in addition to the fact that he is one of these owners, as I'm pretty certain he is.'

'How long have I got?'

'I want you back in time for the team meeting on Tuesday.'

*

Andy Hanna met Sara Hamilton as he came out of the admin office after arranging a Sunday morning flight to London.

'Why London, Andy?'

'The boss got a lead and I'm meeting a couple of people tomorrow, then seeing someone at the SFO on Monday, as well as some financial crime experts in the Met and the City of London Police She wants me back for the team meeting on Tuesday, and her tone strongly suggested that she would have significant parts of my anatomy if I come back empty handed.'

'I don't really think she's like that. She's just determined to close this case. Aisha and I are off to Glasgow tomorrow - I've just been collecting our rail warrants - and I think Fiske expects results from us on Tuesday as well.'

'Any leads?'

'Not as such. We'll talk to some of your colleagues, especially Cam Ritchie. He was really helpful when we were in Glasgow before, when he wasn't trying, successfully as it turned out, to get into Aisha's knickers.'

'Cam's a good guy. She could do worse. And he knows his way around Glasgow politics, student politics in particular. He had a secondment to Special Branch for a while, too. Very bright, and ambitious with it.'

'Good to know. I'll just have to try and keep their eyes on the ball rather than each other! Aisha's a good officer, so I don't really see a problem. Mind you, I doubt if I can resist winding her up. Good luck in London.'

'Thanks. See you Tuesday.'

*

The First Minister looked drawn. She was in her constituency office in Montrose at 0830 hrs on Monday morning, waiting to be interviewed by DCS Esslemont and DCI Fiske. The detectives were shown in by one of the FM's local staff and offered coffee. As usual these days, Vanessa asked for water. Esslemont had black coffee, as did the FM. They were joined by the FM's personal lawyer. The fact that Esslemont had emphasised that the interview was informal had clearly not persuaded her that she didn't need legal support. After the introductions, they sat round a low coffee table. Esslemont led the questioning. Fiske took notes.

'How can I help?', the First Minister asked.

'We need to understand the background to your employment of Paul MacIver who we've charged with conspiracy to murder. It's likely that there will be other charges, equally serious.'

'I'm not sure what you mean, Detective Chief Superintendent.'

'When did you take him on? How did he come to your attention? How much background checking did you do? How much do you know about his friends and associates? That sort of thing. And I would ask you, please, to err on the side of too much information and let us decide what's important and what's not.'

'I became Finance Secretary after the Holyrood election in 2007. I had been looking for a special adviser while I was in opposition, in the expectation that I would be appointed to Cabinet if we won. Paul had been writing analysis and comment on Scottish politics for the *Glasgow Banner* for a couple of years. He was clearly coming from a Nationalist position and a friend who knew him well suggested that I might want to talk to him. I did, I liked him, I offered him a job. He's been with me ever since.'

'Can you tell me the name of the friend who recommended him?'

'I'd rather not. The person in question is not a public figure and I don't see any reason for drawing them into this.'

Esslemont pursed his lips. 'I see. I may have to come back to that, First Minister, but let's leave it for now. How much checking into his background did you do before hiring him?'

'I assume that my staff would have run his name through Disclosure Scotland to see if there was anything on the record. Beyond that, I made my decision on the basis of a recommendation from a respected friend and my own knowledge of Paul's work.'

'Was any more checking done when you became First Minister?'

'Not to my knowledge.'

'Were you aware that MacIver had been a member of the Scottish Freedom Club when he was a student?'

The First Minister stiffened visibly. 'We are all allowed our youthful indiscretions, Chief Superintendent.'

'I'm afraid that doesn't answer my question.'

'I was made aware of that.'

'When?'

'The Permanent Secretary informed me when I became First Minister. He asked me if I wanted any further checks done. I said that Paul MacIver had my full confidence.'

'Was it suggested to you that you might ask Special Branch or the Intelligence Services for a view of his suitability?'

'It was not. And if it had been, I would not have accepted the suggestion. These agencies owe their loyalty to Westminster. They should not have any *locus* here. Had I asked them to investigate Paul's background, I would have conferred on them a legitimacy that they should not have.'

'So, your decision rested on your knowledge of MacIver's journalism, and the recommendation of a friend. The former is in the public domain, so we can form our own conclusions on that. But for reasons that should be obvious to you, we need to know who recommended him to you.'

'I'm sorry, Chief Superintendent, but I am not prepared to divulge that information, for the reasons already stated.'

'First Minister, let me spell it out. We have in custody a man who was at the heart of the Scottish Government for five years, the last year in the office of the First Minister. We believe he has been involved in conspiracy to murder, and possibly in terrorism and cyber-terrorism. If he was "planted", we need to know by whom.'

The First Minister shook her head. Her lawyer leaned over and whispered something to her.

'I am advised that I may be laying myself open to a charge of attempting to defeat the ends of justice. That is a risk I am prepared to take. It is a matter of principle.'

Esslemont was silent for a moment. 'For the record, I did not say that. Nor did I imply it. But, *prima facie*, your lawyer has done her duty to you. I have no more questions. For now. No doubt you will have to make a statement to Parliament regarding MacIver's arrest. Please be circumspect. This enquiry is at a very delicate stage. Should you think is appropriate, or helpful, I will be happy to look at a draft of any statement you propose to make.' But, he thought, when you have to answer questions on it, you'll be on your own.

He rose. 'Thank you, First Minister. We will be in touch if we need to speak to you again.'

*

The accused men were brought to NEC HQ from Aberdeen Prison on Monday morning. MacIlwraith was taken directly to an interview room where Fiske and MacNee and MacIlwraith's solicitor were waiting for him. Mathieson and MacIver were taken to cells in the custody suite. Their lawyers had been told that neither man would be questioned before 1100 hrs.

DCI Fiske began by asking MacIlwraith about his relationship with Simon Mathieson.

'How long have you two known each other?'

'You know the answer to that. We met at university. Glasgow. In 2001.' His lawyer touched MacIlwraith's arm to warn him against showing any emotion in his answers.

'How did you meet? Simon was studying computer science. You were doing history and politics, so you wouldn't have been in the same classes.'

'We were in the same club.'

'What kind of club, Andy?'

MacIlwraith shifted a bit in his chair and reached into his pocket for a handkerchief. 'Political.'

'What kind of political?'

Fiske and MacNee were finding this slow process of discovery pretty tedious, but Vanessa was determined not to do anything that might be construed as leading the accused, much less putting words in his mouth.

'Nationalist.'

'I assume you mean Scottish Nationalist.' MacIlwraith nodded and then, for the tape, said. 'Yes.'

'What was he club called?'

'The Scottish Freedom Club. It was the student branch of the SFP.'

'The Scottish Freedom Party?'

Again, MacIlwraith nodded and said, 'Yes.'

Vanessa leaned forward, looked closely at MacIlwraith, and asked, 'That wasn't the only student Nationalist club, though, was it?'

'No. There was the Scottish Nationalist Association as well.'

'So why did you choose the SFC?'

'I thought they were more serious. More committed to Scotland's independence.'

'More likely to take direct action to achieve it?'

A warning glance from his lawyer made him pause before he said, 'No comment.'

Vanessa indicated to MacNee that he should take over.

'Andy, did you remain active in the SFP after you left university?'

'No comment.'

'Did you stay in touch with Simon Mathieson?'

'No comment.'

'You didn't finish your degree, did you?'

'No.'

'Why was that?'

MacIlwraith looked contemptuous, as if the question hardly merited his attention. 'Because I failed my exams.'

'Too busy working for independence.'

The lawyer touched his client's arm and said, 'I don't think that was a question, Inspector.'

Colin smiled and moved on. 'So you left uni without a degree. Can you tell me what jobs you've had in the last eight years?'

'I've done some voluntary work and some casual jobs.'

'I assume the voluntary work was unpaid and the casual jobs were cash in hand. Have you ever earned a wage or salary?'

'Only when I was living here. In Aberdeen. I worked for a while as a porter at GRH"

'That ended some time last year, which brings us back to where we were when we last spoke. You've been receiving payments monthly into your Co-op Bank account for at least five years. You admitted to me that the payments had gone up from £200 to £750 about six months ago. And I think you were about to tell me who was sending the money. Will you tell me now?'

MacIlwraith looked at his lawyer, who nodded.

'I don't know for certain, but I think Paul MacIver had something to do with it. All it said on my statement was 'SF Club.''

'Thank you, Andy. That helps me a lot. And it may help you, too.'

'When did you last see Paul MacIver? To speak to, I mean.' Vanessa had decided to push the interview along.

'I don't think I've seen him since uni. He was in the SFC as well. But he went abroad and then he sold out.'

'Sold out? What does that mean?'

'He turned out to be a careerist. Joined the SNP. You know the rest.'

Colin MacNee indicated to Vanessa that he wanted a word in private. She suspended the interview, apologised to MacIlwraith and his lawyer for the interruption, and followed Colin into the corridor.

'I didn't want to say this in there, without consulting you, but that sounded to me like a prepared response. Every radical organisation I've ever had anything to do with has used the words "sold out" and "careerist" to describe anyone who works in the political mainstream, especially if they started elsewhere. And he said he hadn't "seen" MacIver, not that he hadn't spoken to him or otherwise been in contact with him.'

'OK. He's pretty well given us MacIver as the source of his funds, but claims not to have seen him. I'll point out the contradiction to him but its odds on he'll now start to "no comment". And I'll have to ask him about his continuing connection with Mathieson.'

DCI Fiske was right. MacIlwraith said he had seen Mathieson "a couple of times" since he left university and MacIver not at all. When challenged about the texts to MacIver's

449

burner from one of his mobile phones, he declined to comment. And he refused to confirm or deny that he remained a member of, or committed to the policies of, the Scottish Freedom Party. The interview was over by quarter to eleven.

*

Mathieson maintained his silence when confronted with MacIlwraith's admission about the money received from the SF Club and his assumption that MacIver was involved. He said that he had known MacIlwraith at university but had lost touch with him after he dropped out at the end of his second year. He was a little unsettled only when DCI Fiske asked him to explain why he had made calls from his mobile to a disposable phone owned by Paul MacIver, but he composed himself enough to say "no comment".

Vanessa then turned to the sophisticated computer equipment that had been found in his flat.

'It's way beyond what's necessary for home computing and I'm told that there's enough computing power there to run a medium-sized business. What were you using it for?'

'I studied computer science at uni. It's a hobby.'

'Expensive kit. How do you afford it? When was the last time you had the kind of job where you pay National Insurance and PAYE?'

'No comment.'

'We'll just assume that MacIver was paying for it and see if a jury agrees with us.'

Mathieson's lawyer touched his client's arm. 'I didn't hear a question, Inspector.'

Vanessa smiled ironically. 'Funnily enough, I'm not hearing many answers. But let's move on. Our IT experts have told me that your laptop is configured to control the rest of your kit and that it's all set up to launch a cyber attack. Are they right?'

'No comment.'

'Did you hack into the systems of a company called Mercury Fulfilment and disable them?'

A trace of a smile and then, 'No comment.'

'OK. That'll do for now. I think we've got enough for the prosecution to convince a jury.'

*

'Mr MacIver, please tell me about your banking arrangements?' DCI Fiske and DI MacNee sat in an interview room opposite Paul MacIver and his lawyer.

The lawyer nodded. 'I have a current account with RBS, that my salary's paid into, and a cash ISA that I pay into monthly by direct debit.'

'No other accounts?'

'No comment.'

'We have found another account in your name, in another bank.' Vanessa quoted the account number. 'Can you confirm that this is your account?'

'No comment.'

'Its got your name on it, so we are going to assume that it's yours. A substantial amount has been paid into it monthly for the last six months. Well over £2000. From an account in the British Virgin Islands.   Who is sending that money and why?'

'No comment.'

'You are also a co-signatory of a third account, this one in the name of the SF Club? Will you confirm that is the case?'

'No comment.'

'The account records show that for the last six months, £1500 has been transferred, immediately after the funds arrive from BVI, to that SF Club account, and then, also immediately, £750 has been transferred to two other accounts, one in the name of Simon Mathieson and one in the name of Andrew MacIlwraith. Can you explain these transactions?'

'No comment.'

'Payments to Mathieson and MacIlwraith go back at least five years, but they increased substantially six months ago, just as the BVI payments began. Can you explain this?'

'No comment.'

Vanessa looked at Colin and shook her head. 'It's pretty clear, Mr MacIver, that you have no intention of co-operating with us. Interview concluded at 11.40.'

*

'So, what now, boss?.' Colin MacNee was in Vanessa Fiske's office, looking over the notes he had taken during the interviews. 'Apart from MacIlwraith partially incriminating MacIver, we're not much further forward.'

'It makes the circumstantial case a bit stronger, but we need more. We need to have another go at Mancuso and Gilbertson.'

CHAPTER TWENTY-TWO

At noon EDT on Monday, 1700 hrs GMT, the board of Burtonhall Inc. met at the company's corporate HQ in Wilmington, Delaware. Richard Seaton, the former US Secretary of State. was in the chair. Cy Packard was immediately to his right. On the left hand side of the table, as Seaton looked at it, sat James Roskill and two other members of the board, the billionaire investor from the Midwest and the Putin-supporting Russian oligarch. The Indonesian politician turned businessman was on the television screen on the wall opposite Seaton and Packard. Jack Eisner, Don Hamnett, Head of Human Resources, General Counsel Magnus Friedkin, and Charlie Fillmorc, the Chief Investment Officer, sat opposite the non-executive members of the board. The mood was sombre. There was no small talk. Meetings of the full board were infrequent and it was unusual, if not quite unheard of, for Packard to insist on a face-to-face meeting in Wilmington. A dispensation had been agreed for the Indonesian because of travel difficulties. The business to be transacted, they all knew, was serious.

'Gentlemen, the CEO persuaded me of the necessity of calling this meeting of the Board. For security reasons, he also persuaded me that we should be – how shall I say? – circumspect about the nature of the agenda. Thank you all for making yourselves available and for attending, as it were, blind.'

Seaton smiled, but there was no warmth in it. He turned to Packard.

'Cy, please inform the board of the business of the meeting.'

'Thank you, chairman. Members of the board are already aware of the' – he seemed to be searching for the right word – 'difficulties that we have been experiencing with two of our major investments in the United Kingdom. A couple of weeks ago, there were two murders in the North East of Scotland. Both occurred at Burtonhall facilities, the Grampian Royal Hospital, which is managed by Hedelco; and the Vermont One oil platform, owned and operated by Ebright Offshore Drilling. Both victims were engaged on inspections of processes and procedures on behalf of the operating companies. The police in Scotland have, apparently, ruled out a purely commercial motive for the killings, but the investigation, and the publicity and politics around it, have caused certain facts that we would have wished to remain confidential to become public. Some of our most important investors have become nervous. But, more importantly, local management has recommended expenditure to deal with actual and perceived shortcomings, at the hospital and on the oil platform, which will make it very difficult – impossible in the case of the hospital – for these businesses to remain profitable in the short to medium term.'

Friedkin and Fillmore nodded in agreement, and Fillmore began to distribute to the board a detailed analysis of the financial position of Hedelco and Ebright.

Packard continued. 'Our prospectus offers potential investors a return on their money within three years. That is not possible with these businesses. In the past, we have divested ourselves of loss making investments, sometimes before they have posted any actual losses.' Packard knew that his colleagues would recognise the significance of this last comment: if losses are real rather than anticipated, the price in the market falls. So far, officially and on the basis of published accounts, both Hedelco and Ebright were in profit. But speculation in the financial press had already undermined their value.

'You will see from the figures that Charlie has prepared that the costs of putting things right at the hospital and on the platform are considerable. And there is no guarantee that the expenditure would produce the kind of returns that our investors expect. We need to respond to the negative publicity by announcing that we will put things right. But I am recommending that, in parallel, we seek buyers for these businesses.'

The American billionaire was first to speak. 'Two things will depress the price we can expect to get. Number one, the fact that we are pulling out. Number two, we have to get the Brits to agree before we can transfer the hospital contract.'

Charlie Fillmore indicated that he wanted to speak. 'On the first, we will test the market as discreetly as we can. And on the second, we will find a prospective buyer before we approach the Scottish' – he emphasised the word – 'Government.'

'Still makes it a buyer's market.'

'Not a lot we can do about that.' Packard said. 'We need to compare any possible loss with what it would cost to keep these businesses, not with what we paid for them.'

The oligarch said that he agreed. The Indonesian indicated, reluctantly, that he would support the CEO's recommendation. James Michael Roskill said nothing.

*

'There are persistent rumours in the City that Roskill is setting up offshore shell companies as vehicles for acquisitions of going concerns, funded partly from his own resources and partly by sovereign wealth funds operating as private equity investors.'

Ben Aaronson and Andy Hanna were in a bistro in Canary Wharf on Sunday afternoon. Aaronson had insisted that he was speaking entirely off the record and that he would not, in any circumstances appear in court to talk about his investigations.

'Then why are you talking to me at all?', Andy asked.

'Because I'd like to nail some of these bastards and I don't think the occasional exposé in the broadsheet press is going to do it.   I blog about it, as do some other members of FRIG - I know, I know, but we couldn't resist it - the Financial Reporting and Investigating Group, but people like Roskill seem just to carry on regardless, moving their money from one tax haven to another, claiming they're doing nothing illegal.'

'Well, usually they're not, are they?'

Aaronson took a sip of his mineral water and looked very intently - scarily so, Andy thought - at Hanna and said, 'You know, I don't give a stuff if it's illegal. It's immoral, it's evil and it's impoverishing people who have little enough already. And if I can help to stop it, I will. That's why I'm freelance and spend nearly half my time working for FRIG.'

Andy was taking notes because Aaronson didn't want to be recorded. He looked up from his notebook, reached for his pint of *Peroni*, and asked, 'How reliable are these rumours?   Are you going to write about them?'

'I may mention them in my blog. I think they're pretty firm but I don't have enough convince an editor.'

'But why would Roskill be doing it? He's already loaded and his directors' fees and what he gets from investments like Burtonhall must produce a pretty sizeable income on top of his pension.'

'Greed. Simple as that. Some people can't get enough, even if they have nothing more to spend it on. I think that Roskill couldn't believe how easy it was to monetize his political career and so he just goes on doing it. Nothing wrong with that except the way he does it. He seems to see nothing immoral about avoiding and evading tax. He's a hypocrite and he deserves to be stopped.'

Andy Hanna was beginning to feel a little unsettled by Aaronson's radical zeal, so he decided to turn the conversation to the practicalities of Roskill's activities.

'How would he go about acquiring these "going concerns"? And why would he want to do it offshore and, I assume, anonymously?'

'The world of private equity investment - buying and selling "entities", as they call them, that are not traded on public stock exchanges - is very dynamic, with firms investing and disinvesting all the time, for all sorts of reasons. One group of investors believes they can't turn a profit where another believes it can, so the "entity" leaves the portfolio of one fund and ends up in the portfolio of another.'

'So, to take a random example', Andy smiled wryly, 'if Burtonhall decided to sell Hedelco, or Ebright, or both, they could probably find a buyer.'

'Oh, yes!'

'Is it possible that Roskill is positioning himself to do that?'

'It's possible. The insider trading rules for publicly quoted companies don't apply to the Wild West world of private equity, so his directorship of Burtonhall wouldn't be a legal impediment. I don't think you need me to comment on the ethics.'

*

Fiske and MacNee knocked on the door of Martin Gilbertson's cottage in Fetteresso at eight o'clock on Sunday morning. Neither Neil Derrick nor Janet MacNee had been best pleased when their partners informed them that they were going to be working on Sunday morning. Colin's children were supposed to be his priority at the weekend and Vanessa and Neil usually had a long lie in. The detectives had used almost exactly the same phrases in explanation: the speed of the investigation was out of their hands; the politics meant that they needed to close the case quickly; even Esslemont was working today.

Neil and Janet may not have appreciated it, but the fact that the DCS was coming into HQ to be available to interview the accused men if information collected from Gilbertson and Mancuso made it necessary to do so, was the most compelling of the reasons given by their partners. It was a very long time since Esslemont had not been on the golf course on a sunny Sunday.

'Good morning, Mr Gilbertson,' Vanessa Fiske said, as a surprised and pyjama-clad Martin Gilbertson looked round the door. 'I hope this isn't a bad time. We need to talk to you.'

Gilbertson said nothing. He opened the door and stood back to let them in. It was a small, recently renovated farmworker's cottage, with a living room and kitchen on the ground floor and a couple of bedrooms and a bathroom built into the roof. Dormer windows had been added back and front, and it looked to Colin as if no expense had been spared on the conversion and modernisation. Gilbertson's salary would have been enough to secure a loan, but it might be useful to know exactly how the bills had been paid and whether there was a mortgage on the house.

'The last time we spoke to you, at your office, you said that you knew who had planned the bombing at Last Cairngorm. You then refused to say any more. We need to talk to you about that again and we need you to tell us what, if anything, you know. I can't promise you anything, but it's unlikely to do you any harm when your case comes up if the court learns that you have co-operated with us in the investigation of a very serious crime.'

Gilbertson looked uncomfortable, even scared. He brought coffee for himself and Colin and a glass of water for Vanessa.

'A couple of months before the bombing, Frank Mancuso told me that his security people had identified a couple of guys with Glasgow accents who were spending a lot of time at and near Last Cairngorm. The complex was partly open. People could view the facilities and see what would be available when it was fully operational; it was part of the marketing plan. These guys were taking more pictures than ordinary tourists and Mancuso's people got some pretty good shots of them.'

'Did you see the photos?'

'Frank brought them to the pub one evening and asked me if I could get my police contacts to see if they were known. I looked at them, but I told him that this was a step to far. Even for me.' He smiled sardonically at that, and stretched out his arms, palms of his hands upwards, in a gesture of resignation and openness.

'So you didn't mention this to Richard Fleming?'

'No.'

Colin MacNee set his coffee mug down on the table. 'Did Mancuso tell you that these men had planned the bombing?'

'Not in so many words, but when it happened he said something about wishing I had done what he asked.'

'Very interesting.' Colin looked unimpressed. 'But if this is true, why didn't Mancuso tell us this after the bombing?'

'I have no idea.'

'You said Mancuso brought the pictures to the pub. Did you actually see them?'

'A brief glance. No more.'

Vanessa reached into her bag for her smartphone and brought up pictures, first of Simon Mathieson and then of Andy MacIlwraith. Gilbertson looked at them in turn.

'I can't be sure, because I didn't look very closely at the pictures Frank brought, but it's possible.'

*

Frank Mancuso lived in a modern loft apartment in a converted mill near the centre of Aberdeen, rented for him by the Last Corporation. He answered the entry phone and buzzed Fiske and MacNee in. It was about 0915 hrs, and the detectives had driven straight to Mancuso's address after leaving Fetteresso.

'Good morning, Mr Mancuso. Thank you for inviting us in. We need to talk to you a bit more about the bombing.'

'Always a pleasure to see you, Detective Chief Inspector, but, as ever, I don't know how I can help you any further. I've been co-operating fully with the investigation at Last Cairngorm and...'

Vanessa interrupted him. 'This is a separate but related investigation. We'll share any information you provide with the Anti-Terrorism Squad and with Special Branch.'

Mancuso tried to look unconcerned, but didn't quite manage it. He invited the detectives to sit down, but offered no other hospitality.

'We have reason to believe that you have withheld evidence that would assist the police in their investigation of the Last Cairngorm bombing. Not only does that impede the enquiry, it may lay you open to a charge of attempting to defeat the ends of justice, and that's very serious.'

Mancuso remained composed. 'I have no idea what you're talking about.'

Vanessa shook her head and tried look more disappointed than angry. 'We think that you have security photographs of two men whom you suspect of involvement in the bombing. It would be in your interests to let us have them.'

Mancuso now seemed rather less comfortable. 'We must have taken hundreds of pictures during the preview openings of the facility. How am I supposed to know which ones you're talking about?'

Colin MacNee quickly calculated that Mancuso had probably worked out where they had got their information. 'You could start with the two that you tried to have checked against police records. And don't even bother pleading ignorance again. It won't wash. And we really don't have time to be pissed about.'

'They're in my office.' He sighed, as if he accepted that it was futile to resist. 'In the filing cabinet. We could drive out and get them.'

'We'll take your word that they're safe. Meanwhile, we'd like you to confirm that these are the men.'

Vanessa brought out her smartphone and Mancuso confirmed that the men in his pictures were Mathieson and MacIlwraith.

'Thank you. Now, tell us what you know about James Michael Roskill.'

*

Andy Hanna and Ben Aaronson continued their conversation as they looked across the Thames. Andy was finding it difficult to distinguish radical polemic from research and analysis.

'I think I understand the mechanics of one fund buying an "entity" from another. What I'm not clear about is how an "insider" could take advantage of his or position during the sale and transfer process, apart from knowing in advance that the "entity" was about to come on the market.'

Aaronson seemed to be examining something on the far bank of the river. 'That brings us back to the question of ethics. Almost everything does. Let's assume that the insider knows that an entity is marginal in terms of profitability, could go either way, into profit or loss. If he could find a way to nudge it towards loss, that would do two things. It would make a sale more likely. And it would depress the price. Any insider could do that, so, at base, it's a matter of personal morality. It's because personal morality is unreliable that insider trading in publicly quoted shares is subject to severe penalties.'

He sounded, Andy thought, like an instruction manual, or as though he were giving an elementary lecture in stockbroking, as though he was trying to keep himself in check. Time to move on.

'Thanks for your time, Ben. I've got to go.'

Aaronson looked puzzled. 'More than time, Andy. I've given you quite a lot of potentially sensitive information. I think there should be a *quid pro quo*. Maybe an early heads-up as your enquiries into Roskill proceed?'

'No such thing as a free lunch,' Andy thought, though he had paid at the bistro. As he turned towards the DLR station, he said. 'Not up to me, but if this goes anywhere, I'll talk to my boss.'
*

On their way back to HQ, Fiske and MacNee picked up the main Scottish Sunday newspapers. With the exception of Aaronson in the Sunday sister of the *Financial Post*, the English-based titles had lost interest in the murders as soon as the arrests were announced. Jason Sime in the *G & T* had followed up assiduously every detail of the murder investigations and related enquiries. Today, his front page story had an exclusive tag, and a joint byline with the business editor:

US Firms Pull Back on Investment in Scotland

The economic fall-out from the bombing at Last Cairngorm and the cyber attack at Mercury Fulfilment continues. The G & T has learned, from sources within the companies, that both companies are reassessing their financial commitment to Scotland.

The Last Corporation has decided to put the second phase of its Cairngorm development on hold until the economic situation in Scotland has stabilised. The decision was, apparently, taken personally by Ewan Last, whose commitment to Scotland is known to have been shaken by the level of opposition to the Cairngorm project.

Mercury is delaying indefinitely its planned expansion in Cumbernauld and, in a move that is likely to cause even more concern to the Scottish Government, they are known to be looking at development sites in Ireland, where generous tax breaks are on offer, easily comparable with the grant aid they have received in Scotland.

All of this, together with persistent rumours that Burtonhall is looking hard at the performance of Hedelco, who manage Grampian Royal Hospital, and Ebright, who operate the Vermont One oil platform in the North Sea off Aberdeen, will make grim reading for the First Minister and her colleagues.

Vanessa Fiske handed the *G & T* to Colin MacNee as they walked across the car park. 'To use the famous headline from *Variety*, it looks as though this one will run and run.'

DCS Esslemont was waiting for them. As soon as he heard what they had learned from Gilbertson and Mancuso, he made two calls. The first was to the Chief Constable to arrange to see him later in the morning. The second was to Aberdeen Prison to ask that MacIver, Mathieson and MacIlwraith be brought to NEC HQ at noon.

CHAPTER TWENTY-THREE

By late on Monday afternoon, DS Sara Hamilton and DC Aisha Gajani, working largely on information from DC Cam Ritchie, had found half a dozen people who had known Paul MacIver at university. They remembered him as being a member of the Scottish Freedom Club, but none thought he had been a leading member. His views on the future of Scotland had certainly been radical - one former associate described him as a Revolutionary Nationalist - but the club had been run by two others. One informant remembered that the organisers had been called Mathieson and MacIlwraith, at least until MacIlwraith dropped out of university.

'Useful corroboration', Sara said as they made their way up West Regent Street to a lawyers' office where one of their interviewees had told them they could find someone else who had known MacIver. 'But nothing we didn't know before.'

The offices of Campbell, Scrivener and McGlone were in a converted Victorian town house near Blythswood Square. It had once been elegant, as had most of the houses of Victorian Glasgow, but it was now functional, with a vestibule leading to a reception area indistinguishable in style from the many solicitors' offices, investment consultancies, architectural practices and public relations companies that now dominated the grid of streets that had once been home to the *haute bourgeoisie* of the city.

Sara and Aisha showed their warrant cards to the young man on reception and asked to see Kate Turnbull. They had phoned ahead, so she was expecting them. They were directed through an internal door. The young man led them up two flights of stairs to a small office. The woman sitting at the desk was in her early thirties with reddish hair and a complexion that marked her out as a native of the west of Scotland.

Sara stuck out her hand and said, 'DS Sara Hamilton. Thank you for seeing us.' She introduced Aisha, and Kate Turnbull motioned them to the two chairs facing her across the desk.

'How can I help?'

'I believe you knew Paul MacIver at university. What can you tell us about him?

'Is this about these murders up in Aberdeen?'

Sara nodded.

'Yes. I knew him. We were exact contemporaries and we took some of the same courses. We were an item for a while after Morven Trask dumped him. He was a good-looking bloke and I couldn't understand - I was just twenty - why Morven had let him go. He made a move on me and I was flattered enough to respond. I moved into his flat and we were together for a year or so.'

'So you got to know him pretty well?'

'As well as anyone ever did, I suppose. He wasn't easy to reach. Too focused on what he always referred to as "The Question of Scotland". I was a nationalist, too. Still am, I suppose. But I quite liked doing other things as well - drinking, dancing, clubbing. After a while, politics and sex weren't enough, so we split up.'

'Who dumped who?'

'I dumped him. I tried to make him lighten up a bit, have a bit of fun, think about something other than "the struggle". He became very intense and tried to make me feel it was my fault for not being committed enough. I remember the moment when I realised why Morven had dumped him'.

'Did you stay in touch after uni?', Aisha asked.

'I saw him around. You know what it's like. It takes a while to stop being a student, so I would see him occasionally in the bars we used to frequent when we were at uni.'

'Did his views change after he left university?'

Kate Turnbull laughed. 'Not so you'd notice! Always going on about direct action, the "respectability" of the SNP, the pointlessness of elections. I told him once that I thought he was trying to bore Scotland into independence.'

'Did you stay in touch for long?'

'Paul went abroad - Canada - a couple of years after he graduated. He wrote to me, which came as a surprise. I assumed he still fancied me. But even his letters were political rather than personal.'

'In what way?

'He was in Montreal and he was spending time with a faction of the separatists. Went on about how much more committed to Quebec nationalism they were than the Parti Québécois and how Scotland could learn a lot from them.'

Sara glanced at Aisha and then said, 'I don't suppose you kept the letters?'

Kate Turnbull smiled. 'I'm a lawyer. I keep everything. And yes, I'll let you see them. Nothing passionate in them except the politics.'

*

On the train to Glasgow, DCs Duncan Williamson and Stewart Todd had agreed that Sara and Aisha should concentrate on MacIver's university contacts while they tried to find anyone who could place either Mathieson or MacIlwraith in the company of Paul McIver. They soon found that they had drawn the short straw. It was very difficult to investigate the backgrounds of two men who had hardly ever had jobs, and whose interests, as far as they knew, were solitary: surfing the Internet in MacIlwraith's case, and playing with computers in Mathieson's.

They started in Glasgow's West End on Sunday afternoon, showing Mathieson's picture around the shops and pubs, mainly Byres Road, trying to find anyone who recognised him. At first nobody did. In the middle of the evening, just as they were about to call it a day, an Asian shopkeeper looked closely at the photograph and said that the man sometimes came in for a paper, or for milk, or bread.

'When did you last see him?'

'Maybe two weeks ago. I remember because he asked me if I sold disposable mobile phones. I sent him to my cousin down the road in Church Street. He sells them, unblocks them, all that stuff. Too complicated for me. I stick to pies and such.'

'Was he always alone when you saw him? Or was anyone with him?', Stewart Todd asked.

'Always alone. No girlfriend.' He smiled to signal a joke. 'No boyfriend either.'

The detectives walked about a quarter of a mile down Byres Road and into Church Street where they found the shop run by the shopkeeper's cousin. It was a tiny place of the sort that used to exist all over Glasgow, before they were wiped out by supermarkets and convenience stores: "wee dairies" selling milk, bread, rolls, and little else. Now it sold disposable phones, phone cards, phone accessories, earphones and the like, and offered services such as unlocking mobile phones and repairing broken screens.

They saw the family resemblance as soon as they went in. The man was younger and more westernised than his cousin. He was also more guarded in his greeting, probably because he guessed they were police officers and because he was running a business that sometimes operated on the edge of the law. Williamson and Todd knew that this kind of enterprise worked on a no questions asked basis.

'We've just been to see your cousin up the road,' Duncan Williamson said as he showed his warrant card. 'He says that he sent this man here to buy a disposable phone. Do you recognise him?'

The shopkeeper took the photograph and looked at it closely. 'Aye. He came here about two weeks ago. He bought two disposables and a charger. Also, a couple of USB cables. I remember because it's not usual for a customer to buy two phones at the same time.'

'Was he alone?'

'No, He was with another man. The other man did not say anything and he stood just by the door and not at the counter, as if he didn't want me to see him. But I had to ask him to move so that I could get the cables, so I got a good look at him.'

'Is this him?' Stewart Todd had taken a photograph of Paul MacIver out of his backpack and passed it over the counter.

'That's him.'

Duncan Williamson told the shopkeeper that they were investigating two murders and that they would have to ask him to make a formal statement. He looked apprehensive, but he nodded and said he would be happy to help.

*

After Sara Hamilton told him that Kate Turnbull had corroborated Morven Trask's information about MacIver's time in Canada, Detective Inspector Colin MacNee arranged to speak on the phone to the Royal Canadian

Mounted Police. He emailed that he was investigating two murders and some other serious crimes and that a 'person of interest' – he did not mention that MacIver had been charged with conspiracy to murder, because he wanted to concentrate their minds on what he was coming to regard as the terrorism aspects of the case – had spent some time in Quebec. He needed to know whether he had come to their attention.

After speaking with the International Liaison section at RCMP HQ in Ottawa, he had emailed Superintendent Pierre Vignault, head of the Integrated National Security Enforcement Team (INSET) in Quebec City. Now, at 1600hrs BST / 1100 hrs EDT he dialled his number.

'Bonjour, Superintendent Vignault, je m'appelle Colin MacNee, et je suis en Ecosse …'

Vignault interrupted 'Detective MacNee, would you prefer if we spoke in English?' Vignault had a strong accent, but his English was grammatically perfect. Colin had thought that courtesy demanded that he try to communicate in French, but he was relieved to change to English, courtesy satisfied.

'Thank you, Superintendent. That would be helpful, if you don't mind.'

'Not a bit.'

'We have a man in custody here in Aberdeen and we think he may have been involved in a bomb attack. He spent a couple of years in Montreal, and it would be helpful to know if he came to your attention.'

'Is this the bomb at Last Cairngorm?'

'Yes. It is.'

'We get intelligence on all terrorist or apparently terrorist attacks. Mainly I just skim the headlines, but Ewan Last has a high profile here in Canada, so I took a bit more interest.'

'The name of our suspect is Paul MacIver and we believe he lived in Montreal around 2004 to 2006. We don't have exact dates. He has a history of radical separatist politics here in Scotland and it would be very helpful if you could tell me if he came to your notice.'

'Do you have a date of birth for him, just to be sure.'

Colin read out MacIver's date of birth.

'OK, let's see. This may take some time. Do you want to hold or call me back?'

Colin said he would hold. It took no more than a couple of minutes, during which he could hear the click of a keyboard as Vignault interrogated the RCMP database.

'The non-parliamentary wing of Quebec separatism has been pretty disorganised since the collapse of the Front pour la Liberation du Quebec in 1970. Occasional attacks amounting to little more than vandalism, but we keep an eye on them. There's a group of ex-FLQ activists and student radicals who hang out in the bars around the Francophone universities and colleges in Montreal. It looks as though your man began to frequent these places in late 2004. We photographed him, ran the picture through the immigration database and identified him as Paul MacIver. He never applied for a work permit, but he did some freelance writing and broadcasting. Probably got paid in cash. Seems to have spent a lot of time with radical separatists.

'When did he leave Canada?'

'May 2006. He left Montreal on an Air Canada flight to Heathrow and hasn't been back. Or if he has, immigration doesn't know about it.'

*

'Right. We've also got some evidence of his activities in Quebec from the RCMP and from an ex-girlfriend found by Sara and Aisha. I'll have to speak to the spooks.'

Vanessa Fiske had been reading an email from Andy Hanna when Colin came into her office after his conversation with Vignault.

'I was going to go to see Esslemont about going after Roskill, but this takes priority.'

She used some old contacts in the Met to get quickly to the right person in the security service. She assured him that she was using a secure line and he asked how he could help.

'Paul MacIver. We have him in custody on a charge of conspiracy to murder, but it looks as though he may have been involved in the Last Cairngorm bombing. This is all pretty sensitive because until we arrested him he was a special adviser to the First Minister. Her closest adviser, in fact. He has a history of radical separatism, including associating with extreme nationalists in Quebec, where he came to the notice of the Mounties' anti-terrorist branch. It would be helpful to know if he has come to your attention.'

There was a pause, then he said, 'I'll get back to you within the hour.'

*

DI Andy Hanna had met Neil Derrick's contact in the SFO for a coffee on Monday morning, and he was cross checking with him Aaronson's take on the behaviour of private equity conglomerates.

'Generally speaking, he's right. Unless they're into leveraged buyouts - financing take-overs by borrowing and taking publicly quoted companies private - there's very little to prevent or deter insider dealing. The Securities and Exchange Commission in the States has been pursuing a couple of private equity funds for insider trading, but their interest has been in how advantage has been gained in either the negotiation of loans or the manipulation of share prices before a take-over. As I understand it, most of Burtonhall's acquisitions have been financed by sovereign wealth funds or high net worth investors, so they're unregulated.'

'So there would be nothing to prevent an insider from trying to influence the price that an "entity" would attract if it came on the market?'

'That's about the size of it.'

*

'The RCMP brought MacIver to our attention when he left Canada in 2006 and we've kept his file open since then. It has to be said, however, that we've added very little to it. He's had no obvious connections with non-mainstream groups in Scotland, and the stuff he wrote for the *Glasgow Banner* was unexceptionable. Some eyebrows were raised when the First Minster took him on in 2007.'

'Did you tell her what you knew?'

'Not directly. We alerted the Permanent Secretary at the Scottish Executive, as it then was, and left it at that.'

'What about when she became FM.'

'We turned things up a notch. We talked to the PS again and suggested, quite strongly, that he advise the FM to request a full security check on MacIver and his known associates.'

'Did she?'

'Not to my knowledge. We weren't asked to do anything, certainly.'

Vanessa tried to keep any sign of surprise out of her voice. 'You mentioned known associates. If I give you two names, can you tell me if they came up on your radar?'

'Go on.'

'Simon Mathieson and Andrew MacIlwraith.'

There was a silence on the line. After about a minute, the voice came back.

'We identified both men as associates of MacIver in 2006. We don't think he met them again, or contacted them electronically, until earlier this year. He met them four times between May and July and has been in touch with them pretty continuously by email and text since then.'

*

Andy Hanna's final contact in London was a self-employed financial analyst, anonymous blogger, and FRIG associate who had recently been to the British Virgin Islands. His name had come up in his discussion with Aaronson, but his number had not been among those given to him by DCI Fiske. Aaronson had suggested that if anything was known about the beneficial owners of secret accounts, he would know it.

'So why hasn't he told you?   You're both part of FRIG, aren't you?'

'We don't share unless we're working jointly', Aaronson had said. 'More secure. He'll blog about what he knows. Eventually.'

They met in a coffee bar in Borough Market at lunchtime on Monday. Andy was hoping to get a flight to Aberdeen from London City in the middle of the afternoon, so he had phoned the number Aaronson had given him before he met the man from the SFO.   The only name he had was Carl, and when they met - he had told Andy he would be carrying a copy of *Forbes* magazine - he volunteered no further identification. Andy mentally noted the irony that someone investigating financial secrecy should so carefully guard his anonymity, but if this led to the single most important piece of evidence that Fiske needed from him, he could live with it.

'A number of us in FRIG have been digging around in the crown dependencies that act as tax havens and host offshore shell companies to see if we can identify any high profile public figures, especially those that have taken a hard line on tax avoidance or benefit fraud, who've been operating accounts through nominee directors. Mates of mine have been working in the Caymans, Bermuda and the Turks and Caicos. I've spent some time in BVI.'

'Did you find anything?'

'Nothing that the mainstream press would publish, and I'd need another source before I would even blog about it, but I'm pretty sure that I've identified two very big names behind a new private equity fund registered by nominees in BVI. But I'd need a very good reason to divulge them.'

Andy decided to appeal to conscience and good citizenship.

'Look, we're investigating two murders and two terrorist attacks, one involving a bomb. We think the perpetrators may have been bankrolled by a very big name who may also be into the kind of insider trading that the regulators can't touch. I can't, for very obvious reasons, give you the name. And I won't be able to tell you if any name you give me matches the names we're investigating. But I can talk to my boss about giving you a call before we go public.'

Andy knew he was pushing his luck. He calculated that if he got the information Fiske wanted, the fact that he had pushed the boundaries of acceptable behaviour would have consequences that he could accept. But it was still a risk.

Carl then used the same justification as Aaronson, saying that he was committed to exposing the activities of "liars, hypocrites and profiteers". He was showing exactly the same single-minded zeal as Aaronson. However, he also said that he had had a close friend who was killed in the 7 July terrorist bombings in London in 2005. Andy thought that this was what tipped the balance towards disclosure.

'The two names I have are Roskill and Carey. Big enough for you?'

Andy Hanna didn't react and he said nothing. He got up, paid for the coffees, and went to find a taxi to take him to the airport.

*

As soon as Fiske finished speaking to Andy Hanna, who had called her on his way to the Airport, she went to see DCS Esslemont to tell him that they should speak urgently to the Chief Constable. If he already thought this case was politically sensitive, he'd need a stiff drink after hearing what she now had to tell him.

CHAPTER TWENTY-FOUR

'Sir, the frequency with which Roskill's name has come up in the course of my enquiries clearly makes him a person of interest. I need to interview him.'

The Chief Constable shifted uneasily in his chair. DCS Esslemont nodded his agreement, but said nothing.

'We spoke before about the need to be able to defend our actions, Vanessa, and to be able to deflect any suggestions that we are indulging in fishing trips. I still have that concern. We are talking about a former prime minister...'

Vanessa interrupted. 'And the current head of the Foreign Office, though I'm not suggesting that I need to talk to him. Yet.'

The Chief ignored the intervention and went on. 'A former prime minister whose reputation as an international statesman and philanthropist stands high? You are suggesting that he is complicit in two murders and two terrorist attacks.'

'With respect, sir, at this point I am saying only that his name has come up in connection with MacIver and that I have intelligence that suggests that he is a beneficial owner of an account in the British Virgin Islands from which a substantial monthly sum has been paid to MacIver for the last six months. I need to ask him what he was buying with that money, a large part of which flowed straight through to the men we have charged with the murders of Peter Keller and Harvey Jamieson.'

'I think Vanessa's right, sir. If any other name had come up in the contexts she describes, we would have had no hesitation about interviewing them, at least informally, possibly under caution. Roskill should have no special treatment.'

'If you do talk to him, it will have to be informal at this stage. And we will have to observe the strictest confidentiality. Special Branch, the intelligence services and Counter-Terrorism will need to be informed.'

Vanessa looked at Esslemont, who nodded.

'Is that really necessary? I agree that I should ask for an informal interview, so I can't see that anyone outside this room, other than

Colin MacNee as Deputy SIO, needs to know. The more people who know, the more likely it is to get out. I've been very careful to pass on to the teams investigating Last and Mercury any material evidence that's come up as we've investigated the murders, and if talking to Roskill produces anything they should have, they'll have it. But we just don't know, until we approach him, whether he'll agree to speak to us, and, if he does, what he'll have to say.'

'In normal circumstances,' the Chief said, 'I'd have to brief the Justice Secretary on this, but I don't think that would be sensible. However, I'll need to talk to the Commissioner-Designate. It's unlikely that this will be concluded before he takes over.'

*

As soon as she had the Chief 's reluctant support, DCI Fiske contacted the Metropolitan Police Diplomatic Protection branch to request contact details that would enable her to make a direct approach to Roskill. The direct telephone number went to the chief executive of *The James M Roskill Public Affairs Trust*, a former diplomat and senior adviser to Roskill during his time as Foreign Secretary and Prime Minister.

Vanessa vaguely remembered his name, and his reputation as a brutally efficient gatekeeper who decided who could see his boss and who could not.

'I'm sorry, Chief Inspector, but Mr Roskill's diary is very full. He'll be in this country very little over the next month or two, so I think it unlikely that we can fit you in.'

Vanessa took a deep breath and told herself not to react to the patronising tone. It's like dealing with the bloody royals, she thought.

'Mr Griffiths,' she said, in as even a voice as she could manage, 'Mr Roskill's name has come up in the course of a double murder investigation and I would very much like to speak to him. I am happy to come to London, or to meet him anywhere else, within reason. At this stage' - she paused to let the implicit threat sink in - 'I am looking for an informal conversation and I am asking you to put my request to him.'

'I know what his response will be. That is my job.'

'Put it to him anyway. I will await your call. When may I expect to hear from you?'

'In due course.' He hung up.

*

'So how have you been?' Janet MacNee was taking Vanessa's blood pressure and looking at her scan on the computer screen. Before Vanessa could answer, she said, 'That's a wee bit higher than I'd like, but still within the proper range.'

'I'm glad to hear it. Given the pressure of this double murder enquiry that Colin and I are leading, I wouldn't have been surprised if it had gone through the roof. But generally, I'm fine. The morning sickness isn't as bad as it was. Funnily enough, it seemed to get better as soon as I told my team I'm pregnant. I could do with more sleep, though, but that's normal. And Neil's been great. Lots of TLC and some gentle sex.'

Janet laughed. 'Lucky you! You'd be surprised by the number of men who are put off by pregnancy.' She caught Vanessa's look. 'Not Colin, of course, since you ask. Have you thought any more about when to stop working?'

'Not really. As you'll know from Colin, this investigation has become very complex, and I really can't think beyond that right now.'

'I understand that, and I wouldn't have expected anything else. But you are carrying twins and that complicates things.'

'How?'

'Oh, come on, Vanessa, don't tell me you haven't been surfing the net for information about being pregnant with more than one baby!'

'I really haven't had time. I think Neil has, but he knows how focused I've been on these murders, so he's probably waiting for a good moment to share his research findings with me.'

'You must know that with twins you may not to go to full term. Expect to go into labour any time from thirty weeks on. You're ten weeks now, so that means you may only have five months to go. That's why you need to think about when to start your leave. You really don't want to start having contractions when you're at work. I'd advise you to plan for between twenty and twenty-five weeks. Day after tomorrow, really.'

Vanessa sighed. 'Thank you, Janet, for being so blunt. I'll work on it. You've given me ten weeks to finish this case.'

*

Griffiths, Roskill's minder, phoned back later on the day of Vanessa's initial conversation with him.

'I've spoken with Mr Roskill and he has asked me to put you in touch with his personal lawyer so that you can discuss with him the details of your request and the matters you would wish to discuss with Mr Roskill.'

Vanessa was very practised at spotting a runaround, and she thought she could see the signs.

'I did stress that I was requesting an informal interview. Involving a lawyer cranks things up a bit, don't you think?'

'That may be so, from your perspective, Chief Inspector. But that's where we are. If you want to progress this matter, you'll have to speak to Lord Cordingley. May I give you his contact details?'

Edmund Cordingley had been Solicitor General throughout Roskill's time as Prime Minister. He was a ultra-loyalist who had deliberately undermined the measured advice about the interventions in Central Asia that had been produced by his nominal boss, the Attorney General. He had left government to go into private practice as soon as Roskill left Downing Street. The Attorney General had been reported as saying that Cordingley was so far up Roskill's arse that he could see Richard Seaton.

'Lord Cordingley? Ieuan Griffiths suggested I should speak to you. I think you know why.'

'Ah, Chief Inspector, I was expecting your call.' The voice was cultured, smooth with the cadences of Westminster and the courts. Behind it, though, Vanessa could detect the accent of Cordingley's origins in West Yorkshire, effaced, but not completely. 'How do you believe I can help with your enquiries?'

Vanessa ignored the touch of sarcasm. 'I doubt that you can. As Mr Griffiths has probably told you, I need to speak with

James Michael Roskill and I understand that you may be able to facilitate that.'

'What would be the nature of your discussion with my client?' The implication of the privileged relationship was unmistakeable.

'That will become clear when I meet him. I would be happy for you to be present. All I can tell you is that his name has come up in the course of my enquiries.'

'I have no wish to be difficult.' The voice oozed insincerity. 'But I will advise my client against meeting you. I will tell him that I have asked you to submit written questions, which he will either answer or provide a written statement in response.'

'You're a lawyer, Lord Cordingley, so you must know that I can't accept that. I recently had to tell a potential witness that we don't operate through intermediaries. But she was an American. You don't have that excuse.'

'I'm not sure I like your tone.'

'I'm sorry about that. But I don't like being obstructed in my enquiries. I will ask again. Will you advise Mr Roskill to speak to me?'

'No. I will not.'

*

In Parliament at Holyrood the First Minister was under pressure from all sides but her own. Even her supporters looked silent, sullen and undemonstrative. Like all successful politicians, she had made enemies and created rivals. Her reliance on Paul MacIver had led her into failure to build the kind of personal alliances that show their value in a crisis. She hadn't dealt with the lingering resentment in some sections of her party about the ruthlessness with which she had deposed her predecessor. And there was already speculation, in the press and in the party, about how long she could survive and who would succeed her. Her statement had been prepared by civil servants and there was no-one to do the political fine tuning that had been MacIver's special talent.

> *Presiding Officer, I undertook to keep Parliament informed on the progress of the various police operations now underway: the murders at Grampian Royal Hospital and on the Vermont One oil platform, the bombing at Last*

Cairngorm and the apparent cyber attack on Mercury Fulfilment.

North East Constabulary have arrested three men in connection with the murders. These men have now been charged with various offences including murder and conspiracy to murder. Other charges may follow.

Enquiries into the Last and Mercury attacks are proceeding.

It would not be proper for me to comment further while enquiries area ongoing.

There was a murmur of incredulity, cries of 'Is that it?, as the Leader of the Opposition got up to speak.

'We now know, as we suspected last week, that one of the men arrested is Paul MacIver, Special Adviser to the First Minister, although I would like to think that he has now resigned from that position. There are persistent reports that MacIver was, at one time, member of an extremist nationalist splinter group known as

503

the Scottish Freedom Party. Will the First Minister tell Parliament what checks into his background and activities were undertaken when she first appointed him while she was Finance Secretary, and what further checks, if any, were made when she became First Minister?'

She rose, picking up her briefing notes from her desk. They shook noticeably in her hand.

'The Leader of the Labour Party knows that we never comment publicly on security matters. For the record, Mr MacIver resigned as soon as he was taken into custody.'

'At a time of national crisis, that is an unbelievably inadequate response. The public will draw its own conclusions from the fact that the First Minister has refused to confirm that security checks were undertaken. So will her party. She knows that I did not expect details, only confirmation that, if may borrow a phrase from the financial sector, due diligence had been

done. If she will not answer my question about security checks on Paul MacIver, will she confirm that she has been interviewed by officers investigating the murders?'

The First Minister remained seated, apparently unmoved by the shouts of 'Answer! Answer!' Members clamoured for a chance to speak. The Justice Secretary, seated beside the First Minister, gathered his papers, rose, and left the Chamber.

*

'Roskill won't see me. I remember learning about the Praetorian Guard that protected Roman emperors. Roskill's got one. I think that the only way we'll get to speak to him is to tell his lawyer that we want to interview him under caution.'

'It may come to that, Vanessa, but let's be sure we've explored all other avenues before we play that card.' Esslemont was as irritated as Fiske with the obstruction they faced, but his caution was a useful corrective to her aggression. 'Let's get MacIver in here again and press him on his links with Roskill. We can start with his search history, move on to the bank transfers, and then hit him with our belief that Roskill is a beneficial owner of the nominee account in BVI.'

'Fine, sir. But I don't want to delay too long. Roskill's in London for board meetings and I'd like to talk to him before he leaves. And it's possible that MacIver will give us something that we can use as leverage.'

It was already late afternoon, and it was likely that MacIver's lawyer, who was a partner in a large Edinburgh firm, would be unable to get to Aberdeen until the following morning.

*

The security correspondent of Channel 4 News had an exclusive. It aired at the top of the news at seven and was posted on the website immediately afterwards.

> *Reliable sources have told Channel 4 News that Scottish police investigating two murders and two terrorist attacks want to talk to former Prime Minister James Roskill.*

Last week, the Scottish political establishment was rocked by the news that the First Minister's closest political adviser, Paul MacIver, had been arrested in connection with the murders of American citizens Peter Keller at Grampian Royal Hospital in Aberdeen and Harvey Jamieson on the Vermont One oil platform in the North Sea. There are believed to be links between these killings, which occurred on the same day just over two weeks ago, and the bomb attack at the Last Cairngorm leisure development in Aberdeenshire and the cyber attack on Mercury Fulfilment in Cumbernauld, near Glasgow.

Our sources say that the Roskill connection involves an account held in the British Virgin Islands, a tax haven noted for its secrecy, and for the provision of nominee directors to conceal the identity of bank account holders. The precise nature of the connection is not known and Mr Roskill has refused a request to be interviewed.

This raises the possibility that the investigating officers will decide to interview the former Prime Minister under caution, which would be almost unprecedented for such a senior political figure.

The remainder of the report filled in the background to the case and named DCI Vanessa Fiske as the SIO, but gave no further details.

Vanessa's mobile rang at home just after seven.

'Sorry to call you at home.' Harry Conival's apologies were frequent but perfunctory and always elicited from Vanessa the reassurance that he shouldn't worry about it.

'Have you been watching the Channel 4 News?' Vanessa said she hadn't.

'You're probably too late to catch it now, but you can get it at eight on Channel 4+1 or right now on the website. They're claiming "reliable sources" for a story about you wanting to interview James Roskill. My phone is already ringing off the hook. I need a brief.'

'Fuck! Fuck! Fuck! You plug one leak and another springs up! I have no idea where this came from so I think we should say that we have no comment to make on unsubstantiated rumours.'

'There you go again. Too many words. We should just leave it at "No comment". They'll hate it and they'll be back, so you'll have to talk to me about it tomorrow.'

'I will, Harry, I will. As it happens, this might not be entirely unhelpful, but you didn't hear me say that.'

*

'Tell me about your relationship with James Roskill.'

Paul MacIver and his lawyer sat opposite Fiske and Esslemont in Interview Room 1 at NEC HQ. Colin MacNee and the Chief Constable were watching through the one-way glass.

MacIver looked at his lawyer, who nodded.

'I have never met Mr Roskill.'

'Are you absolutely sure about that?'

'Yes.'

'There are many kinds of relationship,' DCI Fiske said, 'and most of them don't involve face-to-face contact. In the hope of making progress, let me accept, for the moment, that you have never met Mr Roskill face-to-face. Have you been in contact with him in any other way?'

'Such as?' MacIver was feigning nonchalance, but he failed to convince.

'Email?'

'No comment.'

'Telephone?'

'No comment.'

'Semaphore or Morse code? Don't answer that, I am being unforgivably facetious. And you are being unbelievably unhelpful.'

'Is there a question, Chief Inspector?' This was the lawyer, speaking while resting a cautionary hand on his client's arm.

'My apologies. I have a full analysis of the search history from your personal computer. You have spent a lot of time consulting websites about Roskill. Do you deny having done so?'

'No.'

'A straight answer! I'm so glad this is being recorded. Now, will you tell us why you were so interested in Mr Roskill?'

'He's an interesting man, sometimes with interesting opinions about Scotland.'

'Such as?'

'I can't think of an example offhand.'

Vanessa smiled. 'Let me see if I can jog your memory. I spent a fascinating few hours looking at all the sites you had visited. There was only one reference to Scottish politics. Do you remember it?'

'No.'

'Roskill was speculating on the possible effects on the independence campaign of foreign investors pulling their money out of Scotland. He seemed to think, on balance, that it would help the cause of independence. Do you agree with him?'

'No comment.'

'There's a coded email exchange on your computer between
damascus@easymail.com   and
mike@exflt.com.   What can you tell me about that?'

'No comment.'

'I believe that that you, Paul, are "Damascus" and that "Mike" is James Michael Roskill. Am I right?

'No comment.'

'We've broken the code.   It wasn't very difficult. Interesting though, because the first email in the series was sent from your laptop to "Mike"' and it appears to be following up from a face-to-face meeting. Did you send that email?'

'No comment.'

Vanessa opened the file in front of her and brought out a clear plastic folder with some papers in it.

'These are copies of the bank statements of the Scottish Freedom Club. You are a signatory. A substantial sum has been deposited to that account every month since April. The money is transferred from an account held by a bank in the British Virgin Islands. Who was sending the money?'

'No comment.'

'How would you react if I told you that we have reason to believe that the BVI account is controlled by Roskill?'

MacIver looked down at the table, apparently to mask his reaction and the fact that he had become very pale. He looked at his lawyer, who leaned towards him and whispered in his ear.

'No comment.'

'What was Roskill buying from you for a two thousand pounds a month?'

'No comment.'

'I will be speaking to Mr Roskill very soon, but it would do your case no harm if you were to tell us what you know about these accounts.'

Again, MacIver broke eye contact with Vanessa and turned to his lawyer, who shook his head.

'No comment.'

'What about the £750 each that went from the SFC account to your friends Simon Mathieson and Andy MacIlwraith?   What was that for?'

'No comment.'

*

'He's met Roskill all right. Did you see how he reacted when I said I knew that Roskill controlled that BVI account?'

Colin MacNee smiled, nodded and accepted the large whisky Vanessa had poured him from a bottle extracted from the bottom drawer of a filing cabinet. Vanessa found a bottle of fizzy water in her bag.

'And the whole thing was pretty free of denials.' Colin said. 'He knows we've got him but he's smart enough to know that the case is circumstantial so he's relying on a jury basing its verdict on presumption of innocence and the defence pointing out the almost total absence of forensic evidence.'

'So let's see if we can beef it up a bit. We'll have to interview Roskill under caution. At the very least, he's looking at conspiracy to murder.'

CHAPTER TWENTY-FIVE

In Aberdeen, DCI Vanessa Fiske was on the telephone in DCS Esslemont's office. The Chief Constable's Acting Staff Officer was also there, and the phone was on speaker.

'Lord Cordingley, things have moved on since we spoke before, which is why I have not been in touch. You know that your proposal that I should submit my questions to Mr Roskill in writing was completely unacceptable. I have now decided, after discussions with senior colleagues, that I need to interview him under caution. When would it be convenient to do so? I am happy to come to London, and I should emphasise that the matter is urgent.'

Vanessa was speaking in her most formal tone and had decided that she would not rise to whatever patronising shit Cordingley decided to throw at her.

'I still need to know the nature of your enquiries, Chief Inspector.'

'All I am obliged to tell you is that I believe that your client maybe able to help with my enquiries into several very serious crimes.'

'I'll need more than that before I advise my client to meet you.'

'I am not asking him to "meet" me. I am telling him, through you, which is unsatisfactory in itself, that I need to interview him under caution. If you are not prepared to facilitate that, I will ask my colleagues in the Metropolitan Police to arrest him so that he can be brought to Aberdeen. That may still be necessary after I speak to him, but I would have thought that you would wish to avoid, for as long as possible, the consequences of a formal arrest.'

For a long moment, Cordingley said nothing. 'I will speak with Mr Roskill, as soon as I can, and I will telephone you.'

'Before close of play today,' Vanessa said, using a metaphor that Harry Conival had advised her against, because not much cricket was played in Aberdeen. In London it was, though, and she had a memory of having seen a picture of Roskill holding court in the Members' Enclosure at Lord's. And hadn't he gone to a cricket match immediately after resigning as Prime Minister? Or maybe that was one of his predecessors.

517

She hung up, turned to Esslemont and exhaled deeply. 'I'll go tomorrow, sir. Cordingley knows that if he tries to stall, this will go public. Do you want to be present for the interview?'

The DCS knew that he should probably recognise the significance of interviewing a former prime minister under caution by being there, but he hated going to London.

'No. Take MacNee with you. I'll sit in if you have to bring Roskill here.'

*

In Saltcoats, the SOCOs were re-examining MacIlwraith's house. Colin MacNee had asked for a further forensic search in the hope of finding some physical evidence that would link MacIlwraith to the Last Cairngorm bombing. He was convinced that his browsing history, and the fact that he had downloaded bomb-making instructions, would not be enough to secure a conviction on a conspiracy charge. The PF had said as much. He needed physical evidence to buttress the circumstantial case, and he was certain that MacIlwraith would not have been smart enough, nor careful enough, to eliminate all evidence of bomb making.

'So how the fuck did you miss it first time round?'

Colin was angry and, uncharacteristically, he was showing it. The most senior SOCO had phoned him to tell him that they had discovered, at the back of a desk drawer, a tenancy agreement for a light industrial unit - no bigger than a lock-up garage - on a trading estate not far from MacIlwraith's house. He wanted to know if they should get help from Strathclyde Police to open the unit and search it.

'What do you think?' Colin's tone was sarcastic and incredulous. 'I'll get in touch with Kilmarnock and get them to send round a couple of PCs and some bolt cutters. Just make sure you do it right. Take as long as you need, within reason.'

*

In Glasgow, Dongle Donaldson was working with the cyber crime specialists of Strathclyde Police to see if any more evidence could be extracted from Simon Mathieson's computer equipment. It had been very difficult to make the case against Mathieson in relation to the cyber attack of Mercury Fulfilment any less circumstantial. Mathieson's laptop had been configured to control all his other devices and it could have been used to launch an attack, or to engage in other kinds of hacking. But, as Dongle had expected, a direct link to Mercury Fulfilment had proved elusive.

'When my boss asked me to investigate Mathieson's search history, I only had access to his laptop and, unlike the other guy, he had been very careful not to leave a trail that would incriminate him.' Dongle was thinking aloud over coffee in the canteen in Govan Police Station with two DIs from the high tech squad. 'Did he have any other devices that he might have used for surfing the net?'

'There was a tablet with no history of being used for anything but email, and we checked that the emails were on the same account as the laptop. He had a whole array of hard disks. Any of them could have been hooked up to a keyboard and temporarily configured to get on the web.'

'Did you check them?'

The two DIs looked at each other and then looked down at their coffees. 'Not all that carefully, if we're honest. We were focused on more sophisticated uses of the hardware. We were looking for evidence of cyber crime more than anything. And Andy Hanna wanted us to search for any financial information.'

Dongle decided that getting ripped into them would be counter-productive, and, in any case, they outranked him. His special expertise gave him some leeway with his superiors, but it needed to be deployed carefully.

Dongle spent the rest of the day meticulously searching the various memory devices that had been found in Mathieson's flat. It was time-consuming and painstaking work, especially because he had to be sure that he was recovering stuff that Mathieson – no mean computer expert himself – didn't want anybody to find. He was good, but not as good as me, Dongle thought, as he prepared a report for DCI Fiske.

*

In Edinburgh, the First Minister was preparing for another appearance in

Parliament and another grilling by the opposition. Senior members of her party were openly speculating about how long she could remain in office. The Justice Secretary had not spoken to her since he had dramatically left the Chamber as she answered questions after her previous statement.

In Glasgow, the editorial conference at the *Banner* had discussed the position the paper should take on the First Minister's difficulties. The editorial line had usually been supportive of the government in general and of the FM in particular. In common with other titles, however, it had recalled the abrupt resignation of one of her predecessors. The first leader in the *Glasgow Banner* made uncomfortable reading in St Andrews House:

> *Just over ten years ago, a First Minister was forced to resign over a relatively minor, and as it turned out, technical, breach of the rules governing expenses payable to MSPs and MPs. This newspaper called for his resignation because of the damage that was being done to the reputation of the Scottish Parliament. We now have the unedifying spectacle of a First Minister who, because of a*

conspicuous failure to confirm that she instituted proper security checks on a potential employee, stands accused of not having done so.

Unless she can tell Parliament today that the checks were done, especially when she became First Minister, to ensure that Mr Paul MacIver, now on remand on very serious criminal charges, posed no security threat, she must go. MacIver is widely known to have had connections with radical, even extremist, nationalists. That in itself should have been enough to put the First Minister on her guard.

Let us be clear about the questions she must answer:

Did she request security checks when she was considering the appointment of Paul MacIver as her special adviser when she was appointed as Finance Secretary?

Did she ensure that further checks were undertaken when she became First Minister?

Will she tell parliament who recommended MacIver to her?

Did she act on advice from the Security Services relayed to her by the Permanent Secretary to the Scottish Government that they considered it essential that MacIver be fully vetted?

If the answer to any of these questions is no, the First Minister's position will be untenable.

The First Minister looked up from reading the press cuttings. The only other people in her room in St Andrews House were the Permanent Secretary and her Private Secretary. They waited for her to speak.

'Somebody is briefing the papers, especially the *Banner*. How else would they know about advice from the security services or the question of who recommended Paul to me?'

Neither of the civil servants spoke.

'Should I call the Cabinet before I make a statement?'

'That is entirely a matter for you, First Minister. I would simply advise that you would need to be clear about the purpose of such a meeting.'

What she needed was the kind of advice that she had paid Paul MacIver to provide.

'Draft a statement. Have it here within an hour. Then I'll decide how to proceed.'

*

In Wilmington, Delaware, the Board of Burtonhall had dispersed and, with the exception of the Chairman, Richard Seaton, the board members had been driven to Philadelphia International Airport, where the Burtonhall jet was waiting to take them to their connecting flights: the Russian to New York for a flight to Moscow, via Paris, the American to Omaha, Nebraska, and Roskill to New York to catch the BA First Class Service to London City.

Seaton and Cy Packard, the CEO, were in Packard's office drinking Jack Daniels from the crystal glasses that Cy had been given when he left the CIA.

'James was uncharacteristically quiet today.' Packard said.

Seaton sipped his Bourbon. 'I noticed that. But I didn't know what to make of it.'

'Me either. His whole attitude has been a little strange recently. He was oddly reluctant to approach his old friend Carey to get the Scottish police to stop crawling over us. And he claimed he didn't think there was any need for him to attend the Board meeting. I had to lean on him pretty hard. Almost called you in to persuade him. I have a feeling, an instinct, the kind I used to get sometimes in the Company, that he's up to something.'

'But what?'

'I have no idea. I may have to call in some favours and see what I can find.'

*

In London, Roskill was met by Cordingley at City Airport. Roskill was surprised, and slightly concerned, to see his lawyer waiting for him after he cleared immigration via the VIP line.

'Edmund! What a surprise! I expected to see Vic.'

'He's outside with the car. I had to speak to you immediately and privately. Can we go somewhere quiet? There's a VIP lounge here I take it?'

'You can say anything in front of Vic. Let's just go to the car.'

'No, Mike. This is serious, and delicate, and I don't propose to take any risks.'

Vic was Roskill's protection officer and he had been with him for years. He had heard almost as many secrets as the Queen. Something was up.

They found a quiet table in the lounge and poured some coffee.

'No point in telling you this any way but directly. The Scottish police - Detective Chief Inspector Vanessa Fiske, formerly of the Met - wants to interview you under caution. She'll probably be here tomorrow. You can't refuse.'

'I fucking well can! I am a former Prime Minister of the UK and I do not need to truckle to a minor fucking police officer!'

Foul language, pulling rank and insulting other public servants. Cordingley had seen it before, and always when Roskill was unsure of his ground.

'No, you can't. Because if you do, she'll send the boys in blue round from the Met and you'll be arrested and taken to Aberdeen. And do you honestly believe that the press won't be alerted? I really don't know whether we can keep a lid on this, but I'm sure we can't if you refuse to be interviewed.'

'What's it about?'

'Fiske says she believes you can help with her inquiries into several serious crimes. No further details. I thought you might want to hazard a guess.'

Roskill's denial was perfunctory and unconvincing.

Cordingley shook his head despairingly. 'Mike, if I'm going to help you, I need to know what's going on. I've checked, and Fiske is currently investigating two murders, both in companies owned by Burtonhall. And there are possible links to the attacks on to Last Cairngorm and Mercury Fulfilment.

You have connections to all of them except Last.'

'You can sit in. Then it'll be news to you at the same time as it's news to me.'

There was no point in pressing him any further. They might have another discussion before Fiske arrived, but Cordingley doubted it. His client was in real trouble, but what kind of trouble was known only to the police and his client. And his client wasn't telling.

*

Vanessa got home well after eight. She had spent two hours preparing for her interview with Roskill, which she had agreed could take place at the offices of The James M Roskill Public Affairs Trust in Belgravia the following afternoon. She had arranged a flight in the late morning, which would give her time to talk to Dongle about Mathieson and check with the PF about the possibility of charges against Roskill and further charges against MacIver. She could talk to Colin MacNee on the plane about what the SOCOs had found in Saltcoats.

Neil was in the kitchen - as always, Vanessa thought, with a little pang of guilt - and the smell suggested smoked fish.

'Cullen skink! My Glasgow auntie used to make it, but I don't suppose a nice middle class girl form the West Midlands has ever heard of it.   It's essentially a Scottish chowder, made with smoked haddock - I sourced some smokies from Arbroath -, cream and potatoes. You'll like it. Very nourishing. Very wholesome. My auntie said it would stick to my ribs. She also said it would put hair on my chest, but that wouldn't interest you, I suppose.'

Vanessa put her arms round his neck and kissed him. 'If you made it, I'll love it. Even if it didn't do much for your chest.'

'I decided to be buff, not hairy. If you have any complaints, submit them in writing!'. But Vanessa was already in their bedroom, getting out of her working clothes.

As they finished eating, Vanessa told Neil that she was going to London the next day to interview James Roskill.

'I thought you might be. I had a call today from my contact in the SFO, and it seems that the ex-PM's name is being much bandied about in the City, Nothing very specific, but a suggestion that some of his dealings may be a little less than kosher.'

'You could say that! I think he may have been complicit in a couple of murders and a bit of terrorism. I'll put it to him, but I doubt he'll cough. I've done a bit of contingency planning with the PF. She thinks we might be able to get him on conspiracy to murder and conspiracy to commit terrorism, but the case is far from strong. I'll need to put some pressure on him. Colin's coming with me and I might let loose his moral indignation. Might work. Anyway, it will be fun to watch. He's a terrier when he gets going.'

'My contact also told me that Andy Hanna may have overstepped the mark when he talked to one of the journalists who've been investigating offshore tax havens. Implying that you might provide a *quid quo pro* in return for information about the 'very big names' you're investigating.'

Vanessa smiled. 'Andy's certainly shown the occasional sign of going off piste - Esslemont raised an eloquent eyebrow when he came up with information about cross memberships of the boards of the companies we're looking at.

But what he found was useful. I'll wait until I hear what he's got.'

'You've changed your tune a bit since we had that little spat about how you should treat the gentlemen of the press! Your morality has become a little less absolute.'

'OK, so I over-reacted. Put it down to the pressure of the case. I really, really need to close it, and if Andy's information helps, that's fine. I guess it's unlikely to be the kind of stuff that we can use in court, but if it makes it even a little more likely that we'll get convictions, that's fine too.'

Neil refilled his glass - a nice Chilean Sauvignon Blanc to go with the fish - and took Vanessa's hand in his. 'Do you honestly believe you'll get Roskill in court? A former PM and internationally respected philanthropist?'

'Christ, Neil, you sound like the Chief. You should have heard him talking about the need to be able to defend our actions, not going on fishing trips, bullshit, bullshit, bullshit. At least Esslemont weighed in on my side. No special favours. Treat Roskill like any other "person of interest". Going to him rather than bringing him here is as far as I'm prepared to go in respecting his position.'

'You know it'll get out. Somebody will tip off the press. The Met knows you're interested in him. A lot of people in NEC know...'

'I trust my people and, especially after the Fleming business, I don't think any of them is likely to be indiscreet.'

'I understand that. But you've had to backfill to investigate the Roskill connection, and some of the people you've now got working on it don't owe you anything. Don't mistake respect for your rank and your reputation for personal loyalty.'

Vanessa was quiet for a moment, considering carefully how to respond. She discussed almost everything about her work with Neil. He had been really helpful with the financial aspects of the case. But she bridled when anybody, even somebody she loved, told how to do her job. She decided to say nothing except that she'd think about it.

'Good. Better to be ready.'

*

The First Minister read the draft statement prepared by the Permanent Secretary. It was bland to the point of vacuousness, rehearsing the timeline that had led to MacIver's arrest, and reiterating that the FM had had no reason to suspect that he might have been involved in criminality. She had had no prior knowledge of the arrest and it would be inappropriate to comment further. A reference to the presumption of innocence had been added by her private secretary, but she struck it out even before she had decided not to make the statement.

She asked the Permanent Secretary to come to her office.

'James, this really won't do. If I make this statement, I'll be crucified in Parliament. It says absolutely nothing. The best that can be said for it is that it might do as a holding statement, but I think we are well past the point at which Parliament will accept that. They are out to get me and the silence from the Justice Secretary suggests that he is positioning himself.'

'First Minister, you would not expect me to comment on party matters. But I have to advise you that it would be unacceptable in terms of accountability if you were to let another parliamentary session go by without a statement. If my draft is unacceptable, and you accept my advice that a statement must be made, I will draft another statement. Before I do so, I need to discuss the content.'

'Go on.'

'We have reached the point, First Minister, where you need to answer in detail the questions that have been raised about the vetting, or otherwise, of Paul MacIver. You will need to address the points raised in Parliament last week, and in the press this week. If I may be frank, you need to answer the questions set out in the *Banner*. I have the information to answer three of those questions. The issue of who recommended MacIver to you is a matter entirely for you. On those in respect of which I am able to produce a draft, the answer, in all three cases, is no.'

CHAPTER TWENTY-SIX

James Michael Roskill had decided that charm would be more effective than bluster. He was good at it, and Vanessa Fiske knew immediately that she would have to keep her guard up. It wasn't that she was particularly susceptible to flattery or exaggerated respect. She wasn't, and she would not have acquired her reputation as an effective interrogator if she was. Rather it was an awareness of the seductive and potentially undermining effect of being close to someone who had wielded so much power; who had, apparently without self-doubt, taken life and death decisions; who had, apparently without losing sleep, sent hundreds of his fellow citizens to war. And it was about being in the presence of the kind of self-confidence seldom experienced except among the very powerful and the very rich. Roskill was both.

When Fiske and MacNee arrived at the Belgravia headquarters of the James M Roskill Public Affairs Trust, the receptionist, a stunningly beautiful young black woman with a South African accent, picked up the phone and said they were in reception. They sat down and looked at the various reports and publications on display. All were concerned with the charitable and philanthropic activities of the Trust and all contained many photographs of Roskill, sometimes with the recipients of the Trust's grants, but more often with world leaders, monarchs, and presidents. Colin MacNee thought that Roskill was very careful about his legacy and his legend.

The detectives were surprised when the former Prime Minister came through the door behind reception, thanked the receptionist by name, held out his hand and said, 'Chief Inspector Fiske, welcome to the Trust. Inspector MacNee, good to meet you, too.'

Vanessa appreciated the punctiliousness with which, gender notwithstanding, he had recognised her seniority. It didn't always happen, and the frequency with which Colin was greeted as "DCI Fiske" was a running joke between them. She also noted that he had not thought it necessary to say who he was.

'Please come up.'

They climbed an elegant cantilevered staircase, curved in a style that Vanessa recognised as an eighteenth century signature feature, and were led into Roskill's office. It had been a drawing room and was now furnished in a deliberately modern style. There was no desk. Colin recalled that Roskill had been famous for having no desk in his Downing Street office and for hiring - and firing - people while they sat on a sofa and he stood. There were two modern Chesterfield sofas and three matching armchairs, grouped round three sides a low table. The fourth side ensured that every seat offered a view, through the tall sash windows, of the Belgravia street scene. It would be easy to be comfortable here, but less easy to be relaxed.

A man of about Roskill's age was already in the room, preparing to pour coffee or tea from the pots arranged on a side table.

'I think you've already spoken to Edmund, Chief Inspector, but you've not met.'

Vanessa extended her hand. 'Lord Cordingley. This is my colleague, DI Colin MacNee.'

Cordingley said nothing.

'Edmund is rather highly priced help for pouring the coffee, but he'll turn his hand to most things. I've asked him to be here today.' He paused for effect. 'For obvious reasons.'

Vanessa decided to formalise the atmosphere.

'Mr Roskill, I am going to question you. Before I do so I must caution you. You are not obliged to answer any of these questions but any answers you give will be noted and may be used in evidence against you. In normal circumstances, in a matter as serious as this, I would interview you in a police station and record the interview. In this case, I hope that you will accept that it is sufficient for DI MacNee to take notes, a copy of which will be provided to you.'

Roskill looked to Cordingley, who nodded.

The interview lasted no more than half-an-hour. It ranged from the exchange of emails between damascus@easymail.com and mike@exflt.com, through the nature of any other contact that Roskill might have had with Paul MacIver, his financial interests in Burtonhall and its companies, the bombing of Last Cairngorm and the cyber attack on Mercury Fulfilment, to the beneficial ownership of the BVI nominee account from which substantial payments had been made to MacIver, and which the detectives believed had been used to finance his illegal activities.

For most of the interview, Roskill was calm and impassive, more often denying all knowledge than offering no comment. It was only when the questioning turned to the attacks on Last and Mercury and the possible effects on the market value of the companies, and to the BVI account, that Roskill paused before answering and turned, wordlessly, to Cordingley for advice. Fiske was unsure to what extent the two men had prepared their answers but it was clear that the only lines of questioning that unsettled them were those concerning Last and Mercury and the offshore account.

'I have reason to believe, Mr Roskill, that you are one of two beneficial owners of this account.' She handed him a note of the details as communicated to the bank where MacIver's account was held. 'I believe that I also know the identity of the other owner, but it would be inappropriate for me to name him at this stage. Can you confirm that you control this account through nominees?'

'No comment.'

'Have you any knowledge of the payments from this account, of over £2000 per month over a six month period, to an account in the name of Paul MacIver?

'No comment.'

'What was the purpose of these payments?'

'No comment.'

'Did you, through these payments, help to finance the attacks at Last and Mercury?'

'No comment.'

'Did you conspire with Paul MacIver to destabilise Hedelco and Ebright Offshore Drilling in order to affect the value of these companies?'

'No comment.'

'Thank you, Mr Roskill. I think it is likely that I shall have to speak to you again soon. If I do, you will have to come to Aberdeen. In the meantime, DI MacNee will give you a copy of his notes and, once they have been transcribed, we will send you a copy of the record as we place it in the case file. May I ask you, or Lord Cordingley on your behalf, to sign this to confirm receipt of the copy?'

*

As they walked towards Sloane Square, Colin MacNee gave Vanessa his impressions of the interview.

'He didn't half play on his reputation as a technophobe!' It was common knowledge, because he tended to mention it in every interview he gave, that Roskill could not use a computer, knew nothing about the Internet and had never sent an email. It was part of his persona as a world statesman existing above the common herd.

'But were you convinced? I certainly wasn't. When you were asking him about the email exchanges, his answers seemed to me to show he knew more about the process of emailing than he was ready to admit. I wish we had a tape. My notes are pretty full, though, and he used terminology that would be unfamiliar to the kind of technophobe he claims to be.'

'Such as?' They were entering Sloane Square station to get a train to Paddington.

'"Spam", "domain", "IP address", "server", to name just a few.'

'Oh, come on, Colin. He could have picked up that kind of language anywhere. From his staff, his kids, from books and newspapers. Proves nothing."

'No, boss, it's more than that. He was easy with the language, familiar, more than just aware of it.'

'Would you like to put that to a jury?'

'No, but I would like to put it to Roskill the next time we talk to him. He's mike@exflt.com and he's been emailing MacIver. I'm sure of it. I think we should try to get MacIver to confirm it and then press Roskill.'

'Seems pretty clear that he's behind the BVI account. I think we may have enough to convince the PF to charge him with conspiracy to cause an explosion and possibly to murder. If she goes for it, and she'll have to consult the Crown Office in Edinburgh, we'll have to get Roskill to Aberdeen and into court. Jason Sime of the *G & T* was right: this is bigger than Dunblane.'

*

'There's no doubt that MacIlwraith's lock-up was used to make a bomb. It would be going too far to describe it as a bomb factory, though that's what the tabloid headlines will say. The SOCOs found residues of the "ingredients" listed in the "recipes" he had downloaded. And there was also equipment that the anti-terrorism squad say is consistent with the manufacture of explosives. And he had more rucksacks than a Boy Scout troop.'

While Fiske and MacNee were in London, a verbal report had gone to Esslemont. Colin was now reading from the full SOCO report.

'You'll need to put it to him before we decide whether to ask the PF to change the charges against him,' Vanessa said, 'though it won't matter one way or the other. He's going away for a long time. What's important is that it hugely increases the likelihood of a jury convicting him. We need something like that to be sure of nailing Mathieson for the cyber attack. I think a jury will convict him on the Jamieson murder charge, but I'd like to close the file on Mercury as well.'

'I'll see if Dongle's back from Glasgow.'

Fiske and MacNee had got back to NEC HQ in the early evening after interviewing Roskill. Esslemont and the Chief were unavailable until the next morning. Their report on the former Prime Minister and their recommendation that he be brought to Aberdeen for a further interview and probable charges would have to wait. It was also too late too speak to the Procurator Fiscal, so Vanessa decided to speak informally to Fiona Marchmont, the force's legal adviser. She got her at home just as she was getting her children to bed. She called back about fifteen minutes later.

'It sounds to me as if the only thing that will give the PF pause will be the political sensitivity. The evidence is certainly enough, even if it's circumstantial, to go to court and let a jury decide. But we kid ourselves if we believe that the decision will be simple or very quick. The Crown Office will have to be involved. The security services will need to know. Intergovernmental courtesy will be invoked to tell the Home Secretary and Number 10. You might get clearance to arrest Roskill by the end of tomorrow, but it might be the day after.'

'Can I ask you, off the record, about something else? The other beneficial owner of the BVI account is almost certainly Sir Justin Carey...'

Fiona interrupted and said, incredulously, 'Carey of the FO? Are you sure?'

'As sure as I can be given the secrecy that surrounds everything in BVI, but I don't have anything else on him. No other connection with these cases, except my suspicion that Roskill got him to intervene when we were trying to get the Hedelco emails. I could regard him as a person of interest, but it would be a stretch. Will my case against Roskill be weakened if he is referred to as "A N Other"?'

'I don't think so, but I'll consider it further. It might be better if you didn't refer to him at all. I'm sure you can think of ways of dealing with Carey informally, but very effectively!'

'Fine. And thanks, I may have to talk to you officially tomorrow.'

'Before you go, how are you? We haven't spoken for a while.'

'I'm OK. Knackered, but OK. My blood pressure's up a little, but the morning sickness is better. I just need to get this case off my desk before I can ease up a bit. If Roskill needs to be arrested, I'm bloody well not going to London again. The Met can do it, or if it needs someone from here, Esslemont will have to conquer his dislike of leaving Aberdeen.'

'Good luck with that! I may see you tomorrow.'

*

Vanessa looked at her watch. It was half past eight and she hadn't been able to speak to Neil since getting back from London. As she reached for the phone, Colin MacNee stuck his head round her door.

'Dongle's here. Will I bring him in?'

Vanessa sighed and nodded.

'There are times when I think that Strathclyde runs on its reputation. Turned out that their examination of Mathieson's hardware had been less than thorough. I thought about having a go at them for laziness or laxness or just plain stupidity but...'

'Dongle, just get on with it. We can deal with Strathclyde's witlessness some other time.'

'Sorry, boss, but it didn't half piss me off. Turned out that their examination of the hardware had not included discovering if he had used any of his hard disks - there were seven in total - to access the Internet. They said they were focused on cyber crime and Andy's request for financial records, but they should have...sorry. I spent a long time doing what they hadn't and, as I expected, there was evidence that he had had one of his hard disks configured for browsing. He had tried to delete the browser, but I found it and there was partial history. I got the rest by playing on the hi-tech squad's guilty conscience and getting them to request a full search history.

'Mercury Fulfilment has a number of websites, mainly in the US and here, but also in Australia, Canada, and Japan. Our man had visited all of them, and it looks as if he was trying to get deeper into them than would be necessary to check whether the sweater you had ordered was on its way. I think he was trying to analyse the security protocols, which is what hackers do when they want to disable a site or flood it with spam. Impossible to tell how successful he was, though. And the Strathclyde guys still can't say definitively that his gear was used to attack Mercury.'

'I thought that might be the case. But thanks, Dongle. The case against Mathieson is still circumstantial, but it's now a bit stronger.'

Dongle smiled appreciatively. 'There's a wee bit more. I founds some emails between Mathieson and MacIlwraith, with MacIver copied in. Nothing very interesting in them, as far as I can see, but it does firm up the connections. I'll add them to my report.'

'You do that! Good work! Now, I'm going home to see if Neil still knows who I am.'

*

That afternoon, while Fiske and MacNee were interviewing Roskill, the Scottish political establishment and media were digesting the implications of the resignation of the First Minster. After her conversation with the Permanent Secretary she had quickly accepted that she had to go. She had considered the possibility of simply issuing a press statement and leaving Edinburgh for what the press always calls "an undisclosed destination", but she knew she would have to make a statement to Parliament. The Permanent Secretary had advised her that she should announce who would be Acting FM until the election of her successor and she was fully aware of the politics of that decision. She wanted to avoid giving an unfair advantage to any of the obvious candidates - the Justice Secretary, who was no longer bothering to conceal his ambitions to succeed her; her deputy, who also held the finance portfolio that he had inherited from her; the parliamentary business manager who, like all chief whips, knew where the bodies were buried - so she chose the oldest member of her cabinet, the Education Secretary, who, she knew, had no ambitions to fill the top job and who had, in any case, decided to retire at the next election.

Before concluding her statement she thanked her party for the opportunity to serve her country in its highest office. She said she would play a full part in the referendum campaign, and she announced that she would leave parliament immediately.

The Leader of the Opposition rose. He said that the First Minister had made the right decision because her position had become untenable and that by resigning she had limited the damage to Scotland and its Parliament. The First Minister, and every MSP in the chamber, knew that he was about to twist the knife.

'However, we need to consider what has been left unsaid. Paul MacIver, until recently the First Minister's closest confidante, is currently on remand in Aberdeen Prison on extremely serious charges. It seems likely that these charges will relate to his activities in the cause of independence and that he was engaged in crime both before and during his service with the First Minister. He appeared at her side as soon as she became Finance Secretary and stayed there while she was in the highest office. But where did he come from? How did he come to the First Minister's attention? Was he placed there in order to advance his revolutionary separatist agenda? And if so, by whom? The First Minister told us nothing of this. She moves on, but these questions remain. Will she answer all or any of them? Or will she simply walk out of this chamber and leave the truth

undisclosed, to be discovered by the judicial process or, as I believe to be necessary, by a full public enquiry?'

The First Minister stared straight ahead and did not move. The chamber was completely silent.

The Presiding Officer spoke. 'First Minister?'

She rose. 'It would not be appropriate for me to comment further on matters still subject to police...'

She got no further. A cacophony of jeers and catcalls drowned her out. She sat down as the Presiding Officer called for order. As the hubbub declined, she stood up and tried to continue. But the Leader of the Opposition was also on his feet, gesturing and calling for answers while signalling to his own members to quieten down.

'Presiding Officer, I have not asked questions about the appropriateness of her relationship with Paul MacIver. On that, her resignation is eloquent enough. Nor can she now decide to appoint a public enquiry into matters that relate, in part, to her own judgment and behaviour. But she can say that she would welcome such an enquiry if it were ordered by her successor. Will she now do so?

'First Minister?' The Presiding Officer looked directly at her.

The First Minister shook her head slightly, got up, and left the chamber of the Scottish Parliament for the last time.

*

Ben Aaronson of the *Financial Post* had another exclusive. It went up on the paper's website just as Vanessa Fiske got home. Neil was answering the call from Harry Conival as she turned her key in the lock.

Reliable sources have told the Post *that former Prime Minister James Roskill has been interviewed under caution by police investigating two murders, the terrorist bombing of the Last Cairngorm and the cyber attack on Mercury Fulfilment. Roskill serves on the Board of Burtonhall Inc., parent company of Hedelco who manage the hospital in Aberdeen, where Peter Keller was murdered three weeks ago, and Ebright Offshore Drilling, on whose Vermont One oil platform Harvey Jamieson was found dead on the same day. The former Prime Minister is also a director of Mercury.*

It is unprecedented for such a senior political figure to be regarded as a suspect in a serious crime. Tony Blair was interviewed as a potential witness in a cash-for-honours investigation while he was Prime Minister, but not under caution.

Mr Roskill is believed to have come to the attention of the investigating officers as a result of enquiries into the financial affairs of Burtonhall and its subsidiaries.

The news of the police interest in the former Prime Minister comes on the same day as the resignation of Scotland's First Minister, as a result of the arrest of her close political adviser, Paul MacIver, in connection with the same offences.

Vanessa looked up from the computer. 'His sources are certainly reliable, but they're not here. I'll have to talk to Harry and I'll have to find Esslemont and the Chief. Roskill will have to be arrested as soon as we can mobilise the Met.'

CHAPTER TWENTY-SEVEN

Despite what she had said to Fiona Marchmont, DCI Vanessa Fiske was on the first plane to London City the next morning. She had recalled her conversation with DCS Esslemont about her pregnancy, and her determination that if a former Prime Minister was to be charged in connection with crimes she had been investigating, she would make the arrest. The Chief Constable had insisted that she be accompanied by Esslemont, who had arrived to collect her, driven by a uniformed constable, at 0545 hrs. She came out of the lift at the apartment block where she and Neil lived, carrying her now obligatory bottle of fizzy water, and tried to make her greeting to her boss as bright as possible and her smile less wan than it felt.

'The Chief spoke to the Commissioner, and his acting staff officer has been up most of the night briefing the appropriate people on our behalf. Aaronson's piece probably means that the press will have Roskill's home covered. Special Branch are trying to determine via his protection officers exactly where he is. The Chief and the Commissioner agreed with you that they shouldn't authorise an arrest "by appointment".   It wasn't easy to persuade them that Roskill might be a flight risk, but the seriousness of the offences tipped the balance.'

'So we don't know where he is?'

'We didn't last night, no. We're being met in London by someone senior from Special Branch - name of Bancroft, I think. Hopefully, he'll know more.'

Vanessa smiled.   'It was Bancroft who informed me, when Fiona and I were at the Foreign Office, that we were wasting time and money pursuing the "commercial aspects" of the Keller and Jamieson murders. You should get on well with him, sir.'

Esslemont allowed himself a slight smile. 'I'll not raise the matter if he doesn't. I think we may need his goodwill if we're left with any loose ends after we've arrested Roskill.'

*

DI Colin MacNee was in conference with the Procurator Fiscal, discussing the charges that could be brought against the three men held on remand in Aberdeen Prison.

'I have no hesitation', the PF said, 'in confirming that, so far as MacIlwraith and Mathieson are concerned, in respect of the deaths of Keller and Jamieson, respectively, the charges of conspiracy to murder should be replaced by the more serious charges of murder.'

Colin wondered whether there was a special course that PFs had to take where they learned to speak in complex, constipated prose. Janet had once told him a story about some king, or duke, or count, who, after listening to the first performance of a new concerto, had called the composer to his presence. 'Too many notes, Herr Mozart!', he said. He was wrong, of course, but a variant would aptly sum up the new PF's talent for circumlocution.

'What about Last and Mercury?'

'A little more uncertain, inspector. It is at least arguable that you and your colleagues may have garnered enough evidence to charge MacIlwraith with placing the explosive device at Last Cairngorm to the endangerment of life. If we accept that argument, as we probably shall, I would then have to take a view as to whether it would be prudent also to arraign him, in addition, on a charge of conspiracy, lest the jury should have some difficulty with the more serious charge.'

Colin tried to increase the tempo of the discussion, to no avail. 'Mercury? Mathieson?'

'Ah! I think that we may face even more difficulty there. What you have is worryingly circumstantial and I would be rather loath to prefer charges, under the various telecommunications acts, which would tend to suggest that we believe we have a better than even chance of convicting him of the cyber attack on Mercury. Even a conspiracy charge is marginal.'

'But given the pattern of offences here, and the number of people involved, surely you should take it to court and let a jury decide?'

'Bit of a gamble, I think. I may have to consult the Crown Office on it. I should be able to do that today.'

Colin knew his exasperation was beginning to show, but the charges against MacIver had to be covered.

'Conspiracy to murder, certainly. Probably also accessory before the fact, founding that charge on the payments from the Scottish Freedom Club account to MacIlwraith and Mathieson, supported by what you have on the association among the three of them. I'm less persuaded about his complicity in the Last and Mercury matters. Again, it's circumstantial. I do not entirely rule out charges, but I would like to await the outcome of the arrest and arraignment of Mr James Roskill before I decide. Whatever view I take, we are looking at a very complex and a very lengthy trial. The Lord Advocate will almost certainly want to prosecute personally and to move the trial to Edinburgh.'

Colin didn't care where the trial took place or who prosecuted it. He just wanted to be sure that the charges were the most serious that the evidence would support. 'DCS Esslemont and DCI Fiske are in London to arrest Roskill. I'll come back to you when they're back.'

*

Roskill's main London residence was an elegant detached house in Notting Hill, set back a little from a broad street, with a front courtyard defended by a ten foot wall and electric gates, and a small sentry post for the protection officers that his status as a former Prime Minister commanded. There were, as yet, no satellite TV vans outside, but there was a little group of reporters on the pavement, and others in cars and vans illegally parked on the street. They had started to gather before six o'clock in the hope of snatching a word with Roskill as he left the house. The snappers hadn't arrived, and, as usual, they would come up with the sun.

Apart from a light above the front door, barely visible from the street, the house was in darkness. A few reporters had gone to the house late the previous evening, after Ben Aaronson's story had gone up on the *FP* website, but the only activity they had recorded was the departure from the house, just before midnight, of a figure some of them had recognised as Edmund Cordingley.

Three tabloid hacks, furious that their snapper had yet to turn up, had stationed themselves at the entry to the service lane at the back of the house. No movement there, either, with the exception of a van from Press-Rite, a domestic ironing and dry cleaning company that served Notting Hill and other prosperous districts, which made a brief stop at around 2230.

Cordingley had walked to the gates, waited for them to be opened by the protection officers, and made his way wordlessly to the street. He hailed a taxi, but prudently, if exasperatingly for the reporters, he did not give the driver a destination until he was in the cab and traveling as quickly as the traffic allowed away from Roskill's house.

*

A black Lexus saloon swept through the gates and into the courtyard of the house at about 0930. Fiske, Esslemont and Bancroft had been driven straight there from London City Airport. Bancroft briefed the visiting officers as the driver weaved skilfully through the rush hour traffic. The duty protection officer had confirmed at the midnight shift change that Roskill was at home and that he had spent much of the evening in conference with several aides, including Lord Cordingley, who had just left. The others had gone at various times earlier in the evening, before the reporters arrived, and Roskill was now at home with his wife and a couple of domestic staff. He would have no warning of their arrival. The police officer on duty would contact the housekeeper on the internal telephone and they would be admitted. Once in the house, Roskill would be informed. A helicopter was on standby to fly him to Aberdeen.

*

'Good morning, Mrs Roskill, my apologies for disturbing you. I'm Detective Chief Inspector Vanessa Fiske of North East Constabulary. These are my colleagues, Detective Chief Superintendent Esslemont and Commander Bancroft. We need to speak with your husband.'

Julia Roskill was a slim, fit and very attractive woman of around sixty. She was perfectly groomed, her black trousers and green silk blouse suggesting expensive rather than extravagant tastes. She had a book in her hand - last year's Man Booker prizewinner, Vanessa noted - and she looked at the police officers over half-moon spectacles.

'I'm afraid he's not here.' Just that. No acknowledgment of Vanessa's apology or of her rank. No trace of real apology in her rather stiffly formal response.

Vanessa managed not to seem shocked. 'But according to his protection officers...'

Mrs Roskill interrupted. 'So you've been keeping tabs on him! Maybe you should ask him to wear an electronic tag as well as having a police officer with him wherever he goes. He is a former prime minister. He seems to be paying a high price for having served his country.'

Before Vanessa could respond, Bancroft intervened. 'Mrs Roskill, your husband is a target. That's why he needs protection. It seemed prudent to establish his whereabouts in order to avoid disturbing your routine if he was not here. His protection officers are paid to know where he is.'

Bancroft's emollient tone did not placate her. Vanessa thought that her anger was disproportionate to what, on the face of it, was either a simple mistake or a minor operational error.

'We don't like wasting our time any more than yours, so, if you can tell us where Mr Roskill is, we will leave you to your book.'

Julia Roskill laid the book down on a side table as though holding it somehow trivialised the moment. 'I have no idea, Chief Inspector. I went to bed early last evening and watched the ten o'clock news.' There was a faint trace of distaste in this and Vanessa assumed that her interview of Roskill had featured.

'My husband was in a meeting with Edmund Cordingley and other colleagues in his study. I looked round the door to say good night and he said he'd be up shortly. I woke at half past six and he wasn't here. I assumed something urgent had come up. It often does.'

'Did you check with his protection officers?'

Her look was contemptuous. 'Why would I? I expected a call from him, or from one of his staff, this morning. Still do.'

'We have checked and they have no record if his having left the house.'

'Well, he's not here. You can search the house if you want to.'

'That won't be necessary, Mrs Roskill.' This was Bancroft, again. 'But we will need to spend some time with the protection officers.'

*

The protection officers were adamant. Roskill could not have left the house without their knowledge. Their logs showed that he had returned from his office at the Trust at 1818 hrs the previous evening and had not left. Three aides had arrived at 2000 hrs and left at various times between 2013 hrs and 2220 hrs. Lord Cordingley had arrived at 1930 hrs and left at 2357 hrs.

DCI Fiske did not conceal her anger and frustration, which probably made her proof against any temptation the officers might have felt towards patronising a female officer from a remote Scottish force. She had made sure that they were made aware of her background in Special Branch on royal protection, and even if they knew of her abrupt departure, they also knew that she would be familiar with the protocols under which they worked.

'But he is not in the house. He must have left somehow. The first thing that would have been done when security for the place was being planned was to identify and secure all possible points of entry.' She paused, then added in a tone of profound sarcasm, 'And exit.'

The Special Branch chief inspector in charge of Roskill's protection had been summoned, and he came into the library, where Julia Roskill had suggested they meet.

'Hello, Peter.' Bancroft said, before introducing Fiske and Esslemont. 'I. suppose you know what's happened?'

Peter Mishcon nodded. 'Can we park the question of how my officers managed to lose a former Prime Minister? Believe me, I'll be returning to it. But we really need to concentrate on three questions. How did he get out of the house? Did he go voluntarily? And where did he go?'

'I agree, and it's good to see you again, Peter, whatever the circumstances. I had just raised the entrances and exits question.'

Mishcon turned to the protection officers, one of whom spoke. 'Front gate, front door, back entrance from the service lane. Access to service lane, which has a gate, is by key pad code. We have a list of all those who have it.' Then, as an afterthought, 'Ma'am.' Vanessa could have reminded him that she wasn't the Queen, but she let it go.

'All covered by cameras?'

'Yes.'

'So let's see it.'

The CCTV cameras had caught the Press-Rite van driver keying in the number at the gate and then drawing the van up very close to the back entrance, a reinforced gate in the rear boundary wall. The van was stopped for less than a minute before driving out of the lane through a controlled gate at the other end. The CCTV cameras had recorded a perfect view of the van's roof.

'I think we may have discovered a flaw in our security,' Mishcon said drily.

*

Fiske and Esslemont were driven to Press-Rite's base in North Kensington while Bancroft and Mishcon continued their preliminary investigation of the security lapse at Roskill's house. The driver of the van that did the regular twice weekly collection from the house had failed to turn up for work that morning and there was no sign of the vehicle he had been driving on his last shift, which had been due to finish at 2000 hrs. They got his name and address and, through Mishcon, arranged for Met officers to see if he was there or had been seen there. He wasn't there and a neighbour had seen him leaving around nine o'clock the previous evening carrying a large suitcase. He had wheeled the case round the corner in the direction of Paddington Station.

The missing Press-Rite van was found abandoned under the Chiswick Flyover of the A4 road westward out of London. It was empty, but a forensic examination would collect a DNA sample that was eventually matched to James Michael Roskill. This was less conclusive than it appeared, as the defence would no doubt have pointed out, if a case against Roskill came to court, because the van had often been used to collect laundry from the Roskill house. Vanessa Fiske could imagine his QC, well instructed by Cordingley, leading a forensic witness to a statement that the presence of a minute sample of DNA did not prove that Roskill had been in the van.

Airline records showed that the van driver had been on a late flight to Marrakech from Heathrow. There was no record of Roskill having left the country. DCI Fiske was cynical enough, perhaps wise enough in the

ways of the rich and powerful, to think that
that was not evidence that he hadn't.

CHAPTER TWENTY-EIGHT

'He's gone, Neil. Disappeared. Smuggled out of his fucking house in a laundry van right under the noses of his so-called protection. No record of him on any commercial flight.'

'He's a former prime minister, Vanessa. He can't just vanish.'

'Well he has. And my former colleagues in special branch don't seem to want to pursue him with any enthusiasm. They've alerted Europol and Interpol, issued his picture to border agency staff at ports and airports. They're asked to "identify and report". Straight out of the fugitive hunt playbook. I don't think they give a toss. As far as they're concerned the case is solved, the murderers are in custody, and they can now offer us all assistance short of help. Even Peter Mishcon, who I thought was a mate, seems happy to leave the file open and hope that somebody, somewhere fills it.'

'So get on a plane and come home. You must be exhausted. And in your condition...'

'Christ, you're beginning to sound like Esslemont. I'm perfectly able to do my job.

And I don't like loose ends. I'll be home tomorrow. Or the next day if I go to see mum and dad. Right now I have to talk to Colin.'

*

Mishcon, as the officer in charge of Roskill's protection squad, had suspended the officers on duty on the night of the disappearance, pending a full investigation. DCI Fiske's assumption that he was content to let the matter rest turned out to be a little unfair. He had no more affection for loose ends than she had, and the fact that the former PM had been mislaid by his officers rankled.

'Sir, the FO sometimes provides senior politicians with more than one passport, sometimes in "alternative" names.'

Bancroft and Mishcon were having a drink after Esslemont had been collected to be driven to Heathrow to get the next available flight to Aberdeen. As Vanessa had noted, he was already showing signs of disorientation, even withdrawal symptoms, as a result of having spent a night away. His instruction to her to stay and 'tidy things up" had come as no surprise.

Bancroft nodded.

'Could you find out if Roskill had one and if so, in what name?'

'I could try. But Carey will escalate it to the cabinet secretary, who'll talk to the PM, who'll want to consult the security services, who'll be reluctant to give us the information. Unless we go public about what we think Roskill's done. And that's not a decision for us.'

'It might enable us to find out where he went, and possibly why.'

*

'When I was on royal protection - in special branch - I learned that people like Roskill sometimes have more than one passport and more than one identity. Bancroft's trying to get details, but it may take time, especially if we're right in assuming that Carey is complicit. He's ideally placed to slow things down. And we don't have much time.'

Colin MacNee decided to push things along. "What do you want me to do, boss?'

'People don't usually choose false names entirely at random. I need you to get hold of as many biographies of Roskill as you can find and make a list of all the family surnames they mention. Mother's and grandmothers' maiden names, name changes, adoptions. Places of birth, too.'

'The libraries are shut, but I'll get on to it first thing. When are you back?'

'Not sure. Depends what you come up with.'

'Have you checked this with the DCS? Sounds as though you may be about to go off piste.'

'I'm going to assume that you're speaking to me as a friend. Otherwise, it might be insubordination. Get me on my mobile. I may take a train to Coventry and go and see my parents. They don't know they're going to be grandparents. Might be nice to tell them in person. If I do, I'll book it as leave.'

*

'There's a lot of stuff in the British papers about the interest that the cops investigating the Keller and Jamieson murders are taking in James. Not clear what the connection is, but it won't be long until they mention us.'

Richard Seaton, sitting in his Washington DC law office, looked across his desk at Cy Packard and took a sip of his bourbon.

Packard went on. 'We both think he's up to something. His silence at the board meeting the other day was so out of character. He's usually like a rutting moose, challenging you and me, maybe positioning himself to move into your chair or mine. He's sure as hell up to something.'

'What do you suggest, Cy?'

'As I said before, I could call in some favours. Get some of my old colleagues to see what they can find out. Might take some time, though I'll emphasise that time is money.'

'Unfortunate turn of phrase. Let's hope it doesn't turn out to be prescient.'

*

'Wife's maiden name: Carroll; mother's: Harrington; grannies': Slaughter and Watkins; place of birth: Madelyn,

Staffordshire; wife's place of birth: Sedlescombe, West Sussex.'

Vanessa Fiske sat in her parents' kitchen in Offchurch, three miles from Leamington Spa, taking down the names as Colin MacNee read them at dictation speed. Her mother poured her a second glass of fizzy water, which she accepted, and offered her, using sign language, some toast and honey, which she declined by shaking her head.

'What now, boss?'

'We need to check if any of these names appeared on the passenger manifest of any international flight on the night he disappeared, or the next morning'. Vanessa was being careful not to use Roskill's name: her mother knew to be discreet when she overheard her talking about work, but training will out. 'Let's start with long haul and then go to European if nothing turns up.'

'Do you want to have a punt at the most likely? I suppose I could just go through them alphabetically, but you know him better than me, so you might like to guess what he'd have chosen. We could even have a sweepstake on it.'

Vanessa laughed. 'Harry Conival would run a book. Let me have a look.'

After she finished reading, she laughed again and this time the ironic tone was obvious. 'I'd like to think that he's far enough into black humour to have gone for "Slaughter", but it's too good to be true. Wasn't his constituency in the Black Country? Start with Madely, then it's your call. I'm on leave today.' She looked over to other side of the kitchen, where her mother was wiping surfaces with great concentration. 'I'm going to try to help my parents come to terms with imminent and unexpected grandparenthood. My dad has said nowt so far except "Who would've thought it?" before retreating into his study.'

*

Sir Justin Carey was playing the FO mandarin. 'I'm sorry, Commander Bancroft, but I don't think I am at liberty to confirm or deny that an additional British passport, either in an assumed name or in his own, was issued to Mr Roskill.'

'Sir Justin, we believe that Mr Roskill has been involved in a criminal conspiracy that has led to two murders and possibly to two separate but serious acts of terrorism. He fled from his home just before we went there to arrest him. It is likely that the police and the prosecuting authorities in Scotland will announce today that they intend to charge him. He will be declared to be an international fugitive from justice. He did not leave this country under his own name. We need to know whether he was travelling on another passport, in another name.'

'I have no doubt that your enquiry is both soundly based and legitimate, but I am not prepared to release confidential information, if such exists, about such a high-profile public figure, entirely on my own authority.'

Bancroft considered whether to find a way of hinting to Carey that he suspected his complicity in some of Roskill's activities, but said only, 'Whose approval would you need?'

'I'd need to speak to the Cabinet Secretary. He may have to consult others.'

'Who, for example?'

'Possibly the PM.'

'Do it.'

Carey looked as though he might object to Bancroft's peremptory tone, but he thought better of it.

'I'll try to see the Cabinet Secretary today. I'll come back to you as soon as I have an answer.
*

'We have to say something. There's still a press mob outside his house. The blogosphere is awash with speculation. And the PF is pretty well convinced that we could charge him with several serious counts of conspiracy and possibly with procuring illegal acts. If we could find him.'

Colin MacNee was in the Chief Constable's office with Esslemont, Fiona Marchmont and Harry Conival. The Chief's Acting Staff Officer was taking notes.

'DI MacNee is right.' Harry Conival had spent the seven hours since Esslemont had got back from London no-commenting inventively to an unbroken series of enquiries about NEC's interest in Roskill. He was very good at it, as he was the first to admit, but both his patience and his imagination were wearing thin. 'The least we can get away with is a press release, but it would be better if we put out a statement accompanied by an announcement of a press conference. That might give me and my colleagues a bit of respite. We're a press office, so we can hardly switch the phones to voicemail and go home, tempting as that is.'

'If Roskill had been there when the DCI and the DCS turned up at his house this morning, they would have arrested him, driven him to the Met helipad and flown him to Dyce. We would then have announced that a sixty-three year old man had been arrested in London in connection with, blah, blah, blah. The reptiles would have done everything short of naming Roskill. Some of them might even have taken a chance and done so, calculating that the Crown Office wouldn't cite them for contempt. In any case, we would have had him in court tomorrow morning. So we should ask Harry to put all that in a press release, call a press conference at which we can say all the things we would have said at a briefing after the court appearance.'

The Chief looked less than comfortable. 'I see the logic in that, Colin, but we need to be sure that we do nothing that might be prejudicial, in the event that Roskill ever faces trial. Fiona?'

'There is a risk, certainly, but we might mitigate it by getting the PF to agree to a joint statement.'

Colin MacNee laughed. 'How long have we got? It takes him an hour to say yes or no to the simplest recommendation to prosecute. We can hardly tell the press that we hope to say something by next Tuesday week!'

Colin seldom looked chastened, but the look he got from Esslemont made his expression change rapidly from irritation to regret. "Sorry, sir. Tough afternoon.'

Fiona Marchmont diverted attention from Esslemont's displeasure and MacNee's discomfort. 'I'll talk to the PF. I'll get him at home and go out to see him if need be.'

The door to the Chief's office opened and his secretary came in. 'DCI Fiske on the phone, sir. She needs to speak to the DCS urgently.'

*

'Sir, I need to have one more go at bringing Roskill in, but I'll need your approval.'

'Have you got a lead?'

'I think so, but I'm asking you to trust me to pursue it for a few days. If what I want to do works out, we'll all take credit, but if it doesn't, I'd like you to have "plausible deniability".'

Esslemont thought that sounded like 'Met speak'. 'You mean I'll be able to say I didn't know about it. Don't like the sound of that but, for the sake of argument, if I go along with this, what would I have to do now?'

Esslemont, was not a man for taking risks, not even as the last few months of his career coincided with the demise of North East Constabulary and the creation of the new Scottish Police Service. But, Vanessa Fiske was a good officer whose instincts and diligence had paid off in this investigation and in others. The possibility of still being head of CID when one of his people brought off the biggest arrest anyone, anywhere could remember had its attractions.

'Colin tells me that we're under pressure to announce that Roskill is a fugitive from justice and to say what we want to charge him with. Could you delay that for a few days, three at the most, and sanction some extraordinary travel expenses for me? I'll use my own credit card and claim it back, so we'll be able to decide how to describe it.'

'I don't like the sound of this, Vanessa. I'll delay any announcement of what we intend to do about Roskill, but I'm not giving you a blank cheque. If you go on with this, I'll do what I can, but your expenses may be at your own risk.'

Vanessa knew that this wasn't entirely unreasonable, even if it was consistent with Esslemont's risk averseness. It was the best she was going to get.

'Thank you, sir. I'll keep you informed as appropriate.'

*

Patrick Joseph Carroll had flown to Amsterdam, leaving Heathrow early on the morning after Roskill's disappearance, and connecting to a flight at noon to Aruba. Both flights were operated by KLM and Carroll had flown business class. The booking had been made online - no signature required - and the tickets had been charged to a credit card in the name a company registered in the British Virgin Islands. Nothing to link it to Roskill, but DCI Fiske was convinced enough to book a British Airways flight to Aruba.

'Where the fuck is Aruba?' Esslemont wasn't given to bad language, having come from a Presbyterian home and joined the police before Anglo Saxon became the *lingua franca,* so Vanessa knew he was unhappy. Getting his signature on a claim form for more than a thousand quid that she had spent on the ticket wasn't going to be easy. But his tone also suggested he was impressed that she had, apparently, picked up Roskill's trail so quickly.

'In the Dutch Antilles, off the coast of Venezuela. He may be on his way to BVI, where he has "interests", but I doubt it. He's unlikely end up where we might easily be able to get him and repatriate him. He's on his way to somewhere else.'

'What are you planning? Or don't I want to know?'

'Probably not, at this stage, but I'm hoping that he doesn't know, or has forgotten, that the Americans have a permanent Homeland Security and Defense presence there. Bancroft is contacting them, as well as the local police, in case I need some back-up.'

'You'll only be able to bring him back if he agrees voluntarily. Not likely, is it?'

'Worth a punt, if I can get to talk to him. It'll do no harm for him to know we're on to him.'

*

'Richard, Cy here. Homeland Security has a post in Aruba, in the Dutch Antilles. It's mainly to facilitate US citizens in transit - they can clear customs and immigration before boarding a flight home - but they keep closely in touch with the local authorities. One of my contacts tells me that a Patrick Joseph Carroll arrived in Aruba yesterday. He bears more that a passing resemblance to James and they're considering how to act, given that Interpol has an "identify and report" out on him. They're trying to get a positive ID.'

'Should we try to speak to him, try to find out what he's up to and whether it will affect us?'

'Might be prudent. I could send Jack Eisner to see if he can locate him. Jack can be quite intimidating. If there's anything to be found, he'll find it.'

CHAPTER TWENTY-NINE

At five feet eight, Vanessa Fiske was a few inches too tall to get comfortable in a tourist class seat on a Boeing 747. Making her warrant card visible when she checked in for her flight to Aruba had failed to secure an upgrade. When she disembarked at Queen Beatrix International Airport after a flight of nearly ten hours she was knackered, stiff, and fed up, relying on adrenalin eventually to kick in and keep her going.

'You're where?' Neil Derrick had thought that his capacity for surprise about what his partner got involved in was more or less exhausted.

'Aruba. In the Caribbean. Near Venezuela. Don't ask me why. I'm phoning just to let you know I'm OK, not to tell you what I'm doing.'

'I thought you were at your parents'

'I was. And now I'm not.'

'When will you be back? Or can't you tell me that either?'

He was trying not to sound irritated or unsupportive, but he didn't think he was doing a very good job, so he changed tack.

'Your sister phoned. Very excited about becoming an auntie. She says she'll come to see us soon.'

Vanessa was grateful for the change of subject, but too tired to do much about it. 'That's nice. I talked to her when I was at mum and dad's. Sue's not very good at concealing her feelings and she's clearly astounded that I've got myself pregnant'.

'You didn't do it yourself.'

'No. Sorry. I'm really glad you were involved. I've got to try to sleep. I'll keep in touch. I love you.'

'Love you, too.'

*

Jack Eisner's direct flight from Philadelphia arrived in Aruba a couple of hours after Vanessa cleared customs and immigration, but before she was able to get in touch with the local police. His contacts in the CIA had given him a name to contact in the Homeland Security office. The implication that the person named was covertly a CIA operative had been clear, but Eisner knew better than to press the issue. The geographical proximity of Aruba to Venezuela on the South American mainland, and to Haiti, the Dominican Republic, and Cuba in the Caribbean, made it certain that the Company would have a presence there, but the sensitivity of the island's status as an integral part of a NATO ally demanded discretion.

'Jack Eisner. I was given your name by a mutual friend in the Company and...'

The interruption was uncompromising. 'Why don't we meet for a drink? Where are you staying?'

'The Renaissance, but I'm still at the airport. Not checked in yet.'

'I'll meet you in the Blue Bar at 8.'

*

'Sir Justin, there is some urgency about this. Have you made any progress?'

'I'm sorry, Commander Bancroft, but so far I have nothing definitive to tell you. After you came to see me, I went immediately to speak to the Cabinet Secretary. As I anticipated, he felt that this was sensitive enough for him to consult the PM, who is on an unannounced visit to the troops in Afghanistan, accompanied by the Foreign Secretary...'

Bancroft interrupted angrily. 'But you must have known about that when we spoke...'

'...So there is an inevitable delay in consulting him. He is expected to arrive at Brize Norton later this evening and go straight to Downing Street. The Cabinet Secretary will speak to him as soon as he gets there.'

'And', Bancroft thought, 'He'll want to consult the intelligence services, and if he doesn't decide that off his own bat, you'll make bloody sure somebody suggests it.' He was now in no doubt that Carey was slowing things down to give Roskill more time to get to wherever he was going. Time to put the wind up him.

'You've been very close to Roskill for a very long time, haven't you, Sir Justin?'

'We've known each other, one way or another, since we were at school. I don't see the relevance...'

'Oh, I think you do. It would be - how shall I put this? - unfortunate if you were to allow a personal connection, past or present, to lead you to obstruct or delay my investigation.'

He hung up.

*

As soon as she had checked in and had a shower, DCI Fiske made the required courtesy call to the local police commander. She told her that she believed that Patrick Joseph Carroll had arrived in Aruba within the previous twenty-four hours and that he was in transit to another destination, probably one without an extradition treaty with the United Kingdom.

'I believe that his passport, though not a forgery, conceals his real identity. I hope to persuade him to return to the UK voluntarily. I don't think we'll be able to hold him long enough for an international arrest warrant to be issued and executed. But my first priority is to establish if Carroll is who I think he is.'

'As a matter of course, we photograph the passports of all passengers who arrive here. Would that enable you to make the identification?'

'I'm sure it would. Should I go back to the airport?'

'Not necessary. I can access the records from here. I'll send a car to collect you, if that would help.'

*

Vanessa looked into the Blue Bar as she walked toward the lobby to meet the police officer sent to collect her. Her phone alerted her to a text just as she recognised a familiar figure sitting on a bar stool, sipping bourbon. She read the text just as she walked towards him.

JMR travelling on passport in name of Patrick Joseph Carroll. Bancroft.

''Mr Eisner, what a coincidence!'

Eisner looked up, recognised DCI Fiske and just about managed to avoid spluttering his whiskey all over her.

'Sure is, Chief Inspector! Are you here on vacation?'

Vanessa knew that he was being flippant. With a car waiting for her, though, she chose not to respond in kind.

'I take it we're both here for the same reason, and if I'm right, it would be in the interests of both of us to share information. I have to check in with the local police, but I should be back within the hour. Will you still be here?

'I guess so. I'm meeting a local contact here...'He looked at his watch. '...in about ten minutes. I'll be here most of the evening. My contact may be too. You might be interested in meeting him.'

'Who is he?'

'He's with Homeland Security,' Eisner said, with a complicit smile.

As she walked towards the exit door, Vanessa was aware that the name James Michael Roskill had not been mentioned.

*

It didn't take long to verify that the Patrick Joseph Carroll was James Michael Roskill. New arrivals from the UK were not required to say where they would be staying, so finding Roskill wouldn't be easy. Vanessa reasoned that he was probably carrying a passport in his own name as well as the one on which he had entered Aruba. He would have checked into a hotel near the airport, and it was likely that he was planning to move on as quickly as possible.

'Are there any more international flights leaving this evening?'

'Only one to Atlanta and one to Schipol. There are more in the morning, mainly regional flights to South and Central America and the Caribbean.'
We can check with the airlines, but without a valid warrant we won't be able to detain him.'

'Yes, but if I can discover when he intends to travel, I may be able to intercept him and talk to him. And if I know he's definitely planning to move on tomorrow, I can try to find out where he's staying tonight. You've been very helpful, Commander, but I've stretched your goodwill far enough. Just one more thing. I had to show my passport when

I checked into my hotel. Is that general practice here?'

'Legally, no. But almost all the hotels do it as a check against the credit card shown at registration.'

'Thank you.' That made it probable that he would have checked in as Roskill. He might be carrying plastic in Carroll's name, but the urgency with which he had fled would have made it unlikely.

*

Jack Eisner and his colleague from Homeland Security were still at the bar when Vanessa got back from police HQ. Eisner offered her a drink and she opted for a freshly squeezed orange juice and a fizzy water.

'This is Detective Chief Inspector Fiske, from North East Constabulary in Scotland. David Schulz, Homeland Security's man in Aruba.' They shook hands and said that first names would be fine.

Vanessa took the initiative. 'So, Jack, I think I know, in general, what you're doing in this island paradise - I've been reading the crap magazines in my room - but I'd love to know what brought you here and what, in particular, you hope to achieve.'

'Nothing if not direct, Vanessa. I can't tell you how, but it came to our attention that a member of our board had landed in Aruba and my boss, Cy Packard, and his chairman, Richard Seaton, thought it would be in the company's interests to find out what he's doing here and what his forward travel plans might be.'

'When you say 'the company', do you mean the one Packard works for now or the one he used to work for?' Vanessa delivered the question with a knowing look, which Eisner and Schulz noted.

'Burtonhall. Of course.' But the pause was eloquent and Vanessa took it as confirmation that Schulz was CIA.

She sipped her orange juice and said, 'And?'

'And we don't know where he is except that he arrived, travelling on a passport in the name of Carroll and hasn't left. David's colleagues are trying to find out if he's made any plans to move on.'

'I may be able to help you there, but before I do, I need know that we can trust each other and that we have the same, or at least similar, objectives.'

'Go on.'

'I have a lead position and a fallback. I'd like to persuade him to come back to the UK. Failing that - in fact, in addition to that - I'd like to know what he intends to do with the rest of his life and whether he's working with who I think he working with. In short, I need to find him, and talk to him before he gets on another plane. I have loose ends to tie up.'

Schulz said nothing, and Vanessa sensed he was becoming uncomfortable.

Eisner ordered another bourbon. Schulz shook his head.

'I can live with that. What have you got?'

'I thought at first that we might divide up the hotels between us and try to find him tonight, but some gentle persuasion at police HQ - I played the "both members of the EU and NATO card" - revealed that he's booked on two flights out of here tomorrow. He's on a plane to Miami at 0945 in his real name and on another, as Carroll, to Curacao and Panama City at 0825. The Miami flight has an onward connection to San Jose, Costa Rica. The Panama City connection is to Havana.'

Schulz spoke for the first time. 'He must know that a stopover in Miami is risky. We could have him picked up there if the Brits issue an international arrest warrant. Also, he'll want out of here as soon as possible, even if an intermediate stop at Curacao keeps him in Dutch jurisdiction. Either way, you'll need a warrant to nail him.'

'I don't need to "nail" him,' Eisner said. 'I just need to get a line on what he's up to.'

'He's trying to get to somewhere without an extradition treaty with the UK. I need to get that warrant issued. It's already after midnight in Aberdeen, so even if I felt able to phone somebody, nothing is going to get done until the morning. If he's out of here at 0825, he'll be airside by 0730. If we're going to talk to him, it'll have to be as he arrives at the airport. I'll text and arrange for someone to call me.'

*

It was already 2200 hrs local time and Vanessa had been awake, more or less, for well over twenty-four hours. Her text to Colin MacNee was terse and to the point:

Conf call: you, Chief, DCS, FM, PF, HC: any time after 0700 GMT. Pls confirm asap.

She added the hotel number and room, put her phone on charge on the side table and climbed into bed in the hope of getting a few hours sleep before the call. The text alert woke her at 0400 hrs, which meant she had had just over five hours sleep. She still felt wretched, but it was the kind of wretched that could be overcome, at least for a few hours, by a hot shower and, if she could face it and keep it down, a decent breakfast, which she'd have to order from room service. Colin's text was even more terse than hers had been:

0830 GMT / 0430 AST.

*

'It's a long shot, but I may be able to arrest him at the airport this morning. The local police will provide assistance, but only if we have issued an international arrest warrant. He's booked on two flights, one with connections to Havana and one with a connection through Miami to San Jose, Costa Rica. I think he's unlikely to risk a stopover in the US because he'll guess - don't ask me how I know this - that the American authorities, from Homeland Security to the CIA, are on his case. The other booking has a stop in Curacao, which keeps him in European jurisdiction, so if I can't nail him here, we might be able to have him arrested there. I've booked myself on the same flight, as a precaution.'

'I've already got approval from the Crown Office to issue the warrant, so we can get it to you by email or fax within the hour. Presumably we should send it to police HQ in Aruba?' This was Fiona Marchmont.

'We'll have to look at some of the "administrative"' - the Chief's emphasis on the word was telling - 'aspects of your absence when you get back, Vanessa. For now, the DCS and I are prepared to sanction your proposed course of action. However, you should know that the pressure from the press has hardly diminished. They've done everything short of actually saying that he's a fugitive from justice. I don't think we can hold the line much longer.'

'Harry Conival here, Chief Inspector. Everyone here knows that I think we should have gone public on this before now. We'll have to put out a press statement as soon as the warrant is issued. But we'll need to follow up with a press conference and I assume you'll want to take it, in person.'

'I'm sorry you've been messed about, Harry. Couldn't be helped. If I can't get back in the next forty-eight hours, I'll find a way to do it by videolink. Colin, could you get admin to find out what the options are, given that my travel plans are fluid?'

'I guess that means Aruba, Curacao or Heathrow. Or are you planning any side trips?'

Vanessa allowed herself a laugh. 'Hardly. I don't care if I never see the inside of a plane again. Easiest thing will be to do it from here, sooner rather than later. But that will depend on what happens in the next few hours.'

*

DCI Fiske got into a taxi at just before 0600 hrs and went to police HQ. She collected the arrest warrant authorising the arrest of 'James

Michael Roskill, aka Patrick Joseph Carroll' on suspicion of conspiracy to murder, conspiracy to cause explosions, and conspiracy to breach the telecommunications acts. She was driven in an unmarked police van to the airport, accompanied by the local commander of police and three other officers. By 0615, the van was parked where it could observe, from a distance of about 20 metres, the security-restricted drop off area.

By 0715, Vanessa was becoming both impatient and apprehensive. Perhaps Roskill had, after all, decided to risk the Miami stopover. She had agreed with Eisner, that he should cover that departure and that she would join him if Roskill failed to show for the Curacao flight. The police commander, sitting in front beside the driver, took a call on her mobile and had a brief conversation in Dutch. She ended the call and turned to Vanessa.

'Air traffic control have just alerted us to a flight plan lodged for a private jet plane that arrived last night from the British Virgin Islands. The pilot has requested an early take-off slot, with a routing to San Jose, Costa Rica.'

'Is there a separate departure point for private flights?'

'Yes. They use by a dedicated terminal with its own apron and taxi way. They pay for exit and entry services also. It's expensive, but it means they don't have to use security and passport control in the main building.'

'Let's go!' But Vanessa felt that James Michael Roskill was slipping from her grasp.

*

As the police van turned towards the private terminal, DCI Fiske called Jack Eisner on his mobile. Very quickly, the van had a BMW on its tail and she thought she recognised Eisner in the front passenger seat and David Schulz driving.

As soon as the two vehicles got to the entrance to the terminal, Vanessa and Eisner, closely followed by the police commander and her officers, rushed into the building. Through the full-length windows behind reception they saw a Learjet 70 turning on to the runway. The commander called air traffic control, but the jet had been cleared for take-off. As she put down the handset, Fiske and Eisner watched the plane accelerate along the runway and take off over the Caribbean.

'Any point in checking the passenger manifest?' Eisner asked.

Vanessa shook her head. 'Not really. But I suppose I should confirm what we already know.'

*

Harry Conival's press release, approved by Esslemont, the PF and Special Branch, went out at 1200 hrs GMT / 0800 hrs AST.

ABERDEEN PROCURATOR FISCAL APPROVES CHARGES AGAINST JAMES MICHAEL ROSKILL

The Procurator Fiscal in Aberdeen, having reviewed evidence presented to him by North East Constabulary, has approved the following charges against James Michael Roskill, 63, of Notting Hill, London:

Conspiracy to murder Peter Keller and Harvey Jamieson, jointly and severally with Paul MacIver, Simon Mathieson and Andrew MacIlwraith;

Conspiracy to cause an explosion, to the endangerment of life, jointly with Paul MacIver;

Conspiracy to breach the telecommunication acts, jointly with Paul MacIver.

Mr Roskill was interviewed under caution recently, in London, by officers from North East Constabulary, after which a decision was taken to arrest him on the above charges. Mr Roskill could not be found and an international warrant for his arrest has now been issued. . Assistance is being sought from police services in all countries.

A press conference will take place today at 1700 hrs. It will be taken by videolink by DCI Vanessa Fiske, Senior Investigating Officer, and will be attended by DI Colin MacNee, Deputy SIO, and by DCS Campbell Esslemont, Head of NEC CID.

*

As she was preparing for the press conference, Vanessa took a call from Kenneth Bancroft.

'Julia Roskill has just booked a flight, Business Class, from London to San Jose, Costa Rica, via Atlanta.'

'And we don't have an extradition treaty with Costa Rica?'

'No, we don't, but in very special cases an *ad hoc* application for repatriation may be entertained.'

'This press conference will be interesting.'

EPILOGUE

Seven months later, after MacIver, Mathieson and MacIlwraith had been tried at the High Court in Edinburgh and convicted on all charges, Ben Aaronson and Carl, his otherwise anonymous FRIG associate, interviewed James Michael Roskill at his villa near San Jose, Costa Rica. It had taken weeks of negotiation through intermediaries to set it up. Their first contact had been Edmund Cordingley who, after being interviewed by DCI Fiske and Kenneth Bancroft of Special Branch, but neither arrested nor charged, had given entirely unhelpful but not obviously dishonest evidence at the trial. With MacIver in prison, and his client apparently safe from any Scottish legal process that might try to bring him to trial, Cordingley had finally, but on condition of anonymity, returned Aaronson's call.

Eventually, Aaronson had been told the specific flight on which he and his colleague should arrive in San Jose. When they had cleared immigration, they searched the line of drivers waiting for their clients until they saw a card reading "EXFLT", identified themselves, and were taken, without a word spoken, to a black people carrier with dark windows. Forty minutes later they arrived at the villa, a substantial house overlooking the sea. They had an hour or so with Roskill, who was accompanied by Cordingley, and their "World Exclusive", supported by a picture of the former Prime Minister taken on Carl's smartphone, appeared under Aaronson's byline on the front page of the *Financial Post.*

ROSKILL DENIES IT ALL

In his first interview since leaving the United Kingdom, James Michael Roskill spoke exclusively to the Financial Post. *The full interview appears on pages 4 and 5.*

The former Prime Minister spoke frankly about his business interests, his use of overseas tax havens - "all entirely legal" - and his decision to set up his own private equity company. He has resigned from the Board of Burtonhall and he accepts that his position as a non-executive director of Mercury Fulfilment had become untenable as soon as his name was linked, "completely erroneously", with the cyber attack on Mercury's Scottish warehouse. His contacts with Paul MacIver, former special adviser to the former First Minister of Scotland, had been '"intermittent and entirely political". Reports that he had funded extremist nationalism were "so fantastical as to be hardly worthy of comment".

Roskill explained why he had decided to live permanently in Costa Rica, claiming that the absence of an extradition treaty with the UK was "irrelevant and unconnected" with his move from London. He said he had been impressed by the country's environmental policies, its commitment to world peace as demonstrated by the absence of an army, and its record on human rights. The headquarters of the various foundations and trusts that bear the Roskill name would be moved to San Jose...

*

The day after the trial, Commander Kenneth Bancroft met Sir Justin Carey, the Permanent Secretary, in his room at the Foreign Office. Later that week, Sir Justin, who had been informed by Bancroft of what Special Branch knew of his business activities, and their intention, "if the need arose", to pass the information to the financial regulatory authorities, announced that he would take early retirement, with immediate effect.

*

DCI Vanessa Fiske, in the second week of her maternity leave, was alerted by Harry Conival to Aaronson's interview with Roskill. As she read it on the *FP* website, she tried not to get angry. She laughed at Roskill's description of his relationship with MacIver and she was just about to phone Neil to talk about it when she felt the first twinge.

Seventeen hours later, with Neil at her side, she gave birth, to a girl and a boy, combined weight 8 pounds and 11 ounces. Janet had called it right. She was in her thirty-second week.

Printed in Great Britain
by Amazon.co.uk, Ltd.,
Marston Gate.